NEW YORK TIMES & USA TODAY BESTSELLING AUTHOR

KYM GROSSO

JAX

an Immortals of New Orleans novel

JAX

Immortals of New Orleans, Book 7

Kym Grosso

MT Carvin Publishing, LLC
West Chester, Pennsylvania

Editor: Julie Roberts
Cover Design: Louisa Maggio, LM CREATIONS ©2015
Photographer: Golden Czermak, FuriousPhotog
Cover Models: Jase Dean and Tamara Summers
Formatting: Polgarus Studio

DISCLAIMER

This book is a work of fiction. The names, characters, locations and events portrayed in this book are a work of fiction or are used fictitiously. Any similarity to actual events, locales, or real persons, living or dead, is coincidental and not intended by the author.

NOTICE

This is an adult erotic paranormal romance book with love scenes and mature situations. It is only intended for adult readers over the age of 18.

ACKNOWLEDGMENTS

⁓My husband and kids, for supporting my writing and books. To Keith, you are the inspiration for my sexy stories and I look forward to more adventures with you. From preparing for signings to listening to my audiobooks, I simply could not do this without you. You guys are my world and I love you so much!

⁓To my readers, who encourage me every day to write. Thank you so much for being supportive and patient with me while I wrote Jax's book. You are the reason I continue the series and as long as there are characters whose books need to be written and you would like to read them, I will write their stories. You all are the best readers ever!

⁓Julie Roberts, editor, who spent hours reading, editing and proofreading Jax. You've done so much to help, teach and encourage me over the past three years. You are a great editor and friend. Although the sparkly unicorn you suggested did not make it onto the cover, I promise I will consider it for my next book. I can't wait to come visit you in your new log cabin…just like the one I wrote into Jax's book.

⁓My Alpha readers, Maria DeSouza and Rochelle McGrath. I really appreciate your insightful critique of the storyline and unique perspectives, caring about my characters and books. You both are awesome!

~My dedicated beta readers, Leah Barbush, Denise Vance Fluhr, Janet Rodman, Jessica Leonard, Jerri Mooring, Karen Mikhael, Kelley Langlois, Laurie Johnson, Maria DeSouza, Stephanie Worne, Rose Holub and Tanner Logan, for beta reading. Thank you so much for your dedication to beta reading my books and all the valuable feedback you provided.

~Maria DeSouza, thank you for assisting me and also for proofreading Jax. You have been a great friend and reader, and I appreciate all your help...more than you know.

~Shannon Hunt, Once Upon An Alpha, for promotion and assisting. I cannot thank you enough for all your help during this release. It has been a pleasure working with you, and I'm so grateful for your help.

~Golden Czermak, FuriousFotog, for images and photography. Thank you so much for custom shooting all the images for my Jax release. It was an amazing experience to watch you work, and I am honored to have had you shoot the cover. You take spectacular photos and I love the ones you shot for Jax. The cover and teaser images fit my book perfectly. Looking forward to working together again soon.

~Jase Dean & Tamara Summers, cover models. I am fortunate to have such talented models representing my Jax and Katrina

~To Jase, for being my Jax. I really appreciate how you studied and portrayed my character for the shoot. In every single image, I see Jax Chandler. It was a terrific experience watching you work with Golden and great getting to know you. I will never forget how brave you were wading into the water for the river shots, which turned out amazing. Despite those gators and snakes! Okay, maybe no gators but a few snakes.

~To Tamara, you look beautiful in all the images, and it was awesome having you on another one of my covers. It's been great working with you this year. I love that you've read my books, and I really appreciate your support of the release!

~Louisa Maggio, LM Creations, for cover design. You are incredibly talented and thank you so much for designing another unique and gorgeous cover. I appreciate all the work you did helping me to create the stepback cover as well. I love it.

~Jason Anderson, Polgarus Studio, for formatting my books in both e-book and print. Thank you for doing such great work on another one of my books.

~Ellie Folden, Love N. Books, for model/image acquisition. Thank you so much for all your help with arrangements around the shoot and for recommending Jase as a cover model.

~Nicole Blanchard, Indie Sage PR, for helping to create all the terrific teaser images. You are so talented, and I really appreciate your help with my website and all you do.

~Rose Holub, Read by Rose, for proofreading. Thank you so much!

~Gayle Latreille, my admin, who is one of my biggest supporters and helps to run my street team.

~My awesome street team, for helping spread the word about the Immortals of New Orleans and Club Altura series. It has been a great experience getting to know all of you and meeting some of you in person at signings. I appreciate your support more than you could know! You guys are the best! You rock!

❧ Chapter One ❧

Shackled to the dungeon wall, Jax had never for a second lost focus. *Seized. Tortured.* The Alpha would have his revenge. The beast stirred, calculating its escape. Its blood boiled, raging at the monster that had captured him.

Thoughts of the night he'd been kidnapped flashed through his mind. He'd been sitting in his friend, Finn's, nightclub drowning his troubles in a bottle of scotch, mourning the death of his beta, Nick. Getting drunk hadn't dulled his senses enough to curtail his heroic tendencies. When he'd spied a woman falling unconscious on the dance floor, he'd rushed to her side. Stunned, he'd thought he recognized the injured beauty. *Katrina Livingston.*

At one time, the Alpha had suspected she could have been his mate. They'd met at a holiday party. A simple handshake had pricked a sexual awareness that he'd never experienced with another female. The strange sensation had temporarily abated after he'd thought she'd left, and he'd reasoned it'd been a fluke. But later in the evening, he'd found her on the balcony, taking in the sight of winter's first snowflakes, and they'd connected.

Sitting next to the outdoor fireplace, she'd accepted his jacket. Discussing everything from publishing to ice skating, their conversation had lasted nearly two hours. They'd laughed and discovered they both loved visiting New Orleans. An artist, she'd been born and raised in Louisiana, but had moved to Philadelphia with her brother. He'd asked her on a date, wishing to take her on a tour of his city, but she simply smiled, a sad expression washing over her face. When Jax had gone to the bar to get drinks, he'd returned to find that she'd disappeared.

It wasn't as if he'd known for certain she was his future mate, but the nagging suspicion had driven him to track her down in Philadelphia. At first she'd merely refused to talk with him, not answering his calls. In his typical determined style, Jax had taken it further, contacting her brother, Tristan, Alpha of Lyceum Wolves. When he'd accused him of attempting to force a mating, Jax had been confused. While it was true that he'd aggressively pursued Katrina, he'd never in any way attempted to coerce her into his pack. The disagreement had escalated, nearly inciting a war between him and her brother.

He recalled the fateful night at the club. When he'd witnessed someone who looked like Katrina falling ill, he'd gone soft, rushing to her side. Despite everything that had happened, his protective instinct had driven him to remain with her, insisting he accompany her in the ambulance. The hazy memory lingered, and Jax still couldn't be sure what had happened next. Katrina had transformed into something foreign, something evil. The creature wielded dark magick, injecting him with the poison and rendering him unconscious. During his captivity, it had appeared to him as different people, and he'd questioned his sanity.

Jax licked the crust from his lips; the iron-tanged blood only served to remind him of the pain they'd inflicted. All that had been lost. Nick, his beta, had died in battle, his essence soaking into the bayou mud. Despite the tragedy, his freedom robbed, dignity remained wrapped around the Alpha like a steel cloak. Nothing would change the inevitability of the moment or deter him from his task. Every lash of the whip had sharpened his resolve to exact vengeance upon the perpetrator. Deliberate and calm, he'd strategized his attack. Patience had superseded his urge for reprisal. However, today he'd be free. Dying wasn't an option, but killing a necessity.

A faint cry in the distance heightened his senses. It was the first sign of life he'd heard in weeks. The intermittent whimper echoed throughout the stone walls. Jax drew a deep breath, resisting the distraction that called away his focus. The slice of his canines tearing through his gums honed his attention. He'd deliberately starved himself, forcing his feral beast to the surface. It'd be likely he'd lose control, he knew. A risk he'd take; there was no other choice.

His swollen lids opened, taking in the sight of the approaching guard. Adrenaline pumped through his veins; unable to move, he'd have to lure his prey to his side with a split second chance at the kill. The shuffled sound of footsteps resonated in his ears.

Closer...closer...closer. He slowed his heartbeat, eyes staring as if death had come for him. Every cell in his body feigned surrender, conserving energy.

"Wake up, asshole."

Jax ignored the command and lay limp on the floor, his fangs pricking his own lips. The only thing that mattered was the blood he planned to spill. Tonight there'd be no struggle as the silver laced needle came at his skin. Like a lion stalking his prey in the Serengeti, he'd patiently wait for his prize.

Despite his weakened state, he detected the stench of stale cigarettes and whiskey on the human's breath. The kick to his thigh jolted him into battle, and he launched to attack. Ripping into the guard's neck, the Alpha went feral. The first rush of blood was like water to a dying plant. Jax tore at his flesh, swallowing the meat. Aside from a garbled cough, no sound resonated as life drained from the body. Exercising restraint, he ceased the attack to reach into his victim's pockets and search for the key to his shackles. His forefinger scratched along the serrated edge of the tiny metal implement. Yanking it out of the tattered fabric, Jax freed himself within seconds.

Although the blood and flesh of his captor surged his energy, it wasn't nearly enough to satiate his wolf, to force the shift he'd need to heal. Clawing his way up the jagged wall, Jax shoved to his feet. Dizziness threatened to topple him, but he closed his eyes, willing his balance to return.

His beast growled, urging him out of his cell. The musty

scent of mold choked him as he made his way through the labyrinth of the tunnels. A pinprick in the distance blossomed into a streak of dusty light, and he stumbled toward the faint hope of freedom. Jax tensed in anticipation of the enemy as a shadow to his right stirred. His vision sharpened on the source, a crumpled feminine form tied to a pole.

Jax dug his claws into the doorjamb, a growl gritted through his teeth. *Fuck me. They'll be here any second. Your priority is getting home to your pack, not her.* Jax had lost count of his days in captivity, but his mind had never stopped worrying about the state of his pack. Although he estimated he'd been missing for weeks, his mind remained clouded from the poison, and it could have been more than a month. With no beta to lead in his absence, battles for dominance would begin. Wolves would die in the process. Weakened and distracted, the pack would be susceptible to attack.

Jax cringed as the cry grew louder. Protective, the instinct of the Alpha roared in protest. He crossed the room, ceding to the wish of his wolf. Jax cautiously sniffed at the battered body, investigating the female. Although the faint recognition of a lupine registered in his mind, she was not of his pack. *Don't fucking do it*, he told himself. *The stray wolf isn't your concern. You don't have time.* Near death, she wouldn't make whatever journey lay ahead beyond liberation.

A whimper escaped into the darkness, stopping him cold. Her pain coiled in his chest as if it was his own, and he sucked a breath. Although his mind told him to run, to leave her behind, his heart disagreed.

Confounded, he sighed and looked over his shoulder to reassure himself that they were alone. The demon would soon discover he was missing. It was just a matter of time before they came for him.

"Please..." the pathetic creature uttered, barely audible.

"Goddammit," Jax cursed under his breath.

Lifting her chin with his finger, he tilted her head upward. Her platinum blonde hair, stained with dirt and blood, fell back onto her shoulders. A thin streak of light painted across her bruised cheek. At the sight of her blackened swollen lids, his gut teemed with anger. *Fucking monsters.* Jax stilled as he studied her face. Recognizing the little wolf, the one who'd both aroused and eluded him, he rushed to free her. *Katrina.*

·❧· *Chapter Two* ·❧·

Jax questioned his desire to rescue Katrina. Twice burned, he'd be a fucking idiot to think the third time was the charm. There was no such thing as luck. Jax knew better. *Cunning. Timing. Strategy.* These were the factors that contributed to success. Making decisions based on the heart, not facts, would lead to misfortune.

Jax closed his eyes, concentrating on his surroundings. Unable to detect the scent of his captor, the injured wolf was the only blood that registered. He tugged at the handcuffs that had bloodied her wrists. Her fingers had turned white from lack of circulation. The only thing keeping her alive was the magick within her lupine spirit. Jax scanned the room for keys to her shackles. In the corner, he spied a desk littered with papers and metal implements. He reached for a crowbar, and shook his head in frustration. Not exactly the right tool, but given the circumstances, he needed to make this fast.

"Please...," she begged.

"Listen, princess, if you want to get out of here alive

you'd better keep it down," he told her, spreading her hands apart onto the floor.

"I'm a wolf..."

"Katrina, I don't have time for games. Just hold still if you want to keep those fingers of yours. This might sting..." Jax's anger boiled up as she countered him.

Jesus Christ, he thought, wishing he could leave her without a shred of regret. But despite his reputation, sometimes well-deserved, for being a dick, he was a man of honor. Oh, he'd rescue her all right, but he swore to the Goddess that when this was all said and done, he'd return her ass to Philadelphia as soon as possible. If he never saw Katrina Livingston for the rest of his immortal life, he'd kiss the ground.

The loud bang reverberated throughout the room as he smashed the bar against the chains, cracking them loose. Sparks flashed in the dim light, the scent of metallic smoke swirling into the air. Jax cast the tool aside and caught Katrina in his arms as she tipped toward the floor. Cognizant that she'd lost consciousness, he hoisted her small frame over his shoulder. With no time to spare, he shoved to his feet, tore through the hallway and burst through the heavy wooden door to freedom.

Sunlight hit his face, and the rush of fresh air choked his shrunken lungs. Jax swiftly shielded her behind a tree, concerned the predator that had taken him was monitoring the exterior. Several seconds ticked by before he peered into the forest, assessing his surroundings. Celebrating the rise of the Alpha, cicadas sang throughout the thick woods. He reached for the ground and scooped at the dirt. With the earth to his nose, he sniffed and exhaled a loud breath in relief. There was no mistaking the rich soil of northern New York.

Who the fuck would kidnap an Alpha in his own territory, his own State? Questions spun in his mind as he wondered if whoever had attacked him was an insider. Retribution would come in due time, but today he'd make it his mission to get home, to rebuild.

A snap of a branch in the distance alerted him to the presence of others. Without hesitation, he took off into the brush. His thighs burned as he pressed upward, heading toward the sound of running water. Thorns sliced into the pads of his bare feet and skin. By the time he'd reached the edge of the rushing water, he'd become aware of the staccato beat on his back. *Katrina.*

"What the hell are you doing?" he snapped, setting her onto her feet. She stumbled backwards and he reached for her.

"Please don't hurt me," she begged, burying her face in her hands.

"Katrina." Jax knelt to her, aware that within seconds, whoever was following him would locate them. "You have to help me here."

"No, no, no," she repeated in a whispered cry. She struggled to cover her tattered bra and panties. "Please…please…"

"Whoever the hell kidnapped us is going to be here in about five minutes. If you shift, you'll feel better. Let's go."

KYM GROSSO

Jax stood and stripped off the threadbare boxers he'd been wearing, not bothering to shield his nudity. He closed his eyes, willing his wolf to the surface. Its presence, although sick, snarled in response. As he readied to transform, a whimper distracted him from his task. He blew out a breath and focused on Katrina. "If you're not going to shift, then we've gotta move on foot. Get on with it."

"I'm a wolf but I…" She cowered to the ground, bringing her thighs up to her chest and shaking her head. "Something…there's something wrong with me. Something wrong, wrong, wrong…"

"Jesus, Katrina…we don't have time for this fucking shit. When we get back, I'll hand you over to Tristan and we never have to see each other again. Let's go. Just strip and shift." Jax speared his fingers through his hair, wondering how his instincts about Katrina had been so far off base. She was nothing but trouble with a capital T. Fucked up trouble…the kind you'd find in a back street alley.

"You don't even know what happened to me," she screamed at him, her chin still protectively against her knees.

"I saved your pretty little ass, that's all that matters. But you're not my pack so if you don't shift soon, I can't help you."

"Fuck you," she shot back at the Alpha.

"You'd better stand down, wolf," he ordered.

Jax held his breath, taking in the sight of her battered body. Even though he was tempted to force her to shift,

10

something he knew he could do, it shook him to know someone had beaten her.

"Stay back." With a defiant glare, Katrina pressed to her feet, trembling as she tore off her clothes. Her voice cracked as she fisted her hands and closed her eyes. "And for the record, I'm not doing this because you're an Alpha. I'm doing this for me."

Jax reached for her, having had enough of her antics.

"No, don't..." Katrina attempted to shift. Her eyes rolled up into her head, and she flickered into a transparent state.

Jax fell forward as his hand passed through the air where she'd stood a moment ago. He stumbled, but regained his balance. Shock rolled through him as one of the monsters who'd kidnapped him came into view, black eyes staring back at him. As quickly as it came, it faded.

Katrina eventually transformed to wolf, but was unable to maintain her animal form. She morphed back to human, rolling into the mud and leaves. Naked and shaking, Katrina coughed up blood, her puffy eyes trained on Jax.

"What are you? What?" he asked, stunned at what he'd witnessed.

"Don't." She held a hand up to stop him from touching her.

"Jesus Christ." Jax bent to the ground and scooped her into his arms. "We need to talk about this."

"I told you. I'm a wolf. I'm damaged...broken." A barely audible whisper passed through her lips. "I don't...my name...I don't have a name. Just leave me. I don't blame you."

"What happened to you, Kat?"

"Alpha…" Her head lolled against his chest, warm breath brushing over his skin. "I only know…I know I'm wolf."

"Of course you are." Jax held her tight, cradling her nude body against his.

"You have no responsibility for me…your pack…"

"My pack is not your concern. You may not know who you are, but I do."

Jax had no time to further evaluate what had happened to Katrina. Whatever trauma she'd suffered had affected both her memory and magick. As her tears rolled down his chest, his heart and mind warred. She'd rejected him once, and as Alpha, he owed her nothing. Yet the explosive heat they'd shared long ago was all it had taken to spark his interest. Never mated, Jax knew one day the wolf who completed his soul would come for him. Second chances were opportunities cloaked in failure and as the victor of many a battle, he'd never needed one…until tonight.

"Leave me." Her voice cracked. Contrary to her words, she clutched at his neck, holding on for dear life.

Soft lashes swept butterfly kisses over his skin. Her fear resonated through his wolf, and although he couldn't heal her spirit, Jax refused to let her die. Regardless of *what* she was now, whatever they had done to her, compassion ruled his thoughts.

"We're getting out of here. Sorry, my little wolf. You're stuck with me this time." Jax began running, her body against his. As he leapt over the fallen trees, he took solace in her acquiescence.

From behind, the sound of rustling leaves grew louder and he spied the riverbank to his right. With Katrina unable to run, leveraging nature seemed his best alternative.

"Can you swim?" His eyes darted to the muddy water that swirled downstream.

"What?"

"Don't let go." Instinctively, Jax brushed his lips over her hair, and his stomach clenched as he realized what he'd done. Despite everything she'd said about him, accused him of, there was a weakness she invoked that he'd long forgotten.

The scent of his attackers dusted through the air, grounding his thoughts back into focus. Without further hesitation, Jax plunged into the churning river.

Jax had no choice other than to jump into the freezing water. At first, Katrina had shown signs of lucidity, calling his name in recognition, her eyes lowered in submission. But within minutes, she'd again lost consciousness. If it weren't for his deathly grip around her waist, she'd have drowned. The turbulent ride had lasted more than an hour but they'd eventually settled into a slow-moving current and washed ashore onto a familiar bank.

Trekking the rest of the way by land, Jax carried her until

he reached the secluded cabin. He and his beta occasionally spent weekends at the private sanctuary. Although rarely used, the property was closely monitored by pack security. Located in a remote region of the Finger Lakes, it was hours from the city, but Jax knew they'd be alerted to his presence the second he stepped foot through the perimeter's invisible magnetic security system. Thankfully, the biometric lock hadn't been tampered with or changed. It responded to his scans, allowing him access.

By the time he'd reached the master suite, their skin was rippled in gooseflesh. As Jax gingerly laid Katrina onto the mattress, he noted her once healthy olive complexion had been replaced by a pale sallow tone. Without the warmth of his body against hers, she began to violently shiver.

Fucking hell, Jax thought, taking in the sight of Katrina in his bed. He reached for the comforter and tucked it around her, but she continued to shake. His wolf urged him to lie with Katrina, but logic told him to back away. She'd already accused him of trying to force a mating, and he wouldn't give her reason to do so again. Cautious, Jax set his palm onto her back and gently rubbed his hand in circles until she settled into a calming sleep.

"What happened to you?" Jax asked out loud, aware she couldn't hear him. He shook his head, hoping like hell she'd wake and give him answers.

Jax estimated he had exactly four hours before someone from the pack showed up to confront the intruder, maybe less if the pack was out running. Given that the moon was new, he suspected not. But with the sun setting and exhaustion setting in, it made sense to lock up and spend the night in the cabin. Regardless of who showed up to greet him, he planned on returning to the city in the morning.

Jax stood and stole another glance at Katrina. He shouldn't leave her side, he knew, but he needed time to collect his thoughts. *Five minutes. I need a shower.*

"Why the hell am I so worried about her anyway? Look at her, Jax. Never forget. She betrayed you." He raked his fingers through his dirty hair and took off toward the bathroom. "Great, now you're talking to yourself. Get your shit together."

As the hot spray hit his face, Jax contemplated who'd taken over the pack. Although his friend, Finn, was a strong candidate, others would challenge him. It was likely his adversaries had sent wolves in to fight for the territory. With his return, Jax expected that he'd be forced to exert dominance, as they'd test his power, probing for weakness.

Blistering water sluiced over his roughened skin, and he closed his eyes, focusing on his future. At no time during his captivity had his will wavered. Now freed of his shackles, sweet vengeance simmered in the shadows. His wolf raged, demanding retribution. Goddess help the predator who'd attempted to break the Alpha. Death would be welcome by the time he'd finished exacting justice.

Chapter Three

Katrina stirred from sleep, her thoughts recalling their escape. Memories slammed into her. *The river.* The ice-cold water had burned her flesh. Struggling for life in the turbulent current, she'd clutched at the sole man who consumed her thoughts. *Jax Chandler.*

She had been kidnapped several times over the past three years, and her attackers had threatened that if she pursued Jax, he'd die. The second she'd met the striking Alpha at the holiday party, their chemistry had combusted and she'd suspected he could be her mate. In an effort to protect him, Katrina had immediately returned to Philadelphia. She'd done everything in her power to thwart his advances, but unrelenting, Jax wouldn't stop calling.

When she'd gone to Tristan for help, he'd misunderstood, believing that Jax had tried to force a mating. The two Alphas had never gotten along, and her request only further incensed Tristan's animosity toward Jax. As much as she hated the spiraling rumor, it was her brother's intervention that had temporarily thwarted Jax's advances. Concerned that Jax would travel to Pennsylvania to find her, she'd left for New Orleans. Putting physical distance between them, she'd hid from the demons. Devastated that she'd shattered his affections, Katrina had taken solace in knowing he'd be safe. Leaving Jax had been the only way to keep him alive.

The familiar sound of a shower pattered in the distance. Katrina jolted upright, and her vision blurred as she opened her eyes. The room spun, and she fell back onto the bed, willing her balance to return.

Katrina's mind raced in panic. The Alpha would seek answers, angered by what she'd done to him. Worse, she'd be helpless to resist the attraction, and the demons had warned her that bonding would destroy him. A tear escaped her lids as she considered his demise. She refused to let it happen.

Regardless, they'd come for her. It wasn't the first time. It wouldn't be the last. Katrina sniffed her palm, scenting the death breeding in her veins. The magick that brought her wolf to the surface had been siphoned once again. Although she'd researched the abductions, seeking a way to eradicate her tormentors, she couldn't be certain she'd survive long enough to stop them from killing her.

Calling on her wolf, a small rush of her shifter magick flickered and Katrina forced herself to shift. Thankful she'd transformed, she conserved her energy. Allowing herself time to rest, she curled into the sheets and prayed Jax would leave her alone. So tired, she had no strength to fight the Alpha. *Stay awake...stay awake and heal*, she repeated, but it was of no use. The seductive darkness called to her like a comforting angel. *Be strong, little wolf, be strong.*

"Katrina, it's okay to be afraid," she heard him say as if she were in a dream. "You can shift back now. I'm not going to let anything happen to you." A strong hand stroked over her pelt, and the power of the Alpha flowed through her.

You'll kill him, they'd told her. *Bond with your mate, and he'll die.* Despite what they'd threatened, none of it made sense to her. *Why had they kidnapped Jax?* She'd heard whispers of his name during her beating. They'd wanted her to hear it, she was certain. Nothing was an accident. Every action they took was deliberate, even if cloaked as coincidence.

But as he continued to pet her, she relaxed, destructive thoughts passing like clouds. The warmth of his touch soothed her soul. Her attraction to Jax was so very difficult to fight. For once, she just wanted to forget, to pretend she could have what would never be hers. Deciding to indulge, she leaned into him. Soon enough she'd attempt to escape.

"I know this feels good, but you can't stay like this forever."

She gave a low growl in response.

"Hey now, you know that's not going to work with me. I can see they did something to you...something awful." Jax hesitated, his voice shaken. He shook his head and continued. "Look, Kat, we can rest for a while like this but sooner or later you're going to have to tell me what happened, what you know. You and I…"

Katrina looked up to the great Alpha, wishing she'd never let the rumors of what had happened between them persist. No matter her good intention, the hurt and anger in his voice was palpable. Some mistakes in life could not be undone.

"I don't know why you said what you said to Tristan…shit, I don't want to talk about this right now. I…" Jax closed his eyes briefly and then opened them, glancing away. "What I need to know is how you got into that pit we were in. I need you to tell me every detail you remember about these assholes."

Katrina struggled to remain awake as he spoke to her. Whatever energy he'd given to her had been absorbed and she soon lost concentration. Just a few more hours of sleep, and she could run.

"All right, little wolf. I see this isn't happening now. You can rest, but our time will come," he promised. "You're not going back to Tristan until I'm satisfied you've told me everything."

Jax's words jumbled in her ears. Unable to keep her eyes open, she fell victim to the drugging exhaustion.

Born of an Alpha, her father's blood ran through her veins.

Submission would not come easily for the independent she-wolf. There was only one person she'd ever consider surrendering to...Jax Chandler. It seemed an eternity that she'd denied her carnal craving, but within the safety of her dream, every delicious inch of the Alpha belonged to her. She dragged her tongue over his flesh, tasting her prize. Her wolf rejoiced in response as she owned her mate.

"My Alpha," Katrina moaned, nipping at his skin. Her nipples ached, brushing over his abdomen. As his hardened cock slid between her breasts, his fingers fisted her blonde locks. The sweet twinge of pain to her scalp reminded her of who controlled her, and she smiled.

Katrina's hips straddled his leg as she slowly grazed her lips over his skin. She sought relief for her aching pussy, writhing against his knees, her wetness spreading over his skin. The scent of his masculinity drove her further, her mouth teasing down the muscled ridge leading below his abdomen.

"No, no, no, little wolf." A low growl warned her to stop. Her teeth met his skin in response, unwilling to accept his dismissal.

"Not today, baby," the commanding voice ordered. Katrina sucked a breath as her head was tugged upward by the strong hand wrapped around her hair. "As much as I want you, it's not going to be like this. Call me old-fashioned, but I like my women lucid."

Her eyes flew open in shock as she woke, stunned to see Jax smiling down on her. *What the hell did I do?* She'd thought it all an erotic dream, but as his dick prodded her chest, she realized what she'd done. Katrina attempted to push away with her arms but he held tight.

"Jax," she breathed. "I'm sorry. What did I…oh, Jesus."

"You can call me Alpha." His smile turned cold and Katrina's heart pounded in her chest. She could sense his anger. "I want answers."

"Jax…" she began.

"Alpha." His voice boomed throughout the room.

"Let me go…Alpha," she demanded under her breath. Her hand caught his wrist, tearing it away.

Rolling over onto her back, she pulled at the sheets, attempting to conceal her bare skin. Jax made no move to stop her but neither did he cover his own nudity. Her eyes skimmed over his chest down to his erection and then back to his eyes. She turned her head away, her cheeks heating in embarrassment. Not only had she almost sucked his cock, she'd been unable to resist ogling his gorgeous male form. She'd never seen him nude before, hadn't recalled what he'd looked like when he'd stripped in the woods. But the memory of her night with the charismatic Alpha had been permanently etched in her mind.

As surprised as she'd been to wake with her lips pressed to his flesh, the burning desire for him never faltered. She could escape, move a thousand miles away and the yearning for Jax would never cease. It was a nightmare she couldn't shake. The only resolution was finding a cure to her affliction…one she'd either find or die trying.

Jax shifted onto his side, and Katrina's eyes flashed to his. As much as she wanted to hide, she owed him the truth.

Her stomach churned; she was terrified he'd never believe her excuse for why she'd rebuked his advances, for the rumors that had started.

After she left for New Orleans, Jax helped Tristan locate a wolf that had attacked his mate, and the two Alphas had come to a truce. By the time she returned to Philadelphia rumblings about Jax Chandler had ceased within the Lyceum Wolves. She'd decided at that time not to reopen old wounds, and didn't discuss it further with Tristan.

"You ready to try this again?" he asked, bringing her thoughts back to focus. His piercing stare bored into her, the power of the Alpha filtered throughout the room. "What happened to you?"

"It's complicated." Katrina rolled over to face him, curling onto her side.

"I want to talk about what happened in that prison. I want to know what those things are and why you were there."

"But what I just did..." Katrina's eyes fell to his chest but she refused to look any lower. She averted her gaze, and took a deep breath.

"Oh, don't you worry, Kat. We're going to discuss that, too." He shot her a wicked smile that quickly faded. "But right now, I need to know what I'm dealing with...those things..."

"Demons." Katrina's voice cracked. At the mention of the creatures, she fought the threatening nausea, the stench of their putrid breath fresh in her memory. No matter how many times they came for her, she never got used to the abuse. "I'm not sure exactly what they are. Maybe they're not demons per se. Sometimes...the magick...it feels like witches. I don't know for sure."

"In the days, weeks...shit, I don't even know how long they had me...I just know they looked different. The one that lured me," he paused as if he were embarrassed to admit what he'd seen, then continued, "it came to me in Finn's night club. I thought it was you."

"It looked like me?" she asked, surprise in her voice. Guilt rolled through her at his confession. They'd used her to lure the Alpha.

"Yeah. The strength of these things," he sighed. "That night, she was stronger than a human. They used silver to take me down, keep me down. My power had no influence on them."

"It doesn't," Katrina interrupted. She tucked the covers under her chin and stared blankly ahead. "That's why I think it's some kind of magick. They want our power."

"Wolves?"

"I think so." A tear rolled down her cheek and she didn't move to wipe it away. "Usually, it's just me. The times they've taken me..."

"Wait, are you telling me they've taken you more than once?" Jax's voice grew soft and he slid his hand across the sheets toward Katrina.

She nodded in silence.

"Jesus Christ. Does Tristan know?"

As Jax's fingers touched her cheek, Katrina began to softly cry. *My fault. I should have been smarter. I should have figured out a way to kill them by now.*

"Hey, it's going to be okay. I swear to you."

"No, Jax. You don't understand." Her wet lashes fluttered open and she licked her lips. "These things. There's something about me they want, they've always wanted. I've been trying for so long to make it stop. You don't know how hard I've tried over the years."

"Years?" He shook his head in disbelief.

"Yes, years. A couple now. Their power is stronger every time. They've stolen…" Katrina sucked back a sob. "My magick. In the woods, you saw what happened. Something's happening to me. I'm not right. And my wolf? She's slowly dying. If I don't find a way to kill them…I'm going to die."

"No, that can't be."

"Yes." Katrina shoved up to sit, and brushed both hands over her face and through her hair. She took a deep breath and blew it out, distraught with the agonizing situation. "Look Jax, I've got to go. Just being here now with you is putting you in danger. I'm like poison to you."

"What the hell are you talking about? You were just all over me five minutes ago and believe me, the way it felt…you weren't exactly killing me. What is going on with you?"

Katrina registered the disappointment crossing Jax's face, his lips drawn tight in anger. He'd never forgive her for what she'd done and she didn't blame him.

"Alpha," she began, and lowered her eyes in submission. "I'm grateful you saved me but I have to go."

"No fucking way, Kat. Not this time. I feel like I'm

going crazy here. You and me…Jesus Christ, what you told Tristan. And then just now, you weren't faking that. You may have been sleeping but that was real. What the fuck is going on?"

"Nothing. I need to do this on my own and you can't help me. The longer I'm around you…"

"What? Please enlighten me, would you? What the hell do you think is going to happen? You could have been killed back there, and I saved your ass. You're in the middle of New York. Where exactly are you going to go?" Jax sat up and raked his fingers through his tousled hair.

"I don't know. I just know I have to get out of here. You're in danger as long as I'm here." Katrina pushed off the bed to leave and Jax leapt onto her. His body crushed against hers as he pinned her arms down against the mattress. Like a startled rabbit, she froze. The warmth and strength of her Alpha emanated from his skin to hers and she fought the arousal that she'd buried.

"No running," he told her, bringing his lips within inches of hers. "I will never hurt you, little wolf. But I'm done playing games. You. Will. Not. Leave."

"Jax…" Katrina's chest rose, her eyes locked on his.

"We need to work together to defeat these demons, witches. Whatever the hell they are, I cannot allow you to go alone. Tristan hasn't protected you." His forehead pressed to hers. "I don't know why you said the things you did."

"You'll never know how sorry I am." The whisper passed through her lips, finally a truth. "I don't ever want to hurt you again. Please."

"Don't fight me, Kat. This thing between us…"

"That night at the party…" Katrina struggled to continue as the heat grew between her legs. Ever since that night, she'd kept track of the Alpha, followed him on social media, cried herself to sleep knowing she'd be alone forever. Watching him from afar through a looking glass while he'd dated woman after woman had crushed her heart.

"Your body knows mine, little wolf." Jax leaned in to sniff her neck, his tongue darted out along the hollow of her throat. He growled as she turned her head in submission, giving him access. "We can't ignore this. No fucking way. Do you know why I'm Alpha?"

"You're strong." Katrina ached in desire as he slid the tip of his tongue along her skin. Her chest heaved for breath; she couldn't resist him. Her body lit on fire as his lips pressed to her neck.

"Raw instinct. Knowing when to trust what your gut is telling you. And do you know what it tells me about you?"

"What?" she moaned. Her skin broke out in gooseflesh, his warm breath on her ear.

"When I wake up with your sweet body against mine, you tasting of my flesh, calling my name…that is as real as it gets. But at the same time, I cannot ignore what you've done. Accusing me of forcing a mating? Tell me, why does a wolf do such a thing?" Jax whispered. "I should hate you, despise you for what you've done. But I don't. No, I believe this is a puzzle. None of it makes sense right now, but I will have answers. I always get what I want, Katrina."

"I had to protect you. You and Tristan have never got along, you know that. I needed you to leave me alone, and he misunderstood what I told him. But I swear to you, I never meant to hurt…" She shuddered in arousal as he took her earlobe between his teeth. Katrina cursed her body as she arched up into him. "Ah…Jax."

"This is why I'm Alpha. Instinct tells me I can't ignore this. There's something between us, a reason we're brought together. You and I have things to work out, and you're staying with me for as long as it takes."

"Please, Jax. I'm not good for you," she protested. Her heart fluttered as Jax raised his head to pin her with his gaze.

"What secrets are you keeping? Your lips may lie." His knees pressed her legs open, and he settled between them. "Hmm…your body tells me the truth."

"I want to tell you, but…please…" Katrina tilted her hips upward, his hardened dick prodded her belly.

"Tell me you'll stay, help me find who did this to you…to me…my pack."

Katrina registered the desperation in his words. The desire to be with Jax was overwhelming. Any rational arguments had been slayed by the primal attraction that sizzled over her skin. Her spiraling thoughts justified reasons to stay within the arms of her Alpha. Jax had unlimited resources at his disposal to research the dark society. If they went to New Orleans, it could buy them the time they needed to discover a way to destroy them. Before she had a chance to think any further about the implications, her heart had won the argument.

"Yes." She closed her eyes, the word barely audible on her lips.

As his mouth captured hers, her wolf cried in celebration. Her tongue swept against his as she reveled in the moment she'd dreamed about for years. Never had she imagined it would be under these circumstances. Rescued and enchanted by the Alpha, Katrina lost herself in his touch. She wrapped her legs around his waist, pulling him toward her.

"What is it about you?" Jax asked, sucking her bottom lip.

"I'm sorry…" Katrina gasped as he kissed her again, this time with a passion that speared through her from her head to her toes.

Consumed by lust, she was barely aware of the footsteps coming down the hallway. As Jax tore his lips from hers and shoved her to the back of the bed, she panted for air, her chest heaving.

"Stay back," he warned.

A creak of the door was all the warning she had before it flew open, strangers looming in the hallway. As the Alpha shifted into his powerful black wolf, Katrina's eyes lit in reverence. The majestic beast snarled, its tail up, standing tall in a show of aggression.

Katrina attempted to shift, but her magick faltered; a flicker of her wolf appeared only to disappear. As the intruders approached the threshold, she scanned the room for a weapon. Wrapping her fingers around the base of a brass lamp, she ripped its cord from the wall. Katrina didn't hesitate as she launched the heavy object at the red-haired stranger. The base nicked him in the head and he fell to his knees.

"Jesus Christ, Jax. Get your girl under control," he called, holding a hand to his bleeding scalp.

"Katrina?" She froze as she registered the sound of the familiar voice.

Jax flashed to his familiar form, towering above them all. His loud growl blasted through the room, silencing the din.

"Finn, rise," Jax commanded. "What's he doing here?"

"Saving your sorry ass," Jake quipped, lifting his gaze to meet Jax's.

"Watch your words, wolf," Jax warned.

"Are you hurt?" Jake asked, his voice tense.

"I'm all right," Katrina replied, giving him a small smile. The last time she'd been in Louisiana, she and Jake had grown close, becoming good friends. Although Katrina considered going to him, she cautiously remained on the bed, her focus drawn to the angry Alpha.

"Stay back," Jax snarled. He eyed the wolf, assessing the situation.

"It's, um…it's okay, Jax…" Katrina regarded his pensive expression, but continued, hoping to soothe his concern. "I know Jake. We're friends."

"What the hell happened?" Without asking for the Alpha's permission, Jake intrepidly crossed toward Katrina.

Jax stepped to block his path, and Katrina reached for his hand. Running the pad of her thumb over his palm, she attempted to assuage the protective Alpha. She suspected

Jax remained unaware of their connection, yet his actions spoke volumes.

"He won't hurt me." She lifted her gaze to meet Jax's, noting the vulnerability in his eyes.

"Jax. Please. It's okay. We're just friends. I'm not leaving you." As the words left her lips, she knew she'd said it in all honesty. She'd have to tell him sooner or later about the prophesy. If they completed the bond, he'd die, but it was a conversation to be had in private.

She smiled as Jax leaned in and brought her hand to his cheek. The soft skin of his lips at her palm tickled her skin and she gave a small laugh.

"I need to talk to Finn," Jax told her.

Katrina nodded in acknowledgment and wrapped the sheet around her body. As he dropped her hand and stepped aside, her eyes never left his. Her heart pounded, the loss of his touch leaving her with an odd sense of emptiness.

"How did you end up here? Did he hurt you?" Jake glared at Jax as he passed to his right.

"I'm okay. Really, Jake." Katrina assured him as he wrapped his arms around her. "Jax helped me escape."

"Not again?"

"Yes, again." Jake had seen her struggle to shift on more than one occasion and was one of the few people she'd confided in about the abductions.

"We've got to get you out of here. Somewhere safe. I'll take you back to Logan...protect you. You should have never left New Orleans."

As Katrina pulled out of his embrace, she shook her

head. *No more running.*

"I'm going to stay with Jax." She tried to ignore the look of surprise on Jake's face as she spoke, and although scared about hurting Jax, she couldn't leave him again.

"Now hold on one fucking minute." Jake's voice grew louder. "First of all, Tristan is your Alpha. Second of all, you know you're safer in New Orleans with us. Look, I know this assho…" His eyes darted to Jax and he rephrased. "This Alpha. He likes to shoot off orders like he owns the entire world. You have a home and it's not here."

"Jake, please. I know I said I'd…"

"You'll never be safe here. They'll come again. You know it's true."

"She stays with me," Jax asserted.

"Alpha, I think we'd better talk," Finn interrupted. "We've been searching for you for over a month."

"They're here," Jax commented. "You," he pointed to Finn, "come with me. Jake stays." His eyes focused in on Katrina who held the covers against her chest. "Do not leave the cabin. This is none of your concern."

Katrina sensed their presence. *Wolves.* Although they weren't of her pack, the hum of their magick grew thick in the air. Instinct told her to go with Jax, but his command to remain with Jake took precedence. Before she had a chance to speak, the Alpha shifted, and within a blink of an eye, he'd gone out the door.

You'll kill him, they'd told her. For so long, she'd believed their words. Deliberately avoiding Jax, she'd thought she'd protected him. Katrina brought her fingers to her mouth, his searing kiss lingering on her lips, and she began to question everything she'd thought to be true. No matter her fear, her heart had won; she'd chosen to stay with the one man who she believed was her mate.

⇥❧ *Chapter Four* ❧⇤

Jax pushed thoughts of Katrina to the recesses of his mind as his pack came into view. He'd expected the infighting. A wave of agitation rippled through his psyche, confirming the instability. He scanned the woods but didn't sense any intruders or newcomers to their clan. Yet as he transformed, he took notice of several young males stepping closer, tipping their hands in confrontation.

He waved Finn behind him, happily surprised the experienced wolf had stepped in to lead. While they'd been close at one time, their lives had taken separate paths. Jax had recruited Finn to work with him at his magazine, ZANE. A photographer, he'd been an integral player, creating high profile spreads that brought a unique perspective to the publication. Although talented, Finn chose to leave New York City. He'd gone to Ireland to settle a dispute within his mother's pack. Upon returning, he'd refused to return to ZANE, giving up his artistic passion. Jax had argued with Finn, insisting he was throwing away his life, but supported him when he'd created a New York

City night club that catered to supernaturals.

As he looked into the eyes of his old friend, Jax recognized the blood-thick loyalty that stood the test of time. He considered everything that had transpired over the years, their friendship and the greater good of the pack. Prior to his abduction, Jax had been devastated by Nick's death. He'd grown despondent and refused to name another beta. He couldn't fathom another wolf taking his best friend's place. Yet as Jax stood before his pack, he reached inside himself, drawing on the wisdom that only an Alpha could possess. It was his duty to protect his wolves, no matter what turbulence affected his own life. With the decision made, he'd bury the pain and announce his edict.

"Agrestis Wolves, I stand before you today as your Alpha," Jax addressed them. He waited patiently as they flickered back into their human forms. A glint of moonlight appeared as silver shadows on their skin. "You are not without your leader."

"You were captured?" a voice called out.

"Yes, I was attacked, but I prevailed and stand before you today." Jax sought to ease their concerns, mindful they'd be shaken. It wasn't as if dangerous supernatural beings didn't exist, but it was rare one was powerful enough to kill an Alpha.

"And what about Nick? He's dead. You didn't protect him," he charged.

Jax's eyes flickered red with rage as the brawny wolf, Arlo, spoke Nick's name. On the verge of losing his temper, the Alpha forced his pulse to steady. Jax had long recognized

Arlo's antagonistic nature, but this was the first time he'd been aggressive enough to challenge the Alpha. As the pack stirred, Jax sensed their acceptance of the defiant wolf. In the Alpha's absence, he'd assumed a position of authority.

"Shut the fuck up about Nick." Jax's voice boomed throughout the forest. Several wolves reverted to their animal form out of fear, cowering in submission. "What happened in New Orleans was a battle. People die in battle."

"Maybe you should care a little more about what happens here in your own pack," Arlo countered. He stepped forward, fisting his meaty hands. Dirt clung to his sweat-covered flesh.

"We've gotten along without you," Easton, a second wolf, yelled. He, too, eyed Jax and made a move toward the porch.

In his peripheral vision, Jax spied Finn stripping down. The sight of the strong redheaded male preparing for a fight gave confidence to the Alpha's choice. Jax stared down his pack and set forth with his announcement.

"Agrestis Wolves. I hereby name Finn Cavanagh as my beta." His eyes darted over to his friend, who remained impassive. If it weren't for the tick in his forehead, his somber expression would have concealed his irritation. "This is my pack and mine alone. If you challenge me, do it now, but there will be no discourse."

"I smell the bitch." Arlo stroked his flaccid cock and sniffed up into the air. "That's right, Chandler. Her scent is in the wind. You going to let us all have a go?"

"You'd leave your own wolves to go fuck a Lyceum

whore?" Easton laughed.

A surge of rage exploded within as the Alpha shifted. The threat toward Katrina had been the trigger; his reaction swift and forceful. Lurching forward, Jax attacked. Although Easton had managed to transform, Jax pounced onto the grey wolf, slicing his teeth into his neck. Blood rushed into his mouth, feeding his fury. The whimpering wolf rolled onto its back in submission, its paws drawn tight to its body. Despite his frenzied state, Jax maintained control. Granting the wolf mercy, he turned his focus to Arlo, whose teeth were firmly embedded into his hackles.

Forcing his body backward, Jax slammed the large brown wolf into the dirt. Arlo had always been a skilled fighter, but he was no match for the powerful Alpha. Jax had ruled for over thirty years, and he'd demonstrate his dominance yet again. In the heat of battle, no compassion would be granted to the wolf who threatened his rank. The Alpha never took killing lightly. Yet tonight death would blanket the forest, its foul stench a reminder to those who challenged him, of who exactly led Agrestis Wolves.

Growling, saliva and blood sprayed into the air as Jax secured his hold. Arlo snapped in an attempt to dislodge the fierce Alpha. Unrelenting, Jax pierced his fangs deep into his opponent's fur, shredding the skin. The tenacious wolf shoved upward, refusing to submit. With his forepaws, Jax pinned the wolf immobile and lodged his jaws further into Arlo's neck. Releasing the supreme strength of an Alpha, Jax vigorously shook his challenger. Bones snapped as he crushed its spine, the sanguine essence rushing down his throat.

Jax absorbed the magick as the life drained from the wolf. Raging, he shifted to human and sprang to his feet. A mournful, triumphant howl tore from the Alpha's lungs, and his wolves rose to meet his call. Overcome with emotion, he both celebrated his victory and grieved the loss of a pack member. For the greater good, blood had been spilled to protect them all. Jax wiped tears from his face, satisfied when Finn nodded and joined him. *My new beta.* No longer divided, Agrestis Wolves were united once again. *The Alpha had risen.*

Jax shoved the cabin door open, and Finn followed. They'd run with the pack for over an hour and had returned exhilarated but exhausted. Although Jax had known leaving Katrina was a risk, his wolves took priority over the woman who'd nearly started a territorial war. The attraction between them was undeniable, but he struggled to reconcile his feelings with what she'd done in the past. No matter how beautiful she was, he didn't yet trust her. Instinct may have urged him to keep her close, but logic told him to question whether she was friend or foe.

The attractive little wolf caused him angst, an emotion he was not at all used to feeling. A curious pang of jealousy had stabbed through him when he'd observed the interaction between Katrina and Jake. His gut twisted as he speculated on the nature of their relationship. She'd told him that they were friends, but was she telling the truth?

Jake was a good friend to his sister Gillian's mate, Dimitri. He'd shown aggressive tendencies from the moment Jax had met him in New Orleans. While Jake displayed irritation toward him, it was clear the young wolf hadn't tried to establish himself as Alpha nor had he challenged Finn. On the contrary, his new beta appeared entirely comfortable with the Acadian wolf, welcoming him as a guest.

Jax turned on the kitchen sink spigot and submerged his head in the flowing water. The icy stream did little to thwart the churning thoughts of Katrina, Jake and the challenge. Jax reasoned he'd need a long shower to wash away the death lingering on his skin. Finn's rough voice drew him out of his contemplation. He jerked his head upward, droplets spraying throughout the kitchen.

"Jesus Christ, Jax. Do you think you could have taken five fucking minutes to ask me to take Nick's place?" Finn glared at his Alpha.

Jax caught the look of disgust that crossed his beta's face and shrugged. While the debonair Alpha was usually the epitome of a gentleman, he had trouble shaking off the feral tendencies the challenge had brought forth.

"This shouldn't be a surprise." Jax grabbed a dishtowel and wiped his face. "You're my beta."

"What the hell is going on with you?" Finn gestured to the wet tiles.

"What?" Jax glanced to the floor and chose to ignore the

mess. "It's just water."

It had been over a year since Jax had visited his private home. While the décor of the cabin was upscale, its exposed beams and soapstone kitchen counters gave it a slightly rustic feel. The great room, with its vaulted ceilings and skylights, soaked in the light of the moon. Despite not visiting there often, he'd utilized a service to keep the home well stocked with supplies.

Naked, Jax strode across the room to the bar, where he reached for a bottle of Lagavulin. Setting four glasses onto the smooth surface, he uncorked the scotch and began to pour.

"Seriously. Have you lost your shit?" Finn snatched a throw blanket off the sofa and wrapped it around his waist.

"What is wrong with you?" The caustic liquor burned his throat as he downed a shot and poured another glass. Offering Finn a tumbler, he handed it off and fell back down onto the black leather sofa.

"Really, you gonna just lie there? Letting it all hang out?" Finn took a swig and wiped his mouth with the back of his hand.

"What do you want me to say?" Jax closed his eyes and opened them, taking a deep breath. His mood grew dark and he continued. "It had to be done. I could not allow Arlo to challenge me further."

Jax lifted his gaze to meet Finn's. He wasn't waiting for judgment. They both knew what he'd done was in the best interest of the pack.

"I'm not talking about that. He was an asshole. He's

been fighting me since the day you went missing, but Jax…fuck. How was I supposed to take over?"

"Did Tristan show his face?" the Alpha asked, stretching his neck from side to side.

"You kiddin' me? After what went down with Katrina, you think I was going to tell him who I saw in the club? Fuck no. If he was lookin' for her, I wasn't volunteering information. He would have been up here tearing the entire city apart."

"Smart move." Even though Jax and Tristan had established peace, a truce of sorts, the issue with Katrina had never been resolved. He still believed that Jax had gone after his sister.

"It was Logan who called. Gillian was behind it. Holy shit, man. I'd call her a pit bull but that would be an insult to the breed. The tiger in her…she would not give up. She kept calling here for you and next thing I knew, I had the Alpha of Acadian Wolves threatening me."

"She's my sister. The Alpha genes are strong in that one. She won't submit, you know that, right? Dimitri's got his hands full with her but I can't help but be proud. She doesn't take any shit."

"Yeah well, tiger girl got Logan involved and before I knew it, Jake was here. Between the two of us, we were able to manage things, but Jax…" Finn took a deep draw and coughed. "What happened to you…you've got no idea how fucking happy I am you're back. But tonight…"

"Ah, the beta thing…" Jax swirled his drink, taking note as the legs ran down the sides of the glass.

"Yeah, that." Finn shook his head and threw it back against the back of his chair.

"You would have been my choice of beta if you hadn't left." Jax lofted the statement in silence, waiting for Finn to acknowledge it, to finally tell him what had happened over in Ireland that had kept him from coming home. He'd never been the same.

"Look, you know I had to go. And hell, I've been back for a while now. But your beta?"

"It's done. Nick was my best friend, you know that. He, uh…" Jax's voice cracked as his sorrow rose to the surface. He swallowed the last of his scotch and choked back his emotions. "He's gone. I love him, but there's no going back."

"He was a great guy."

"And so are you. What's done is done. Finn, this makes sense. You're the only one I can trust. We've been friends a long time. It was the right decision."

"You could have told me. To just put it out there like that. It's not like I wasn't ready to fight tonight. Seriously, I was ready to tear the shit out of Easton and Arlo. Those dickheads have been challenging me since the day you left, but hell, to just do it like that…not tell me."

"How long have you known me?" Jax stood and went to the bar.

"A long fucking time, that's how long." Finn stared at his Alpha, his eyes bloodshot.

"This is why I'm Alpha. I make decisions. There is no wavering. It's what I do." Jax didn't expect others to always understand his responsibility. It was the ultimate burden and opportunity. The lives of hundreds of wolves and the future of their pack rested in his hands.

"I can see you're going to give me more of your Alpha mumbo jumbo, so let's move to the next topic. What the fuck is up with your, uh," Finn gestured to his friend's dick. His mouth curled up in a half grin, "your lack of clothes? Because I know Jax Chandler, and this is not him."

"Perhaps I don't give a fuck what anyone thinks tonight. I'm going back to my nature. I'm raw." Jax pounded on his chest with a closed fist. The killing had surged a virile energy within him that he struggled to contain.

His thoughts turned to Katrina. The fresh scent of coconut shampoo lingered in the air and he wondered where Jake was. Had he watched her while she ran the soap over her smooth skin? An unfamiliar possessive urge crawled inside his belly and his lips drew tight in agitation. He didn't want to care who she fucked or what she did.

Jax curled his fingers into the mahogany bar, his claws scratching the wood. *Fuck it all, I need to see her now*, he thought.

"Jax." He heard her voice softly call to him. As he raised his eyes to hers, the beast inside stirred. *Mine.*

❧ *Chapter Five* ❧

The sight of Katrina standing in the hallway took his breath away. She appeared fragile, her wet hair combed behind her shoulders. Her once brunette locks had turned blonde, and he wondered if the change was related to her abduction. His eyes darted to Jake as he brushed by Katrina, giving her a small hug as he passed. The brief but intimate interaction reminded him that no matter his visceral attraction, he didn't trust her.

"Everything all right?" Jake asked.

"Kat." Jax ignored the question, his eyes locked on Katrina's.

"Everything's great, Jake. Thanks for taking care of my pack while my sorry ass was captured, Jake." The Acadian wolf gave a smirk, his voice laden with sarcasm. He snatched a tumbler and poured a scotch. "You're welcome, Alpha. No problem, Alpha."

"Sometimes showing trust is a form of appreciation." Jax gave a brief smile to Jake and turned his attention back to Katrina.

As he drew closer to the she-wolf, he noted no other scent on her. As much as Jake grated on his nerves, the confirmation he hadn't touched Katrina ameliorated the Alpha's concerns. After Jax had fought to save Dimitri and Gillian, he considered that Logan had returned the favor by sending an honorable wolf to help Finn watch over his pack.

"Sometimes a simple thank you works too, but whatever." Jake stole a glance at Jax's bare ass. His eyes darted to Finn, who laughed in response. "And sometimes…just putting on some clothes is a great way to show appreciation. You look like you work out. I'll give you that. But dude, I don't need to see your junk all day long. How 'bout some threads?"

Before Jax had a chance to retort, Katrina approached, distracting him. Her petite form swam in his black cashmere bathrobe. The lapels drifted open, and his eyes fell to the swell of her breasts. A warm hand on his roughened cheek stunned him into silence. His eyes lifted to meet hers.

"Clothes do not make the man. The Alpha can do as he wishes." Katrina smiled.

"Don't listen to her, Finn. She grew up with Tristan. That one never gets dressed either," Jake retorted.

Katrina glared over to Jake for only a second. Jax never lost focus as she spoke to him. Although he towered over her, she commanded his attention.

"Death is never easy," she told him.

"I'm fine," he began.

"I smell it on you. Never forget, Jax. I am an Alpha's daughter. An Alpha's sister. A death within the pack destroys a wolf to renew the lives of many. The wolves...they're settled now?"

"Yes. And you are..." He leaned into her touch, within inches of her lips. Jax's cock jerked as he breathed in her scent. A devious smile crossed his face. "You smell delicious."

Jax's chest tightened as Katrina's expression grew somber. He wanted to trust her. He'd never thought it possible that anyone besides another Alpha could understand what it was like for him to kill during a challenge, yet she stood before him unafraid, undaunted by the fatality he'd caused. There had only been a handful of occasions when he'd been forced to take the life of a brother. Each time it came with a price, and the cost was high on his soul. Yet this was the responsibility of a leader, and the pack rejoiced in the peace and stability of an established Alpha. They'd mourn the loss, perhaps some would harbor resentment, the family and friends of the deceased, but they'd also come to acceptance. It was the culture of the wolves: their past, their future, how it always would be.

"I know I said I'd stay, but maybe Jake is right. Maybe I should go. After what I did to you...your wolves...they won't understand," Katrina explained, her voice gentle.

Her soft palm on his skin soothed the bitterness of the past. Confused by his mixed emotions, he blinked and the memory of what she'd done flashed through his mind. A fresh surge of anger surfaced. Until she confessed what had happened, why she did what she'd done, he couldn't forgive her. His hardened dick told him to forget about it, but reason prevailed. *Don't let the temptress fool you.* Jax wrapped his hands around her wrists, closed his eyes and shook his head.

"We need to clear the air." He lifted his gaze to meet hers, his brow furrowed and tense. He forced himself to remember everything that had happened, and his tone grew firm. "Until I know everything, and I mean every last fucking detail about what is going on with these demons, you aren't leaving. Consider yourself a guest. Or a hostile witness. Whichever you prefer...doesn't matter, because you're not leaving."

"You can't keep me against my will."

"Oh, I can and I will. What you did..." he growled.

"Things aren't how they seem," she offered.

"And just how are they?" Finn rose and approached them. "You accused Jax of forcing you to mate with him."

"I told you..." Katrina's eyes darted from Finn to Jax. "You have to believe me. I never told Tristan you tried to force me to mate with you. But I was trying to get you to stop coming after me. I was trying to protect you from these things. You and Tristan...you've never gotten along. When I told him that you wouldn't stop coming after me, the rumors started. I know I should have stopped it but then Marcel died. It was just easier. You left me alone. You were safe. I'm sorry, Jax. But it's not what you think."

"Really? Because people almost got killed over your little accusation. Who does that?" Finn asked.

"Someone who's desperate, that's who," Jake interjected, crossing the room to Jax and Katrina.

"How would you know? You were down in NOLA. It's not like you were here when it happened," Finn countered.

"I know Kat and there's no way she'd do that without a reason." His eyes went to Jax. "Let her go."

"Really, just how well do you know her?" Finn questioned, his question laced with implication. "Are you lovers? Friends with benefits? Fuck buddies? Do tell, wolf."

"Enough!" Jax yelled, without letting go of Katrina.

"You know her presence in this cabin causes trouble in the pack as we speak. It's part of the reason Arlo is dead," Finn said accusingly.

"What?" Katrina's eyes widened. Unsuccessfully, she attempted to break free of Jax's hold.

"That's right, baby. They could smell you on him." Finn poured a shot and downed it. "They were going after you. And he defended your pretty little ass."

"No…Jax…please…you have to let me go." Katrina shook her head, continuing to tug her wrists from his grip.

"I said enough!" Jax yelled. "All of you. You will not blame her for Arlo's death."

"Please just let me go. I'm not good for you," she protested.

"Finally, someone in this goddamned room sees reason. I don't know why you are so set on keeping her. It's like you aren't even thinkin' straight." Finn tunneled his fingers through his ginger locks. In a moment of recognition as to what was happening to his Alpha, his eyes landed on Jake, who shook his head no.

"I need to go back to New Orleans. I'll find answers

there. They won't stop. If I stay here…"

"I'm warning you. Do not challenge me," Jax commanded. Although he'd loosened his grip, he hadn't released her. "I already told you earlier, we're going to work things out between us. What happened in that cave and when you went to shift, no…this is fucked up. I saw what happened. That night in the club, the person who kidnapped me looked like you, but it wasn't. In the ambulance…they changed. I want to know what the hell we are dealing with. Why are they after you? Why me?" Jax released Katrina and threw his hands up in frustration. She rubbed her wrists, tears brimming in her eyes. Her rage emanated from her like a beacon, stabbing through his chest. "No, you're not leaving New York until I have answers, and if there's something in New Orleans that you know about that's going to help us, then I'm going with you."

"Jax…" Katrina's shoulders slumped in defeat. She looked to Jake for help but he shrugged, deferring to the Alpha.

"We can't stay here. I've got to get back to the city, check on ZANE. Fuck." Jax blew out his breath, the realization that his multi-billion dollar corporation, while probably still running, had been ignored. Assuring the publication subsidiaries were still intact was a priority. "Finn. I need you to round everyone up. We're going back home."

Jax turned away from Katrina, needing space. As he strode down the hallway to go shower, guilt rushed through him. Jesus Christ, she was pushing him to his limits. He wanted to fuck her senseless until they both couldn't breathe. She'd kill them both. The way she tested him drove him insane, yet his beast celebrated her defiance. When his wolf demanded her submission, she'd give it freely and the moment would be all the more sweet.

Jax stepped into the shower, letting the cold spray pelt his skin, and prayed his body's reaction would subside. He hadn't wanted to escalate the argument further. If she hadn't lied to Tristan, why had she allowed her brother to continue to think he'd attempted a forced mating? Although her excuses were like poison on her lips, the woman's compassion touched his soul. He despised that she appeared to care, that her touch calmed his wolf in a way that no other woman had. Jax glanced to his erection, and cursed it. With his arm leveraged across the tile, he tugged at his cock and stroked himself. Like a punishment, he pumped it with vigor, angry that she did this to him, enraged he'd lost control. *Goddamned, motherfucking…*As his seed erupted, he cried out in frustration and smashed his fist against the wall. The crack of the tiles did nothing to change his decision. When they got to New York, he'd interrogate her to his satisfaction and send her home to NOLA with Jake.

~❀· *Chapter Six* ❀~

Katrina stared out the tinted window of the limo and wondered how the hell she'd survived the past three days. After they'd returned to the city, Jax had insisted she stay in his home. She'd argued, unsuccessfully, that she'd be safer in a hotel, when in truth it would be Jax who'd be safe from her.

Her guest room, located on the first level of the three-story Central Park West penthouse, had become a prison cell. She'd considered escaping, but Finn had been assigned to guard her. While he'd initially spoken to her with contempt, he'd softened toward her after he'd found her crying on the balcony. A weakened moment, she acknowledged. Katrina didn't usually lose her composure. But the sand in the hourglass was spilling out fast; soon they'd be out of time.

Jax had isolated himself on the third floor, ignoring her but to say good morning and good night. When she'd attempted a conversation, he'd summarily dismissed her, claiming he was needed in a meeting. The more time she spent away from Jax, the more her magick dissipated. If the demons didn't make a move to abduct her, she suspected she'd die anyway.

Earlier in the day, Katrina had called Tristan to explain that she'd gone to New York and had been in contact with Jax. As much as she loved her brother, she almost felt relieved when she'd found out he was out of town, traveling to an emergency meeting in Seattle to help settle a dispute among allied Alphas. Over the past couple of years, she'd told Tristan about her kidnappings, but there'd never been enough evidence for them to find a perpetrator. Until recently, she'd always been able to immediately shift. Healing quickly, no physical evidence remained of her abduction. When she'd asked Tristan to help keep Jax away, he'd been quick to assume that he'd attempted to force a mating. Although she'd denied it, the rumor had settled within the pack. When she'd left for New Orleans, their relationship faltered. Soon after, her brother Marcel, died, leaving Katrina devastated. Despite moving back to Philadelphia to be with Tristan, they'd grown further apart.

Their phone conversation had been brief but she assured him that she was safe. Tristan, however, insisted he'd be flying home within the day. Regardless, Katrina knew the only place she'd ever felt remotely safe had been New Orleans. But she knew Jax would never let her go nor would he be satisfied until he had the answers he sought.

As they stopped in midday traffic, Katrina smoothed the silky printed fabric over her thighs. She wondered if Jax had selected the stylish wrap dress himself or had simply hired a personal shopper. The day after she arrived, her closet had been filled with a selection of clothing, all in her size. Food of her liking was cooked by his personal chef, delivered by butlers. He'd spared no expense seeing to her comfort. In her gilded cage, she grew miserable, desperate for his touch.

The car lurched forward, reminding her of their final destination. Jake called her name, interrupting her contemplation.

"You okay?" he asked.

"I'm fine," she lied. Her stomach clenched in anticipation of seeing Jax. "I don't get why I have to meet him here. He comes home at night. We've been in New York for days."

"He's busy. The business, it hasn't been doing as well without him," Finn offered. "Nick was in charge of operations. So now Jax has been training someone to take over but it's intensive work. Most of his established corporations are doing well, but ZANE...the magazine is a delicate operation. It was Nick's baby. It's important to Jax that it doesn't tank."

"Is it in trouble?"

"He's been gone for a month and a half. It's doing okay but Jax doesn't settle for mediocre."

As they came to a red light, Jake moved over to sit next to Katrina and took her hand in his. "Listen Kat," he began. "All this shit you've been through over the past couple of years, we're going to find a way to make it stop."

Katrina looked out the window and took a deep breath. No words could fix the situation. They needed to get to

New Orleans and search for a spell, a weapon against her attackers.

"Look, I know what's happening between you and Jax. I'm not sure why you've fought so hard to stay away from him. But I've spent time with you. Long nights in the bayou. You're the real deal. Lying isn't your style. So whatever reason you've got going on for putting distance between you and Jax…"

Katrina's eyes flashed to his. She sighed, considering his point, but didn't answer.

"You need to talk to him. You know I give Jax a hard time. There are times when the two of us butt heads. He can be a son of a bitch, for sure. But he's Alpha of this pack for a reason. He was there for Gillian. He helped her shift to a wolf for the first time. I saw him fight down in New Orleans. He would have given his life to protect any one of us, a pack that isn't even his. And Nick paid the price. What happened to Nick…" Jake's mouth drew tight as he recalled what had happened. "Fuck, he didn't deserve any of it."

Katrina glanced up at Finn, who appeared stunned by Jake's account of the night his friend had died. It hadn't occurred to her that his wolves hadn't known the details about the death of their beta.

"So my point is, he might be an asshole at times but you can trust him with whatever you have brewing. I can feel your magick draining. Maybe Jax hasn't been around you enough to feel it but he damn sure will. Let him help you."

Katrina, at a loss for words, nodded in agreement. She closed her eyes, searching for her wolf. No longer could she hide the truth. Denying her mate, her Alpha, would torture her. But if they could find a way to destroy the demons, bring them down one by one, they'd both have a chance of living.

You can do this, Katrina told herself, rehearsing her speech. For fifteen minutes she'd worn a hole in the carpet of the spacious office. Located atop the Midtown Manhattan skyscraper, floor to ceiling windows lined the walls of the octagonal-shaped room.

Katrina ran her fingers over his sleek desk, noting how not even a pen was out of order. How could she be the mate of such a highly organized person? She laughed, recalling how her office was littered with pens of every color and half-filled sketch pads. Creative, she drew, painted and created. In Philadelphia, she'd been involved in the arts, and had opened a salon, enjoying doing the hair and makeup of local celebrities. But after her last abduction, being forced to return to New Orleans, she'd opened a gallery featuring several of her own paintings as well as work from local artists.

The door creaked open, and Katrina jumped. She cursed her jittery nerves, but her attention was soon distracted by the laughter of a female. Katrina turned to find the source running her hands over Jax's forearms. Her wolf snarled, and she fought to maintain an impassive expression as they entered the office. Jax faced Katrina, his eyes locking on hers. In a suit and tie, he was every bit as spectacular as he'd been raw and naked in the bedroom. For a brief second, she imagined tearing off his tie, ripping the buttons off his shirt so she could continue what she'd started in the cabin.

Katrina swore she felt his fierce beast growl. With her palms flattened against the window, she struggled to stand as his power washed over her. She couldn't be sure if he was deliberately exerting control or if somehow, in her weakened state, she was unconsciously absorbing his magick. She sucked a breath, and blinked, attempting to remain upright.

"Katrina, hey." Jax reached for her arm, and slid his hand behind her back, supporting her. "It's okay. I've got you."

As the warmth of his breath brushed her cheek, Katrina thought she'd melt. The draw of the Alpha was impossible to fight. As Jax set her down into a chair, he broke contact. Her heart pounded in her chest, and she inhaled, attempting to regain her composure. *I can't do this*, she thought. *I need this man, in my life, in my bed.* None of it made any sense, she knew. She had to confess everything before she gave in to the urge to run out of his office.

"I'm okay," she managed, staring up into his blue eyes.

"Jax," the woman interrupted, annoyance in her tone.

"You scared me," he admitted, never taking his sight off Katrina.

"Jax," she repeated, louder this time. "The upcoming photo shoot. Are we going with five girls or—"

"Later," he dismissed her.

"But sir, the models will be here in an hour."

"London, go find Adam. He'll help you with the details. You're ready to prep this one on your own. I'll be down in an hour."

"But I thought—"

"Discussion's over. Go find Adam. Now."

His focus on Katrina never wavered as he sat on the edge of his desk. Katrina unconsciously reached for his hand, the urge to touch him overwhelming.

"Yes sir." The staccato beat of heels echoed in the distance, and Katrina startled in her seat as the door smacked shut. Although the woman hadn't slammed it, she'd closed it with enough force to make a point, demonstrating her irritation. Katrina fought the envy that flittered in her mind.

"What's wrong?" Jax asked, his tone soft but firm.

"I'm fine."

"No. More. Lies."

Katrina shuddered as his voice boomed around her, his power washing over her like a tidal wave.

"I told you before." She lowered her eyes. While she didn't intend to imply submission, her body hummed with the energy of the Alpha. Breathing deeply, she sought to control what was happening to her. "My magick...they've stolen it. I can't...please stop."

"Stop what?" Jax asked as he walked to the bar. He retrieved a bottle of water from the refrigerator, opened it and offered it to Katrina. "Drink this."

Katrina defiantly met his gaze, her lips pursed in anger.

How could he not know what he was doing? She'd known Tristan could release his power on a whim, influencing the pack.

"It's overpowering me…your energy."

"Drink it." Jax nodded, waiting on her to obey. "Not a request."

Katrina brought the rim to her lips and did as he told her. Jesus almighty, if she'd felt better, she'd have knocked this Alpha on his ass. It wasn't as if she hadn't gone head to head with Tristan on occasion. Torn between ripping off his clothes and dousing him with the contents of the bottle, she silently counted to ten.

"Your energy. Control it," she told him in the most even tone of voice she could conjure. "I don't know what's going on. I told you…they've done something to me."

"I'm not deliberately sending it to you, Kat." A curious expression crossed his face as if he didn't believe her. "I'm not saying it's not possible. I'm saying that I'm not trying to hurt you. Believe me, if I were forcing it on you, you'd know it."

Katrina's eyes flashed in recognition of his threat. Today, they'd have it out and one way or another, she'd move on.

"Why are we doing this here?" Katrina scanned the room, and brushed a lock of her hair behind her ear. "I've been at your house for days and I've barely seen you."

"Because." Jax paused. As he rounded behind her, Katrina stilled, frozen like a frightened deer. The wolf towered above her, the heat of his body emanating onto her skin. Firm hands rested on her shoulders, and she closed her eyes, as he continued. "This is where I attend to my business matters, and as much as I want you for pleasure, and make no mistake, I do…you're currently business. You see, negotiations are a tricky thing. Much like poker, the players conceal their weakness, their strengths. At home, you have me at a disadvantage. I seem to have trouble controlling myself around you."

Katrina gasped as his lips brushed her ear, her nipples stabbing through the silk.

"I…" At a loss for words, she opened her eyes, afraid to make a move.

"That's right, my sweet little wolf, you're in my world now. And while I still find it difficult to resist you, I will have answers. The truth. All of it."

Jax stood and walked away, leaving Katrina's body on fire with arousal.

"My company. My office. My rules. I can't tell you how much I'd love to punish you for your indiscretions. Ah, to spank your ass while you scream for mercy….well, that does sound lovely. Not today, though." He smiled and sniffed the air.

Katrina tightened her legs together, aware he'd scent her desire. It wasn't as if it was a secret she was attracted to him, but hell, just imagining his firm hand on her cheek, the loud slap to her flesh, provoked wetness. Embarrassed by her own fantasy, she averted her gaze.

"You are a naughty one, aren't you?" he teased knowingly. "Don't you worry, I promise someday, just not today. No, today is for discovering truth."

Katrina fought a small smile, wanting so badly to take him up on his offer. But if they made love, it would only be a matter of time before their instinct drove them to mate.

"Feeling better?" He raised an eyebrow at her and extended his hand. "Take it."

Jax was in his element. Katrina knew not to test him as she placed her small hand in his. He led her around the large black desk, and while curiosity urged her to ask what he was doing, she resisted talking. *Answers. The truth. It's all he's ever wanted.* He'd either believe her or not, but the exhaustion of protecting him could no longer be sustained. One thing was certain; challenging the Alpha wasn't in her best interest.

"Like this," he told her, reaching for her hips.

Her face registered surprise as he backed her up against the edge. When his firm hands went to her waist, she held her breath.

"Up you go. Business first, then play."

"What are you doing?" Katrina's hands went to his shoulders as he lifted her up onto the flat surface.

"Very nice." He gave a wicked grin as he ran his fingers down her arms. His soft touch left a trail of delight on her skin. Taking her wrists, he carefully set her palms flat onto the surface so she leaned back at an angle. Katrina went to move, and he placed his hands on top of hers. With a tilt of his head, he warned her. "Don't move."

"What are you doing? Why am I on your desk?" Katrina's pulse raced as he sat back into his chair, studying her like she was on display at a museum.

"I'm leveling the playing field. Something about you," he drawled. Removing his suit jacket, he hung it on the back of his chair. "It distracts me. I simply cannot have it. I won't fall victim to the half-truths that spill from those luscious lips of yours. No, I can think of much more pleasant things that should be coming out of your mouth."

"Jax…" A picture of Jax's chiseled abdomen flashed into Katrina's mind. Recalling how his cock pressed to her skin, she imagined sucking him down her throat. A new wave of desire rushed over her, and her face flushed.

"That's right. I'm very much looking forward to having you on your knees." He smiled as if he'd read her mind. "But first, we talk."

"What are you…?" As his hands glided over her thighs, her skin rippled in gooseflesh.

"We shall start at the beginning. Why, dear Katrina, did you tell your brother that I tried to force a mating?" Jax pinned her with his stare, his voice low and firm. Despite the lingering fingertips atop her knees, Katrina heard this question as an order; the request came from the Alpha, not a lover.

"I already told you the truth. I asked Tristan to help me keep you away. You wouldn't leave me alone. Once you called him, it just confirmed it. He was angry at you, and it all just spiraled out of control. I'm sorry I let it go so far, but I was trying to protect you," she explained, her body tense with arousal. He silently listened without interrupting, so she continued. "These…demons. The things that have taken me. It's happened six times over the past three years.

At first," Katrina paused and looked out the window. A firm hold on her chin directed her gaze back to Jax and her heart raced. "They told me that my mate, an Alpha…that I'd kill him. What they've done to me, they'll take it from my mate too. They've been waiting, hoping for it to happen."

Katrina lifted her hands, and was swiftly reprimanded.

"Do. Not. Move," Jax ordered as his hands moved to her knees. Katrina's heart slammed against her ribs as he spread her legs. His fingers lingered on her inner thighs, but all the while, he never took his eyes off hers. "You have one chance to set things right with us. This is it. Don't you dare lie to me."

"I'm not," Katrina protested. She refused to cry, no matter the desperation that bubbled in her chest. "I know you think I'm crazy. Why do you think I haven't told anyone? Tristan suspects I've lost my mind."

"That doesn't make sense. He's your brother. Why doesn't he know what's going on with you?"

"It's not like Tristan can't feel if I'm in trouble, but every time they took me, I wasn't gone for long. I never had trouble shifting. I'd recover quickly. This time, though, things are different. It's a total loss of time…loss of magick."

"If you never lied to Tristan about me, why let the rumor continue? How exactly could you protect me by staying away from me?"

"Because, Jax…" Katrina shook her head, exhausted with keeping secrets. "You're an Alpha. You are *the* Alpha. *My* Alpha."

"Are you trying to say that we're mates? How would you

know for certain? We've never made love."

"Between my father and Tristan, I've attended summits, met nearly every standing Alpha in the country. It wasn't Logan. I mean, I spent enough time with him when he was my brother's beta. No…the night we met…"

"The party?"

"Yes. I'd known about you for some time."

"You stalked me?" he asked, amusement in his question.

"Not really." Katrina rolled her eyes, a small smile formed on her lips. "Maybe a little cyber stalking, okay? But what was I supposed to do? Put yourself in my shoes. You know how it is for wolves. We have no idea who our mate is, let alone if we'll ever even meet them. And then this 'thing' tells me I have one and that when I meet him, I'm going to kill him. I suspected it was you. There's part of me…I still don't know for sure."

"Let me get this straight, some sicko abducts you, beats you, steals your magick and you believe some mumbo jumbo they tell you?"

"And this is exactly why I didn't tell you." Katrina seethed. She'd had enough of his games. If he didn't believe her, he could go to hell. She'd find a way to kill these demons on her own. As her hands flew up off the desk, he struck as fast as a cobra, snatching her wrists out of the air. Desperate, she screamed at him. "You want the truth? I'll give you the fucking truth. I didn't stop Tristan when he misunderstood. I let them continue believing the lie so you'd stay far away from me. That night at the party? I wanted you so bad I couldn't breathe. But I left anyway. I did all this to save you from me…me, the person who will ultimately kill the great Alpha. The one who might be my mate."

"Put your hands back where I told you, now." Jax loosened his hold, returning her hard glare.

"Make me," she challenged.

"Hands on the desk," he growled.

"I'm only doing this to prove a point." Katrina yanked her arms away from him and set her palms flat. "Do not misread this as my submission."

"Believe me, little wolf, when you submit, we'll both know it." Jax slid his hands underneath the hem of her skirt, slowly grazing his fingers up to her hips. His expression softened as he spoke. "This thing between us…ah, Kat. I wanted you too. And when I thought you'd lied. I was so angry. Confused. I've dated a lot of women, but that night…it was like there was no one else."

"Jax…" Katrina licked her lips, recalling his searing kiss. She could no longer abide her craving for the one man she'd gone so long without. But neither could she give in to him without him acknowledging the truth, believing her words. "You have no idea how much I've wanted to be with you. I'm sorry I left. I really am so sorry, but…I don't want to hurt you…I won't hurt you. I don't know why this is happening to me. But I'm trying to fix it…looking for a way to stop them."

Jax paused, his eyes locked on hers. Katrina's stomach fluttered as she waited on his words.

"I sure as hell wish you'd told me what was happening

instead of running. But are we really mates? Meant for each other? There's only one way to find out. You know it. And I know it." Jax's lips hovered inches over her knee, his warm breath on her skin. "I should send you back to Tristan, but I just can't."

Katrina hissed as his lips brushed her inner thigh. She knew why he wouldn't let her go; for the same reason she hadn't run. As the tip of his nose edged under her dress, she took pause, aware that she wasn't a hundred percent certain he was indeed her mate. After all she'd done to protect him from the curse, what if she was wrong?

"These things…these demons…they're going to have to go through me if they think they're taking you again. You need to learn to trust me." Jax raised his eyes, pinning her with his stare. In silence, his fingers hooked around her panties.

"I never meant to hurt you…" Katrina tilted her hips, allowing him to remove her underwear. As the cool air hit her damp pussy, she arched her chest.

"Time for pleasure, my little wolf. I've waited so long to have you…open your dress," Jax told her.

Barely cognizant of her surroundings, Katrina scanned the office. Although alone inside, employees milled about outside his door. She focused back on Jax, his wolfish grin greeting her.

"That's right. Someone could see us."

Katrina sighed, her desire spiking as he flittered his fingers over her mound.

"Do it now," he ordered, pushing the fabric over her

hips, exposing her pussy.

Katrina smiled. Her Alpha wanted to play, to test her limits. While it would take more than teasing to make her submit, she'd give him what he asked. Sliding her palm over her breast, she reached for the buttons, slowly opening her dress. Without waiting for instruction, she brushed the sleeves down her arms and peeled off her bra, baring herself to him.

"You're more beautiful than the first time I saw you," he groaned.

Katrina yelped as he cupped her ass, pulling her toward him. She cried out loud as he took her breast in his mouth. Spearing her fingers through his hair, she guided his head. Her nipple swelled in response, his bite nipping its tip.

"Jax," she breathed.

"You…are exquisite." His fingers slid through her wet folds and flicked at her clit. "Hmm…is this what you want?"

"Ah, yes." Katrina's energy surged. As his mouth went to her other breast, her pussy ached with need. So long she'd waited for his touch, and now she was certain she'd never be able to leave him.

Jax caressed her ripe flesh in his hand, and captured her mouth with his. As his tongue brushed against hers, Katrina tasted her mate, allowing her mind to calm, to forget all the trauma she'd suffered. His strong lips overpowered her own, and she relented, reveling in his devastating kiss.

"Please, Jax…" she cried as he drove two fingers inside her readied core. She gasped as his lips moved down over her chin, peppering kisses down her neck.

"From this moment, things will never be the same," she heard him mumble. "Open for me, little wolf."

Katrina leaned back, doing as directed. The slick stone cooled her pussy as he pressed her knees wider still. Her patience wore thin as he brought his head between her legs, blowing air over her taut nub. As he dragged his tongue through her labia, Katrina moaned his name. His fingers curled inside her and she nearly flew off the desk.

"Jesus, you taste better than I ever imagined," he spoke into her lips, gently lapping at her sensitive hooded bead. "Tell me you'll never lie to me."

"Jax…" Katrina heaved for breath. For years she'd avoided the man she'd desperately craved. Coming alive for the first time in her life, she'd give him anything he wanted.

"Say it," he pressed. Sucking her clit between his lips, he drank of her essence.

"I swear it. I swear to you. But we can't bond…I won't hurt you." Tears streamed from her eyes, her gut torn with the guilt that she could destroy him.

"Never," he repeated.

"Ahh…please…" Katrina's orgasm crashed around her and she cried for mercy, shuddering with every lash of his tongue. She wrapped her legs around his shoulders as she exploded in pleasure and fell back on to her elbows. She screamed, forgetting where they were, and jolted back into reality as she heard the crash of a door slamming open.

"What the fuck is…?" Finn asked.

Katrina lifted her head forward to see Jax smiling from

between her legs.

"Out," he ordered.

She closed her eyes, and for the first time that she could remember, she laughed. Katrina scented both Jake and Finn at the entrance but chose to ignore them. Instead of being embarrassed, a sense of liberation washed over her.

"You'd think those two would know not to come in here." Jax pressed his lips to the top of her bared mound, and withdrew his fingers.

"Maybe they like to watch," she suggested with a sexy smile.

"Something you're interested in, perhaps?"

As he brought his wet fingers to her mouth, she smiled, neither confirming nor denying his provocative question. He cupped her chin, sliding his thumb into her mouth. Katrina moaned, tasting herself, nipping at his fingertip. With the softest touch, he rose to kiss her, and she opened to him. As his lips took hers, gently sucking and biting, Katrina softened into his strong embrace, his power rejuvenating her wolf, infusing her with his magick.

She opened her eyes as his lips lost contact. Her Alpha gazed at her with the possession she'd expect from her mate. Although Jax hadn't admitted the connection, his kiss was all she'd needed to confirm her suspicion. It both thrilled and scared her that Jax Chandler, one of the most dangerous and cunning Alphas in existence, was destined to be hers. But if they didn't find a way to destroy the demons, she'd be the wolf who exacted his demise.

Chapter Seven

Jax had always suspected that Katrina Livingston could be his mate. After he'd met her in New York, he'd gone feral with lust for the one woman he couldn't have. Unable to stop thinking of her and desperate to get in contact, he'd called Tristan. But after she'd leveled accusations, Jax swore that no woman could do that to him and still be his mate. His instincts had always been dead on until that moment in time.

But her claim that she'd never told Tristan he'd forced a mating resonated as truth. Jax and Tristan had a turbulent past. His father had never favored Tristan's more liberal views regarding supernaturals and humans. A brutal ruler, he'd deliberately incited wars with Lyceum Wolves. When Jax assumed the position of Alpha, he quickly learned that Tristan would never trust him. The tension never dissipated after his father died. Occupying bordering territories, the two Alphas reluctantly coexisted.

With Katrina in his home and office, exposed to his satisfaction, his emotions swirled inside his chest like a tornado. From the second he'd met her, Katrina had incited his beast's hunger like no other. There was no denying how responsive she was to his touch. Feasting between her legs, his cock turned to concrete, her essence bringing him to life. Like the devil himself, she tempted him and he fantasized, looking forward to seeing how far he could take her.

When his office door had opened and they'd been interrupted by Finn and Jake, she'd simply laughed, altogether focused on him. As he looked up into her eyes and caught the flicker of delight, his heart seized, cognizant that no matter what had transpired, he'd give her a second chance. Unable to control the explosive chemistry between them, his wolf sure as hell wasn't going to let her walk out of his life again.

As he broke their kiss, he inwardly reprimanded himself for his lack of discipline. It wasn't as if he'd planned to fuck her on his desk. *Jesus, I'm losing it.* The sugary taste of her pussy on his lips left him wanting more, and he fought the craving. A soft brush of her fingertips to his cheek broke his contemplation, and he placed his palm over her hand.

"This thing between us…" At a loss for words from desire, he forced his concentration to business. His comfort zone lay with strategy, planning the attack. "I need to know everything you know about these things…this society. What do they do when they take you? Do you ever go anywhere else? How many of them?"

"I, ugh…well, sometimes it's hard to remember," she answered, her voice soft.

Jax knew he'd taken her off guard. As he shifted from

lover to inquisitor, he sensed the change in her demeanor. She withdrew her hand, and his wolf recoiled at the loss of her touch.

"Even if it's small, it could be important," Jax answered.

His eyes fell to her glistening mound, and his painful erection strained against his trousers. He'd never wanted to make love to anyone more in his life than at that moment, and it took every ounce of self-control he possessed to tug at the hem of her dress, covering her bare skin.

Jax shook his head, both irritated and aroused. Attempting to shake the lustful haze from his mind, he stood and crossed to the window, leaving her alone at his desk. With his palm glued to the glass, he scanned the cityscape. He was a cold bastard, he knew, for walking away, but if he didn't put some distance between them, he'd be buried inside her for hours.

"A few months ago, there was a vampire…" she began.

"A vampire?" Jax kept his response calm even though the hairs on the back of his neck pricked in alertness. Out of the corner of his eye, he spied her sliding her arms into sleeves. Averting his gaze, he forced his line of vision back out the window.

"Yes, he was only there for a few hours. He's very strong."

"You spoke to him?" Jax turned to face Katrina. Conflicted, he knew they needed to focus on a solution to the demons that'd kidnapped them, but as he registered the hurt in her eyes, he changed the subject back to their relationship. "Kat…what just happened with us…this isn't finished. I have a shoot to go to…" *Fuck, you sound like an inarticulate fool. Look at what she does to you.* He took a deep breath and attempted a recovery. "Please don't take this the wrong way, but if we are mates, and I'm not saying that we are, we need more time. I need more time."

"I'm fine," she replied, her fingers nervously sliding down her lapel as she adjusted her dress.

Jax plowed his fingers over his impeccably coiffed hair. He took note of her somber expression. She'd interpreted his actions as rejection. Holy shit, he didn't think he could screw something up more than he already had. Yet the more words that spewed from his lips, the more he managed to fuck up the situation.

Katrina's presence in his life threw him off balance. Feelings and emotions were not something Jax did well, and clearly Katrina fell into that category. Deciding to avoid the conversation that would inevitably come, his thoughts drifted back to the vampire.

"Tell me about the vamp."

"I told you, he's strong," she replied.

"They're all strong."

"No, he's the strongest. More than Léopold."

"You know Léopold?" Jax didn't conceal the surprise in his question. Léopold Devereoux, one of the most dangerous vampires on the east coast, was ancient and ruthless. He'd been known to kill all creatures, including wolves.

"Yes," Katrina answered without hesitating. "He's an ally to the Acadian Wolves. Jake knows him."

His wolf grew agitated at the mention of the virile, unmated wolf who'd become Katrina's confidant. Jax suspected she'd baited him, and shoved the distracting thought away. Focused on acquiring information, he'd ignore it…for now.

"Does the vampire have a name?" he pressed.

"Quintus. His name is Quintus." Katrina's eyes flashed in fear. "But Jax, I don't think we should go after him."

Jax heard the quiver in her voice, and appreciated her apprehension. *Quintus Tullius.* A mercenary over the centuries, the elusive vampire was a force unto himself within the supernatural community. Guarded and lethal, he'd exiled himself underground. The seductive vampire was well known for his sexual exploits.

"Tell me." Jax approached Katrina. She blinked up at him, stoic in her composure, as if they'd never touched. With the scent of sex fresh in the air, his wolf stirred, yearning to inflame her cool demeanor. Jax restrained the urge to rip off her clothes and claim her. He balled his hands, straining to concentrate. "Did he touch you?"

"Whatever does that have to do with anything?"

"Because I know Quintus. I'm asking you again," he said, slow and deliberate. "Did. He. Touch. You?"

Katrina's hand reached for her neck, and Jax's stomach dropped. He couldn't be sure if they'd made love, but with her silent gesture, he was certain Quintus had bitten her. His beast raged at the thought of it and threatened to snap. Desperately trying to remain rational, Jax turned on his heel and took a deep breath.

"You want to know if he touched me?" Katrina asked in confusion. "Where are you going with this?"

When Katrina's hand reached for his arm, he froze. The woman had him torn up inside. He needed to get his shit together before he made yet another mistake.

"Yes, yes…he bit me, okay? But it was nothing. He was weak. And I needed to get the hell away from those things. I fed him. What is wrong with you?"

As Jax turned, his gaze on hers, he noted the innocence in her words and shook his head.

"What? Wait, you thought I…" She gave a half smile. "I'm not saying I haven't been with other men, but never Quintus. I only met him once."

"But he's tasted you?" Jax pressed.

"Yes, and I'm not sorry for it. It helped him heal, and we escaped. I won't say he's not attractive, because that would be a lie and I think we just established," her gaze went to the desk and back to Jax, "that I'm not going to lie to you anymore. But I won't feel guilty for saving myself. Or him. Now that being said, Quintus…even though he was nice to me that day, he can be dangerous…unpredictable."

"Indeed." Jax restrained his anger. When he questioned Quintus, he'd discover if he'd taken advantage of Katrina. "What was he doing in that hellhole?"

"I don't know. Like I said, he was only there for a few hours." She paused in contemplation. "They were foolish to leave me with him. He could have killed me if he'd wanted to, but he didn't. He saved my life," she admitted. Katrina fingered her skin and shivered. "You know vampires, Jax.

They only have two ways. Pain or pleasure. And all I'm going to say about it is that he didn't hurt me."

"We'll go see him." Jax reached for his jacket and slipped it on. Retrieving his cell phone from its inner pocket, he slid his fingers across the glass.

"Do you really think this is such a great idea? No one even knows where he is. Besides, I just told you that he's dangerous. If you confront him, he'll see you as a threat. He might even try to hurt you."

Jax glanced up at Katrina, giving her an amused smile. She had no idea just how powerful he really was. Returning to his task, he scrolled through his contacts.

"What's so funny?" Katrina asked, her hands on her hips. "I can assure you that there's nothing funny about Quintus. I get that you're Alpha but he's really old. He can do everything Léopold can do plus a host of other things we can't conceive of. This isn't a good idea. We should leave him be. I have contacts in New Orleans."

"And we'll use those as well, but Quintus? We're going to see him. You must learn to trust your Alpha, little wolf."

"You're not my Alpha yet."

"I will be," he replied with confidence.

As he sent the text message, his spirits lifted. Whatever had stolen away Katrina's magick, it had to be destroyed and he was one step closer to annihilating it. He glanced at Katrina, and his beast stirred once again. He knew he'd have to have her soon.

The truth. Today, for the first time, he'd heard it from her lips. One small step toward trusting her again. But first,

she'd have to learn how to trust him, and he looked forward
to teaching her.

~⚜ *Chapter Eight* ⚜~

"Quintus Tullius?" Jake asked.

"Right pocket." Finn aimed at the shiny blue ball. He pecked at it, and it went careening into the hole.

"Tell me why we're doing this again? I've been around Léo and let me tell you, he's one badass vamp. If this guy made him, he must be a real prize."

"I'm the king." Finn fisted a hand into the air.

"Yeah, yeah. How is it that you make it every single time?" Jake smiled and shook his head.

"Because I'm the king." The ginger beta eyed the billiards table, scouting his shot.

"Sure you are, big guy." Although Jake was six-three, Finn had him by a few inches, his muscles bulging. "Look, I'm not saying we shouldn't go but I'm just sayin' maybe we should at least call Léo before we do this."

"I only take orders from one wolf. No offense, dude, but it ain't you. Jax wants to go see this vamp? I'm there. This pack has been through hell the past month and there's no way I'm challenging him. Not happenin'. So you can either come with us or go back to New Orleans." Finn rounded the corner, attempting to case a better view. He tilted his head and pointed to his next target. "One ball. Get ready to bow to the king."

"You suck." Jake took a swig of his beer and set it on the bar, watching his opponent sink another ball. "For the record, I think Katrina should stay back here."

"You'll get no argument from me. But Jax seems to have other plans." Finn shook his head and chalked his stick. "Look, I know you're friends with Kat, but this thing with her and Jax…"

"Red, let me give you a bit of advice. I think we both know what's happening here between them. I can't say I'm thrilled about how this is goin' down, but I can say that number one, this mating shit…I'm going to run like hell if it happens to me. It's messy, complicated stuff. You do not want to even try to understand it. And number two, you need to stay clear of Kat until they actually do mate, because until they do, Jax is going to be one possessive son of a bitch. Oh, but it will happen. The easy way. Or the hard way. I'm not willing to take bets as to when."

"How the hell can't he see what's going on? And why the fuck did Kat go and tell her brother he was forcing a mating, when they are mates? It makes no fuckin' sense. Orange stripe. Center pocket."

"It sounds to me as though she went running to Tristan and then somehow this whole thing got blown out of proportion. She's protecting Jax from something," Jake noted. "But I can't say exactly what's going on."

"Well, that's a helluva way to do it. We all were confused because none of us had ever even seen her except for that one party."

As the ball sunk into the leather catch, Jake rolled his eyes. "I refuse to call you King but you're pretty damn good at this."

"I'm the king all right," Finn laughed.

"Kat's not what she seems. Down in the bayou, she, uh, she just had a way about her. You know she paints. Sculpts too. She's really talented. She started working with all the kids, teaching art clubs, giving back to the pack. I wish she'd stayed."

"Sounds like maybe you like her. Did you guys ever…?" Finn left the question open ended and held the pool stick up suggestively.

"Fuck no. I mean, yeah, if she had wanted to, I would have, but no, we never got that far. And besides, things were already complicated enough for her. You know, she came back down to New Orleans with Luca. But nothing was going on between them at that point."

"A vampire, huh?" Finn laughed. "Now, that's interesting."

"She's all wolf. Trust me. I've seen her. I think she was just doing it to keep Jax away."

"Well, it appears she has a mate now."

"That she does."

"One who may go down kicking and screaming."

"Wait up. I don't get that. Didn't he call Tristan about her?"

"He did, but I think he just wanted to see her again. Then all these allegations got stirred up and you know how that story ended. It was a serious no go after that. The man didn't skip a beat. It's not like he's pussy deprived. He's an Alpha. More women after him than he knows what to do with. Some who aren't going to be very happy when they find out about Kat."

"I guess she's not going to go over too well with his pack," Jake surmised.

"Like a lead fucking balloon." Finn pointed to the eight ball and smiled. "Hearts are going to break. Maybe some heads. Before it's all said and done, I think you can expect a fight. I mean, not only do some of these women think he's theirs, well, they just don't like Kat after what happened. It's messy."

"Good times ahead." As the black ball disappeared, Jake held a congratulatory palm up in the air. "One of these times, I will win, you know."

"Ah, but for now..." Finn smiled and slapped his opponent's hand. "Crown me, baby."

"I'm gonna warn ya, I'm not going to let anything happen to her. It's why I'm still here. And as for Jax? Yeah, I busted his balls down in New Orleans. But after what happened to Nick, seeing the Alpha fight..." The memory of watching Nick die washed over Jake and guilt settled in his gut. "The bottom line is that whatever these things are, they came after him too. No way am I leaving him hangin' either. I've seen a lot of shit over the years. Witches. Magick. Demons. But Jax is tough. He's got this."

"I appreciate your support." Jax rounded the corner, a small smile crossing his face.

"Hey now, don't go getting a big head." Jake rolled his eyes.

"You just remember who's Alpha and we'll get along fine."

"You take care of Kat and we will," Jake responded, the smile gone from his face.

"You like her?" Jax picked a marble ball up off the table, tossed it in the air and caught it.

"I do like her. She may not be my mate but she's my friend." Jake eyed the confident wolf. His commanding presence thickened the air, his power rolling off him in waves. "We do this together. I don't want her hurt."

"Don't get in my way, my friend. Like I said, just remember who's Alpha and all will be well." Jax set the orb on the table and rolled it forward.

"You don't get what she is to you, do you?" Jake pressed.

"Katrina?" Jax paused and smiled. "There's something between us. She told me she was trying to protect me. That I'm her mate. These things, the demons…they told her if we mated, I'd die."

"I knew there was some reason she'd gone to Tristan." Jake said. "But let's say they told her they'd kill you, why would she believe these things?"

"Good question. Tell me, Jake. If you were an Alpha, what would you do?" Jax posed the question rhetorically and continued. "I'd like to think she was scared. They only abducted her for short periods of time, never long enough for Tristan to notice she was missing. It's not like she's a child. She goes weeks at a time without seeing him. Eventually when she tells him what's happening, she has no proof. To be fair to Tristan, without evidence, this can be a difficult situation. Does he divert resources to a crime where there's no evidence except for maybe her bruises? But even then, she's shifted, healed. As it is, Katrina's finding it hard to grasp what's happening to her."

"She's alone," Jake added.

"Or she perceives she's alone? Doesn't think Tristan believes her."

"They threaten her and go through with it."

"Yes, they steal her magick. So then when they threaten me?"

"She believes they'll go through with attacking you," Jake concluded.

"I think that's exactly what happened. Think about this. If they've threatened to kill her only potential mate, she's going to do what she has to do to protect me. Of course this gets tricky. Does she know for sure I'm her mate? No, but she suspects it. Same is true for me. Do we absolutely know yet? No, but sometimes our instinct is all we have. Would you risk the life of your mate even if you didn't know for sure? I wouldn't. So now we have some decisions to make. Mating is serious business. To deny one's mate, it can be done, but not easily."

"Hey man, I'm not mated, but Dimitri? Logan? It was pretty intense. I've never seen a wolf deny their mate. So if that's what you are looking to do, I can't help you there.

And honestly…" Jake blew out a breath. After everything that had happened with Nick, he felt indebted to Jax. The Alpha had suffered a great loss to help his own pack. "I think you need to explore this thing with Kat. I won't lie, I care about her a lot. But she's not mine. And denying her as yours, I think it could hurt you every bit as much as it would hurt her."

"I never said I planned to deny her. But what Finn said is true. My pack, they'll resist her. She'll have to earn her way. I cannot do this for her."

"Kat's strong. You need to give her a chance to show you what she's made of."

"It's true she has Alpha blood in her veins. I suspect she's every bit as difficult as my sister." Jax gave a small chuckle.

"Yeah, well, Gillian doesn't really do submission." Jake laughed.

"She'll fight me on this." Jax smiled as if he'd enjoy finding out if she'd submit to him. "But I cannot compromise who I am."

"If you're worried about her ability to establish rank, she's tough. It's not like she didn't take out a few wolves in New Orleans and that wasn't even her pack. You already said it all. She's Alpha born."

"We need to discuss Quintus. You must let me deal with him tonight, do you both understand?" Jax changed the subject abruptly. "It concerns me that he's tasted of Katrina. He's deadly. Could kill both of you in a blink. Don't fuck with him. Stay close to me and keep your dick in your pants. This place," Jax paused, a serious expression washing across his face, "it's dark. Seductive. Everything Quintus enjoys. Remember at all times that this is the vampire who created Léopold. Whatever happens, do not engage with him. Follow my lead, even if it is in opposition to what you believe is right. I'm not your Alpha, Jake. But I will send you home if you challenge me tonight. I'd prefer not to send you home in a body bag."

Jake nodded, hearing Jax's words, surmising that the Alpha had had previous interactions with the dangerous vampire.

The sound of footsteps in the hallway alerted Jake to Katrina's presence, and his eyes locked on Jax, who smiled with his typical cool confidence. As she rounded the corner, all attention went to the radiant she-wolf.

·❀· *Chapter Nine* ·❀·

Katrina contemplated what had happened in Jax's office. Having told him the truth, she finally felt free. She wasn't certain he'd believed her but it didn't matter. For the first time in years, hope penetrated her thoughts. She considered how he'd blasted her with his energy and then denied it. The sensation had left her invigorated yet confused as to what had really occurred.

His seductive interrogation rocketed her into ecstasy, but when he'd withdrawn, she'd been disappointed. Although she'd always known that her actions would have long-term consequences, she still wasn't prepared for the distance he tried so hard to put between them. Her wolf couldn't accept it, and even though she'd spent so much time avoiding Jax, her thoughts were consumed with the Alpha.

Conflicted, she prayed that what the demons had told her wasn't true. *Could they have lied to me about Jax? Why do they care if I mate with him?* There was no denying that being intimate with the Alpha had supplemented her own magick.

Feeling energized, she was ready for whatever battle lay ahead.

Quintus. In truth, she'd never expected to see him again. The captivating vampire had treated her with both compassion and respect during their short time together. When he'd bitten her, she'd come undone but in spite of her induced state of arousal, he'd never taken advantage. With her blood in his veins, he recovered within minutes.

She recalled the dizziness that ensued as he transported them out of their prison. It'd been the only time in her life that she'd experienced materialization, the intense magick overwhelming her body and mind. A kiss to her forehead was all she remembered when she later awoke inside her condo. It was only afterward that she'd discovered how deadly the ancient vampire truly was, and she considered herself lucky that she hadn't ended up dead.

Katrina scanned her elegant guest bedroom, appreciating how opulent Jax's lifestyle was in comparison to hers. It wasn't as if she didn't have money. On the contrary, she'd been gifted a considerable trust. But not wishing for unwanted attention, she'd chosen to live modestly. Her simple two bedroom condo in the city had always been enough for her, and when she moved to New Orleans, she took up residence in an apartment in the French Quarter situated over her newly renovated art gallery.

As she turned off the light, and went in search of Jax, butterflies fluttered in her stomach. Katrina couldn't be certain the kindness Quintus had shown her still existed. Or perhaps he'd be utterly ruthless, the stone-cold killer his reputation portrayed him to be.

Voices filtered through the hallway, and she caught her name on Jax's lips. Committed to her sworn honesty, she'd never lie to him again. She'd admitted the vampire had tasted her blood, and she'd known it would draw the Alpha's ire. She couldn't be sure if he was jealous or if he simply thought less of her for feeding Quintus, but she refused to be ashamed of what she'd done; she'd survived.

As expected, their conversation quieted as she entered the billiards room. Although she was aware of both Finn's and Jake's eyes on her, Jax was the only one who commanded her attention. His black t-shirt hugged his contoured pecs, jeans hung low on his hips. Katrina noted how his typically Nordic blond hair had darkened to a light shade of brown. Unconsciously, she fingered her own locks, reminded of the power of the demons and how they'd changed her.

Her eyes went to his lips, which curled up in a sexy smile. Confident and casual, Jax was sex personified. The Alpha's gaze upon her skin made her feel as if she wasn't wearing any clothes. She brushed her palms over her white tank top, assuring herself that she was dressed. The memory of what he'd done to her in his office flashed in her mind. She struggled to thwart her arousal and crossed her arms over her chest, hoping to hide the hardened peaks that strained against her bra.

Jax approached, his expression serious and sensual. As he reached for her hand, his touch seared her flesh. He brushed his lips to her cheek, and she closed her eyes, inhaling his masculine scent. Acutely aware of the rush of his power, she accepted it, reveling in his strength.

"You ready to go see Quintus?" Katrina heard him ask, his breath on her ear. Her chest rose slowly and she attempted to focus, to shake the desire that Jax incited.

"I'm not convinced he can help us," she responded, avoiding his question. As he stepped away from her, Katrina bit her lip, anxious about seeing the vampire.

"If there's one thing I know, it's that if Quintus was bested by these things, he's going to want revenge. And I can sure as hell guarantee that he knows more than we do." Jax brushed a hand over his hair, certitude in his eyes. "Stay with me. Understand? You belong to me in this place."

"But I... it's not true," she refuted him.

"You're under my protection, therefore you're mine. Do not give him any indication otherwise." Jax took out his cell phone and tapped against the glass. "Cael's got the limo ready."

Mine. Katrina's face heated as he said the words, her emotions already turbulent. He hadn't acknowledged her as his mate, but as his hand grazed the small of her back, she saw the smile on his lips and her heart caught. Jax Chandler was a force unto himself, one that, try as she might to control his influence on her, she was struggling to contain. Drawing on her inner strength, she steeled her nerves. Not convinced she belonged to the cunning Alpha, she'd hold her own in the presence of Quintus. If he truly held the keys to her freedom, she'd play the game to discover his secrets.

As they pulled into Central Park, Katrina struggled to see where they were going. Of all the places in the city, she couldn't fathom how Quintus could remain undetected in one of the most vibrant sections of the park. The driver opened the door, and in silence they exited the car. Although it was nearly midnight, and the crowds had long since dissipated, she sensed a few stray humans roaming the grounds.

The limo's headlights flashed off, and Katrina adjusted her vision. The Angel of the Waters stood majestically guarding Bethesda Terrace, the reflection of the moon in the rippling lake. Katrina peered down the stone staircase, its arches leading into tunnels through to the fountain. In the safety of daylight, she suspected not a soul would give the area a second glance except to marvel at the beauty of the attraction.

Jax held a finger to his lips, silencing their small party. He stilled as they came up to a large stone pillar. A carved owl had been etched into its center. The three-dimensional bird stood proudly as if it could come alive at any moment. Small bats on either side kept company, their ominous blank eyes staring out onto the trespassers.

"Remember what we discussed," Jax told them, reaching his hand behind the chiseled figure.

As his fingers entered the recess, Katrina's pulse raced in anticipation and she inhaled deeply, attempting to slow her heartbeat. Her eyes darted to Jake and back to Jax as a small glow the size of a firefly appeared. A grinding rumble commenced, the pillar cracking wide open, revealing a staircase.

Jax gestured for them to descend, and Katrina looked up to him, uncertainty registering in her expression. In her human form, as lupine, she could see in the darkness, but she'd never willingly step into a pitch black cavern, one that appeared as ancient as the vampire they were going to visit. Trusting the Alpha, she followed him into the confined space, startled as the exit sealed shut behind them. With her hands on Jax's shirt, she blindly put one foot in front of the other.

The sound of the heavy bass alerted her that they were no longer alone. A splash of scarlet-red light appeared as they stepped into a vestibule. Katrina took in the sight of the black granite lobby. White silk fabric lined with strings of lights hung in columns from the ceiling. A clatter echoed in the foyer as a thin tall man passed through a waterfall of iridescent glass beads. Dressed only in black satin pants, his pale skin appeared translucent. He addressed Jax, but made no eye contact with Katrina. Black and silver flecks floated in his red irises. As he spoke, he licked at the crusted brown substance in the corners of his mouth. He shot her a vile smile, and she noted the black lines running down his teeth.

Katrina didn't scare easily. Over the years she'd been exposed to many different creatures in her brother's nightclub. From vampires to witches, she'd interacted with both good and evil. But as she watched the creature speak to Jax, the hair stood up on the back of her neck, chills rolling over her skin. Sensing an otherworldly vibe from the maître d, she wondered if he'd been possessed. Her hand found its way to Jax's shirt. Seeking contact with her protector, she breathed out the dread that had crept over her. Comforted by the warmth of Jake at her back, she never took her sight off of the macabre greeter.

"He's expecting you, Mr. Chandler."

"Indeed," Jax replied.

"This way." The thin man granted Katrina a sinister stare before turning back through the beaded entryway.

"Stay close," Jax whispered in her ear, taking her hand.

Katrina nodded, suspecting that whatever lay in the other room would be both dark and abominable. She caught a glimpse of Jake's tense expression, but Finn remained impassive. With her curiosity piqued after Jax had easily gained them entry, Katrina resisted asking how well he knew Quintus.

Her questions faded as they pressed through the shimmering baubles and entered the bar. The pulsing bass of techno music resonated under the soles of her boots. Unshaken, Katrina scanned the club for the vampire. Brick walls adorned with rusty hooks and chains surrounded a triangular bar, its shiny tinned surface littered with glasses and ashtrays.

Patrons of various ages ignored their entrance. Katrina noted that most of the women wore little clothing, baring their breasts, and the men followed suit. Her attention went to a woman who stood spread eagled atop bar stools. With her hands bound to the ceiling, each high-heeled foot was set firmly onto a seat. Men took turns licking between her legs. A trickle of blood ran down her thigh, a vampire at her hips. Screaming in ecstasy, she writhed toward the waiting mouths.

They weaved their way throughout the sea of dancing bodies. As they approached the back of the club, a woman, perched on her hands and knees, grunted, her fangs solidly embedded into the arm of a waif who lay dazed on a red velvet sofa. From behind her, a man buried his cock into the vampire, his eyes glazed over in a hedonistic frenzy.

Katrina's heart pounded against her ribs, her breath quickening. A firm stroke of Jax's thumb to her palm told her he sensed her unease. He responded with a wave of power, reminding Katrina that he'd protect her. Whatever happened, Jax Chandler was every bit as deadly as the creatures that slithered in the night.

In an instant, the music rolled back into a quiet thump, and flaring lights blinded Katrina. Disoriented, she held tight to Jax, immediately detecting the vampire's presence. *Quintus.*

"Jax," Katrina heard a distinctive male voice call. The familiar Italian accent caught her attention.

Jax released her hand, readying to approach the dark figure. He nodded to Finn and Jake, who immediately flanked Katrina, taking her hands.

As his face came into view, Katrina recognized the attractive vampire. Dressed in black leather, he appeared larger than life. His beard had been trimmed close, the penetrating gaze of his black eyes bored into her. She noted the brief glint of recognition that flashed right before he diverted his focus to Jax. Despite the tension, instinct told her he wouldn't hurt her.

"Quintus," Jax nodded, acknowledging his presence.

"Fucking with demons isn't good for your health, my friend," Quintus commented, his attention darting to Katrina and back to the Alpha.

"I hear they captured you as well," Jax countered.

"It's been a long time, Alpha." A corner of his mouth ticked upward.

"That it has. Perhaps this time, we work together?" Jax glanced to Katrina, who tore her hand from Jake's.

"Ah, Katrina, my lovely little savior." Quintus smiled.

"She's mine, Quint. These things…" Jax stepped in front of Katrina, blocking her view, "…they must be stopped."

"You'll get no argument from me. However, my existence is unaffected by their actions. It seems to me that you're the one with the problem. You see," Quintus gave Jax a slick grin, easing toward Katrina, "it's the Alpha's sister they want. She's special."

Katrina's heart raced as he brushed his roughened finger over her cheek. Before she could respond, Jake had shoved her out of the way, clutching Quintus' arm. She screamed as the vampire took Jake into his grip. With his arm around the wolf's neck, he dragged his fangs over his throat, drawing a bubbling line of blood.

"No!" she screamed. Katrina attempted to rush to Jake's aid, but was restrained by Finn. "Get off me."

"Quintus, no," Jax ordered.

"This wolf," Quintus stated, licking the sanguine fluid over his lips. "He's not yours. His Acadian blood…how I do love the taste of a virile wolf."

"Leave him be," Jax insisted. "He's learning, testing his new role. It's Katrina. He's protective of her. Please, show mercy so we can continue."

"Don't hurt him," Katrina cried. With a strength she didn't realize she possessed, she elbowed Finn, breaking free of his hold. But as she went to run to Jake, Jax commanded her.

"Do. Not. Move." Jax held his hand out to stop her.

The rush of his command slammed into Katrina, and she heaved for breath. She'd never experienced the negative energy that could be utilized by an Alpha. Clutching her gut, her eyes teared. Despite the passion she'd felt earlier for Jax, she hated him for attempting to force her submission. Refusing to lower her eyes, she glared at Jax in defiance.

"No, Jax." Katrina stopped cold, her voice a shaken whisper. Although he'd overpowered her, she refused to submit when Jake's life was at stake. "Maybe I was wrong about…"

"Don't interfere," Jax warned.

"Quintus." Katrina's scolding tone morphed into a soft plea, begging for mercy. "Please. Jake is my friend. He meant no harm."

"Ah, bella, what they did. I could not let them have you." Quintus' hold on Jake loosened and the wolf gasped for breath.

"I never expected you to save me that day." Katrina wiped the moisture from her cheek as she recalled what had happened. "I just knew I had to save you. One of us had to get out of there."

"Cara mia, I was a fool. I should've known when I saw her…it was too good to be true." Quintus shoved Jake to the floor, and took a seat in a large leather chair.

Katrina noted the change in the vampire's demeanor and speculated that he spoke of someone he'd lost long ago. Slowly, she backed away, noting that Jake was unhurt. Jax's eyes narrowed on her, his displeasure evident.

"I need your help, Quint," Jax stated, his gaze remaining locked on Katrina. "*We* need your help. This thing, these demons, whatever the fuck they are…they're trying to kill her."

"I see, and your interest in her?" Quintus spread his legs open, lounging backward. He paused, contemplating his words, and stroked his beard. "What is she to you? Don't fuck with me, Jax."

"Why do you need to know? Katrina's relationship to me is no concern of yours," Jax growled.

"Interesting," Quintus mused with a small smile. "Why does the great Alpha answer my question with a question?"

"All you need to know is that she's mine. She belongs to me."

Katrina seethed at his statement. After tonight, their future was uncertain. She would not mate with an Alpha who could not trust her, one who'd use his power to force her into submission.

"We've been friends a long time," Quintus continued and barked a laugh. "Maybe that's a stretch. Perhaps, we have a mutually beneficial relationship. Regardless of what you call it, I know you, Chandler…perhaps better than you think."

"Then you'll tell me everything you know?" he pressed.

"Sit." Quintus pointed to the chair next to him. "These two," he gestured to Jake and Finn, "we talk alone."

"Go get a drink. Don't leave her alone," Jax ordered.

Jake's mouth closed tight, his lips pursed in anger. Finn's temple pulsed in concern but he didn't challenge his Alpha. Finn gestured for Katrina to follow Jake.

Jax expected her to obey, to allow them to talk without her. Katrina's anxiety rose as she debated her next action. Defying Jax twice would further anger the Alpha. Quintus called her name, requesting her presence, and without asking, she stepped forward.

"She stays. Tell them, Alpha."

Katrina noted the amusement in Quintus' eyes even though his mouth revealed no emotion. Jax nodded in acknowledgement, his eyes going to hers. Although he didn't speak, she sensed his irritation with the vampire.

"I'm fine," she assured Jake, in the hopes he'd go willingly with Finn.

Jax sat next to Quintus, in a set of matching intricately carved mahogany chairs. The plush leather seats, embroidered with fleur-de-lis, reminded her of New Orleans. With no room to sit, she stood in front of the small round coffee table, protectively crossing her arms.

"Shall we begin again?" Quintus tapped the wood with his fingers and smiled up at Katrina. "Which one of you would like to tell me the nature of your relationship? How exactly does the sister of the Lyceum Wolves' Alpha come into the company of Jax Chandler?"

"Katrina and I are together because we both were kidnapped," Jax explained.

"That may be true but there is something else. Now what could that be?" Quintus extended his hand to Katrina. "Come, bella."

Afraid to look to Jax for approval, she allowed the vampire to take her palm in his. As he pressed his cool lips to her skin, her wolf growled in warning. Katrina attempted to jerk her arm away but he held tight.

"Quid pro quo, my friends. I shall help you in exchange for the truth. And," he gazed at Katrina and then to Jax, "a taste of her blood."

"No fucking way." Jax lurched to his feet. "We're leaving."

"Jax, please. We need to know. We need his help," Katrina pleaded.

"Have you lost your mind?" Jax gritted out, his eyes flared in rage.

"I can tell you about the demons who seek to steal her magick." Both Jax and Katrina were silenced by his statement, and focused on him. "That's right, my friend. Her magick." Quintus brought her palm to his nose and sniffed. "She's strong this evening, but she's filled with *your* energy."

"No, that can't be," Jax protested.

"Ah, it's true, isn't it? You've been feeding on his strength, haven't you? Maybe unable to control it? You're sucking it up like a beautiful little sponge, but sadly," he reflected, "your own magick, the very essence that makes you shift, come alive into the beautiful creature you are… it's weak."

Katrina's eyes blurred with tears as Quintus confirmed what she'd suspected. She'd felt stronger but it was Jax who'd invigorated her being. She drew on his power, and without him, she'd be unable to sustain her own magick.

"I don't know what's happening," she admitted, her response quiet.

"No, don't listen to him, Kat. He just wants to feed from you."

"Indeed I do," Quintus quipped. "She's lovely."

"She's my mate," Jax declared.

Katrina shook her head no, wishing he hadn't provided the information to Quintus.

"Really now?" Quintus laughed in amusement. "But you haven't mated? She's unmarked. You didn't claim her right away. Hmm…well, now, what does that say?"

"It says nothing." Jax shook his head in annoyance. "It says we're still trying to figure out what in the hell is going on. Look, Quint, if you can't give us answers, we're done here."

"No," Katrina interrupted. If they didn't get the answers they sought, they might never be free. Even in New Orleans, where she'd been less visible to the demons, she suspected they'd eventually find her.

"I said, no. We're leaving," Jax replied.

Quintus released a hearty laugh. "The Alpha has indeed met his match. Refreshing to see the almighty Jax Chandler challenged by such a lovely creature. This tells me she must be deadly." His expression went serious as his gaze washed over Katrina. "You must be careful, my friend. Like many of the world's most beautiful plants, she could be lethal."

"This is over. Come on, Kat. We'll go to New Orleans." Jax stood.

"No, please." Katrina tugged her hand away from Quintus and slowly reached for Jax. By the time her palm touched his face, her body hummed with his energy. "He's right about me. This is your magick you feel, not mine. I need answers. We're running out of time. Let him bite me. Anything I feel, I will only ever feel for you. It's not real."

"I can't let you do this." His forehead pressed to hers.

"That's the thing, Jax....you don't *let* me do anything. As much as I want you to be, you aren't my Alpha yet. I know you don't want me to get hurt, but I can't let these things kill you or me. We need answers. And if that means sacrificing, then I need to do this. Please understand."

"This isn't a good idea." Jax's focus went to the vampire as he considered her argument.

"I want to be free," she maintained.

"Jesus, this isn't right. But if we do this, I'm going to be right here with you."

Katrina gave Jax a small smile as he reluctantly granted his permission.

"Quintus, I give you my blood only. Nothing else, do you understand? Don't force me to shift," Katrina warned, unsure what would happen if she panicked. The demons had changed her, and the incident in the woods with Jax served to remind her that they'd infused her with whatever evil they held.

"Jax, you can't let her do this," Jake called, hearing every word of their conversation. Finn held him back, and while she understood his concern, there was no turning back.

"Jake, stop." Katrina held her hand up to him, and focused on Jax. "Stay with me. Don't leave my side. Quintus won't hurt me." Katrina paused, catching the delight in the vampire's dark smile. "Will you?"

"As a man of honor, I swear it. There's one thing you should know about me, and I'd think my friend Jax would know this by now; no action is without reason. And your blood," Quintus reached for her wrist and brought it to his nose, "it's no different. You saved me once and I save you in return, bella."

"Tell me now. How do we kill these things?" she asked.

"We're agreed, Alpha? Knowledge for blood?" Quintus asked, continuing to press his nose to Katrina's skin.

"Katrina..." Jax began.

Katrina sensed his hesitation. As her eyes locked on his, she attempted to push her magick back at him. Hoping he could feel her strength, she prayed he'd trust her. Although not marked nor bonded as mates, she knew his wolf would likely go feral having any man touch her. But with little choice, desperation sliced through her chest.

"It's just blood," she said, her tone confident. No matter how shaken she was inside, she'd never show fear.

"Just blood," Jax confirmed. "Do not touch her, Quint. It will be the last thing you feel before you die."

"Agreed?" the vampire asked, raising an eyebrow.

"Yes," Jax bit out. "Go. What do you know?"

"Circe," Quintus stated.

"What?" Katrina asked, confused.

"It's a who. Greek mythology," Jax responded, his focus trained on the vampire.

Quintus laughed. "Ah, I always knew you were a smart one."

"A goddess," Jax continued.

"Of magick. It was said she turned men into animals. Which is interesting, as you shifters are animals." Quintus smiled up at Katrina and licked his lips.

"Would you stop with the cryptic answers," Jax demanded.

"Circe worshippers. They harbor magick, stealing it."

"But why would anyone do that? Why not just go to witches? They conjure it naturally, both good and bad."

"Who's to say they aren't witches? Some say witches. Some say demons. Not much is known. What you see is an illusion. They shift, indulging in the deception. The torture they practice, the pain and fear, the energy it elicits. They use it."

"What in the hell for?" Jax asked, scrubbing his chin.

"They have a dark master, one who hasn't been able to break free of the underworld."

"Circe? But she can't be real," Katrina countered.

"I cannot say one way or another." Quintus' tone resounded low and rough. "Whispers. Rumors. Blah. In the end, all the three of us know to be true is what we saw in there. And even then, the illusions…they're so very real."

Katrina's arm broke out in gooseflesh as the chilling tone of Quintus' voice rolled over her. "Why take me? I'm just a wolf."

"An Alpha's daughter," Quintus told them, his words slow and deliberate. "An Alpha's sister."

"An Alpha's mate," Jax finished his sentence.

"But that happens sometimes. It's not unusual to be all three," Katrina stated.

"An Alpha's daughter or sister? Yes, that's fairly common. But for you also to be the mate of an Alpha? All three? Not so much," Jax countered.

"There may be something else. Something about you. Assuming there are others, why do they come for you? Why Jax, for that matter?" Quintus pondered. "Perhaps your family hides secrets."

"Tristan wouldn't do that. I've told him what happened," she protested.

"But he hasn't stopped it, now has he?" Quintus pointed out.

"My brother's a busy man. He has many things to attend to on any given day. Tris might not have completely believed me, but he'd never lie to me."

"Well, now, I'm no expert on Tristan Livingston. But I saw you the night I was captured. I saw what they did to you. The bruises," Quintus reflected with a lilt of compassion in his words. "No one could withstand what they'd done to you. Yet not only did you survive, you fed me."

"I'd shift," Katrina argued. "I was never gone for long. A day at most. Sometimes only hours."

"Something about your magick. It's special to them. Potent." The vampire once again reached for her hand and turned it over, inspecting her palm.

"Why let me go then? Why not drain me dry?" Katrina questioned. Her voice grew louder as she tried to contain her panic.

"Because they are letting you heal," Jax told her.

"They sow the field and wait for it to grow again. Then they come back to yield the crop. But like an overplanted field, your ability to replenish grows weak. But there is something unusual about the Alpha. Why do they attack him? Why risk the wrath of his pack?"

"How do we kill them?" Jax interrupted.

"Tricky business. I suppose you must figure out a way to stop them from sucking away her essence."

"You mean like a vampire?" Jax raised an accusing eyebrow at him.

"Now, now...no need to toss around insults." Quintus brushed the back of Katrina's palm over his beard. "We are not so different, after all. You know full well that vampires are born of the same magick as wolves. Immortality. Our ability to transform. Unlike wolves, who thrive on the cycles of the moon, vampires drink the blood of humanity itself.

Their magick, however, is neither good nor evil. It simply exists."

"So what are these things? Like drones?" Jax growled, his eyes on Katrina's hand. "Get to the short of it."

"Testy aren't we, Alpha?" Quintus laughed and continued. "My guess is that they're like mages, driven by the demon itself, working collectively to escape. They seek the assistance of witches who need favors."

"What kind of favors?"

"The kind of favors that lie deeply entrenched in black magick. Spells that are so very difficult on their own, they seek the help of the demon. The price is high, I imagine."

"What kind of a demon has the power to control these things from the underworld?" Katrina asked, as a chill ran up her spine.

"That is the question, my sweet dove. Something strong. Destructive."

"Something or someone," Jax added. "What's your part in this? Why were you there with Katrina?"

"Simply put, I danced with a witch, a very nasty one. But that's neither here nor there. The creature that appeared to me that night…" His voice trailed off, and Katrina noted the sadness that flushed his expression. As if someone had slapped his face, he blinked and continued. "She appeared…it appeared as someone I'd known long ago. I should've known better but sometimes matters of the heart can obscure reason."

"What's the name of the witch? Who did you fuck with, Quint?"

"Doesn't matter," he grumbled. "No need to speak her name. The last time I saw her in New Orleans…"

Katrina startled as Quintus jerked her arm; her feet stumbled back.

"I'm afraid we're out of time." The ancient vampire's eyes flashed red, his voice lowered into a whisper. "Your Katrina is like a beacon. They're coming."

"What do you mean, 'they're coming?'" Jax rushed to Katrina, wrapping his hand around her waist.

"No more time, Alpha. I need her blood now. I will get us out of here."

"How are you going to do that?" Katrina yelled. "What is happening?"

"They're here. Come. I'll get you out. But first…her blood?" Quintus sought the approval of the Alpha.

The room began to quake, and Katrina fell back onto Quintus' lap. Bits of cracked bricks sprayed from the ceiling in the far corner, and a small tunnel of light poured onto the dirty stone floor. Jax fell to his knees in front of her, and his eyes met the vampire's.

"Do not touch her. Blood only," Jax repeated.

Katrina's pulse raced at the realization that they'd come for her again. *You can't have me again.* She tore at her blouse and ripped the fabric, exposing her shoulder. With her gaze locked on Jax, she grabbed tight to his hands.

"Do it now!"

She screamed as the vampire's fangs pierced her flesh. The room spun, suction at her neck. The searing pain transposed into desire. With her hands on her mate, she moaned in ecstasy.

"Jax," she cried. "Please help me."

Clutching at his lapel, she pulled him to her. As his lips met hers, her world went dark.

⤙⤏ *Chapter Ten* ⤐⤚

Jax fought the nausea as they materialized onto his bedroom floor. He blinked, and checked his surroundings, quickly realizing that Quintus had transported them back to his penthouse. Although the shifty vampire had saved their lives, his fangs remained lodged in Katrina's shoulder.

"Get the fuck off her!" As Quintus raised his head, Jax's fist landed directly on the vampire's nose. The vampire hissed, bringing his hand to his face. Blood sprayed onto the cherry hardwood floor. "Jesus fucking Christ."

"What the hell is wrong with you? I just saved your goddamned ass. Fuck me." He licked at his lips.

"I'll tell you what's wrong. Look at what you just did to her." Jax scooped Katrina in his arms and inspected her skin. Two tiny red bumps protruded from her pale flesh, the wounds healing. Jax sighed, shaking his head. Katrina's head lolled in the crook of his arm, and he glared at Quintus. "What's wrong with her? What did you do?"

"You're an ungrateful asshole. Same as all those years ago," Quintus spat, leveraging the bed to shove to his feet.

"Really? Are we back to that? She never wanted you anyway." Jax blew out a frustrated breath.

He'd known Quintus for over fifty years. They'd fought off the rise of a human sect that sought to destroy all supernaturals. Allies, they'd survived battles, shared meals and women, but one woman had come between them. *Margot Tremainne.* At the time, Jax had been a neophyte Alpha, seeking to assert his role. He'd thought it a game to best Quintus, winning the affection of the flirty French mistress.

"Si, amico mio. It's about trust."

Jax laughed. When his friend reverted to speaking Italian, he knew he was in trouble.

"Jesus, Quint. I'm sorry, okay. Fuck. It was a long time ago. I was a dick, is that what you want to hear?"

"Si. You are." Quintus brushed the dirt off his leathers. "Those shitheads made a mess."

"What did you do to Kat?" Jax pressed his cheek to hers. Despite her being unconscious, she appeared well, her heartbeat strong, her breathing normal.

"She'll be fine."

"Does she look all right to you?" Guilt flooded Jax; he'd allowed him to bite her.

"You know damn well that dematerializing isn't easy, even for someone as good as me. I had to take both of you. That takes a lot of magick, and I needed nourishment, if you will. Katrina's blood," he paused as if he'd enjoyed a meal at a five star restaurant, "she's the very best. Must be the Alpha in her. I'm not quite sure but si, she's delicious."

"You seriously need to get the fuck out of here before I stake your ass."

"Jealousy is an ugly emotion."

"You hurt her."

"Pfft. She's fine. Just resting. You're well aware that materializing is difficult on you wolves. And the humans?" He rolled his eyes and checked his hair in the mirror, smoothing a strand back into place. "Don't even get me started. So weak. They're pathetic. I will not apologize for saving you both. I would have never been able to get you both out at the same time if I hadn't drank from her."

"Yeah right, like I'm supposed to believe that shit." Jax brushed his lips to her forehead, and pulled the fabric of her shirt together, shielding her bra from Quintus' view.

"Believe what you want. One thing is certain, you must find a way to stop these demons."

"Tell me the name of the witch. Who did you screw with?"

"Why do you want to know so badly? I escaped, didn't I?"

"Yeah, but you needed her." Jax glanced to Katrina and sighed. "Just tell me. I need a starting point. Whoever the witch is, she knows more about these things than we do. If I know what I'm dealing with, I can destroy it."

"Fine, but it's your funeral. Her name's Ilsbeth. The bitch…"

"Ilsbeth," Jax interrupted with a disgusted laugh. "It fucking figures."

The powerful witch had last been seen in New Orleans.

After casting a spell on Dimitri, robbing him of his ability to shift, she'd disappeared. Logan had suspected that Léopold had killed her.

"Si. She's not one to be trifled with."

"Yeah, well, she's dead."

"Has this been confirmed?" Quintus asked in surprise.

"One could wish. But no." Jax slid his arms underneath Katrina. Cradling her to his chest, he pressed to his feet. "After tonight, it's obvious we need to get to New Orleans sooner rather than later. Logan will help me. He owes me."

A pang of grief stabbed at him, the mention of the debt cleaved through the thin veil of his healed emotions. He'd protected his sister, fought alongside of Acadian wolves, but it was his brother who had died.

"Ah, I heard about Nick. Sorry, amico." The sympathy in Quintus' statement was evident, but out of respect, the vampire remained far away from the Alpha's mate.

"Look Quint. I've gotta take care of Katrina. Jake and Finn…"

"They'll be home safely. They're after her, not them." Quintus turned to leave. He paused, looking over his shoulder. "This demon, it grows stronger. Finding her tonight, it broke through my wards. New Orleans is safer. With all the witchcraft buzzing in the Quarter, it may have a harder time finding her."

"My home is always protected with wards, but I agree…we'll leave tomorrow."

"If you need me…you know where to find me."

"Hey, Quint," Jax called as the ancient vampire passed

through the doorway.

"Yeah?"

"Thanks, man."

Quintus nodded and gave a wave in silence as he dematerialized.

Jax glanced down to Katrina, his heart heavy. The great Alpha had failed those closest to him, and a seed of doubt crept into his mind as he wondered if he could keep her safe. He studied her face, noting how her pink lips curled into a smile even in her sleep. She moaned and buried her nose into his shirt, her hand traveling over his shoulder. His cock stirred in response, and he knew he was in trouble.

What the hell was I thinking? Jax settled into the oversized tub, adjusting his steel-hard dick. *Clean her off. Get her into bed. We'll all get a good rest and leave in the morning.* It all had seemed a good idea when he was formulating his plan. After he'd run the soap over her arms, he'd grown aroused. With her head lying flat on his shoulder, he held a firm hand around her waist, contemplating his next move.

Taking a deep breath, he closed his eyes, reflecting on the scene in the club. He'd considered refusing Quintus her blood. But not only did they desperately need information, he'd known the vampire wouldn't hurt Katrina. The bastard may have held a grudge but they'd been through enough battles for him to know that he could trust him. Although he'd been grateful to Quintus for saving them, the memory of his teeth embedding in her creamy skin made him sick. *Mine*, his beast growled in disagreement, but human reason had agreed to the act.

Is she really my mate? The question danced in his mind. Instinct told him she was but until they made love, he couldn't be completely certain. It was getting more difficult to deny his wolf's craving. It bared its fangs, warning him not to wait. *Take her now,* it urged. Although Jax had always been a patient man, her slick nude form against his left little room for restraint.

Katrina's eyes fluttered open, and he breathed a sigh of relief.

"Jax," she whispered, licking her lips.

"Shh, little wolf, I've got you. You're safe." Brushing a stream of warm water over her belly, he stroked her skin.

"But Quintus." Panic laced her words. "He bit me…"

"You must learn to obey your Alpha." His dominance rose to the surface. A soft hand grazed over his thigh, and his cock swelled in response.

"Why are we in water?" she asked, ignoring his statement. As she went to sit up, Jax held her tight to him.

"Because we were covered in dirt and you were unconscious. Seemed the easiest way to clean us both." Jax gave a small laugh.

"Hmm…that's it, huh?" Her hand reached for his. "I guess I can think of worse ways to wake up."

As she wove her fingers through his, Jax smiled. When he'd stripped her bare to bathe her, he'd known it could go one of two ways. She'd either be as aroused as he was, or she'd come out scratching like a wildcat. But it was apparent from her reaction that she, too, continued to fall victim to the unrelenting attraction.

"We need to talk about what happened tonight." If she was his mate, she'd have to submit; there was no other way.

"What?" she asked innocently.

"Kat," he gritted out as her bottom slid over his hardened dick. "Tonight with Quintus…you could have been killed."

"Me? He was about to kill Jake," Katrina responded with a demure tone. She pressed her thumb into his palm and teased the soft skin between their fingers. "Did you expect me to stand by and watch? I had to do something. I know what you did. Your power…"

"I won't apologize. I wasn't going to let anything happen to you."

"But Quintus…"

"Quintus is a friend, but he's dangerous. I'm well aware of how lethal he is which is exactly why I ordered you, forced you back."

Jax reached into her hair, gently pulling her head to one side, revealing her creamy white neck. Her lips parted, and he couldn't tell if it was in arousal or surprise. With his eyes on hers, he grew serious.

"You will learn not to test me." Jax grazed his nose over her skin, letting her scent infiltrate his mind. His wolf snarled, demanding submission.

"You can't change who I am. Jax…I…" she breathed.

Her back arching, the rosy tips of her nipples broke through the bubbles.

Jax lost control, and with the speed of his animal, he flipped her over onto her back. The sound of splashing water resounded throughout the dimly lit room. Swirling puffs of eucalyptus-scented steam floated into the air, and Jax delighted in the gasp that escaped from Katrina's lips.

He pinned her arms to the flattened surface surrounding the tub. With his chest pressed to hers, their wet skin sizzled with the heat of passion. The tip of his cock pressed through her folds, teasing her nub. She moaned as he licked the hollow of her neck.

"I will have all of you or none at all, Katrina," he told her, his lips at her neck. "You know our ways. You were raised as one of us. Why do you continue to challenge me?"

"You need to understand. I've been on my own a long time. Aside from Tristan, I don't take orders from anyone. What you're asking…it won't be easy. Ah…" she cried as he dragged his tongue up over her skin.

"Are you mine?" he asked.

"I…I…" she stuttered.

Jax lifted his head, meeting her gaze. "Are you mine? It's simple. You feel this."

Jax took her lips with his, passionately demanding her decision. His tongue sought hers. She wrapped her legs around his waist, bringing him closer. His wolf roared, yearning for her submission, but with his control weak, the urge to be buried deep inside her superseded all else.

Shadows danced in the candlelight as he shoved out of

the stone tub, water dripping off their silky flesh. Making his way into the bedroom, Jax groaned as she bit at his lips. His calves brushed the mattress, and he tore his mouth from hers. Gripping her waist, he tossed her onto the bed. The fire in her eyes drilled through him as she backed up on her elbows, her swollen pink mouth parted.

"Are you mine?" he asked again. The planes of his muscled physique tensed, his cock jerking as blood rushed into it.

"I…I…I want to say yes…" Her hand brushed her long mane out of her eyes.

His eyes drank in the sight of her bared on his bed, the beaded moisture rolling down her abdomen. She licked her lips and brought her hand to her breast, teasing her nipple between her fingers.

"Say yes to what…that you belong to me?" Jax pounced on the bed. She startled only slightly but continued to caress her tip. On his knees, he straddled her torso. His tight balls brushed over her stomach, and he took his cock into his hand, stroking it. "That you're mine?" He inched forward, and grazed the tip of his seeping head through the valley of her breasts. She released her nipple, and her hands crept up the front of his thighs. Her sexy smile drove him to press her further. "That you'll fuck me? Which is it, princess? Because this is happening tonight."

"You know I want you," she breathed, never taking her eyes off the Alpha. "But I won't hurt you, Jax. I can't make promises I can't keep. Not now…not until we have answers."

Although he knew why she hesitated, he was convinced more than ever that whatever they'd told her about her killing him was bullshit. The more he was around Katrina, the stronger their connection grew.

Jax pumped his hardened dick through the swell of her mounds. Her hips lifted, and he knew she sought relief for the ache between her legs. She'd admit she was his before he gave her what she needed.

"Is this what you want? My cock inside you?" Jax smiled, brushing the crown over her nipple. He delighted as the ripple of her shiver grazed his inner thighs.

"You're torturing me…making me wait."

Jax eyed the seductive beauty. Goddammit, she was going to drive him fucking crazy. With his skin against hers, his wolf howled, recognizing his mate. The Alpha needed to hear the words from her lips, that she felt it too, that she was his.

"Say yes, Katrina. Say it. Say you belong to me. Or I swear, I will get up and walk away right now." He slid closer, thumbing his seed over his shaft.

"Jax…please." Katrina blinked, running her hands up his ripped abs. "Please…yes. Yes, I belong to you."

Jax knew she was scared of hurting him, would resist the bonding until she knew otherwise. His hunger had reached a precipice. The dam broke, the Alpha's power burst, and he fought to retain the tendrils of energy that threatened to spiral from his body.

Guiding his glistening head toward her mouth, he swiped it over her lower lip. Her pink tongue darted out and swept over its slit, eliciting a tremor through his body.

"Suck it," he told her, his eyes locked on hers.

Her lips opened at his request and he pressed into her wet mouth. The suction around his shaft increased and his hands went to the headboard. Clutching onto the wood, he plunged into her warmth. She hummed, the vibrations traveling from his tip to his root, and he cursed.

"Fuck, yeah." As he continued to pump in and out of her, his wolf claimed her as his own. Resounding and unequivocal, the call for his mate registered. No male would touch her without his permission; she'd be his for all of time.

A small purr came from her throat, and he hissed as she dug her fingernails into his ass. He laughed, noting her aggression. Her tongue twirled over his head, and he fought the urge to erupt.

"Oh no, I'm not coming in your mouth. I've gotta be inside you." She released a small whine as he withdrew.

"No…" she protested.

"See that's the thing, baby. This wolf is your Alpha, not the other way around and…" He paused. Sitting back on his knees, he spread her legs wide open, and admired her slick mound, her lips swollen in arousal. "…this pussy." He ran his crown through her slippery folds, brushing it over her blossoming clit, its shiny bulb beckoning to him. "Oh, shit, yeah. See how wet you are for me." Pressing his cock to her entrance, he lifted her legs. "My woman. My mate."

"Yes," she cried.

Plunging inside Katrina, Jax grunted, sheathing himself

fully. Her quivering channel pulsed around his shaft, and he sucked a deep breath, willing himself not to come.

Palming his cheeks, she pressed her fingers into his mouth. Jax sucked her, tasting, feeling, consumed with his mate. His wolf celebrated, urging the Alpha to bite her. He rocked in and out of her, all the while licking at her thumb. He'd thought he'd take her roughly, but as he descended into rhythmic thrusts, he gently spread her knees to the side. Seeking her mouth, he brought his lips to hers. With each long stroke, he kissed her, desperate to claim her. His hand found her breast, caressing her soft swell.

Together they moved in harmony, and all Jax could think about was how he'd never in his life been with someone who challenged him, met his dominance with vigor and passion. His wolf called to him to mark her. He tunneled his fingers into her hair, and she gave a small squeak as he wrapped them around her locks.

With his eyes locked on hers, his gut clenched as she willfully bared her neck to him. Although her sign of submission registered, Jax wasn't foolish enough to interpret it as her embracing their mating. His wolf, on the other hand, feral for his mate, lost control. Jax pounded into her, accepting the consequences of his actions. Katrina Livingston may have once drawn both his lust and ire, but tonight in his arms and bed, she willingly gave herself to him.

As his fangs descended, he allowed his beast the control it sought, biting into the soft flesh of her neck. With the only shred of restraint he possessed, Jax resisted drawing blood, which he knew would initiate bonding. He heard her cry his name as he held her in place, his teeth marking her skin. Katrina convulsed underneath him in orgasm.

"Mate," Jax grunted, stiffening as his release tore through him.

"Yours." Katrina shuddered with ecstasy, clutching to her Alpha.

"I've wanted you forever," she admitted. "I can't lose you."

"I'm here, baby. It's going to be okay," he promised. Warm tears brushed his cheek, and his heart melted. A rush of emotion coiled in his chest. "I'll keep you safe. I swear it."

No matter what she'd been told by the demons, he knew in his heart that she could never destroy him. Her sacrifice in keeping them apart had crushed her spirit, denied her wolf. In his arms, her energy splintered apart. Like fireworks, she'd come alive.

Jax rolled to his back, bringing her with him. Her small sob quieted and he wrapped both his arms around her, cradling her to his chest.

"Katrina, this is meant to be. Fighting it, running from it like you've done…it limits your strength, expends energy you need to conserve."

"If something happens to you…" she began.

"Let me worry about that now, will you? The rush you've felt; maybe you are absorbing my power, but I feel stronger than ever. And just now," Jax wiped a tear from her cheek with his thumb, "my wolf is calm, content that his mate is claimed."

"I can't believe you marked me." Her small fingers grazed over his chest, her voice shaky.

"I'm not going to fight nature when we have other things to fight. We need to do this together. I'm not buying this shit about you hurting me. I don't know why those assholes told you that, but I'm telling you that I feel amazing."

"I never knew what it would be like. Making love to you...my wolf, she claims you as her own." Katrina pressed her lips to his chest.

"I wasn't sure either. But that first time we met our connection was so strong. I suspected. It's why I kept calling. Talked to your brother. I couldn't just let you go. But when you ran and I thought you'd lied, well, hell. I know mates don't always get along but that made me question my sanity." Jax speared his fingers through his hair. "I've been Alpha a long time. I trust my instincts. And my instincts told me that you could be mine. So to have them be so far off base...and now, together like this? It makes so much sense to be with you. Look." Jax lifted her chin with a finger, exposing her neck. "It's unbelievable."

"What?" she asked, her eyes lighting up.

"My mark on you, it's ever so slight but it's there."

"Really?" She smiled.

"Really. And it's beautiful...like you." Jax brushed his lips to the top of her head. "But do be warned, little wolf."

"Hmm...what?" Katrina's words grew sleepy, her thigh coming up over his legs.

"I wasn't joking earlier. You'll learn to obey me within

my pack. There is no other way."

"I love the way you feel inside me," she responded without acknowledging his statement.

Jax gave a small smile, aware that she'd ignored his statement. But Katrina underestimated the determination of her Alpha. She'd learn to trust him. While she'd bared her neck, he suspected that she'd test him the first chance she had. His cock twitched, as he fantasized about the erotic ways he'd teach his little wolf to embrace her submission.

Within his arms, Katrina succumbed to slumber, and he prayed to the Goddess that he could keep her safe. With dawn approaching, he'd have just enough time to assign Finn to watch over his anxious pack. As he drifted off to sleep, Quintus' words played through his mind. *New Orleans.* Tomorrow they'd depart for the Big Easy, and search for the keys that would unlock their future. They'd finally get answers, seeking a weapon against the enemy that never rested. The demons had found her tonight; time was running out. *Tick tock. Tick tock.*

-ఆ Chapter Eleven ☜-

"What did you do?" Finn asked, staring at the inside of the refrigerator.

"Nothing. Not a damn thing," Jax lied.

"I may have been your beta for all of fucking two days, but I know you. We grew up together, remember?" He reached for a carton of milk, opened and sniffed it.

"I haven't known him for as long as you, but something is up," Jake commented, smearing cream cheese on his bagel. He took a bite and smiled. "Only in New York."

"What the hell is with you two anyway? I come out here to get some coffee and you've taken over my house. Why don't you tell me how you got home?"

"Nice, by the way." Jake pointed his pastry at the Alpha. "Whatever…just disappear. And letting Quintus bite Kat? Don't even get me started."

"I wouldn't go there if I were you," Finn warned.

"Oh I'm goin' there. He let that vamp bite her right there in front of everyone." He swallowed, and waved his butter knife in the air as he spoke.

"I'm in a moderately good mood this morning, Jake. Let's not ruin it." Jax smiled and held his nose to his latte, inhaling its delicious aroma. He opened the lid and peered inside. "Don't you love how they make these cool little hearts?"

"He did not just say that." Finn rolled his eyes and snatched a bagel out of the bag. He threw it onto the black and white speckled granite countertop.

"Hearts? No, no I did not notice. You're joking, right?" Jake shoved the round dough into his mouth, continuing to talk as he chewed. "Please tell me he's joking."

"What?" Finn rummaged through a drawer and slammed it shut. Scanning the kitchen, he spied a serrated knife from the wooden block and retrieved it. "We got back fine, by the way. I can see you cared so much about what happened."

"These things are after Katrina, not the two of you. Besides, you're no worse for wear. You even had time to bring by breakfast, which was very thoughtful, by the way," Jax commented.

"You're welcome." Finn sawed through the bread.

"You're a tough guy, and him," Jax's eyes darted over to Jake and then fell back onto his drink, "he's preparing for his own time."

"Preparing for his own time?" Jake asked. "What the hell is that even supposed to mean? Have you been drinking?"

"No, my friend. Just observant." Jax smiled as he took a long sip of his coffee. "Hmm, I missed these."

"What's wrong with him?" Jake glanced to Finn.

"Did you know that Alphas sometimes run in families?" Jax reached for his iPad that he'd set on the counter, and joined Jake at the kitchen table. He gazed out the floor to ceiling window which looked out onto Central Park, and smiled. He loved his city more than ever, and it'd be here he'd rule with his mate.

"No shit," Jake replied, his answer laden with sarcasm.

"But sometimes, it doesn't. Sometimes an Alpha is just born. He's made." Jax slid his fingers across the glass, opening his email, then paused. "I cannot bring you the answers you seek. I can only guide you."

"Look, I don't even know what that means. All I'm sayin' is that you let Quintus bite…"

"Enough." Jax waved a dismissive hand in the air.

"She must not really be your mate, because damn, if she didn't challenge you right there," Finn noted.

"Oh, she's my mate." Jax laughed. She'd kill him, but she was indeed his. Her true submission would be sweet when it came but it would not happen easily.

"She sure as hell didn't act like it last night. Who the hell thinks she can go up against someone like Quint?"

"Someone who's desperate, that's who." Jake nodded at Jax as if to give him support. "Someone who was trying to save me. She's brave."

"See there, he also has instinct," Jax noted with a smile.

"Instinct? I think the both of you have lost it over that she-wolf." Finn attempted to stuff the bagel into the toaster, but it wouldn't fit. "Fuck."

"Katrina is tough. As wolf, she's one of the strongest I've

seen. I'm talking 'Gillian strong'. She's pretty badass." Jake shrugged and gave a nod.

"Her father was an Alpha. Her brothers." Jax blew out a breath and looked over to Finn. "And her mate as well. There's something extraordinary about her."

"By extraordinary, do you mean crazy? Because she's kind of crazy for challenging an Alpha. That's special all right. The pack is going to have a field day if you don't get her under control." Finn managed to insert the bagel into the slot. His finger sizzled and he jumped. "Shit. That's fucking hot."

"Yes, genius. It's a toaster," Jake jibed.

"Fuck off."

"Cold water," Jax suggested.

"Ice," Jake told him.

"Cold water," Jax repeated. "Or shift."

"He's going to shift over a boo-boo on his little finger?" Jake gave a small chuckle.

"You're both assholes." Finn toggled on the spigot and shoved his finger under the stream. "It's cold water, by the way."

"Whatever." Jake reached for his orange juice and took a swig.

"The Alpha is always right." Jax laughed and focused back on his screen. "Tell me about last night."

"Nothing happened. You three vaped out of the basement and the earthquake stopped. Whatever was on its way in must've sensed you were gone. After that, we left the same way we came in. The place was a disaster, but we got home, that's all that counts." Jake leaned back in his chair and stared out onto the city. "Nice place, by the way."

"Thanks. It's home. Speaking of which…today we're going to New Orleans."

"What about the pack?" Finn asked.

"You're in charge while I'm gone. I should only be a few days."

"What about Katrina?" Finn wiped his hands dry on a towel.

"She's going with us." Jax trained his vision on Jake, who met his hard stare. "Ilsbeth. We're going to find her. I don't know exactly what happened between her and Quint, but she's wrapped up in this shit storm."

"There was a time," Jake reflected, "she wasn't all that bad. But what she did to Dimitri, to his wolf? When I think back on it, I just don't get it. I know she wanted D, but there are rules we all play by. The witches? The vamps? They all know the score with us wolves. We can't commit to others who aren't our breed."

"Friend em'. Fuck em' at your own risk, but emotions? It's trouble," Finn added.

"It's none of my concern why she did what she did. I just need to know how she knew about the demons. So we're going back to New Orleans." Jax's voice grew contemplative. Returning to the city would bring up memories of Nick's death, but he had no choice.

"Hey Jax, you know Nick, he, uh…that night." Jake paused and rubbed his chin. "Chaz, he'd hurt your sister…would have killed her. He's a hero. He died protecting her."

"That night you almost died too, my friend," Jax noted. "I took Nick's death hard. But I can't lose control of my emotions again. You both know that the pack, the energy of an Alpha, it affects everyone. When I was missing, I'm sure all hell broke loose. I took no pleasure killing Arlo."

"He was a dick anyway," Finn began.

"Perhaps, but that wolf...he was a brother. An uncle. A son. Killing during a challenge? The death it brings. It always comes at a cost, don't ever think it doesn't. But this is our responsibility. To lead. There is no other path for us." Although Jax dare not speak the truth of his suspicion regarding the young wolf, he hoped someday Jake would realize his destiny. "I've already called Logan. He knows we're coming and why. Jake will remain at my side. Finn. You're needed here."

"You still haven't told us about Katrina. The pack..." Finn shook his head, hesitating.

"She's my mate." Jax shoved out of his chair, and moved to stand at the window.

When he'd woken, he'd found her quietly sleeping on his chest, wrapped around him like a blanket. With their turbulent past, he didn't expect an easy road to their mating. He needed to convince her that bonding wouldn't hurt him. But with his mark blossoming on her skin, his wolf celebrated, content she'd been claimed.

A laugh drew Jax out of his contemplation and he turned to see both Finn and Jake, shaking their heads.

"What's so funny?" Jax asked.

"I just never thought I'd see the almighty Jax Chandler fall so hard. All the women over the years? Shit, I remember that little vamp from LA you dated. She had her fangs into you...literally." Finn laughed. "And London? Holy hell. She's going to lose it when she finds out you've found a mate."

"You one hundred percent sure you guys are mates?" Jake asked.

"Of course he is." Katrina stood in the entryway to the kitchen, a sheet wrapped around her.

Jax smiled, unsure of what to say. A laugh escaped his lips, as he thought about how she'd turned his life upside down in two days. The articulate Alpha had been rendered speechless. As he took in the sight of her bright eyes, her tousled hair, his cock jerked. Holy hell, he was in trouble.

"He marked me. Can you see it?" she asked, trailing her fingertips over her neck. She blinked and gave Jax a sexy sleepy smile.

He went to her, setting his coffee on the table. Jax ran the pads of his fingers over the lines. The quarter-sized intricate design had grown a deeper shade of pink.

"It's beautiful. How do you feel, baby?"

"Baby, my ass..." Finn commented under his breath.

Jax ignored him, cupping her cheek. She turned into his touch, her lips brushing over his skin.

"Come here," he told her, bringing her into his arms.

"Hmm..." Katrina nuzzled against his chest.

"Jake and Finn brought breakfast." The Alpha spoke into her hair, inhaling her scent. A mixture of coconut infused with mango still remained and he recalled their interaction in the tub. Lifting his head, he met her gaze and trailed his thumb along her bottom lip.

"Sounds good." She snuggled into his embrace.

"Hungry?" His dick tented the thin fabric of his pajama pants, detecting her arousal.

"Yes," she purred, her palm sliding over his bare chest.

"Really, people? We're right here," Finn pointed out. "Maybe you all need to go get a room, as they say."

"Hey, speak for yourself." Jake leaned back in his chair with a wide grin. "Kat. Jax. Don't listen to the big guy over there. I'm up for a show."

Jax caught the amusement on Jake's face and knew he was only half kidding. He'd heard from Gillian how she'd helped him heal after he'd been shot, having made love to both Dimitri and Jake. While he couldn't be certain he'd share his mate, he'd happily let him watch. Jax suspected her interest in the idea, pushing the envelope sexually. Undressed in his office, his little wolf had responded with arousal to the intrusion. Jax had always been sexually adventurous, and after making love to Katrina, he looked forward to exploring her fantasies.

"Seems we have an audience this morning," Jax laughed.

"Ah," Katrina peeked around his shoulder and winked at Jake. "It appears we do."

Jax put his arm around her and ushered her to the table, unfazed about revealing his erection to the others. Some things were meant to be concealed, but his sexual prowess and his interest in his mate wasn't one of them.

"Finn, call a pack meeting. Announce that I've left for New Orleans on official business. Meeting with Logan and my sister."

"And if they ask about Kat?" Finn stood from the table, combing his hair back with his fingers.

"Tell them she's a person of interest in custody with our pack." Jax smiled at Katrina, who laughed. "Tell them I'm interrogating her, ensuring she provides us with information leading to the capture of my kidnappers."

"Interrogating, huh?" Finn shook his head and gave a lopsided grin.

"He certainly has perfected the craft." Jake smiled at Katrina and Jax. "I mean, all that *interrogating* he did in the office yesterday and then last night obviously led to more *interrogating*, hence the marking. The Alpha's been busy."

"You guys aren't going to make this easy on me, are you?" Jax asked, picking up his coffee.

"Nope. Not even a little bit." Jake pressed his lips together, stifling his laugh.

"Yeah, no, not going to happen," Finn agreed with a smirk. "Hey, don't feel too bad, Alpha. While you were doing all that *interrogating*, Jake and I were bonding."

"You got it, brother. We had to save ourselves."

"You two are hilarious." Jax shook his head and sighed.

"They are pretty funny," Katrina admitted. She reached for a pastry, her eyes on Jake.

"Go tell the pack. Also, do me a favor and call the helicopter. I want to skip the traffic. I've already texted Rhys and called up the plane."

"Okay, I'm outta here." Finn began to walk toward the foyer but stopped and paused. "You gonna be okay without me? The last time…"

"I'm not going to tell you that we aren't going to run into trouble. But Jake's going with me. Logan and Dimitri are there too. I've gotta find out what Ilsbeth knew. If I find the witch, I have a better shot figuring out how to stop these things." Jax blew out a breath and pinched the bridge of his nose. "I really need you up here, Finn. The pack has been through enough shit the past month. One of us has to stay to keep order, and that, my man, is you. I'm trusting you to do this."

"I got it. I'll text you later with a status." His new beta gave a wave and turned on his heel, leaving the room.

Jake gave a sideways glance to Katrina and back to Jax. "So, uh, just to recap about last night. Everything's okay? Quintus looked like he bit you pretty hard."

"My mate doesn't listen well." Jax slowly spread the cheese onto the bread, his eyes trained on his knife.

"You're both overreacting. I'm perfectly fine." Katrina unconsciously reached behind her neck, where Quintus had bitten her.

"Very soon she'll experience a lesson that she will not forget," Jax warned. His eyes went to Jake, who nodded his head in agreement.

"I'm sorry but I wasn't going to let Quint kill Jake," she replied.

"You know I love ya, Kat, but Jax is right. There's a reason he's the Alpha of this pack. You can't just ignore him when he tells you what to do in these situations," Jake asserted. "It's worse that you challenged him. You're his mate."

"We're not bonded yet," she contended.

"We will be soon." Katrina's words cut through Jax, and he couldn't identify the emotion that followed. Anger? Arousal? The growl of his wolf reverberated in his mind, urging him to take her again. While he hadn't known her long enough to fall in love, the commitment would come in time.

"You know what will happen if we mate. I can't risk anything happening to you." Katrina pursed her lips and set her food on a plate. "And as far as me not listening, as you put it. I've lived a long time on my own with no master. I'm an Alpha's daughter, a sister. Tristan doesn't force me into antiquated rules. What makes you think submission to your will is in my blood?"

"Because, my little wolf…" Jax didn't miss a beat as he drove his fingers through her hair at the nape of her neck. Tugging her locks, he tilted her head backward, exposing her throat. He leaned in, his lips inches from hers. "That little mark on your neck is mine. You are mine. Our mating will happen. Don't. Test. Me."

The tense whisper of his statement died as Jax captured her lips. His bruising kiss was met with passion. Katrina gasped into his mouth, returning his advance, biting and sucking at her mate. Fingernails raked down over his shoulder, tearing at his skin, and the sting reminded him that Katrina harbored a wild nature, one that might be impossible to tame.

"And I think that's my cue to leave." Jake laughed and pushed up from the table. "As much as I enjoy a good show, I can't figure out if this is going to be super-hot or more like gladiators. Yeah, I'll catch up with you guys later."

As Jake left the kitchen, Jax forced his libido under control. He'd torn his lips away from his mate, frustrated with her refusal to accept her fate, their mating. After making love with her, there was no doubt in his mind that the bond would make them stronger. But without her trust, he'd need proof before she'd consent.

Jax heard the water running, and was reminded that Katrina had gone to shower. His cock hardened as the image of her perfect nipples dripping with water formed in his mind. *Goddammit. For the next year, I'm going to have a perpetual hard-on.* He adjusted his erection, but resisted the urge to stroke it. As much as he loved that the Goddess had given him an attractive mate, it was going to make it damn hard to concentrate on business.

The doorbell rang, breaking his concentration. On any other day, he'd have his staff attend to it, but he'd dismissed his butler and the rest of the staff, unwilling to risk Katrina's safety or theirs. As he opened the door, he sensed London's presence. He waved her into the foyer and retreated into the great room.

"Why are you here?" Jax had been grooming her to take over day to day operations. London had been working with Nick for several years and knew the company inside and out.

"Finn said…well, if you're leaving, I need to get your input on these first." She sat on the sofa and flipped open her tablet.

"I just sent you my feedback. We didn't have to do this in person. Go with the black and white on the cover. Follow up with the color spread."

"I just thought…"

"Why are you really here?" Jax asked, already suspecting why she'd insisted on visiting him at his penthouse.

By now, the pack already had their suspicions about Katrina's role in his life. After their romantic interlude on his desk, half the company probably had heard her scream in orgasm. Although he'd found his mate's lack of inhibition refreshing, he'd thought better of what he'd done afterward. He needed more time to work through Katrina's introduction to the pack. Going down on her with the office door swinging wide open wasn't exactly the optimal way to do it.

Jax ignored London, who slowly put her things back into her bag. With thick raven hair, green eyes and a razor-sharp mind, she'd caught the attention of many men, humans and supernaturals alike. Although Jax hadn't slept with her, they'd shared an intimate moment. In a moment of weakness after Nick's death, they'd kissed in the nightclub. Despite the fiery interaction, he hadn't expected more than a fling. Despite not being his mate, the females in his pack often sought the attention of the Alpha.

As he leaned back on the sofa, he pretended to be engrossed in his email. With Katrina already vulnerable, he wasn't ready to divulge information to his pack.

"There are rumors," he heard her say. Jax kept his head down but lifted his gaze to meet hers.

"You shouldn't believe everything you hear."

"Everyone knows she's here." London scooted toward the Alpha, closing the distance. "So she isn't staying? That bitch from Lyceum wolves is finally going home?"

"You need to check yourself." Jax's eyes flared in anger and he struggled to conceal his irritation. "Katrina. That's her name. I suggest you use it. Not a request. And yes, she's staying here. For as long as I say she stays."

"Jax, please." London's voice softened as she edged closer, her knee brushed his. "We haven't talked about what happened. The night you disappeared. At the club. Our kiss." She closed her eyes and drew a breath, her chest rising and falling slowly. Gradually she opened them, and continued. "There's something between us. I don't know what it is. I know I was with Nick before and maybe that's an issue, but he's gone."

"I don't want to talk about Nick. I don't want to talk about that night. It was a kiss. It was nothing more. I'm sorry, London." Jax shook his head and set his iPad aside. Jesus, he hadn't expected this conversation today. In the distance, he noted the shower had stopped running.

"Then maybe…" London gently laid her things on the

table. "You need to give us a chance."

Before Jax knew what was happening, the brunette had swung her thigh over his. Straddling him, she pressed her groin to his.

"What the hell?" Jax exclaimed. Because Katrina hadn't claimed him, her wolf would lose it if she saw him with another woman. "You need to get off me right now."

"That night...you kissed me. I'll never forget it. If you just give us a chance I know..."

Jax sensed the second Katrina entered the room, but it was the growl that drew his attention. The small white wolf bared her teeth. With her hackles raised, she gave no doubt as to her intention to attack London.

"Get off me right now. Easy now." Jax lifted her by the waist and tossed her onto the sofa. He held up his hands defensively, aware that Katrina had gone feral. "Nothing's going on here, Kat. London's just confused. She's missing Nick."

"What the hell is wrong with her?" London backed into the corner of the couch, pulling her knees to her chest. "Really? She wants a challenge? I'm not shifting right now."

"No one is shifting. Get your things off the table and slowly walk out of the house."

London moved to collect her tablet and Katrina stalked toward her, continuing to growl.

"Kat. This is not what it seems. You need to trust me." A rush of satisfaction filled his chest, observing his mate possessively claim him. But he couldn't let her kill London. "You need to back off. Let her leave. She's got to get back to the office."

"I can't believe you let her in here," London lamented.

"Let her go," Jax commanded.

Katrina whined. Her fangs exposed, she settled to the floor. Although she hadn't ceased her aggression, it would have to be sufficient. Jax's gaze moved to London, who'd already begun to stand. "Move slowly and get out now. Keep moving. And not a word to the pack, London."

"Seriously?" London asked.

"I'll be back in a few days and if I hear you've been talking, your employment will be in jeopardy. Leave here and go back to the office. Go now!"

Jax towered above the petite wolf, breathing a sigh of relief as London slammed the door behind her. He looked to Katrina, who continued to show the whites of her teeth.

"What you just saw here," Jax held his palms upward and swiveled, looking around the condo, "this was nothing. A misunderstanding. My pack...they don't know about you, baby."

Katrina transformed into her human form. Standing bare, she glared at Jax.

"This thing between us...you know we both have pasts. You can't go around trying to kill every woman I ever dated." Jax laughed. "You haven't even marked me yet. Your wolf, she's not going to be very happy until she gets what she wants."

"Who is she?"

"No one. We work together."

"You fucked her?"

"No, but I did kiss her. Jesus, why am I even explaining myself to you? You know what, Kat? You're going to have to learn how to trust me."

"Really? You do realize you just had a woman straddling you, right?"

"And you need to learn how to listen." Jax drank in the sight of his mate standing nude before him. From her fierce eyes to her full breasts down to her cream-colored painted toenails, she exuded sexuality. She brushed her long blonde mane behind her ears, and licked her lips. The defiance caused his dick to thicken.

"Are you kidding me?" she continued. "You were the one with a female in your lap."

"And you," Jax approached her within two broad steps and gave her a devious grin, "are the one who continues to challenge me."

He wasn't sure whether it was the tip of her pink tongue brushing over her swollen lip or the way she crossed her legs, attempting to conceal her own arousal, but he lost control. Katrina squealed as he placed his fingers on her waist and hoisted her over his shoulder.

"What the hell are you doing? Put me down."

"My dear, dear, Katrina." Jax ran a strong palm over the back of her thigh. "I realize we don't know each other very well yet, but you, my lovely mate, you must learn to trust me."

"I do trust you." Katrina didn't fight as he lifted her and set her in front of the back of the sofa.

"Really? Because on more than one occasion I've given

an order and you not only ignored it, you fought me. And this," Jax smiled as he turned her around, her bottom brushing over the front of his thighs, "is the perfect opportunity for us to have this discussion."

His cock lengthened as he ran through the scenario he planned. He'd always enjoyed a little bondage. Today, he'd test Katrina's limits. The defiant little wolf needed a lesson and she'd learn why he was Alpha.

~❦· *Chapter Twelve* ·❦~

Katrina yelped as Jax bent her over the sofa. He spread her legs wide open, the cool air rushing over her pussy. She reached to balance herself, her palms flat on the soft leather.

"What do you think you're doing?" she asked, her emotions vacillating between pissed as hell and aroused. A smooth palm cupped her ass and she sighed, deciding on the latter. "Just because my body responds to you, that doesn't mean I'm forgetting that bitch you let in here."

"Trust," he began.

Katrina gasped as his warm breath teased her bottom. His fingers dug into her hips.

"Even animals born without the magick to shift understand that trust is essential to life. You should know better. There's structure within our lives that protects all of us. Without it, there is chaos. So this is why our wolves value order. Challenges to my position aren't tolerated." Jax slid his grip over her smooth ass and squeezed gently. "Disobedience…"

"I know full well what it's like to live within a pack, but

this situation isn't life and death." Katrina's pussy ached as his soft fingers traced a line down between her legs, grazing over the outside of her labia. Growing wet, she shifted her position, attempting to move. Her action was rewarded with a firm slap to her bottom, the sting leaving her skin tingling. "Hey…"

"As I was saying, disobedience is not tolerated. Wolves, they choose willingly to submit to their Alpha, accepting their position within the pack. Because they know…" He paused and smacked his palm against her other cheek.

"You can't just spank me," she protested. Guilt rose as arousal flooded between her legs. She'd never allowed a man to spank her, yet the twinge on her skin left her wanting more.

"The pack knows," he continued, ignoring her statement. He trailed a finger through her wet slit, eliciting a moan, "that by giving their submission, they're protected. As a whole, we are stronger than individuals. We cannot do that without collaboration. This is what unites us."

"I don't know what you want from me," she sighed. Her aching clit swelled as he brushed over it. Katrina pushed up on her toes, but was unable to move, as his hands held her firmly in place.

"You're not going anywhere." The Alpha bit gently at his mate.

"What do you want from me? Ah…" Katrina sucked a breath as his teeth nipped at her flesh, leaving her quivering with pleasure and pain. "You could die if we…Jax…"

"What do I want?" he growled. His warm breath teased

her skin. "I want everything. You. Us. This."

"I can't..." Soft lips brushed over her bottom, silencing her. Painfully aroused, she knew it'd be minutes before she was begging him to fuck her.

"You can feel it, can't you?" He cupped her mound, tapping his fingers over its smooth surface. "Your Alpha knows you better than you know yourself. That is part of my responsibility. To care for you...to protect you."

"Jax, please..." Katrina tilted her hips, seeking relief.

"That's much better, my sweet little wolf. I love to hear you beg." Jax rose, nestling his erection into the crevice of her ass. Sliding a hand down her back, he fisted her hair and tilted her head up until her gaze met his. "I've got a little surprise for you."

"But...oh Jesus, you can't leave me here like this." Katrina's heart pounded against her ribs. Whatever he was planning couldn't be good and with her body already on fire, she breathed through her unmet need. She considered running, escaping the dominant Alpha, but the truth was that she couldn't resist his challenge. Whatever erotic game he planned, she'd play, but true submission wasn't a prize she was willing to give just yet. Her wolf paced, urging her to mark him, and she shook her head, refusing the demand. The desire to protect her mate outweighed the possessive need to claim him as her own.

A rush of cold air caressed her skin, making her aware he'd left her.

"Don't move," he warned, his voice low and commanding. A shiver of anticipation ran over her body.

"What are you doing?"

"I want you exposed and open to me. You don't seem to listen very well and I can tell you're thinking of challenging me right now."

"How do you know what I'm thinking?"

"No lies." He arched an eyebrow at her in warning. "Wolves…we choose our Alpha. Our pack. We choose to submit for the greater good. Even the strongest wolves, they do not challenge for the sake of challenging. This brings discord. It puts us all in danger. Last night…"

"We needed to get the information. He was going after Jake," she began, but went silent as he settled pillows underneath her torso, supporting her weight.

"It was dangerous. You didn't know what Quintus would do. I happen to know him very well. He's an old friend."

"But you didn't tell me that. How was I supposed to know?" Katrina hugged the cushions, unsure whether she wanted to let Jax proceed. Her heart raced as she caught sight of the black cuffs and dangling brass chain.

"Trust, Kat. Because I'm your mate and Alpha. You can always be assured that I will protect you and do what is in the best interest of this pack." Jax gave her a devious smile as he reached for her wrist and began to fasten the soft leather. "You understand I would never hurt you?"

Katrina had never let anyone restrain her, but found herself nodding as he asked the question. Jax had never given her reason not to trust him. It wasn't as if Katrina didn't understand his argument. She'd never directly challenged Tristan, but her brother didn't push her the way Jax did. Katrina had lived for decades independently of pack politics and did what she pleased.

As he fastened the leather to her wrists, his eyes never left hers. *I must be crazy*, she thought. *Why on earth am I letting him do this?* Deep within her soul she yearned for what he demanded. Although the Alpha drove her wolf wild, it was the woman who couldn't resist his test.

"The point of this is that you are making a decision to listen to me." Jax eyed the legs of the heavy marble coffee table and deftly wrapped the cord around the base and secured the clasp.

"Is this really necessary?" She laid her cheek onto the soft pillow, resting her head.

"Yes, because this is your choice. We both know full well that you could shift and escape if you wanted." He ran his finger over her cheek, his lips hovering over hers. "You are choosing to stay here, because you want this."

Katrina's heart caught. His mouth crushed onto hers, and she tugged on her restraints. Her sensitive nipples grazed over the chenille fabric as she wriggled against it. Katrina moaned as his tongue gently swept against hers. His hand stroked over her hair, and she blinked up at him, objecting when he tore his lips away. She heaved for breath, her body igniting with desire.

"Do you have any idea how much I've wanted you? How much my wolf needs you?" he asked.

"Oh Goddess…" Katrina's thoughts spun, regretting how much time she'd lost with her mate. She knew damn well how hard it had been for her to not only leave Jax, but to force herself to date other people, to escape all the way to New Orleans. A slow form of torture, she'd unsuccessfully attempted to put him out of her mind. No matter how many times she told herself she was protecting him, her heart ached to see him again.

Under his touch, she could no longer deny the raw emotion, the chemistry that churned with every word he spoke. Her Alpha commanded her, she knew. Admitting his victory, however, would be difficult. It meant she'd agreed to the mating, that she'd given in to her wolf's desire to claim him as her own. If she lost control, she feared she'd do more than mark him. Her fangs ached, yearning to slice through his skin, allowing the magick of his blood to flow into her, solidifying the bond.

The soft brush of the head of his cock against her bottom broke her contemplation. Her skin pricked in awareness as he slid it down the cleft, teasing her entrance.

"This," he slapped her cheek again, and Katrina cried aloud, "will be mine, and do you know why?"

"No, Jax...don't say it." As he spanked her again, her pussy tightened. "I can't..."

"You're a difficult one. But look how responsive you are to this." The sound of a crack rang out in the room as he delivered another blow. "Tell me why...why will you be mine?"

"Because," she whispered. She'd give her soul to surrender to the mating, but refused to hurt him.

"Ah..." Fingers slid between her folds, brushing over her

clitoris.

"You fight your own happiness." Jax pressed a finger inside her slippery core and she clenched down on him.

"I can't do this…"

"Fuck, you're beautiful." Jax reached around her neck, sliding his thumb over her bottom lip. "So stubborn. But do you want me to stop, Katrina?"

"No, no, no," she told him as he plunged in and out of her heated channel. She parted her lips, sucking a breath.

"This moment. Look at you. You choose submission. You display your trust. Why do you deny me otherwise?"

"You know why," she breathed, her lips wet with saliva. As he added another finger inside her, she quivered around him. "Don't stop."

"Don't you dare come," he warned, withdrawing his hand. "Why do you submit to me here?"

Katrina's body shivered as he retreated. Her wolf howled, begging her to claim him, to say the words. In her heart, she knew she couldn't go without him another day.

"Because…" As he slammed his fingers back inside her pussy, applying pressure to her clit, she came apart. "You're my mate. Please Jax…I don't want to ever hurt you, but fuck…ah yes, don't stop…you're my mate."

"Your Alpha." Jax removed his fingers and slammed his cock into Katrina.

"Yes, yes, yes," she cried, as his shaft entered her from behind.

All Katrina could smell, feel, and see was Jax. As he stretched her wide, she dug her fingers into the couch, bracing herself as he pounded into her tight channel. She shuddered as his fingers found her swollen nub.

"You are everything I need, Katrina. Do you hear me?" he told her.

"Jax I…" she panted, her body alive with energy. The strength of his magick filtered through her veins. As she felt the pad of his thumb circle her puckered flesh, she tensed.

"You need to trust me," she heard him tell her. The pressure built as he slid over her skin, igniting a dark arousal she'd never experienced. "No challenging."

"I promise. Yes, ah, yes, oh…please, please," she repeated as he slid it into her back hole.

Full with pleasure, she embraced his erotic touch. Katrina screamed Jax's name as her climax crashed down on her. She splintered into a thousand pieces. Quivering in ecstasy, her toes dug into the carpet. His fingers moved to her hips, and she heard him grunt, giving a final thrust.

"Kat," Jax cried, pressing his lips to her neck.

Katrina went limp, floating within the relaxation of her submission. His kiss, his touch, it was all she'd ever needed. Surrendering to the Alpha, she prayed she wouldn't destroy him.

Within seconds, her hands were freed and he lifted her, cradling her against his chest. As they fell onto an adjoining sofa and she rested within his arms, Katrina grazed her lips to his chest.

"My Alpha," she whispered. With her heart and soul, she swore she'd fight to keep him, not just for a night, but forever.

⊷❀ *Chapter Thirteen* ❀⊶

My Alpha. Jax closed his eyes, his mind whirling with emotion. He'd never understood how a mate could take a man's world, shatter everything he thought he knew and then end up molding it all together in a spectacular masterpiece.

When Katrina walked in on him and London, Jax had known she'd lose control. No matter the control she'd exercised, until she'd marked Jax, her wolf wouldn't accept another woman touching him. The instinct to own her mate would far exceed any rational thoughts. Although they'd explored her submission and she'd said the words out loud, her fears about losing him drove her to resist mating.

He hadn't planned on cuffing her to the table. Although he'd used the restraints on occasion, the act had been more than simple bedroom play. She could have shifted, broken free at any point. He knew it. She knew it. But she'd chosen to stay within his confines, accepting the situation on his terms. It was a lesson she'd need to learn out of the bedroom as well.

Jax buried his nose into her hair, pleased with his scent on her skin. He weaved his fingers through hers, and brought her palm to his lips. His heart squeezed in his chest and in that moment he realized how vulnerable he'd become. Upon Nick's death, his emotional reserve had been depleted. Without knowing that day who he had rescued, Jax had found Katrina. She'd begun to heal the cavern in his heart that had been left in the wake of Nick's passing.

Katrina curled against his body, bringing his hands into the warmth of her breasts. Adrift within a peaceful haze, she moaned, and it reminded him that she hadn't fallen asleep.

"Jax," she whispered.

"Hmm…are you okay?"

"Very okay." She laughed. "More than okay."

"Me too," he agreed with a kiss to her head.

"My wolf knows. She knows you are her mate," she admitted quietly.

"And you?" He forced himself to breathe calmly as he waited on her answer. After everything they'd just experienced, he hoped the lesson had taken hold.

"I'm sorry for challenging you. The vampire…I didn't know you knew him. I know that's not reason enough, but you must know I'm desperate. If he'd killed Jake? I couldn't live with myself. He's protective of me. But it's more than that. I just feel so out of control."

Jax stroked her hair gently and inhaled.

"When I'm with you, your magick…I can feel it. You make me feel whole again. They've changed me, though. Remember in the woods?"

"Yes."

"My magick, they siphon it, poison it with whatever evil they manage to get from this thing they worship. I don't think they just want my magick, though. I think they want me. They want me to be like them."

Katrina shivered against his chest. Although he suspected it was the topic causing her to shudder, not the temperature, he reached for a throw blanket and spread it over her.

"Whatever this is, the only way we can fight it is together. I know you're tough, Katrina, and I'm glad you are." He gave a small laugh. "Well, of course, I'd have a mate to match me. It's not like I don't understand why you've done some of the things you've done. I get you want control because control's been taken from you. But you need to let me help."

"Jax…that night we met at the party." Katrina blinked, her lashes tickling his chest. "I knew. I saw you across the room. When you touched me…it's so stupid. I didn't think it would be like that. I just knew you were my mate."

"I remember that night. I won't ever forget it."

"I've never felt that way. Just this immediate connection with you. I can't explain it." She shook her head and reflected. "You know, I'm not a young wolf. I was born in the early 1800s. I've lived through many bad times. These things, yeah, they hurt me, but it's not the first time I've been tortured."

"I didn't realize…" Jax attempted to conceal his shock at her confession.

"No, it's okay. It was a long time ago. There was this woman, Simone. She, uh, got off on killing women. Was into some kind of black magick. Tristan had to go to Kade Issacson and Luca Macquarie for help." Katrina's voice grew serious, her eyes focused on their intertwined fingers. "They both found me."

"I'm so sorry, Kat." Jax reasoned that if her brother had been forced to seek assistance from the New Orleans vampires, it had to have been a dire situation.

"The things I saw Simone do? I just…it's not right." Katrina closed her eyes and sighed.

"Jesus, I wish I'd been able to protect you. Things will be different. I promise you."

"It wasn't until recently…these things came for me. Of course, when they told me I'd meet an Alpha, my true mate…I didn't believe them at first. I mean, when so many years pass, you just stop believing that it will happen. You take lovers, try not to get too involved because you know if you meet your mate, you will hurt the other person. But that night, everything changed."

"I know what you mean. I've been around for quite a while too." Like Katrina, Jax had lived a long time, experienced the loneliness. He'd casually dated. Sex was easy. Relationships, however, were entirely too complicated. Unable to mate with humans or witches, he'd kept his interactions to one night stands. Within the confines of wolves, he'd grown close to few females. They understood the inevitability that would come for all wolves. If another met his or her mate, they'd better accept the situation when they were forced to separate. "Something about your eyes. Your smile."

"My smile?"

"Yes, do you remember what we talked about?" he asked, wrapping a single strand of her soft hair around his finger.

"Ice skating. You were trying to talk me into going to Rockefeller Center."

Jax laughed. "You told me you were an Olympic champion."

"Give me a few more years and I might be."

"What happened to your hair?" Jax regretted asking the question as soon as it left his lips. He suspected it had to do with her abductions. The impulsivity of his comment was evidence that he'd lost the ability to restrain himself around his mate. "Sorry, I didn't mean to ask."

"No, it's okay. This last time…I wasn't there that long. You saw me. It's not just about beating me, forcing me to submit. It's about their chanting…like spells or whatever. It feels like…" Katrina brought his hand to her chest. Her voice trembled. "My hair isn't the same. What they are doing is changing me from the inside out."

"You don't have to talk about it."

"I want to tell you, but it's hard to explain. It's like a drill in my chest…the noise of their words. I want to cover my ears but I can't. It gets louder and louder and it feels like my blood is draining out. But it's not my blood. It's my magick…it pours out of me. I can't control it. And now…"

"What?"

"When we were in your office, your power overwhelmed

me. It was almost like when an Alpha gets angry. You know how it works. You can push out your emotions, your power. Force wolves to submit."

"I can control the flow of my magick. As my mate, you may have some of the same influence I have. You know that, right? Your energy…the pack will sense you. Us together, how we are feeling affects everyone."

"I think it's what Quint said. Maybe somehow because I'd lost my magick, and now, because you're my mate, I take yours. All these years I've waited." Katrina stifled the tears which filled her eyes. "And when I think back to when I first met you. How you made me feel? To know it could be real, that I had this mate? I was overwhelmed."

"Happy?" he asked with a kiss to the top of her head.

"So happy," she agreed. "And you were funny. I wasn't expecting that. You weren't this arrogant man that they write about in the headlines."

"They say that? No, I've never heard that before," he joked, trying to lighten her mood.

"I know, hard to believe, right?" She gave a small laugh. "Seriously, going home…asking Tristan to help keep us apart? I'm telling you, it broke my heart. But I couldn't risk hurting you."

"We're compatible." He changed the subject. "You seemed to enjoy your little lesson tonight."

"I've never done that before," she admitted.

"Hmm…in two hundred years you never had a little spanking?"

"Truth?" Katrina pushed up onto his chest, meeting his

gaze.

"Yeah." Jax brushed a hair behind her ear, surprised she didn't immediately agree.

"I've been with other guys, but not many. And I haven't ever let anyone tie me up. Oh, no. To let someone do that? First of all, even though I could have easily gotten out of the restraints, it takes a lot of trust to let someone do that. And second, well, as you've already noticed, I'm not necessarily submissive. But when I'm with you? It's like I want to do all kinds of things I've never done. You make me feel free. You should know, though, Jax, I have been bitten before, and not just by Quintus."

Jax held his tongue, attempting to remain calm. It had been bad enough that Quintus had tasted of his mate. The act of drawing blood, allowing someone to drink from her was extraordinarily intimate.

"Luca…he…it's never been serious. He's just a friend." Katrina hesitated. "But back to your original question, no I've never been spanked. Nor have I ever let anyone tie me up. Not until you."

"I'll push you further," Jax responded. Katrina may not have been with many others but he suspected his little wolf enjoyed experimenting as much as he did.

"Seeing you with that other woman tonight…I'm hanging on by a thread. We need to find answers, because, Jax," her eyes fell, sorrow washing across her face, "I almost lost control tonight and bit you."

"It's natural. She wants to claim her Alpha. I know it took a little lesson to get you there, but…" His cock hardened as he recalled how she'd screamed his name as he slammed into her pussy.

"No, Jax. Not just mark you. My wolf…she wants your blood…to complete the bond."

Jax smiled, his chest tightening with emotion at her statement. Their connection grew stronger, weaving itself together. The way she'd protested bonding, he hadn't considered how strongly the instinct to mate would affect her. She'd restrained her beast for too long, denying it the craving it sought.

"I keep going back to this, Kat. And I know it's hard for you to just blindly trust me, but you have to learn, or at least try." Katrina flashed her eyes at him, her cheeks still flushed from lovemaking. Jax cupped her chin, tracing his thumb under her swollen lower lip. "I wasn't fooling around when I told you about instincts. It's one of the benefits of being an Alpha. The chemistry involved in mating is strong, and I'd be naïve to think it isn't influencing my desire to keep you in my life. I know what these things told you, but I don't want you to be afraid of mating, completing the bond. I'm telling you, when I'm around you, I've never felt stronger in my life. Whatever power or energy you're getting from me, I don't know…maybe it's just that we somehow are working together. But the longer you hold off on marking me, the harder it will be for you. It's natural that your wolf is not just going to want to mark me, but bond with me. But no matter how I feel about this, I'm not going to force you. Your wolf, on the other hand, she may have the last word."

"I want to believe you. To have a chance at a life with you? To be mated? You don't know how many times I had to stop myself from dreaming about it. It just hurts too much."

"It's okay to dream, baby." Jax leaned toward Katrina. His eyes went to her lips and then met her gaze. Every second he spent with her, he grew more determined that he needed her in his life. "We're going to find answers in New Orleans. If I have to search every inch of this earth to find that damn witch, I will."

She gave him a small smile, and it was enough to tell him that a seed of hope had been planted. Trust would come in time and so would her submission to their mating. If he could keep them both alive and destroy the evil that came for them, they'd have a future together.

Jax peered up at the once majestic Garden District mansion. The clean slate staircase had been obscured by overgrown Oleander hedges. Although it had been nearly two months since Ilsbeth had gone missing, the coven home had quickly fallen into disrepair. The enormous pentagram perched above the main entrance was draped in fine white webbing. It was as if death itself emanated from the house.

Jax had crossed paths with the infamous witch a few times over the years. He'd been wise not to ask for any favors, aware that she always expected a greater one in return. Over the years Ilsbeth had grown powerful, establishing her influential coven. Until recently, the witch had been relatively benevolent to most creatures. However, her bitter jealousy led to dark magick and lies. Believing she was deeply in love with Dimitri, she'd become convinced that if he was no longer a wolf, he'd never mate. The despicable act had nearly cost Dimitri his life.

Jax called Logan on the flight down to New Orleans. Rumors of shape shifters had twisted through supernatural circles but no one had actually claimed to have seen one. Although Dimitri and Gillian had insisted on coming with him to Ilsbeth's home, he'd refused, and had sought Logan's order to keep them at home. Whatever information Jax sought was his responsibility alone. He would not risk the life of his sister and her mate.

Luca stood waiting on their arrival. His wife, Samantha, who belonged to Ilsbeth's coven, had agreed to assist them in their search for the manipulative sorceress.

A squeeze to his hand brought his focus to Katrina. She gave him a warm smile, and crossed her long slender legs. Tucking a stray hair into her casual bun, she removed the sunglasses that had been pushed up onto her head. He inwardly laughed, thinking about how ridiculous it was that they were about to go into a dangerous situation and all he could think about was fucking his mate. Her black cotton dress rode up her thigh tempting him further, and he reasoned he'd be lucky if he didn't bond with her before the week was through.

His eyes darted to Jake, who watched them in the

rearview mirror. The car came to a stop and he turned his attention back to his little wolf.

"You ready to do this?"

"I think so. I know I'm ready to get answers, that's for sure." Her eyes lit up as she caught sight of Luca and Samantha. "They're here."

"Gilly wanted to come but there was no way I was letting her get hurt. Not after last time," he told her, his focus distracted by the vampire.

Jax observed Luca's expression. The corners of his mouth had been drawn tight with tension. He didn't blame him for not wanting to be in the middle of witchcraft central. But Jax suspected that the vampire's cool demeanor had more to do with his presence.

"Hey, are you going to be okay?" Her voice softened as she ran her hand over Jax's cheek.

"Yes." Jax buried his emotions, taking notice as Katrina smiled at Luca through the glass.

Although she'd told him about their relationship, their silent interaction gnawed at his gut. This man had been with his mate, tasted of her blood. Until Katrina, he'd never been possessive of a woman. He didn't want to ask, but couldn't stop the question before it left his lips. "Are you and Luca still good friends?"

"Well, yes, somewhat, but he's..." The engine cut off, and Katrina was silenced as the door swung open, and a large masculine hand reached to assist her.

"You don't know how to stay out of trouble, do you?" a deep Australian accent asked.

Jax tensed as she exited, falling into the arms of the imposing vampire. He exchanged glances with a petite redheaded woman who was burgeoning with child. Katrina, as if realizing her actions, broke free of the embrace and extended a hand to the witch.

"Samantha. You look beautiful."

"Thank you." Samantha smiled warmly.

"Luca. Samantha. This is Jax Chandler." Katrina hesitated and looked up into his eyes. "My mate."

"Oh my. Congratulations," Samantha exclaimed.

"When I heard you were coming, and with who," Luca said, his tone serious, "I know you've wanted this, but Kat, are you sure? Did you complete the bond?"

"Luca," Samantha reprimanded him, a gentle slap to his arm. "What kind of question is that? They're wolves. I may not have been around very long but even I know how it works. They have no choice."

"Not true," Jake interjected.

"Jake." Luca nodded.

"It's so good to see you again." Samantha took his hand in hers and gave it a squeeze.

"Hey, Luca. I'd say it's nice to see you…but yeah, I know you're not exactly a fan. No offense, Sam, but the big guy here can be a bit…particular."

Samantha and Katrina laughed in response.

"What you call particular, I call civilized. Stripping off my clothes and turning into an animal for fun? Let me just say I can think of a hundred other things I'd like to do." Luca sniffed.

"As I was saying," Jake continued, ignoring the cantankerous vampire. "Although wolves are given a mate, the ultimate choice is ours and ours alone. Should we choose to ignore fate, it's painful, nearly impossible, but it can be done. That being said, I've known a few wolves who managed to refuse the mating. Wasn't pretty."

"Sometimes we learn through pain," Luca commented, giving Jax a hard stare.

"It's none of your concern," the Alpha replied.

"That's where you're wrong. You listen to me, Kat here is my…"

"Luca, please." Katrina placed her hand onto his arm and kept her voice soft. "So many years. Goddess knows I wouldn't be here without you, but you must let us try. You know what I did was wrong."

"You survived. How is that wrong? Jesus, we both lied to Tristan."

"We didn't lie. Granted, we could have tried to tell him otherwise. But you and I both know that Tristan never liked Jax. My brother's smart. It's possible he even knew the rumors weren't true, and thought it best that I stay away from him for other reasons. Tristan knew and we both knew that sending me to New Orleans was the right decision at the time. What's done is done."

"Maybe you're right, but you and I…"

"This isn't the place to talk about this." Katrina's eyes went to Samantha, who gave her a sympathetic smile. "We don't need to rehash history."

"Samantha knows everything. There're no secrets

between us." Luca glared at Jax. "Can you say the same about you and the wolf?"

"It's not that simple. You know that it's not. Jax and I have only been together a few days." Katrina closed her eyes and took a deep breath. Opening them, she pinned her eyes on Luca. "I love you, you know that, right?"

"Yeah," he agreed with a heavy sigh.

"I've been alone forever. You need to let me have this." Katrina's voice wavered as moisture brimmed her eyes. "As much as I tried to deny what's going on between Jax and me to protect him, it's simple, I don't want to anymore. I want him in my life. Every second I'm with Jax, I'm more convinced that he's the only one who can save me. These things are trying to kill me. It's not just about them stealing my magick. This is about my life. Please understand," she begged.

"The bottom line here is that you have no say in our relationship. Discussion's over," Jax interrupted, glaring at Luca. He didn't wish to hurt him, especially considering he was expecting a child, but neither would he tolerate another male interfering with their bond. Without giving him time to argue further, he took Katrina's hand in his and stepped toward the mansion. "Let's get going. We need to get in the house. Samantha? Did you open up the wards?"

"I removed them temporarily. But once you leave, you won't be able to get back in the house. The wards will go back in place, and it'll be locked up," Samantha warned.

"Wasn't this a coven house?" Katrina asked, glancing up to the huge stone mansion. "Where are all the witches?"

Samantha's gaze went to Luca. He nodded and she turned her attention back to Jax and Katrina.

"After Ilsbeth disappeared, there was a bit of infighting. There's another house in the French Quarter. It's where I trained. This place," Samantha gestured to the porch, "this was Ilsbeth's home. She held parties here for special occasions and holidays. She usually only let a couple of others stay with her."

"So you just closed it up?" Jax asked. "Has anyone else been inside?"

"Not exactly. There's a warlock. He's taken over."

"Goes by the name of Mick Germaine," Luca added.

"He asked me to set wards to keep others out. I figured since this belonged to Ilsbeth, it was the right thing to do."

"I can't imagine the other witches are happy about that," Jax speculated.

"Well, yes, some weren't pleased. But they had no choice. Mick...he's very powerful." Samantha nervously stroked a hand over her belly as Luca wrapped a protective arm around her.

"A few of the witches still live in the Quarter but most have moved out of the city. Mick's got a setup there." Luca hesitated, his eyes darted to the mother of his child and back to Jax. "Look, I'm not saying the guy's evil, but you should know he's being watched. Kade and I keep tabs on him."

"I try to stay away from the conflict. Negativity isn't good for the baby. She needs peace," Samantha told them.

"When are you due?" Jax asked. He caught a glint of pain in Katrina's eyes, and he took note to explore that further.

"This month. Any day." She laughed. "Honestly not many people know vampires who've had children. So we're kind of playing this by ear."

"Anything else we should know about this place?"

"I'd go in with you but…" Samantha shrugged.

"No way," Luca growled.

"Thank you for doing this." Katrina smiled. "We really appreciate you coming today, helping us."

"I'm glad to help." Samantha reached for Katrina's palm. Her eyes widened as she wrapped her fingers around her hand. She gasped, refusing to release Katrina. "What happened to you?"

"Oh God…let me go. I don't want to hurt you." Katrina's voice rose with panic as Samantha's grip tightened.

"What the hell?" Luca grabbed both of their wrists and attempted to separate them, but Samantha held up a silencing hand.

"No. I'm fine. Leave me be."

Jax rushed behind Katrina, and slid his hands around her waist. The irises of Samantha's eyes swirled in shades of silver and he grew concerned that whatever had taken Katrina was hurting the witch.

"Your magick…it's not like a wolf. No, no, no…how can this be?" Samantha sucked a deep breath and blew it out.

"I…they did something to me," Katrina admitted softly. As Samantha released her arm, she snapped it into her chest.

"Did I hurt you?"

"No, not at all. But Kat…I've never felt anything like you. You're almost like a…but no…that can't be." She shook her head in confusion.

"Almost like a what?" Jax asked.

"Her magick, it's so strong. But not like a wolf. Whatever these things are doing…they're changing you. Your hair." Samantha brushed her hand over Katrina's head. "This isn't of your doing."

"No. The last time…well, if Luca told you everything, you know…they're taking my magick. Once it comes back, they take me again. Something about this last time. I don't know. It felt different. I didn't recognize Jax. I didn't know who I was."

"I think it's best we let you look through the house." Samantha slowly backed away from Katrina, holding onto Luca. "I've got to go call Mick and let him know you're here."

Jax studied the witch, aware she'd sensed something about Katrina that frightened her. It worried him that she'd suggested his mate was anything other than wolf. Aside from the incident in the woods, her difficulty shifting, she'd been stronger than ever. With his mark on her skin, even her scent grew more like his. Despite his desire to ignore the witch, deny her suspicion, instinct told him that she had no motive to lie. He glanced over to Jake, who scrubbed his chin in worry, and he knew he wasn't alone in his thoughts.

Luca and Samantha gave them a parting wave before they settled into their car, and Jax's attention went to

Katrina, who appeared preoccupied.

"You sure you want to do this?" he asked, gently brushing his hand over the small of her back. "You don't need to go in. Jake and I can handle this."

"No." She took a deep breath and exhaled. Driving her fingers into the back of her hair, she grimaced. "Samantha knew something just now. Don't tell me you didn't believe her, either. I don't know what the hell's going on but I'll be damned if I'm going to lie back and take this shit. No way. If Ilsbeth sent Quintus to that prison, she had to have known something. She's tied in with these things. She fed him to them. We have to find her and make her tell us what she knows."

"Let's do this, then." Jax weaved his fingers into hers and brought the back of her hands to his lips.

As they made their way up the stairs, Jax prayed like hell there weren't any surprises inside Ilsbeth's funhouse. He wrapped his fingers around the cold metal door knob, the loud click confirming the home was unlocked. Jake flanked Katrina and pushed the door wide open.

The musty air rushed outside, causing them to cover their noses with their hands. A streak of light shone through the doorway, illuminating dancing specks of dust that swirled in its stream. Jax reached for Katrina as she rushed to enter, but she slipped through his fingertips. Both he and Jake followed in after her, but stopped dead in their tracks. The loud screech forced them to put their hands over their ears. Jax wore a confused expression as he glanced to Jake, who shrugged in response.

"Do you hear it?" Katrina asked. She spun in a circle, her hands outward as if she was catching the luminous rays. "It's beautiful."

❧ *Chapter Fourteen* ❧

Katrina's magick ruptured, flowing through her fingertips as the classical music filled her chest. She twirled in the midst of the symphony around her. Caught up in the wave, she reveled in the cacophony.

"Where is it coming from?" she yelled. Katrina turned to find both Jax and Jake on their knees, holding their palms over their ears. They grunted, doubled over as the music grew louder.

Katrina couldn't fathom why the concerto wasn't affecting her in kind. Her wolf threatened to shift as her mate agonized on the floor, and she attempted to calm her own magick. Closing her eyes, she concentrated, absorbing the harmonic tones. The sweet melody continued and she suspected that Ilsbeth had set a spell. A scream tore out of her lungs, calling on the witch who had set the trap. "Stop it, now!"

"Holy shit," Jax exclaimed.

"Fuck me." Racked with dizziness, Jake tumbled over, and the Alpha caught him in his arms.

"Jax! Are you okay?" Katrina knelt and put a hand to Jax's forehead, his skin heating her palm.

"Yeah, but he doesn't look too good. What did you do?" Jax coughed and inspected Jake's eyes.

"I didn't do anything. I think it was a spell or something. It was…it sounded magnificent."

"Why'd you run in here?"

"I don't know. I was outside and then I saw the sunlight coming through the stained glass. I just…something just drew me in. I can't explain it." Katrina's chest tightened in guilt. She didn't even know Ilsbeth but when the door opened, a force called to her and before she knew what she was doing she was inside, dancing. Demanding the witch cease her attack had been as natural as breathing.

"Jesus, Kat." Jax wiped the sweat from his brow, and locked his eyes on hers. "This isn't good. You know that, right?"

"I…I don't know what to say. It just happened." Jax's penetrating stare told her they'd discuss what had happened later.

"Hey sweetheart." Jake stirred and he blinked, smiling up at Katrina. His eyes darted to Jax. "You too, big boy. I'm feeling loved."

"Yeah, right." Jax went to push him off but hesitated as Jake groaned.

"Are you all right?" Katrina asked Jake. "Do you think you can walk?"

"I was just enjoying that righteous rock concert. Must have passed out. Waking up to your beautiful face, though?

Worse places to be. Just sayin'." He winked and brought his hand to his head. "Fuck, that hurt."

"Okay, smartass, you ready to get up now?" Jax glanced around the foyer, its cathedral ceiling adorned in hanging crystals of various shapes and colors.

"I don't know. I kind of like being held. I'm reliving my childhood."

"Goddammit, Jake." Jax shoved him away, and stood. He extended a hand to Katrina, who brushed a kiss to Jake's forehead before she accepted his assistance.

"You saw what she did?" Jake pushed onto his knees and blew out a breath, steadying himself before getting to his feet. "Not the kiss. Although that was nice. Very nice. I mean the other thing."

"Yeah, I saw it all right and I don't like it one damn bit." Jax walked toward the staircase, and scanned the room.

"I didn't do it on purpose." Katrina stifled the panic that rose in her throat. Never in her life had she controlled magick outside her own wolf, nor had she conjured psychic connections with physical objects. But there was no doubt in her mind that her command had ceased the music.

"It was kinda cool if you think about it." Jake shrugged and patted her on the shoulder.

"Scary? Yes. Cool? Not so much," Jax disagreed.

"Hey Alpha, did you ever hear that expression, 'look on the bright side of life?'" Jake winked at Katrina and brushed the dust off of his jeans. "You gotta loosen up, man."

"I'm just tryin' to keep us alive. I know you're used to all this voodoo shit down here, but I prefer my mate to be a wolf," Jax replied. "No offense, Kat."

"I am a wolf. Just what the hell are you trying to say? You believe Samantha?" Katrina tore her hand from his and put her hands on her hips. *I knew it. He thinks something is wrong with me.*

"I'm sorry. I didn't mean it like that. It's just that…" Jax sighed and exhaled loudly. "Look, something just happened here and I don't know what it was. I know you're a wolf but I don't have a good feeling about this. I really don't want anything happening to you."

"Let's just look for whatever we came for," Katrina told him, hurt that he doubted her. Granted, she knew what she had done wasn't normal but it wasn't as if she didn't have a wolf inside her. Since being with Jax, she'd felt stronger than ever.

Katrina stared up at the spectacular curved staircase. Streaks of sunlight reflected off its mahogany banister.

"This place is huge. Where should we search?" Jake asked.

"Everywhere," Jax responded.

"It's somewhere in here." Katrina ran her palm along the wall, its rectangular insets appeared in an artistic geometric pattern. The cool wood tingled her skin, and as much as she didn't want it to be true, a voice inside her head told her the mystery would be found within the grand home. "I want to see Ilsbeth's bedroom."

"So did a lot of people. Dimitri used to joke that was where the magick really happened," Jake laughed.

"That turned out well," Jax noted.

"No, he's right." Katrina started up the stairs.

"Where the hell are you going?" Jax asked.

"To get answers." She stopped on the third stair and turned back toward Jake and Jax. "Where do women keep all their secrets? We keep them close to us. If it's not in the bedroom, my guess is that it's somewhere special to her. She was passionate."

"Crazy is more like it." Jake gave a smirk.

"She was a lover spurned. Fueled by passion," she surmised. "Sometimes when a person is desperate, they're not thinking clearly."

"Hey, I'd like to give that bitch the benefit of the doubt as much as the next person, but seriously? She almost killed Dimitri's wolf. He would have lost everything, including his pack. She might as well have just killed him." Jake shook his head. "No, I'm sorry. Sometimes you cross a line and you can't go back. You say something, in her case, do something, something really, really shitty and you can't just call 'take backs'. Not buyin' it."

"Sometimes people are redeemable, Jake. Sometimes we do things for reasons people don't always understand." Katrina's eyes met Jax's. "And we deserve forgiveness."

"I know you're talking about what went down with you and Jax, but this is different. You didn't try to kill Jax. I knew Ilsbeth over the years, yeah, sure there were times when she'd get her freak on or help people out, but she was one fucking scary witch. You did not want to get in her way. I'm sorry, Kat, but we're just going to have to agree to disagree on this one."

"Don't you want to find her?" Katrina felt the energy emanating through her palm as she caressed the railing. A dynamic vibration hedging between benevolence and anger reverberated within its otherwise lifeless timber and Katrina pulled her hand away. Concealing her reaction from Jax, she wasn't ready to disclose what she'd sensed. She prayed whatever supernatural phenomenon she was experiencing in the house didn't follow her home.

"We all want to find her," Jax agreed, following her up the steps.

"I don't," Jake admitted.

Katrina caught the hard stare of disbelief Jax gave him.

"We do want to find her. And so do you," Jax told him. "Ilsbeth has answers. Who knows what we're going to find here today? All I know is that it would be a helluva lot easier if we could just ask her about what she did to Quintus instead of playing Sherlock Holmes."

"I get your point, oh-great-one, but after what went down with D, I'm good without seeing her again."

Katrina heard Jax growl under his breath as they ascended. A hum sounded in her ears, and neither male took notice. The closer they came to the bedroom, the stronger it became. She found it ironic that, for the first time, her body and mind were responding to a witch she'd never known. Despite rumors of Ilsbeth's death, Katrina knew in her heart that she was alive. Whether she was well or not was another question entirely, but her vibrant spirit filtered through the hallways. As she opened the mistress's bedroom door, she became more convinced her salvation lay hidden within the mystical estate.

Upon first glance, nothing appeared sinister. To the contrary, the well-decorated room gave off an air of comfort. The room's amethyst-colored walls were offset by pale bamboo hardwood floors. A circular bed with a satin padded headboard sat in the center of the pentagram-shaped room. Above it, a web of beaded crystals hung from a chandelier, its strands connecting to each of the corners. A life-sized painting of a nude mermaid covered one of the walls. Its sparkled canvas flickered in the waning sunset.

Along the far side of the room, a built-in bookshelf was filled with hundreds of books. Katrina scanned the collection, running her fingers over the spines. From Shakespeare to romances, it appeared Ilsbeth was an avid reader.

Katrina considered the impeccable state of the bedroom and noted how everything appeared in its place. The witch had been particular, she speculated. From the brush and mirror set on the dresser to the matching floral notebook and pen sitting on her desk, its perfect décor could have been found within a design magazine.

Spying a closet door, Katrina crossed the room and turned its handle. She flipped on the light switch and stepped into the large walk-in wardrobe. To the left, an entire wall of neatly stacked shoes sat on wooden shelves. She glanced to the right, finding racks of clothing, sorted by colors. An enormous bronze floor mirror rested along the far wall. A garland of dried pink roses draped over its grand arch, bringing a sense of nostalgia to the room. Everything had been properly arranged, including a set of matched luggage in one of the corners, which further convinced Katrina the witch hadn't planned on leaving.

She heard a laugh come from the bedroom and peered through the door to find Jake dangling a pair of black panties from his finger. He stood in front of the chic dresser, its drawers opened. Katrina almost felt guilty for rummaging through Ilsbeth's things but self-preservation prevailed. The only way to find clues to the witch's whereabouts was to thoroughly search everything.

"D always said she wasn't exactly vanilla. He sure as hell enjoyed the kinky witch before all the shit went down." Jake inspected the delicate lace and ran his finger through its seam. "Oh, yeah. Crotchless. And beaded. Nice. That's one way to get a wolf."

"Seriously?" Katrina rolled her eyes.

"Hey, am I lying?" Jake laughed and gestured with the undergarment up into the air toward Jax.

"I'm with Jake on this one. Sexy. Easy access." Jax shrugged and gave a smirk.

"Maybe you need to get Kat a pair," Jake suggested, holding them to his nose. "Hmm…smells nice. Gardenias. No, wait. Lavender."

Jax sniffed. "Definitely, lavender."

"Maybe I don't need him to buy me anything. Maybe," Katrina paused and cocked her head to the side, giving Jake and Jax a wicked smile, "I already own a pair. Maybe a couple of pairs."

"Oh, yeah…now that I'd like to see." Jake tossed the

underwear back into the drawer, closed it and opened another one.

"Not going to happen." Jax combed through the desk and flipped through some loose papers.

"I've already seen her au natural." Jake retrieved a pair of handcuffs and waved them at Katrina.

"Ah, but that's not the same," Jax countered.

"Jax is right. Shifting doesn't count." Katrina shook her head and laughed.

"How's that?"

"It's the allure of the chase. Sometimes what we can't see is far more arousing than what we can." Jax smiled at Katrina, who winked at him.

"Maybe if you're a good Alpha, I'll give you something to chase later," she teased. Katrina studied the intricate pattern of the wallpaper. The seams appeared to come together in the shape of a door. "Hey, look at this."

Katrina ran her finger over the brass circle. Jax reached for it, admiring its intricate pattern.

"I'm not sure what it is. Hold up. Wait." He extended and inserted a long claw into an edge and it clicked open, revealing a solid ring. "It looks like a door knocker. Now what the hell would that be doing here?"

"Hey, it's in the bedroom. Looks like you could clip something to it. Maybe it was for BDSM play. You could definitely tie something onto it."

"Yes, you could," Jax responded. "But I don't know. It's in an odd location. If you were going to install these in the bedroom, you'd want them higher up."

"And you would know this because?" Jake laughed.

"It's a door." Katrina glided her palm downward, kneeling onto the floor. Jake followed her action, while Jax continued to manipulate the metal.

"She's right. It's cold. There's definitely something here." Jake rapped his knuckles on the wood.

"There's something else…" Katrina felt more than just air. A twinge of magick seeped through and she shivered in response. "We have to get inside."

"You sure that's a good idea? Secret door. Bondage ring. I have a bad feeling about this." Jake watched as Jax tugged on the ring. "I've seen a lot of horror movies and this doesn't usually turn out well."

"Maybe there's a key?" she asked.

"Here…let me try," Jake suggested.

"Be my guest, but I'm telling you I just almost yanked the thing out of the wall and it's not budging." Jax pounded on the wall with his fist and although a hollow sound resonated, the sturdy surface didn't budge. "I think Katrina's right. There must be a key or something."

"We haven't searched the rest of the house. Maybe we should just move on to another room." Jake grunted, pulling and pushing on the brass sphere. It made no movement, but he stepped up his efforts, and continued. "I've been here a couple of times, and there're other places we should look. The office, for one, is a place we should search. She's got an entire wall with nothing but ingredients. I'm talkin' a huge antique apothecary cabinet. I bet the thing has dried worms from the 1700s along with ashes from the French Revolution. She once took blood from a naiad right in front of Léo. Dimitri even gave her his wolf hair." Jake gave a great heave and snapped his fingers away. "Goddammit."

"I don't know." Jax speared his fingers through his hair. "We all know there's something back there."

"Jax." Katrina removed her hand and stood. Besides the magick, there was nothing else she could detect. "Whoever would have gone to such lengths to build some kind of secret wall surely has something hidden behind it. Maybe we could find a tool in the basement to open it up."

"We could check out the garage," Jax suggested.

"After we get done breaking into the super-secret playroom, can we please go downstairs?" Jake asked, his voice laden with sarcasm. "Seriously. That set up she has, it's the real deal. Hundreds of drawers."

"Maybe he's right. I'm sure she does have stuff down there," Katrina reluctantly agreed, frustrated the door wouldn't open. "But I want in here."

"How about you stay here with Jax and I'll go look in the garage for something to open it? I've been in there, too. It's mostly tools and stuff."

"It's beautiful, though." Katrina observed the ring. Her eyes were drawn to the antique object. She hadn't noticed it at first, but what she'd thought were geometric shapes were miniscule horse heads intertwined, fitting perfectly together.

"What is it?" Jax asked.

"Do you see it? They look like little ponies…" Katrina's

fingers drifted to the object, and a jolt of preternatural energy ripped through her body. As if she'd been electrocuted, she stood frozen, unable to move her hand. She felt the pinch of Jax's fingers wrapped around her wrist, his loud voice telling her to let go. But the longer she touched it, the stronger the draw to unlock it. A click sounded in her ears, the door falling free of her palm.

Katrina sucked a breath, willing her dizziness to end. Strong arms caught her as her legs gave out, and she breathed in the scent of her mate. Her eyes blinked open and she deliberately attempted to slow her pulse.

"Hey, baby." Jax pressed his lips to her forehead. "You okay? You scared me."

"Scared us," Jake exclaimed. "I'm shitting my pants right now. How the hell did you do that? Both Jax and I tried to open that thing and you just…"

Katrina caught the glare Jax shot Jake, and she knew it was because he didn't want to address the elephant in the room. For some unexplainable reason, Ilsbeth's magick was influencing her. As much as Katrina wanted to believe it was just the house, the shock on Samantha's face and her foreboding words warned her that something more insidious was happening.

But given the urgency, they didn't have time to speculate. As the door swung wide open, it occurred to Katrina that if it had opened that quickly, it could shut and lock as well. She forced herself to wake up from the spell, and right herself.

"Where are you going?" Jax asked, refusing to let her go.

"The door. We need to get going."

"Maybe you need to rest a minute. I'm not going to pretend to know what just happened here, but it obviously did something to you. You almost fell."

"I gotta go with Jax on this one. What the hell is going on? First the music. Now this." Jake held the door with his foot.

"I don't know. I..." Katrina stuttered. How could she explain what had happened when she had no idea what was affecting her? She accepted Jax's assistance and held his hand as she regained her balance.

"How can't you know? You saw what just happened, right?" Jake pressed.

"Let her be," the Alpha growled. "We'll discuss it later. The sooner we find something, the sooner we get out of here."

"Fine. But I'm just sayin' it's not natural."

"Leave it," Jax told him.

"You know I'm right," Jake insisted.

"Just stop." Katrina had had enough. The air in the room thickened, making it difficult for her to breathe, and she suspected that whatever was inside the house, it was forcing her to move. She put her hand on her chest, and took a step toward the dark entrance. As she ventured into the darkness, the pressure lifted and she couldn't be sure in that moment whether the flutter in her stomach was caused by relief or dread.

Katrina breathed in the scent of sage as she entered the great room. Awestruck, she held tight to the railing as they made their way toward the wooden spiral staircase. Floor to ceiling built-in bookshelves circled the oval balcony. She stopped momentarily to gaze up at the stars through the cathedral ceiling that was made entirely of glass. Katrina wondered why it couldn't be seen from the front of the home, but guessed that Ilsbeth had enacted a spell, creating the illusion of solid stone, which had hidden it.

"This is unbelievable." Jake ran his hand over the books. "Now this is what I call a library."

"It must be some kind of a ceremonial room," Jax noted.

Katrina remained silent as she glanced down into the space, empty save for an altar.

"I'm pretty sure Ilsbeth held coven gatherings out in the gardens, but y'all know it rains quite a bit in New Orleans."

"Sure does. This place looks pristine, though." Jax led their party down the steps. He held his arm out, keeping both Katrina and Jake behind him. "Not only that. Do you see any other exits or entrances?"

"No way in or out but through the portal," Jake agreed.

"It's special," Katrina told them. As Jax stepped onto the granite floor, she brushed past him and moved into the center, taking in the sight of her surroundings. "It's a perfectly closed oval."

Antique velvet-covered sofas and chairs were set around its perimeter. The scarlet-colored walls on the lower level gave a warm contrast to the cool stone beneath her feet. Katrina approached one of the many paintings adorning its walls.

"I can't believe this. No, these can't be real." Her heart pounded with excitement, noting the canvas that had been set into an ornate filigree gold frame.

"Gauguin," Jax acknowledged.

"Monet," Jake called from across the room.

"It's quite the private collection." Katrina slid a finger across its border, but unlike what had happened in the bedroom, she felt nothing. She turned her attention to the altar that faced the north side of the hall. Her eyes darted to Jax, who gestured with his hand as if reading her mind.

"Look at all the granite." Jake slid his toe across the floor. "Some religions consider it sacred. It has magnetic properties."

"I always thought witches preferred limestone," Katrina said, approaching the wooden structure.

"Ilsbeth never did anything small. She's been around for hundreds of years." Jake came up behind Jax and Katrina and sighed.

"Everything in her bedroom was unique. This hall. The furniture. The paintings. It's all very personal." Katrina pointed to the altar cloth. Its detailed embroidery depicted naked women; one in particular was a larger size. Her platinum blonde hair fell to her feet.

"She's one of a kind. And this place? It looks like no one has ever even been in here," Jax surmised.

"Maybe." Jake nodded. "We can check with Dimitri and

Leo to see if they know anything else, but neither one of them has ever mentioned this place to me. The only times I've been to her house, we either met in the yard or her office."

"I've been around plenty of witches over the years," Jax told them.

"Bet you're bummed you missed out on Ilsbeth." The corner of Jake's mouth curled, but his eyes remained on alert.

"What she did to my sister's mate is unforgiveable." Jax picked up a candle, studied it and set it down. "But I suspect like with many people, she's neither all good nor all evil. Witches, wolves, vampires…they often skate the edge of both."

"I don't know how you could say that after what happened to…" Jake began. Katrina shot him a glare and shook her head no.

"What happened to Nick wasn't Ilsbeth's fault entirely," Jax continued.

"They attacked Dimitri, and he was unable to shift. I saw what she did to him," Jake countered

"True, but he may never have met Gillian otherwise. My sister is formidable." Jax fingered through a brass incense bowl and sniffed it.

"I didn't know Ilsbeth, but the feelings I'm getting from being in this house, from touching her things…" Katrina paused and caught the wide-eyed expression of both Jake and Jax. "What? Can we just acknowledge that something is off with me and leave it at that? I'm not saying I'm some kind of psychic, but I'm not going to lie to either one of you. Maybe Ilsbeth has some kind of spell set so she can make contact with us?"

"I don't like it." Jake picked up a copper disc and observed its pentagram design.

"A pentacle," Jax noted.

"How come you're so willing to give Ilsbeth the benefit of the doubt after what she did to Dimitri? And Quintus for that matter?" Jake tossed the object not so delicately back onto the table. "You don't seem like the forgiving type."

"Because, my friend, Alphas learn to be the judge, the jury and executioner. We must be prudent in our interpretation of the facts. Sometimes things aren't as they appear. Take Quint." Jax lifted a small bronze statue of a horned woman and inspected it. "We've been friends a long time. Long enough for me to know he wasn't going to kill my mate. But he's impulsive. He's not always a nice guy. In fact, he can be a very nasty vampire at times."

"Are you honestly trying to tell me that he deserved what Ilsbeth did to him?"

"No, what I am saying is that he may have done something equally as atrocious to Ilsbeth and without knowing all the details, I can't judge. For all I know, his actions may have been even more egregious than hers. So in the absence of facts, an Alpha must rule on the side of caution. You need to evaluate all the evidence and should it be missing, you can decide whether or not you will take action."

"Well, I'm not the Alpha. All I know is that she fucked

with D. Therefore, ipso facto, evil bitch."

"All I can say is that you'll learn what it's like someday."

"Many witches are benevolent with their spells. But these horns?" Katrina gestured to the large headdress that sat in the center of the altar. A pair of antlers extended from the headband. "It gives me the creeps."

"She's the high priestess," Jax answered. "They belong to her."

"Not anymore. There's a new sheriff in town," Jake said in his best western accent. "Mick Germaine. That should be interesting. Would love to get Logan's thoughts on that."

"How's that?" Jax asked.

"Nothin'," Jake sighed.

"Doesn't sound like nothing." Katrina reached for a small silver bell, but paused as Jax cocked his head and made an observation.

"Now that's interesting."

"What?" she asked

"That bell there…"

"Yeah?" Katrina pinched its tip and rang it; the audible chime sounded loudly. She looked inside and ran her finger against the smooth metal before setting it down.

"Well, there's only supposed to be one of those. I've been to a few ceremonies. Granted they weren't typical, in that it was a special occasion, but the bell? I recall them ringing it at the beginning and end. That there," Jax pointed to an object. Its oxidized metal finish bubbled in shades of red, "that looks like another bell."

"Well this one here is just an ordinary bell. And this

one…it looks…it's an antique. Maybe it's why she has two." Katrina reached for it, and the second her skin touched its surface, the energy hummed through her hand. "Oh my God…"

"Let go," she heard Jax order but compelled, she held tight.

Katrina gave a firm shake and although nothing sounded, a small item fell onto the cloth below. The rusty article, smaller than a quarter, rolled toward Jake, who snapped it up with his fingers. As Katrina released the bell, it dropped onto a knife handle, the tip of which tipped upward, slicing her finger.

"Ow." Katrina snatched her hand away from the altar.

"What the hell?" she heard Jake exclaim.

She turned her attention back to the table. The sickle-shaped instrument glowed where her blood had stained its shiny blade.

"Are you okay?" Jax asked. He tore off a piece of his t-shirt and reached for her hand.

"It's just a tiny cut." Katrina bit her lip, the sharp pain resonating up her arm. "What is that thing?"

"It's a boline," Jax commented, tending to her wound.

"I thought they used an athame?" Jake lifted the knife into the air, where the color slowly returned to its original state.

"It's not used for the same purpose. They use it for cutting things other than flesh. You okay?" Jax wrapped the torn cloth tightly around her pinkie.

Katrina nodded and brought her bandaged hand to her

chest. "What fell out of the bell?"

"It's a ring." Jake inspected the rusty metal object. "I'm pretty sure it's a poison dispenser."

"What would that be doing on the altar?" Katrina's heart raced. "Something about these things…we need to figure out what's going on. I could feel the energy in it."

"They go back to the medieval times. Pretty clever really." Jake fingered the ring. "This one? My guess is early fifteenth century."

"But why would Ilsbeth own one of those? It's so…*human*. She's a powerful witch. She could probably poison someone much more easily with a spell." Jax pinched the bridge of his nose. "This isn't making sense."

"True, and look at this house. Ilsbeth has money. I was in her closet. Designer clothes. Every last shoe in its place. I can't exactly see her wearing that ring," Katrina said.

"Maybe she didn't wear it." Jake attempted to jar the circular bulb, using his nail to scrape away the dirt. "Like everything else in this damn place, not opening."

"Maybe she collected it like the paintings, but after what just happened here, my gut's telling me it's important. Jake, get the boline and the bell too. We've already been in here an hour and we still need to search the rest of the house." Jax turned to Katrina and gave her a sympathetic smile. "You sure you don't want to go sit in the car? I'm almost afraid to see what other tricks this witch has going on in here. I don't want you to get hurt."

"No. After what happened in the foyer, I don't think it's a good idea for me to leave you guys alone." Katrina scanned the room one more time, almost expecting Ilsbeth to materialize before them. "This house. I don't know why, but I'm meant to be here. It wants me here."

They exited in silence, and Katrina suspected both of them thought she was losing her mind. Although they'd had the decency not to comment further about how the magick affected her, she grew convinced that she was connected to the witch. Despite what Ilsbeth had done to Dimitri, Katrina didn't sense malevolence within her home. These objects, the music, even her spilled blood had been an intentional act, one designed to communicate.

As they entered the secret passageway, Katrina gave a parting glance to the special place Ilsbeth had taken great care to create, and she wondered what other secrets lay within the walls of the mansion. The energy she'd felt previously had dissipated, but they were one step closer to finding answers. Through the tunnel, the exit into the bedroom was revealed, the last streams of light from the sun lancing through the darkness. With salvation on the horizon, she breathed in hope that one day she'd awaken in the arms of her mate, free from the evil that plagued them.

⤞ Chapter Fifteen ⤝

Jax palmed the tarnished piece of jewelry and considered what had transpired at Ilsbeth's mansion. For over three hours, they had searched. Jake had been correct about the office contents. From everyday herbs and crystals to more rare substances such as a vampire fang, the apothecary contained Ilsbeth's treasured ingredients. But Katrina hadn't experienced any other psychic connections after they'd left the bedroom.

On the short ride back to his Burgundy Street home in Quarter, they'd sat in silent contemplation. Jax had bought the recently renovated early nineteenth century mansion sight unseen, but justified the purchase with the intention of spending more time with Gillian. He surveyed the empty living room, admiring the hand-carved cream-colored crown molding. The plaster walls had been painted a distinctive robin's-egg blue. Matching silk curtains hung perfectly from the twelve-foot-high ceiling. A grand fireplace sat against the wall to the right and Jax set the ring and other items they'd collected on its mantle. He reached for the switch, igniting the gas, and watched as the flames roared to life.

A rattle overhead told him Katrina had turned on the shower. He'd resisted pressing her about what had happened at the house. In the pit of his stomach a nagging thought persisted. What if his mate was changing? What if she changed into something to the point where they'd be unable to bond? Samantha's shocked expression was all he needed to tell him that something was terribly wrong with Katrina's magick, more than he'd suspected. While she no longer experienced trouble shifting, her behavior and experiences in Ilsbeth's mansion had bordered on the inconceivable.

Jax attempted to shake the troubling thoughts from his mind and made his way into the kitchen. With no time to decorate, the only furniture he'd ordered had been for the master bedroom and a kitchen table and chairs. Jax searched through the cabinets, thankful he'd had the forethought to ask his butler to stock the home with food and drinks. Snatching a couple of snifters off the shelf, he set them on the counter. He reached for the bottle of cognac and uncorked it, the classic notes of vanilla and cinnamon wafting into his nostrils. Jax held the tumbler up to the light, swirling the well-aged liquor.

Like its circular motion, his mind spun, strategizing. They needed a witch to help them figure out the significance of the poison ring. He'd texted Luca on the ride home, but the vampire steadfastly refused to let him see Samantha again. Jax didn't blame Luca for not wanting his pregnant fiancée involved in their business. They'd all seen how the black magick was affecting Katrina. Bringing the mystical objects to Samantha and possibly risking her baby's safety was not an option.

If you want something done right, take it to the boss. Unfortunately, the boss, Mick Germaine, was an unknown player in the convoluted supernatural world. Unlike his acclaimed counterpart, Ilsbeth, the warlock hadn't impressed Kade as ally or adversary. Luca told him that Mick had left New Orleans, taking up residence an hour outside of the city toward Bayou Goula in Iberville parish. Jax had convinced the vampire to set up a meeting with the head priest. Tomorrow night they'd go see the warlock.

Tonight, however, Jax would tend to his mate. His wolf had grown anxious, yearning to taste her again. Katrina's tenacity never ceased to amaze him. He shook his head and gave a small laugh. She fought him at every turn, yet he'd caught her every glance, watching him.

As he put the rim to his lips and let the spicy tonic flow over his tongue, Jax decided to test his little wolf further. There would be no secrets between them, nor any limits he didn't test. He gathered the glasses and set forth to the bedroom, looking forward to the pleasure he'd find within the arms of his mate.

Stalking his prey, Jax quietly cracked open the bathroom

door. In contrast to his ultra-modern New York City penthouse, everything about his new home was ingrained with a classic elegance. Mini brass gas lamp sconces illuminated the walls. The enormous shower sat center, its clear walls in a perfect square. Exposed copper piping emerged from the floor, curving into the oversized circular showerhead.

Jax sipped his cocktail and kicked off his shoes, observing the way her back arched as she ran water through her long hair. With one hand, he yanked his t-shirt over his head and tossed it aside. Katrina pretended not to notice him as he circled the steam-filled enclosure. Her eyes closed, she teased him, running her hands down over her breasts. *Ah, how my mate enjoys being watched.* Perhaps he'd give her the opportunity to do so for Jake, he mused with a small smile.

He unzipped his jeans and shrugged out of them. The sound of Katrina's sigh told him she was every bit aware of what he was doing. Her arousal filtered into the air, and he lost patience. Jax set the drinks on the counter and took his dick into his hands. Unable to wait a second longer, he paced toward the door.

Steam swirled around him as he stepped into the glass-encased shower. He came up behind Katrina, the warm mist brushing over his face. His cock brushed the small of her back and he slipped his arms around her. Her head fell back onto his shoulder and he heard a soft moan.

"Hmm…Jax."

"You were expecting someone else?" He held her close,

his hands sliding over her stomach.

"Why is it that, in such a short time, I'm starting to feel like I've never been without you?"

"Because we've known each other our whole lives. Our wolves, their minds have always been one. It is us who have to learn to adjust. They simply do what nature has taught them."

"How is it you know everything?"

"How come you answer questions with a question?"

"Have you ever been in love?" she asked.

Jax's chest tightened at the question. So many years had passed, but he'd thought he'd been in love only once.

"I thought so," he replied.

"You have?" she asked, a lilt of surprise in her voice.

Jax detected pain in her response and he knew he shouldn't have said anything. But given he expected the truth from her, he wouldn't lie.

"It was a long, long time ago. There was a girl. I was just a teenager. Foolish."

"We all do things in our youth we regret."

"Some later in life," he noted. "But what I did? We mustn't pretend we can marry humans. It is not our way."

"You broke her heart?"

"My father insisted." Jax grew silent. Aside from Gillian and Nick, he hadn't discussed his family with anyone.

"I see." Katrina's arms wrapped over his.

"Have you been in love?" Jax diverted attention away from his own situation. In truth, he sought answers about the vampire.

"I've had lovers, but I've never been in love."

"And Luca?"

"Luca? It's complicated," she sighed.

"It always is. But, my mate, I want to know what I'm dealing with. Do I have competition?" he half joked, wrapping her wet hair around his hand.

"I told you that Luca rescued me." Katrina blinked away the moisture. With her head tilted backwards, she met Jax's gaze. "Sometimes, for whatever reason, you meet someone and there's just this connection. We've been lovers on and off over the years, but was I in love with him? Not really. Not like you mean. We're just friends."

"He still cares about you," Jax observed, selfishly relieved that she hadn't fallen in love with the vampire.

"I care about him, too. Samantha, she's been good for him. Softens him up a bit. He can be a bit cranky." She laughed. "He's not exactly fond of humans…as in not at all. Frankly, I'm surprised he bonded with a witch. I only say that because he's not tolerant of other supernaturals. He cooperates with them only because Kade's his maker. He makes him help the wolves at times. But he and I? I don't know. He was never like that with me. When we first met, he was unjaded. We were both still very young."

"I want you to know that even though I said I thought I was in love," Jax paused and carefully selected his words, "I've never felt this attraction, not like what I feel when I'm with you. When I first heard you laugh, I just…if you hadn't left, I would have chased you for the rest of the night. And now that I actually have you? I'm never letting go."

"I don't want you to let go."

"We'll get answers tomorrow from the warlock. This thing is far from over." Jax traced his finger over his mark and his lips tightened in determination.

"We may be out of time," she whispered. "Samantha. She knows."

"Knows what?" he asked, aware of what she was insinuating.

"I'm changing. I can still shift, but inside," Katrina brought her fist to her chest, "something is happening. Tonight at the house…I don't know how I did what I did. I've never even met Ilsbeth. But the magick? It's almost as if she knew me."

"It's going to be all right, Kat." Jax spoke with conviction. It terrified him that something evil had rooted inside his mate, but he wouldn't let her see his trepidation. "Tonight…all I want to do is be with you."

Jax's hand found her breast. He took a slippery tip in between his fingers and let his other hand dip in between her legs.

"Jax…I want…this," she breathed.

"I need to be in you again," Jax admitted. Claiming her hadn't been nearly enough to sate his wolf. He yearned to make love to her over and over, marking her with his scent, his touch.

Katrina cried out loud as he slid a finger deep inside her core. Her head lolled forward and she braced her arm against the glass.

Jax smiled. He'd never been with a woman so responsive

to his touch. Made for him and him alone, his mate shuddered in pleasure. Her breath quickened and he knew she was close. Driving two more fingers deep inside her channel, he pumped into her, his thumb circling her clit. He wrapped his hand under her chin, and she parted her lips, her tongue laving at his thumb.

Jax's shaft strained against the crevice of her ass. The thought of fucking her, taking her in every conceivable way hardened his cock to concrete. Nothing would be off limits with Katrina, and the excitement of exploring how far they could go sent shivers through his body.

A small whimper escaped her lips as her core spasmed. He didn't relent as she came, plunging his fingers in and out of her pussy.

"Yes, yes…that's it, baby. Let go. You don't need to hide from me," he encouraged her, as her small cry became a scream.

"Yes, yes, yes…" Katrina's voice echoed in the shower.

Jax withdrew and spun her around toward him. Lifting her by the waist, he grazed his cock through her wet folds. He stumbled backward, his back slamming into the side wall. Katrina held tight around his neck and slipped her hand down between them. Jax hissed as she took his shaft into her hand and stroked it.

"Mine," she whispered in his ear and guided it into her pussy.

"Fuck, yeah," Jax grunted as he drove up into her. Her channel fisted him and he sucked a breath, the sensation quivering over his sensitive skin. "No, no, no…don't move, don't move."

"You feel so good inside me. Please, I need this. I need you," she told him.

The bite of her nails digging into his shoulders took the edge off and he slowly withdrew and rocked inside her again. Moving together as one, they made love. Water dripped down their faces, their lips crushing together. He'd never get enough of this woman, he knew. Tonight was just the beginning. Every time she revealed a slight vulnerability, she countered with a strength that could only be found within the arms of an Alpha's mate.

His tongue swept against hers and he drank in her loving kiss. As she sucked his bottom lip ever so gently, he increased his pace. Thrusting up into her, he grazed his pelvis against hers, and felt her shake beneath him.

"Oh, Jax!" Her deafening calls urged him and he pounded up into her.

"That's it. Fucking come, baby. Oh shit," Jax cursed. From his root to its tip, her sheath tightened around him, and he called out her name as he came deep inside her.

Her teeth scraped down over his shoulder, and he noted how she'd been careful to avoid marking him. Despite her control, he suspected she'd snap soon, marking him regardless of whether she intended it or not. Her wolf would have its due.

As he slipped out of his mate, and gently set her on her feet, he locked his eyes on hers. Jax recognized the tears brimming on her lashes, and his heart caught as she wrapped her arms around him tightly, holding on for dear life.

"I don't want to give you up," she whispered.

"It's going to be all right, Kat." Jax meant the sentiment even if he hadn't figured out how to make it happen yet. In time, he'd find answers. In time, she'd be his forever. No one would take her away from him, not when he'd just found her.

Jax reached for the spigot and shut off the water. Not willing to break contact, he simply stood, letting the heat from their bodies warm them. Katrina went to pull away and he cupped her cheek. She closed her eyes, resting her head in his palm.

"As long as I'm alive, I'll protect you with my life. This thing...whatever it is, we'll face it together. You're not alone anymore."

She blinked her eyes open, and gave him a small smile. A flicker of hope flashed in her eyes, and he knew that was all people sometimes needed to keep going. No one had said finding and keeping his mate would be easy, only that it would happen.

Jax held tight to her hand and opened the door. He grasped the edge of the towel and wrapped the cottony fabric around Katrina. She went to take it from him but he shook his head no. Without argument, Katrina allowed him to do as he wished.

Here and now, he'd tend to his mate. Jax patted the moisture from her chest and pressed his lips to hers, sucking the stray droplets into his mouth. Silence filled the room save for her gasp as he kissed along her collarbone, carefully drying her. Gentle swipes over her arms were met with moans, his lips finding her breast. He continued slowly, tasting her and moving the towel over her hips.

Stopping to lift his gaze to hers, he knelt before her, bringing the fabric down over the swell of her ass, then weaving it through her legs. As he glided it over her thighs, he exposed her bare mound. She whimpered as his lips brushed over her inner thigh, leaving her shivering in anticipation.

Her fresh arousal drifted throughout the room, her sweet scent tempting him. Jax ran his palms up the back of her thighs until her fleshy globes rested in his hands. Breaking eye contact, he brought his face to her abdomen. He inhaled deeply, hearing the rush of air escape from her lips in response.

"You're beautiful," he breathed, his lips ever so slightly grazing her pussy. "From the minute I saw you and now..."

"Ah...Jax." Katrina's muscles tensed as he teased her with his touch.

"So perfect." He dragged the tip of his tongue through her slit, flicking it over her swollen nub. Her honeyed essence coated his lips and he hummed in delight. "Perfectly made for me."

Jax smiled as she raked her fingers into his hair, fisting it. The prick on his scalp heightened his arousal, and as she tilted his head upward, he momentarily allowed her indulgence to take control. Her heated stare confirmed what he'd known. His little mate not only wanted to be watched but she loved watching his mouth on her.

With a growl, he drove his tongue through her folds. She

cried out but held tight to his head. His hands dropped to her pussy and he used his thumbs to spread her labia wide open, granting him access to his prize. But instead of sating her yearning, he mercilessly teased her, licking along the sides of her clit, but never providing her the full friction she sought.

"Jax...please. I can't wait," Katrina panted. "In me...please, I need you in me now."

Jax heard the soft thud as her head rested back onto the wall. Her hands fell to his shoulders and she widened her stance.

He smiled and rewarded her by sucking her clitoris between his lips. As she went onto her tiptoes, quivering with pleasure, he spoke into her wetness.

"Easy, baby...hold on, now."

"Jesus, Jax...please...oh God..." Katrina lost her words as Jax stretched her open further with his fingers and drove his tongue up into her core.

Jax stroked her sensitive ridged channel and delighted as her sweet juice coated his lips. She writhed onto his face, quivering under his touch. Struggling to breathe, Jax didn't relent as he applied pressure with his thumb to her clit. She rocked atop him, heaving for breath. A scream tore from her lips as she convulsed, her orgasm slicing through her. With her palms pressed flat against the glass, she attempted to brace herself against the onslaught of spasms rippling through her.

Jax sprang to his feet, his mouth capturing hers. He wanted her to taste herself on his lips, to savor the exquisite flavor of her arousal. As the Alpha possessed his mate, she returned his branding kiss with fervor. Never in his life had he been more terrified and exhilarated at the same time. His mate, Katrina, owned his soul.

❈ *Chapter Sixteen* ❈

Katrina's heart pounded as if she'd run a marathon. Her thoughts spiraled as he picked her up off her feet and carried her to the bed. When they'd returned from Ilsbeth's, she'd grown contemplative within her own reflections on the experience. But from the second her mate stepped into the bathroom, the concerns about everything they'd found, her future, all of it, if for only a brief respite, disappeared. Her emotions were replaced with arousal.

She felt his eyes on her, watching and waiting as she washed her hair, bubbles sluicing down her back and over her breasts. Like a lover's hands, she'd cupped her breasts, tweaking her tips into swollen points. After he'd made love to her in the shower, emotions surfaced once again. The magnificent man who'd taken her completely was so much more than a passing phase. As each intimate second passed, she'd exercised every last shred of self-control not to mark him as her own. As thoughts of losing him rushed back into her mind, she was unable to contain the tears that escaped.

But once again, he'd assured her he'd protect her.

Yearning to hear the words, she wanted more than anything to believe him. Spoken with conviction, nothing but truth resounded in his statement.

When he'd fallen to his knees in front of her, the sight of her great Alpha took her breath away. His long locks fit perfectly into her hands, guiding his mouth to her pussy. Both vulnerable and ripe with a strength she'd never known a man to possess, he played her body, the maestro leading her in a symphony of pleasure.

She attempted to focus and catch her breath as he set her on the bed. The fire in his eyes told her he was far from finished making love. Her chest rose and fell in anticipation as she watched him stalk to the dresser and retrieve items. *I'll test your limits*, he'd told her and she expected nothing less from the commanding wolf.

Although the lights were dimmed, she caught the blur of an object in his hand. She shivered in excitement, her fingers drifting over her stomach.

"I want you. All of you, Katrina." His low and sensual voice washed over her as he climbed up onto the bed and straddled her legs. Her eyes darted to the item he held behind his back.

"Presents? And it's not even my birthday." She licked her lips and gave a nervous laugh, as a wicked smile crossed his face.

"You could say that. Do you like surprises?" His head dipped to her breast. She arched her back and mewled as his rough tongue swept around her areola. Without warning, he drove two thick fingers into her pussy. "Hmm…I see you do."

Katrina gasped at the intrusion and moaned as her channel quivered around him.

"Jax…what are you…?" Katrina lost her thought as his teeth tugged on her nipple, the pleasurable sting bringing her attention to his mouth.

"You make me lose control, woman," he growled. His fingers slowly pressed in and out of her slick core. "Everything about you…"

Katrina smiled as he lifted his head and she caught the mischievous glint in his eyes. His thickened shaft lay heavy on her thigh, and her pussy clenched around him. As much as she wanted to move, to seek his penetrating arousal, she thought better of it. Her palms moved to cup his unshaven cheeks and he turned his lips to her fingers, sucking them as if he were making love to them. His eyes never left hers as his tongue swirled over them, nipping softly as he let them slip from his mouth.

"I'm going to make love to you," he promised. Katrina nodded as he withdrew his fingers and pressed his thick head to her entrance.

Jax smiled, and she gazed into his penetrating eyes. The sight of her magnificent Alpha stirred excitement throughout her body. Katrina had waited a lifetime to feel this way about someone. To be so utterly consumed by a man, his kiss meant more than breathing. Hundreds of years had passed and no one mortal or wolf had possessed her the way Jax Chandler had in a matter of days.

Seconds felt like hours as his lips hovered above hers, his

warm breath on her mouth. His whispered name was all she managed before he kissed her. Melting underneath him, she brushed her tongue against his, reveling in the taste of her mate. His rough whiskers brushed her face, reminding her of the wild soul that lurked within his gentle kiss.

Her legs wrapped around his waist as he slid inside her core, inch by inch, slowly filling her. She protested as he tore his mouth from hers. His weight rested on her and he braced himself up onto his elbow, spearing his fingers into her hair. Her eyes blinked open and she caught him staring at her, his heated gaze causing her heart to flip.

"Don't be afraid," he told her, and she knew he was referring to losing him.

"I…I…Jax." Katrina tilted her hips up as he rocked in and out of her.

"You can't deny your wolf forever."

"I can't resist much longer." She didn't want to say the words out loud. She suspected that she'd mark him soon, unable to resist the lure of her mate.

"This, us, it's everything."

"I want to…" Katrina's words faltered as he increased his pace, and she lost herself within his eyes. *Her lover. Her mate. Her Alpha.*

Before she knew what was happening Jax withdrew and rolled her on her stomach. Katrina squealed as he lifted her bottom into the air. She braced herself on her elbows and heard him command her.

"Like this," he told her. "Hands and knees, princess."

"Jax, please." She wiggled and a firm slap to her bottom

rewarded her sass. "Ah…yes."

"Time to play, little wolf."

"Please, just…" Katrina breathed as he slid his ridged shaft into her glistening pussy, stretching her open as he filled her.

"Don't move even a little bit," Jax grunted.

Katrina's head rolled forward and she moaned, her sheath contracting around his rock-hard cock. She heard him exhale, and startled as the cool gel dripped down her cleft.

"I told you not to move," he warned, gliding his palm down over her cheek. His thumb circled her puckered flesh, igniting every cell of her body with desire. "Right here, Katrina. I'm going to have you soon. But first…"

Katrina heard his soft chuckle. She turned her head and caught a glimpse of his devious smile as he waved a shiny gold object in the air, holding it by its looped handle.

"A new toy just for my mate. I told you in New York when I had you indisposed," he paused and laughed, "tied up so nicely. Jesus, it makes me want to fucking come just thinking about it. Hmm. But I digress. As I was saying, I told you I planned to push you, my sweet wolf. My tastes…they aren't exactly vanilla. And I suspect that yours aren't either."

Katrina sucked a breath as the smooth metal surface brushed over her bottom. Although she'd fantasized over the years, there'd been no one she'd trusted to indulge. Tonight, she'd give herself over to her commanding Alpha, the one who'd settle for nothing less than raw honesty.

"I've always wanted…" She stilled as he probed her back hole, the tight ring resisting its entrance.

"Easy, now. Relax and trust me, Kat. I'd never hurt you." Jax removed the tip and replaced it with his thumb. Wiggling it slowly, he pressed it into her bottom, stretching her muscle. "We've got to move slowly."

Katrina closed her eyes, allowing him to prepare her. Her hips rocked forward and back, sliding him in and out of her pussy. Ripe with arousal, she moaned, "More."

"There you go. See how good that feels. That's a girl. Just push back. Look how amazing you are," Jax praised. He withdrew his finger and gently inserted the plug. "I can't wait to fuck you in your beautiful little ass."

"Ah…slow…slow…oh…" A tiny twinge was soon replaced by a delightful fullness that she'd never experienced. "That feels…ah yes. Don't stop."

"It's almost all the way in. You're doing great," he praised. "Just feel me. Let this happen. Let us happen."

Katrina relaxed into the dark intrusion, accepting a pleasure she'd only ever allow her mate to give her. She reached for the headboard of the canopied bed and braced herself as he withdrew his cock and penetrated her core.

"Jax…so full. Please, yes," she cried.

"You feel so good…" Jax muttered. "You're so tight around me."

Katrina gripped the wood, unable to think of anything but the pleasure rippling through her body. Strong fingers grazed through her slick folds, and she gasped. As he stroked her clitoris, Katrina shook, losing control. The most violent, mind-numbing release of her life crashed over her, leaving her body tingling all over. Her core contracted, fisting Jax, bringing him with her. She moaned as he clutched her shoulders and slammed inside her pussy. A triumphant call tore from his lips as he gave one last forceful thrust.

Katrina panted, her body going limp as he removed the toy. They fell onto their sides and he immediately wrapped his arm over her, his lips gently peppering her collarbone with his kisses. She breathed into his embrace as his leg draped over her hip. Katrina's heart crushed, her wolf crying into the night, begging to mark her mate.

She'd opened her body and mind to Jax but still held the tiniest but most precious sliver of herself back. Without a doubt, she could fall hard and fast for the wolf who'd exposed her secret desires and accepted her for everything she was. But until she knew for certain that she couldn't hurt him, she'd never claim him as her own. As she drifted off to sleep, a solitary tear ran down her cheek and over her lips, the taste of regret bitter on her tongue.

Although the heaviness of slumber called her to curl into the sheets, the warmth encasing her body had cooled. *Jax.* Katrina blindly swept her hand across the bed, grasping the blanket. Her eyes went to the large antique wooden wall clock, its brass pendulum reflecting the street light. It was nearly four thirty in the morning and she wondered where

Jax had gone.

Giving a yawn, she shoved up to sit on the bed and glanced around the bedroom. Katrina peered through the cream-colored translucent fabric that hung from the rungs overhead, and smiled. Her Alpha had chosen a romantic décor for his elegant home. It reminded her that there was so much to learn about her mate. In spite of their heated sexual tryst, only time would unravel his mysteries.

A shiver ran over her arms, the air conditioning cooling her skin. Instead of searching for clothes, she simply tugged at the sheet and wrapped it around her body. Katrina swung her legs over the bed, and steadied her feet onto the cold hardwood floors. As she made her way down the hallway, a flicker of light reflecting into the walls told her Jax had gone downstairs.

She padded down the grand stairway and her thoughts drifted to another era. Having grown up in the early 1800s, she recalled long ago when a home would be lit by candles, the warm breeze of spring pouring through the windows. Although there had been no modern conveniences, it had been a simpler time in many respects.

Rustling papers drew her out of her contemplation and as she rounded a corner, she spotted Jax sitting on an area rug in front of the fireplace. Wearing only a pair of jeans, her shirtless Alpha appeared lost in rumination. He held a small wooden frame in his hand; a large cardboard box sat next to him. Afraid to startle him, she kept quiet. She smiled when he whispered her name, realizing he'd sensed her presence.

"Katrina." Jax set the picture into the box and patted the floor.

"Whatcha doing?" She eyed the container.

"I couldn't sleep, so I thought I'd check things out."

"Everything okay?"

"Everything's great. This place," he glanced around the empty room, "I bought it after seeing it online." He laughed, his eyes meeting hers. "I called my realtor and told her I wanted it. Never even stepped inside it until today. Pretty crazy, huh?"

"It must have been special," she commented, trailing her fingers over his shoulder.

"Maybe. Not really. It wasn't so much the house. It was Gillian. This is going to sound strange, because my pack is my family. But to have a blood member? It changed everything for me. My mother and father...they aren't alive anymore." Jax shook his head, his face pensive. "When Gilly came into my life, I swore I wouldn't be some long distance relative who sent holiday cards twice a year. No, that isn't going to happen. I want to be close to her. I want her close to me. I want..."

"A family?" Katrina's heart broke for him, sensing how lonely he'd been. It wasn't as if she didn't understand the anguish of solitude. After decades of watching others find their partners and have children, she'd buried the painful dream of finding her mate, forced to accept her solitary existence.

"Yes, a family." He reached for her hand and covered it with his. "I don't want to scare you, Kat. I mean, shit, it's not like we have exactly had an easy go of things. We aren't even bonded yet but you need to know…"

"Jax…I can't promise you forever, because I don't know what will happen to me. But I'm your mate. I belong to you. I'm your family now." Katrina gave him a warm smile.

"I already told you, I'm not letting you go," he replied and changed the subject. "This box. I guess Samuel sent these things here before I went missing."

"Things?"

"Yeah, you know. Family photos, stuff I've collected over the years. Gillian stayed with me for a while after Nick died. We went through some of it. As you can imagine, I have a lot of shit." He blew out a breath and picked up a well-worn cream-colored domino. He fingered it, running his pad over the blackened dimples. "Samuel got some of my family things mixed up with Nick's."

"You need help sorting them?"

"Nah, not right now." He held the trinket up to the light. "It's made of bone. Wood on the bottom."

"Yours?" She smiled.

"Yes and no. Nick collected them over the years. This one's an antique. We used to play…a whole lifetime really. Nick loved these damn things." He reached for her hand and tugged her toward him. "Come join me."

Katrina settled next to him, and picked up the frame he'd set back into the box. She studied the black and white photograph. A young woman stood stoically, her long dress brushing the ground. Katrina recalled owning a similar garment in the 1840s. The dress she'd worn had been fashioned in a royal blue damask fabric. Although it had revealed her bare shoulders, the long sleeves covered her arms.

"Who is she?" While the girl didn't smile, Katrina noted a glint of happiness in her eyes.

"Phoebe." Jax gave a regretful smile and retrieved it from her hands.

"A friend?" *A lover?* Katrina sensed the sorrow from her mate as if it was her own, and she realized that from now on, his wellbeing would be tied to hers. Her fingers once again traveled to her shoulder, his mark tingling on her skin.

"I thought I was in love." He laughed and shook his head. "So young. I must've been around seventeen. I might as well have been a baby."

"She was human?" Katrina's wolf let out a low growl, and she stifled the displeasing emotion. To be jealous of a dead girl was ridiculous, she knew. But with her Alpha unclaimed, the irrational thought surfaced.

"Yes."

"Things were different back then." Katrina recalled her mother's warning to stay within their pack. When Tristan became Alpha, he'd been a more progressive leader, allowing interaction with humans. Regardless, wolves learned to be cautious of falling in love with others, expecting they'd someday meet their mate.

"My father was a strict man. He, uh," Jax sighed, "he didn't tolerate any breaking of rules. It was more than just submission. My mother, she doted on him like a king. It was never enough. That day…"

"What happened?"

"He'd caught me with her. I was foolish. I knew better. We'd never even had sex, you know. Just kissed. But it was enough. He scented her on my clothes. He beat me that day."

"Oh, Goddess…" Katrina caressed his back. The thought of any father abusing his child made her sick to her stomach. But to know her mate had been mistreated; she wished she could go back in time and kill his father herself.

"He got the best of me. He knew that I was growing stronger, that the Alpha within my soul was strong. Sometimes I think it was the only way he thought he could survive. I'd either have to leave the pack or challenge him."

"What happened?"

"My mother, she went into a depression after that day. She took care of my bruised body, but she couldn't repair the damage that had been done to our family. She'd begged me to submit, to accept that no matter what my father asked, I'd have to give in. But that's the thing, Kat, when you're Alpha, you don't get a choice. You are born Alpha and when the opportunity comes, you seize it."

"But Logan, he didn't challenge anyone. He was Tris' beta for so many years. Granted he was a leader but I never expected he'd take over Acadian Wolves."

"Tristan knew. I guarantee it. We all can sense the Alpha within others. Now it's true that some wolves suppress it. Something in their lives happens and they just decide life is better without responsibility. But for most of us, it's an overwhelming call. We cannot deny it, any more than we can deny breathing." Jax scrubbed his palm over his tousled hair and shrugged. "But Phoebe? She never asked for any of this. Hell, she didn't even know I was a wolf."

"You stopped seeing her?" Katrina asked.

"That's the thing. I didn't stop seeing her. I wasn't going to let that bastard tell me who I could or couldn't see. He'd been telling me my whole damn life what to do. I'd watched him lead, he bullied pack members. And the girl? I wanted her more than anything. Jesus, when I think about it…shit, I was just like any other teenager."

"Horny?" She gave a small laugh.

"Hell, yes. She was beautiful and just the sweetest girl in town. And I was an asshole, a selfish prick who should have known better."

"No, don't say that. There's no way you could have known anything. We all were teenagers once."

"I killed her." Jax's voice grew soft and he traced his finger along the rim of the frame.

"What? No." Katrina's eyes widened, her heart rate sped up at his declaration. There was no doubt in her mind that her Alpha could kill, she'd witnessed the aftermath at the cabin. But deliberately murder an innocent? No way.

"My father ordered her death and his beta killed her. No one suspected anything. Her body was found in the woods a week later. He made it look like she'd been mauled. Her fault, they'd said. Stupid girl had gone where she shouldn't have. But I knew better. My whole pack knew."

"Oh Jax," she gasped. "I'm so sorry."

"It was my fault. Her blood," Jax extended his palms and

stared at them as if they were dripping before him, "it's on my hands."

"No, Jax. You didn't…"

"Yes, Kat. It was my first lesson in being an Alpha. Patience. Restraint. These qualities of mind are every bit as important as the brute strength and cunning needed to win a challenge. I," he paused, brushing both of his hands over his head, "did not have the patience. Nor did I consider the consequences of my actions. I underestimated the power of my opponent. Had I had patience, I would have waited for the day when I would become Alpha. My self-indulgence cost Phoebe her life."

"You were just a kid." Katrina fought the tears, choosing to be strong for her mate. "I'm not going to pretend that you haven't been carrying around this guilt for a long time, but you need to let it go. Your father sounds like an awful person, a complete psychopath. I know you know this. I've watched you lead. I've been on the end of some of your 'lessons'. There's a difference between teaching and punishing. And there sure as hell is a difference between punishing a teenager and murdering an innocent girl who did nothing more than fall in love with a boy."

"My mother had already been hanging on by a thread. She, uh, only lived a few more years. You know, they talk about the spirit within us. I'm pretty sure it's what killed her will to live." Jax set his eyes on Katrina, who took his hand in hers. "The day she died, I left the pack. I only returned later…when I was stronger. After Gillian had been born…"

"Does Gillian know about your father? What he did?"

Jax shook his head no.

"You didn't tell her?" Katrina eyed him with concern.

"It's not like I didn't want to tell her but hell, I'd just reconnected with Gilly. How am I supposed to tell her that her father, this great warrior, just so happened to be a ruthless murderer? From what I can tell, Mirabel, her mother, hasn't told her either. She managed to escape. When I came back to the pack, things had only grown worse. He'd stolen her tiger. Pack members were terrified. We were on the verge of territorial wars with others because his behavior had become more aggressive. He didn't exactly believe in diplomacy."

"You returned? What happened?" Katrina instinctively knew what words he'd confess even before he said them and she'd already made the decision to support him. No man deserved what his father had done to him.

"I killed him." Jax closed his eyes and blew out a deep breath before continuing, his voice calm and low. "I'd had enough. Someone had to stop him. And I was Alpha. I am Alpha."

"A challenge?"

"Yes. I almost died that day. But I wasn't going to give up. Not for one second. Even as blood was pouring out of me, my flesh in his claws and teeth, my conviction never wavered. This face," his eyes went to the photo, "she was in my mind. That day, she was avenged. Her blood may be on my hands but I did what I had to do to set it right. I am not my father."

"No, you're nothing like him at all."

"Tristan doesn't think so. You know that's why he doesn't trust me. I don't blame him. But Phoebe? I didn't mean to get her killed."

"Come here." Katrina brought Jax into her embrace, his face rested on her breast. As she cradled his head and caressed his hair, she felt the stress drain from his muscles. Her heart broke for her great Alpha. "None of this is your fault, Jax. Do you hear me? You are nothing like your father. Nothing at all. You may have been born of an Alpha, but you grew into the leader you are today. I watched my father. Marcel. Hunter. Tristan. Great men make mistakes and learn from them. I'll tell you this." She pressed her lips to his head and spoke softly. "*You* are an amazing man. You're honorable. Courageous. Compassionate. And you're mine. I am your family. Me. You're not alone."

Jax raised his gaze to meet hers and Katrina cupped his cheeks. He'd bared his heart and soul, trusting her. She leaned in and kissed away the moisture on his lashes. She'd always known Jax was a striking if not beautiful man but it was his sensitive heart and mind that took her breath away.

She grazed her lips down his cheek, finally settling on his mouth. As the sheet fell away and she gave herself to him, the decision not to claim him became all the more difficult. Falling for Jax Chandler was as inevitable as the sun rising, and she was helpless to control it.

~❦· *Chapter Seventeen* ·❦~

Jax blinked his eyes open, smiling as the sight of Katrina resting on his chest came into view. Although his wolf stirred, restless she hadn't claimed him, the man delighted in the peaceful bliss. Confessing the nature of Phoebe's death and the beating at the hands of his father had incited a cathartic awakening. Not only had Katrina soothed his battered soul, she'd accepted him for who he was and who he would become.

It was true that living pack members had witnessed the challenge, with some holding him in a higher reverence. Newer members, however, hadn't lived through the bitter history, the significance of what had occurred lost on them. He knew he'd have to tell Gillian the truth someday but it'd have to wait. His sister had already texted him five times since he'd arrived, and he'd insisted she stay clear of him until it was safe. He hoped Dimitri had resumed some control over his mate but suspected it was unlikely, given her nature.

A stream of sunlight stabbed at his eyes and he yawned.

He glanced at the time, and wasn't surprised they'd slept until three in the afternoon. A loud bang sounded from afar, and he cursed under his breath. *What the ever loving fuck?* He'd given Jake the security code so he could come over whenever he was ready. But listening to the racket coming from downstairs, he couldn't fathom what the damn wolf was doing.

He pressed a soft kiss to Katrina's forehead and carefully peeled her off him. She mewled as he tucked the blanket around her, and he smiled in response. Jax brushed away a hair from her cheek and took a long minute to drink in the sight of his mate. Her swollen pink lips curled into a small smile and he hoped she was having the best dream of her life. Although she'd been pale, she'd developed a tiny hue of color in her cheeks after only being in the sun for the day. Her long blonde hair spilled out over the black sheets like a majestic waterfall, tempting him to wake her just so he could run his fingers through the silky strands.

After using the bathroom and throwing on a pair of jeans and a t-shirt, he padded down the hallway in his bare feet. The ruckus filtered throughout the house as he descended the steps, the spicy scent of pepper filling his nostrils. By the time he reached the landing, the melodic beat of zydeco grew louder.

"Hey, bro," Jake called from the kitchen.

"What the hell?" Jax's eyes went to the sink, which was filled with half a dozen bowls. A large cauldron boiled on the gas stove.

"Mudbugs, man."

"What?" Jax reached for a cabinet door, opening and shutting three of them before he found the mugs. "Have you lost your goddamned mind?"

"Mudbugs. Crawfish, Yankee boy."

"What?"

"Got a boil goin' baby. Secret family recipe. Oh, yeah." Jake waved his wooden spoon in the air, and gave a hip roll to the music. He laughed and turned to his concoction.

"I'm going to wake up from this nightmare." Jax scanned the room and made a beeline for the coffee machine. "Have you been drinking? Please tell me you've been drinking, because I don't think there is any other reason for your babble."

"As a matter of fact, I've got a pitcher of Bloody Marys ready to go, my friend."

"You do realize I just woke up?" Jax poured his coffee, sniffed it and took a sip.

"Uh, that falls in the category of don't care. I've been up for a while now." Jake picked up a loaf of flaky French bread and pointed it at Jax. "While you've been gettin' busy, I went and got myself a good rest. Being that my ass has been in Cali and New York for the past two months, I'm missing my roots."

"There's something wrong with you, you know that?"

"I'm hungry and you're grumpy. Want some?" He tore off a chunk and crumbs flew up into the air.

"You're a slob."

"You love me and you just can't admit it, can you, Alpha?" Jake joked.

"Toss me the bread." Jax gave him a smirk and caught the loaf as it flew across the room, white flecks spraying everywhere. "I'm not cleaning this up."

"As if you would clean? Let's get real. I'm sure Samuel is on his way down here now."

"No, he isn't, smartass. I told him to stay home."

"Backup maid?" Jake smiled broadly and nodded.

"I'll text him." Jax retrieved his phone and sent a message to his butler. He hoped he could find someone to tend to the mess after they'd left the house.

"Good deal. You're going to love me big time in a few minutes," Jake promised.

"Crawfish for breakfast? I highly doubt it. Are you always this cheery in the morning?" Jax sipped his drink.

"It's technically the afternoon but yes and yes. Positive attitude. It's what it's all about."

"Really? Is that what you demonstrated yesterday?"

"Hey, easy there. First of all, that witch is one scary bitch. You don't even know the half of it. And second of all, Kat's reaction to that house...well, that kind of speaks for itself. We all may have pretended like it didn't happen, but you know that shit's not right. And that redheaded witch knew the score. Fucking Luca, man. He's got a stick so far up his ass he's like one of those marionettes."

"He's not going to let us see her, so just give it up. Mick's next on the list."

"Are you sure you really wanna go there? I like running in the bayou at night as much as the next wolf, but I'm not so sure about this freak fest this warlock has going on." Jake sat down at the table with Jax and tapped a beat on it with his spoon, then paused. "I've met Mick before, ya know? He's, uh, how should I put this? He's kind of a free spirit. If you'd met him, you would never think he was some big and powerful warlock. He's a player."

"A player?"

"Yeah, you know. A player. With the ladies," Jake sang, a lilt of amusement in his tone. "And I'm not just talking witches. He's charismatic. Really good-looking."

Jax raised a questioning eyebrow at him in silence.

"For a guy." Jake glanced to his steaming pot and then focused back on the Alpha. "My point is that we better have a plan B. It's not that I doubt what Samantha's sayin'. Logan confirmed that Mick has taken most of the coven outside of the city. But from what I gather, it's more like a big ole voodoo orgy. There's magick happenin' all right, if you know what I mean?"

"So he's a flake? It's better than hearing we're going out to talk to some mage who practices black magick." Jax shrugged. It wasn't the best situation but it wasn't the worst. In the end, it didn't matter, because he was going to get answers if it was the last thing he did.

"I'm just setting expectations is all, which are pretty low."

"It's quite simple. If Mick doesn't have answers, I'm going to Logan and there'll be an all-out war with the vamps. Because that will mean that Samantha really is the only one who might be able to help. Granted, I get why Luca doesn't want her around this black magick stuff. Or

Katrina right now for that matter. I don't want her or her baby hurt. But I'm not buying that she doesn't know what we found. And even though she may be a new witch, she must be pretty damn influential if she has the keys to Ilsbeth's private home. I wonder if she's even taking orders from Mick." Jax reached for the butter and sliced off a slab, smearing it onto the bread.

"You can be stone cold sometimes, you know that, right?"

"You misinterpret things, Jake. Come on, you've been around Logan and other Alphas, right? It's not your first time at the rodeo."

"Yeah, but they're not as bold as you, no offense."

"None taken." Jax bit into the bread.

"I'm not sayin' this is a bad thing, it's just that you are a little more intense than most Alphas. That's all." Jake shoved out of his chair, and went to the refrigerator to retrieve the pitcher. He set it on the table and searched the cabinets until he found glasses.

"What you describe as intense, I would describe as thoughtful. I've learned the hard way not to be impulsive. At the same time, as Alpha, one must be decisive." Jax shrugged. "You'll see."

The young wolf had no idea of his own power, Jax mused. From the second he'd met Jake, he'd known he was special. Yet, Jax resisted telling him. *All things in good time.* Until there was a need, it would be best for Jake to learn on his own.

"And," Jake pointed his glass at the Alpha, before setting

it in front of him. "You're a cryptic son of a bitch. You wouldn't happen to be related to Léo, would ya?"

"A vampire? Ha. Ha. You're hilarious." Jax's stomach growled and he peered around Jake to eye the pot on the stove. "That done yet?"

"Ah, ha! I knew it. You gettin' ready to show my cookin' some love?" Jake poured the thick red liquid over some ice and inserted a crisp celery stalk.

"Maybe." Jax laughed and reached for the cocktail. "Don't tell anyone, though. I'd hate to ruin my rep."

"You're badass. I don't think a little happy time with my mudbugs is going to make people think you've gone soft." Jake focused on his meal and didn't hesitate, changing the topic. "So, uh, speaking of soft, how's Katrina?"

"Nice segue."

"Hey, I try." He laughed.

"She's good."

"Good? Trouble in paradise already?"

"It's complicated." Jax coughed and set the glass down. "Damn, these are strong. What the hell did you put in them?"

"Again. Secret recipe. Besides, it's good for you. Veggies. Kinda like a salad in a glass."

"That would be a smoothie."

"Close enough. So what's the deal with Kat?"

"It's nothing really." Jax sighed, contemplating how much to share with the wolf who was becoming a friend. He enjoyed Jake's company, his continual petty challenges akin to a puppy biting at his heels. He saw a more innocent version of himself and hoped that with guidance, he and Logan could give Jake what he needed to be a great leader.

"You know I love Kat, I mean like a friend," Jake was quick to qualify, "but she's been on the run for a long time."

Jax nodded.

"She acts strong. Hell, she is strong, but she's scared."

"She won't mark me." Jax's eyes met Jake's as he confided in him. "Fucking demons, whatever they are. She's convinced she's going to hurt me."

"I don't know much about mating, but watching D...let's just say it doesn't seem like you get a whole lot of choice. I mean he was resisting it, worried he'd kill Gilly's tiger and then the next day? Boom. They're mated. Now, this thing with her magick...it's not right."

"I know. I can feel it. Sometimes," Jax paused, and glanced over his shoulder. He heard water running upstairs, which told him she was awake. "Her magick, it can be strong, just like it should be for someone who's an Alpha's mate. But then, there are other times when it just feels different. I mean, we both know wolves aren't mediums. They don't touch objects and *feel* something. We're wolves. We shift. Yes, the pack can sense me and my feelings, and I can get a general vibe on my pack, but this is completely different." Jax sighed and swirled the celery around the spicy mixture before extracting it. "I don't know if it's Katrina and what they did to her? Or maybe somehow Ilsbeth did something and it's just that house? Maybe she set up a spell so that only Katrina could find the clues?"

"Let's say that's the case. That would mean that Ilsbeth

somehow knew about what was happening to Kat. Someone would have had to have told her, because Kat never even met Ilsbeth."

"You said D was sleeping with her?"

"Yeah, but he's true blue with the pack, man. He'd never let secrets slip out over pillow talk."

"Ilsbeth knew about these things, because she sent Quint to the prison. And so that means she probably knew about them before Kat ever came down to New Orleans."

"How would she know what was going on in New York?"

"Because she's like Léopold. She travels a lot. I've met her several times at charity functions in Manhattan."

"You've met, huh?" Jake raised a suspicious eyebrow at the Alpha.

"What?" Jax shook his head and took a bite of celery.

"Just how many times have you met her?"

"What the fuck is that supposed to mean? I don't know. A few times. A half dozen times tops."

"Just wondering why you're so willing to forgive the bitch. Oh, did I just say that?" Jake held his finger to his mouth, his eyes wide. "Sorry, I meant witch."

"We've been through this, okay? I get what she did to Dimitri. I'm just saying, and this is the Alpha speaking, got me? The Alpha can see the big picture. Ilsbeth has done some good things over the years. She's helped Kade. Even Léopold. Granted they're vampires, but she performed tasks in goodwill. So that tells me that on occasion, she can take the right path. Now as Gilly's brother, I want to kill her for what she did. It's fucked up." Jax sipped his drink and blew out a breath. "But that's the thing, as Alpha, I don't just get to be her brother. I must see the big picture. And it tells me that she's not all bad."

"She's not all good," Jake countered.

"True. But what happened last night? Something…instinct is telling me that Ilsbeth is trying to help us. Maybe something bad happened to her."

"One can only hope." Jake threw a stack of newspapers on the table. "Can you spread those out for me?"

"What?"

"Spread em' out. On the table. Bugs are up." Jake slid oven mitts onto his hands and lifted the metal colander out of the boiling pot.

Jax unfolded the papers and continued his train of thought. "I'm just saying, maybe she went away to lick her wounds…"

"Or hide because D was going to kick her ass from here to the moon."

"More like Gilly. Stop interrupting." Jax gestured to the covered surface. "This good?"

"Yeah, thanks."

"The thing is, just because Kat didn't know her doesn't mean she didn't know Kat. She's shrewd. She might have known what was going down. Maybe she even knew that she'd need Katrina to help bring these assholes down."

"Heads up, Sherlock," Jake instructed, dumping a steaming pile of red crustaceans onto the papers. "Look at that! That's a slice of heaven right there."

"I'm just sayin'. You need to learn to look at the big picture, Jake. Jesus, those things do smell good."

"Told ya."

"Not as good as…" Jax turned to find Katrina standing in the doorway.

Wearing nothing but his white dress shirt, his mate smiled at him and shifted her weight from one hip to another, inadvertently flashing a hint of inner thigh. He made a mental note to thank Samuel for making sure his closet had been stocked with his clothing. *She's the only sustenance I need, not a damn crawfish.*

"Hey, Kat." Jax inwardly laughed, realizing how nothing else seemed to exist in her presence. Pushing onto his feet, he reached for her hand. She giggled as he took her into his embrace. Although she'd showered, he could still smell his scent all over her skin and his cock hardened in response.

"Hey," she responded back, her voice soft and husky.

Her smooth palm ran under the fabric of his shirt, grazing over his abs. She gazed up into his eyes and brushed her thumb over his flat nipple. Jax lost his words, and his eyes fell to her lips. Smiling, his mouth descended on hers.

The kiss was gentle, like a soft breeze in summertime. More than aroused, he was comforted by the support she'd given him when he'd told her about what had happened with Phoebe and his father. His heart tightened as she relaxed into his arms. He could fall for this woman, and although he'd known it would happen, the rush of adrenaline running through him confirmed how much he cared about her, about his future with Katrina.

"You guys are killin' me, ya know that, right?" Jake teased.

Jax smiled into her lips and slowly opened his eyes, pleased with the come-fuck-me-now expression his mate wore. A pity it had to wait. But the way his thick shaft strained like a steel beam against his zipper, breakfast would have to be fast. A set of fingernails combed down his back, and he sucked a breath as they delved down inside his pants, cupping his ass.

"Hmm...now that's the way I like to wake up," Katrina purred.

"Baby, you're tempting me." Jax laughed as her other hand glided down between his legs and gripped his straining erection, stroking it through the denim. "Ah, shit. Not fair."

"Who said life is fair, Alpha?" Katrina pressed a kiss to his cheek and glanced to Jake, who shook his head.

"Really? I am right here." Jake gestured to his chest.

"Hmm...I think Jake likes to watch," she quipped.

"You're wicked." *My little minx wants some public fun, does she?* Jax hadn't thought it was possible, but her statement sent a fresh rush of blood to his already painfully erect cock.

As she spun in his arms to open a cabinet, he gave a devious smile to Jake.

"Let me help you," Jax said sweetly. Without releasing her waist, he came up behind Katrina and lifted her shirt, exposing her bare bottom.

"What are you doing?" She laughed. As she reached for a coffee cup, she jumped as he roughly clasped a rounded cheek.

"My mate is very poorly behaved, don't you think? Teasing you like she did." Jax looked over his shoulder to Jake. "I think it's my little wolf who likes being watched. Perhaps you should come see her?"

Jax knew he was playing with fire, inviting him to play. Allowing Jake to bring Katrina pleasure wasn't an option. His wolf would lose it, and he risked shifting. Unmated, his wolf growled in warning, but the Alpha's pulsing dick won the battle.

"You're serious?" Jake shot him a look of surprise, and dropped the pot holders onto the counter.

"Did you know that my mate enjoys being spanked?"

"Jax," Katrina hissed, wiggling under his touch.

"Isn't it amazing how the Goddess sees fit to give me such an adventurous mate?" Jax nuzzled his nose into her thick locks and teased the back of her neck with his lips. The fresh scent of her coconut-scented shampoo reminded him of her wild nature. "You know, my sweet princess...the sooner we complete our mating, the sooner we can explore all the possibilities."

As Jax kissed her skin, he sensed her wolf yearning to claim him. Although Katrina kept her restrained, the tether strained tight, fraying apart where he'd worn it thin. Like a game of chess, he'd strategically play his new mate, breaking her will until she set her wolf free. He suspected when she finally did, they'd bond.

"She's always been beautiful." Jake cautiously approached.

The Alpha lifted his head, meeting his gaze. As expected, the young wolf knew better than to reach for her.

"She," Jax smacked her ass, the slap sounding throughout the kitchen. As he expected, Katrina moaned in arousal, not making an effort to move, "is amazing. And very, very hot."

Jax's fingers grazed down her cleft until he cupped her mound, giving it a light tap.

"Jax...we shouldn't do this," she panted.

"Jake was nice enough to make us breakfast." He winked and gave a small chuckle. "And you came down here teasing us with something far more delicious. Should we give him a taste?"

"I...I..." Katrina's gaze went to Jake. "Ah..."

"Hmm? What was that? I can't hear you." Jax plunged two thick fingers into her, causing her to cry out in pleasure. He marveled at how aroused she'd become at having an audience. "She's dripping wet. And such a naughty wolf. You like him watching, don't you? Tell him, Kat."

"Jax...just...oh please," she breathed. Bracing her arms on the outside of the cabinet, she spread her legs wider, giving him better access.

"You need to answer when I ask you a question. Seeing that my hands are busy, would you mind assisting me in teaching Katrina how to answer me?" Jax glanced to her ass and nodded at Jake.

Taking his guide, Jake gave him a grin. "Yes, Alpha."

As Jake slapped Katrina, her tight channel clenched around Jax's fingers. "Oh yeah, she likes that, all right.

Don't you, Kat?"

Her hips began to thrust forward seeking relief, and Jax thought he'd come from the sound of her moaning. Jake spanked her again and she yelped.

"Yes, goddammit, I like it. Please…I can't take this. Fuck me." Katrina bit at her own skin and squirmed as Jax withdrew his fingers.

Jake fell back against the granite counter as Jax moved behind his mate, and unzipped his jeans. His eyes went to Jake, who undressed.

"Look at Jake. Look what you do to him." Although unsure if he'd ever share his mate fully, the idea of making Jake watch turned him on as well. Jax slid his palm over his thick cock. Thumbing its slit, he brushed his seed over his shaft. He lifted her shirt once again and positioned himself, pressing his crown to her entrance.

"Oh my God…" Katrina grunted as Jax plunged into her.

Sliding a hand up under the flowing cotton, he reached for her breast. His other hand reached around between her legs, his middle finger spreading through her labia.

Her pussy pulsated around him as he rocked in and out of her slick core. Katrina glanced to Jake, who stroked his dick. Jax gave her a wicked smile as her gaze finally drifted to him. He never took his eyes off of her as he increased the pace. In all his days, he'd never been so impulsive. Fucking her in the kitchen, let alone in front of Jake, had been the furthest thing from his mind when he'd woken up, but there was no way he was stopping now.

"Fuck me…harder, Jax, harder," she urged.

Taking her clit between his fingers, he gently pinched, gradually tightening his hold. The sound of his flesh smacking against hers rang in his ears as he thrust into his mate. Jax bit his lip, struggling to keep his orgasm at bay. Her tight channel spasmed around his rigid length, hurling him into release. He erupted, a loud grunt tearing from his lips. Katrina screamed in ecstasy, repeatedly saying his name. Spent, Jax collapsed against his mate and wrapped his arms around her, pressing his lips to her shoulder.

In a short time, his entire life had become about Katrina and her only. If she liked being watched, he'd give her anything and everything she wanted. She was like a force of nature that had swept him off his feet, spinning him up into a cyclone, and he didn't want to set his feet on the earth again. Her terrific storm had smashed apart his reality, setting forth a new world where he did nothing without her.

A warm washcloth touched his hand and he accepted it, cleaning both himself and Katrina. He tossed it into the laundry room, but never lost contact with his mate. She slowly turned in his arms and fell into his embrace. The soft rise and fall of her chest synched against his. Both were left breathless from their heated encounter. He smiled, kissing her hair, blissfully aware that he'd lost complete control of the situation.

For the first time as an Alpha, he realized that from here on out, there was one part of his life he no longer ruled. When it came to Katrina, she drove him over the edge, testing his judgment, but there was no denying his mate would bring him to new levels of pleasure he'd never known.

Jax tore the tail off the tiny crawfish and glanced to Jake and then back to Katrina. *Sex in the kitchen?* Par for the course. *Swallowing the innards of a small crustacean?* Uncivilized.

"Just do it," he heard Katrina tell him.

"It tastes good," Jake coaxed.

"I've lived a long time. Hunted as a wolf. Eaten all kinds of delicacies. Sushi? Yes. Escargot? Yes. Shrimp brains? Uh…" He sighed and looked at the tiny antennae. Its eyes stared up at him, and they weren't screaming 'eat me'. *Why did I let them talk me into this?* "Can't I just eat the tail? It's how I get them at home."

"Don't be a baby. Just suck it." Jake laughed.

"Don't rush me."

"You already did the hard part. Now just suck." Katrina brought the little red head to her lips and slurped. "Hmm…see? It's good."

"That's right. Your woman knows how to suck a head."

"Fuck you." Without dropping the slippery treat, Jax punched Jake on his arm, who feigned injury.

"He's getting violent," Jake teased.

"Duh, he's an Alpha." Katrina's voice softened, and she gave him a warm smile. "You can do this, dear."

"You two must have been barracuda shifters in another

life, because you're both relentless." Jax stared at the crawfish and shook his head. "Sorry, little guy, but they say you taste good." He quickly brought the shell to his lips and sucked the fluid down.

"Yay!" Katrina clapped as Jake broke out in a hearty laugh. "He did it!"

"So?"

"I won't lie." Jax paused. He fought a smile, attempting to fool them. "It was…great. Spicy, like liquid fire. What the hell is in that stuff, anyway?"

"Secret recipe." Jake winked at Katrina.

"Load me up." Jax handed his plate to his friend, who shoveled the tiny red creatures onto it.

"So…tonight. Do you think we'll find out anything from this warlock?" Katrina asked.

Her question immediately broke the humorous mood that had followed their erotic interlude. Jax's gaze went to Jake, who deferred to the Alpha. Although instinct told him that tonight they'd get answers, he couldn't be certain of the situation they'd encounter.

"The weather's supposed to be bad. Rain," Jake noted.

"We'll take the SUV." Jax peeled away a shell.

"Sometimes the roads get shut down. We should leave early."

"What kind of place is this?" Katrina asked. Her eyes darted to Jake.

"I told Jax already. Mick's kind of a free spirit. I'm actually pretty surprised that he's the cream that rose to the top." He stood and began to crumple up the used newspaper. "But it is what it is."

"There're many different kinds of witchcraft. Just because Ilsbeth chose to run her coven a certain way, that doesn't mean the witches agreed. I've seen it happen before. You know, something happens to the high priestess and pandemonium lets loose." Jax shrugged.

"I guess it's not that much different than wolves. While you were away…" Jake hesitated. "Well, no use in rehashing that. It wasn't pretty."

"And that's how it's always been. It can happen with the vampires too. For as long as I can remember, Kade's been down in New Orleans. But in Philly? Alexandra was the queen bee until Tristan shut her down." Katrina stood and began to clear the dishes. "What a bitch that one is."

"She is a piece of work," Jax commented, raising an eyebrow.

"But now he has his hands full with them in his club. They fight over the humans, with no one to put an end to it. From what I hear, Léo's trying to intervene." Kat rummaged through the drawers, finally retrieving a dish towel.

"So you can see how tonight could be unpredictable." Jake turned on the sink faucet and began to wash dishes.

"I'll dry," Katrina added.

"Yep, Alexandra was a sick one, all right. But on the flip side, she kept her vamps in check. Léo will take care of it eventually." Jax sighed and took in the sight of the mess all around him. He considered that this was the first time in months that he'd gone for any length of time without thinking of Nick's death, and now both Jake and Katrina had given him that gift. A simple meal had brought them together.

Even in the midst of a bad situation, the universe always had a way of working out the details. Nick had passed, and the devastation that followed hadn't been pretty. But as he watched the young wolf and his mate at the counter, she turned and gave him a smile that would melt a glacier. In that instant, he knew that life was coming full circle.

❧ *Chapter Eighteen* ❧

Katrina's nerves danced as they pulled up the long winding driveway. The row of Southern live oak trees greeted them, Spanish moss hanging from the branches. Hundreds of glowing orbs speckled the lawn. The luminaries flickered with candlelight, their illumination brightening as they approached the buildings. To the side a dilapidated plantation house sat in need of repair, its wooden porch appearing to sag in one corner. Yet the shadows in the windows told her that its inhabitants hadn't abandoned the deteriorating structure.

A thunderbolt rocked the car and Katrina stifled the shiver that ran through her body. As they drew closer to the valet, she rubbed her hands together. The tingling in her fingertips traveled up her arms and over her scalp. As during her experience at Ilsbeth's, she sensed the magick in the air. Although she'd thought to keep the disturbing sensation to herself, she chose to disclose it. Tonight they entered as a team and secrets could cost them their lives.

"Jax." She never took her eyes off the entrance as she

placed her palm on her mate's shoulder.

"You okay?"

"Remember what happened to me at Ilsbeth's? I feel something in my hands. It's not my wolf either. It's something else."

What's going on?" Jax immediately turned to face her from the passenger seat and took her fingers in his.

"Just kind of this thing. I don't know how to explain it." Katrina withdrew her hands and stared down at her palms, her expression serious. "It, uh, it feels warm. Almost like caterpillars. Goddess, that sounded stupid."

"Whatever's in you, Kat...I'm not going to lie and tell you it's nothing to worry about. But you haven't been weak since we got to New Orleans. No episode like in the woods that day." Jax brushed his knuckles over her cheek and she closed her eyes, relaxing into his touch. "The good news is that both of us are still strong, and I've marked you."

"But I haven't claimed you yet. My wolf..." Katrina knew she wouldn't last much longer. She suspected her wolf would take over her will, outweighing her humanity. Every time they made love, she grew one step closer to making him her own. If her teeth sliced open his skin and she drank of his blood, the bonding would commence.

"She's stronger than ever." Katrina noted the flicker of happiness in Jax's eyes, and it broke her heart that she'd waited so long. But she'd die first before she hurt Jax. She held a silencing finger to his lips. "I know what you're going to say. Don't you ever think I don't want this, because I do...you..." Moisture rose to her eyes along with her emotion. "You've changed everything. I just can't do it until I know you're going to be safe. It's killing me not to claim you."

"It's going to be all right, baby. I promise you. All of this. You. Me. Your magick. Remember what I told you about instinct. We're about to pick up another puzzle piece, and very soon it's all going to come together."

"Hey guys, I don't mean to break up this special moment, but I think our main man just came out to say hello."

Jake turned into a grand arched car port. The elaborate cedar structure had been carved with intricate patterns. As Katrina zeroed in on it, tiny skulls, chiseled into the wooden beams, in different sizes and patterns alike, came together like a fine painting. Although it struck her as creepy, the arrangement did have an artistic flair.

For but a second she reminisced, missing her gallery, being able to freely create without fear of abduction. The vehicle jolted to a stop and her focus was drawn to the man who stood watch over them at the entrance. Bright lights in hues of purple streamed around the stranger. He had the appearance of a tall, thin angel, and a shiny translucent fabric hung loosely from his outspread arms.

The car door clicked open, and she took Jax's hand. The rush of his power flowed through her skin. He winked, and she knew he'd deliberately sent the calming energy to her. No matter what happened in the next hour, she'd be with her Alpha.

"Welcome, welcome, welcome," The violet-colored

stream morphed to lavender, finally dissipating as the warlock came into view.

Mick Germaine. Wearing a long silver robe embroidered with silver sequins, the shirtless mystic smiled broadly. Katrina studied the handsome stranger. She considered that he looked like he could have been one of the models in Jax's magazine. His piercing gray eyes drew her focus, accentuating his chiseled jawline. The sides of his head had been shaved, his long dark hair brushed up into a ponytail. Barefoot, his tanned legs peeked through his holed jeans.

"Come, come." He gestured toward the door, and then extended a hand to Jax. "Alpha, I am humbled by your visit to my Shangri-La."

Katrina held tight to the crook of Jax's arm. Waves of energy poured over her. As if she were standing in a waterfall of flowing magick, it rained down from above. The humming power whirled around her, and she struggled to concentrate. Inhaling, she breathed out the tension, allowing her body and mind to adjust to the increased activity. Jax's low, commanding voice brought her attention back to the conversation as she heard him introduce her.

"This is my mate, Katrina Livingston." Jax stood protectively in front of her but she managed to extend a hand.

"Ah...Kitty Kat," Mick trilled. As she placed her hand in his, she watched his eyes light up in surprise at her touch. "You're in transition, I see. Come. Let's talk inside."

Katrina's palm sizzled within his grasp and she snatched her hand back to her body. "Thank you, but I'll stay with my mate."

"But is he now?" Mick challenged. With an outstretched arm, he ushered them into the building. With the body of a well-trained athlete, he conveyed deliberate strength with every step.

Katrina reached for Jax, and took in the sight of the great room. Its brick walls rounded upward, wooden beams spearing up into an apex. Streaming swatches of red and black velvet draped from the ceiling. Shelves of various heights supported thick candles, which illuminated the room in a dim sensual light. Scantily clad women and men danced to a slow rhythmic beat upon a limestone dance floor. As if in a trance, the mass of zombie-like witches swayed, their bodies moving in a well-rehearsed ballet.

As they weaved their way through the sea of people, Katrina held tight to Jax. Mick led them through a pair of heavy swinging Cyprus doors, and as they shut, the din ceased behind them. The small circular foyer appeared to break off into two hallways. Katrina strained to see where they led as Mick turned to address their group.

Her focus drifted to the enormous chandelier that hovered above them. The hand-blown glass fixture took on the appearance of a modern octopus. White extensions radiated from its striking royal-blue interior. Having spent hours in antique and specialty stores over the years, Katrina estimated the piece to be well over five thousand dollars. Although Mick had retained the rustic nature of the building, it was apparent that he'd infused opulence in the details of the décor.

"As much as I'm looking forward to our little chat, I do believe I should be a good host and show you around my new spread." He gave a broad smile and lowered his voice. "This is a very special place."

"Look Mick, we appreciate you meeting with us, but y'all know it's about to get to stormin' out there. And we'd like to get back home," Jake told him.

"We don't want to get stuck out here," Jax added.

"No one gets *stuck* in paradise, my friends. You see, when Ilsbeth went walkabout, I was forced to take on her coven. This, as you know," he nodded toward Jax, "is a great responsibility."

"Mick, please, we just need…" Katrina began, but was interrupted.

"Patience is a virtue. It's part of the reason we're in the bayou. Back to nature where we belong." He took a dramatic breath and flicked his ponytail. "I did not ask to become a high priest. Oh no, no, no. But all these bitches are far too weak to take over. So when Ilsbeth left, I thought to myself, 'self, where should you go to be one with nature? Where should you go to commune and get back to your roots?' and my meditations led me here."

"Why leave the city?" Jake asked.

"Because our very essence comes from the soil. The air. The water that falls upon us tonight. And the great blazing sun of Louisiana. Oh yes," Mick held his palms up to the air as if in worship, "the city, I am afraid, while ripe with magick, is polluted." He held out his fingers and counted off his reasons. "The ground. The air. The water. This is where the coven is meant to be."

"We're just gonna have to agree to disagree there, warlock, because I think it's pretty damn fine where it was," Jake countered.

Jax shot Jake a look of irritation for engaging with the eccentric witch. Jake rolled his eyes in response.

"This coven is for the pure of heart. For those looking for happiness within nature." Mick gave Katrina a wicked smile.

Although he was attractive, Katrina's keen sense warned her away. She found herself moving closer against Jax, and tugged on the back of his shirt. Mick's eyes painted over her from head to toe, undressing her. Under the black light, the tattoos over his body danced. An illusion, perhaps, a flock of birds along his flank of muscular abs flapped their wings.

He smiled at her, and her eyes flared in acknowledgement. Her wolf went on alert, unsure of what he'd do next. Katrina concentrated on calming her beast. The magick inside her teetered on explosive, and she grew concerned that if she shifted, it wouldn't be her wolf that appeared.

"Ah…I know you sense my energy, Kitty, but it is not me you have to fear," he blithely commented.

Before Katrina had a chance to respond, he waved a hand and a chart appeared on the wall, its lettering stenciled in calligraphy. From one to thirty, rooms were labeled in order with a notation of occupied or vacant.

"The city is stifling. Here in the woods we can conjure the pure magick that Mother Nature provides. And what is the most potent of all energy?" he asked rhetorically, giving a maniacal laugh. "Sex. Love. Hate, of course, however that is not the kind of negativity I wish to bring into my circle. My counterpart, the great Ilsbeth, she had a much more traditional approach. And as you know, she was quite the destructive force. I choose benevolence."

Jax rolled his eyes. Katrina interrupted, aware her Alpha was losing patience with the warlock.

"Mr. Germaine, we need your assistance with…"

"Ah, so the dear, sweet Samantha has told me. I'll never know how such a darling witch could marry that overbearing set of fangs." He sniffed. "To each her own, I suppose. First the tour, Kitty. Then we chat. As you have noticed, the weather grows turbulent. Excellent energy for our celebration but as you've pointed out, we get to havin' travel issues out here. And seeing as how you arrived by car this evening, you may be spending the night with us."

"That's not happening," Jax countered.

"Alpha, you're not from the south, so please defer to the experts." He gestured to his chest and laughed. "As I was saying, my barn…my special place…I've created rooms for my coven as well as guests. The left side is reserved for my witches. The right, where you are standing now, is for guests. Follow me."

Katrina shook her head at Jax, whose mouth had drawn tight. His jaw ticked in anger, but given no choice, he followed. Through a labyrinth of darkened hallways, they eventually passed several closed doors. Mick paused at an empty room; a flicker of candlelight danced inside it.

"And this, my friends, is where our guests can rest for a few hours or for the entire evening. I present to you the Voodoo room. A bit cliché, I know, but I thought the Alpha would enjoy it." Mick laughed and continued walking. "This here is our looking-glass room. As you can see, this offers entertainment for our voyeurs. Tell me, Kitty," the warlock turned to Katrina and gave her a sensual smile, "do you like to watch?"

"It's none of your business," she snapped. Her eyes darted to the window display. A foursome inside paid their party no mind as they made love. A woman lay on her back sucking her partner's cock, while another woman attended to her pussy. A second man fucked her from behind.

"Tsk, tsk...that answer won't do at all," he sneered. "Negative thoughts are not welcome in my space. I'm afraid if you want answers, tit for tat."

"Now just wait a damn minute," Jax began.

"Yes, but you won't ever be involved," Katrina spat. "Now can we hurry up? I am aware of how the weather is down here and we're running out of time."

"Ha! Very good, Kitty. You like to watch...hmm...I knew it!" Mick turned on his heel, squealing in delight as if he'd been given a birthday gift. "And this is another play room. Of course I have my own private dungeon but we must make sure our guests have options."

Katrina peered inside at the various instruments of pleasure and pain. A St. Andrew's cross rested in the corner, and the thought of tying up her Alpha flashed in her mind. As much as she'd enjoyed submitting to Jax in bed, she imagined she'd enjoy dominating given how out of control her life had been. She caught Jax staring at her and wondered if he could read her thoughts. Averting her gaze, she looked to Mick, who waved them into an office, where a perky brunette greeted them.

"Come in, come in. 'Tis time for business. This is Avery. She's one of my very special witches." He blew her a kiss, which she caught in the air and pretended to bring to her mouth. She moaned as her fingers seductively trailed between her breasts, her eyes set on Jax.

Katrina's instinct to attack was thwarted by both Jake and Jax who reached for her wrists. The silent cue interrupted her vicious thoughts. She looked to Jax, but he shook his head, warning her back. With a huff, she yanked her arms free and glared at the witch.

"Kitty doesn't like to share? What a shame. You wolves are very possessive creatures, almost as bad as the bloodsuckers. Sit. Please." Mick gestured to a set of scarlet crushed velvet sofas. Rounding his swirled marble desk, he threw himself into a white leather chair. He propped his feet up onto the edge and steepled his fingers.

Katrina reluctantly sat, taking in her surroundings. Brick walls adorned with antique farm tools were countered by the modern technology that rested along an extended console. She detected the faint scent of coumarin. The herbaceous odor lingered in the air, and she spied a small bowl of black tonka beans on the end table.

A giggle bubbled behind her and Katrina's eyes flew to Avery. Dressed in a black see-through corset, she slinked over to Mick. The opaque stripes trailing down over her breasts did little to cover the rosy nipples that strained through the mesh fabric. Garters snapped tight to her thigh-high stockings, long legs pinned into patent leather pumps. Her eyes locked on Katrina, and she pursed her cherry-stained lips at Jax.

Rooting her feet to the ground, Katrina struggled to stay calm. Jake mouthed the word 'no' from across the room. Her wolf growled, urging her to attack. Her hands fisted in frustration but she knew losing control within a love shack of witches was a bad idea. Silently counting to ten, she prayed the meeting would be over within the hour. Mick cleared his throat and her focus was brought back to the warlock.

"Boring you, am I?"

"I'm sorry, what?" she asked.

"You need to claim him, you know?" he responded.

"How do you know I haven't already?" Katrina's heart pounded in her chest; she had not expected to discuss the topic with Mick.

"Running, running, running. Don't think Ilsbeth didn't take notice, ah, because she did. These things…they've always been troublesome."

"What do they want?" As Katrina's pulse raced faster, her curiosity bloomed. Until now, no one had had answers.

"Demons, quite a bother really. Always trying to escape as such. There're many levels. Some walk among us, simply bringing negativity. Others possess the bodies of the dying. And some…" Mick paused, his eyes narrowed in concern.

Gone was the flighty host, replaced by a more serious individual, who appeared concerned for his own wellbeing. His voice rasped in both a cold and thoughtful tone. "They want to possess the living. But you see, they are not meant to do so. They reap pestilence and death, and once allowed to walk among us, they'll take over this realm. So you understand how it is imperative to stop them."

"Yes, I heard these tales as a child, but these things, the ones that kidnapped me, they take new forms."

"It's true. We don't know much. The Méchants. The 'evil ones', loosely translated. I can smell their influence on you." His gaze went to Katrina. "But back to your mating. Now what did they tell you?"

Katrina hesitated. Jax nodded and took her hand in his. "It's okay, Kat. Tell him."

"They told me." Katrina swallowed. A gentle squeeze of her hand from her Alpha imbued her with the warmth and confidence to continue. It had sounded ridiculous, but she'd believed them. "I didn't know at the time about Jax. I mean, they just said my mate would be an Alpha. But there aren't many Alphas and some are already mated. I'd been following Jax."

"You stalked him? That's lovely." Mick clapped his hands.

"No, I just, I don't know...I was attracted to him. I'd seen his pictures. Then one night. Happenstance really..."

"There are no coincidences," Jax commented.

"Your Alpha is correct," Mick acknowledged.

She returned Jax's warm smile and continued. "The

second we met...I suspected he was the one. I wouldn't be able to resist mating with him. I could kill him. Running was the only way to protect him from me." She sighed and shook her head, lifting her eyes to meet Mick's. "This thing. It changed me. When we escaped, I shifted. But it wasn't me. I was weak, and even now, I know it's Jax who fills me with strength."

"They have done this to you on purpose," he told her. "They confuse you. They've opened a portal to your essence, your energy. And each time they take you, they harvest the spirit of an Alpha's lineage, sucking it out of you like a farmer milks the cow. But, my dear, they cannot close the hole. It's like a flat tire after being punctured by a nail, it closes tight, but not quite tight enough. The air slowly leaks. It's the same with your magick."

"But why do they need her magick? Why not just take any wolf? You'd think they'd be getting a fresh wolf instead of using her over and over," Jake asked.

"Why not just kill me?"

"How much do they need?" Jax went solemn, as if he'd come to a revelation.

A shiver ran down Katrina's arm, and she sucked a quiet breath. *What the hell is coming for us all?*

"Let me start with the why. Well, three is of significance. Unlike what you might think, not many are born of an Alpha, sister and mate. That is quite obvious. But a better guess is that one or both of your parents has a tie to this demon. A favor, perhaps?"

"How can that be? Tristan would have known if our

family owed a demon. If it weren't for Jax actually being there…" She gave an exhausted sigh. "I can ask Tristan again."

"Do ask quickly, Kitty. You're running out of time." Mick leaned over his desk toward them. "The hole…the very one I told you about. You must feel it. Your magick leaks…and your mate," his eyes trained on Jax, "your Alpha, he fills you with his."

"But I don't feel weak," Jax said in denial. "I'll admit I can feel the slight transfer but nothing is wrong with me."

"But your mate? She doesn't just have your magick. Something grows within her, it eats at yours. They want to use her."

"They implanted a chip in her?" Jake asked. "Or is this more like one of those amoebas that eats away at you?"

"What the fuck?" Jax scolded him.

"What? I'm just sayin'. Tell me you haven't watched the videos where they extract the bug that laid eggs inside of someone's skin."

"Really? You had to go there?" Mick shook his head.

"Ew, no, that did not happen," Katrina protested, and rubbed her arms. The thought that something else could be inside her made her nauseous.

"No, my dear." Mick glared at Jake. "You wolves can be so uncouth at times. I'm all about nature, but seriously?"

"Say what you want, witch-boy, but if she's got somethin' growin' inside her, well…my mind jumps to larvae."

"Don't listen to him," Jax told her, and pinned his eyes

on Jake, who shrugged. "Shut it now."

"Katrina has something inside her. Not a bug per se." Mick shook his finger at Jake. "A seedling of dark magick. Something that only witches have. Mages. The ability to change form? Demons have long been able to do that nifty trick."

"And how do you know all this shit anyway? You seem to know an awful lot about demons and Katrina." Jake leaned back into his chair.

"He has a good point. How do we know you're not involved?" Jax asked.

"Very good question. I can only offer you my honesty, and have no proof of my innocence. I do know that the high priestess had interactions over the years with the Méchants. Favors here, favors there. Ilsbeth's magick was not without reproach. Take for example," he paused and leaned back in his chair, "Dimitri. One does not steal magick easily. And in doing so…there's a price."

"I imagine a very high price," Jax added.

"Indeed," Mick agreed.

"So wait." Jake leaned forward, shook his head and scrubbed both hands through his hair. "Are you telling us that not only did Ilsbeth try to kill Dimitri's wolf, but that she did it by getting help from these things?"

"There are only so many things we can do with our magick. At some point, we require special ingredients. It's no secret that she was known for her collection of elements. A menagerie if you will."

"I hope that bitch is burning in hell as we speak." Jake

crossed his arms across his chest.

"Look, we get that Ilsbeth took unconventional paths to get her way, but at the end of the day, all I care about is my mate."

"As you should. So, first things first. How do we fix Kitty?" Mick set his sights on Katrina. "These demons…you know they will lie. So let's start with the obvious. Mating will not hurt your Alpha. I cannot be one hundred percent certain, but I have done my research. No need to thank me," he buffed his long fingernails upon his pants and then admired them, "but this leak. I'm afraid this is a problem."

"What makes you think I can…?" Katrina began.

"This leak. This energy. The sexual essence that is generated between beings. It can purify." Mick stood and made a sweeping gesture with his palm. "But you must have the assistance of an Alpha."

"Wait." Jax shook his head. "Are you saying what I think you are saying?"

"Are you saying I have another mate? No, that's not possible," Katrina insisted.

"I'm saying exactly what I said. It's an energy healing. Nothing more. Nothing less. But, as you pointed out or should I say, may have guessed, the Alpha can help to prepare her for her true goal."

"Dimitri and Gillian healed me," Jake blurted out.

"I don't want to hear this." Jax stared at the wall, refusing to look at him. It wasn't as if he didn't know what happened between Gillian, Jake and Dimitri, but he preferred not to discuss his sister's sex life, let alone in front of the warlock.

"Jax, come on. You know how wolves are. Don't even try to tell me that you and Nick didn't share," Jake challenged him.

The statement pierced through Katrina like a knife in her gut. Her claws dug into the couch, tearing at the fabric. The idea of Jax being intimate with another woman sent her wolf into a frenzy.

"First, don't bring up his name here," Jax told him. "Second, I just don't see how this will work to help us. And third, where the fuck am I supposed to find another…"

Katrina's eyes went wide as Jax's voice trailed off. She couldn't tell where his thoughts had gone but she suspected he'd found a solution, one she couldn't be certain she'd like.

"Once Katrina has stopped siphoning your magick and leaking her own, you both will be strong enough to face them, to use whatever you brought me to defeat them." Mick smacked his hands onto his desk. "So let's see it then. Show and tell. I've told you what you need to do and now it's time for show."

Katrina's head spun, wondering how the hell they'd be able to carry out his instructions. She'd known something was off with her own magick, but the solution Mick proposed seemed ludicrous.

"Before we show you what we found, I think it's important to note that Katrina," Jax's eyes darted to his mate and then back to the warlock, "she had some unusual experiences in the house. It was almost like Ilsbeth or the house was trying to communicate."

"Hmm…interesting." Mick smiled up at Avery and feverishly rubbed his hands together. "Come on now, the suspense is killing me."

"There is a ring. It was inside this bell." Jax retrieved the rusty items from his pocket, and set them on the desk. "There's a boline, too. I know it looks normal, but it accidentally nicked Kat and her blood smeared onto it. And then the damn thing glowed. You could see something written on it. It made no sense."

Katrina slipped her hand into the purse that was strapped against her shoulder and carefully removed the sickled blade. She'd been afraid to touch the ring since the incident at the mansion. Although she'd been cut by the knife, the coldness of the object elicited no energy or emotion. She unwrapped the cloth napkin and carefully set it down on the marble.

Mick lifted the jewelry into the light. Sliding open his drawer, he retrieved a magnifying glass and studied it. "It's a poison ring. Very clever."

"Fifteenth century," Jake added.

The warlock shot him a questioning look.

"History. It's kind of my thing." Jake gave a half smirk.

"The vampires always underestimate wolves, but never me. Oh, no." He took a deep breath and sighed, placing it on the desk. Mick's attention went to the knife. "Looks like a simple boline to me." Holding the hilt he spun it around, examining all the sides. "You say it glowed, huh? A simple spell. But what is not known is whether or not Katrina's blood did this alone? Or does it work for everyone? Just wolves?"

"We don't know."

"Did you find anything else?"

"Just the bell, but otherwise, no," Jax answered.

"When I was there…" Katrina's eyes widened as she recalled the experience, how the electricity had hummed through her hands. She held her palms upward and stared at them, "…it was just this feeling. Like a tingling. That bell. I couldn't let go of it until the ring fell out. Ilsbeth wanted me to have it."

"We don't know for sure what's happening," Jax added.

"You don't have to believe me. I may not have known Ilsbeth but I know as sure as I'm sitting here that she wanted me to have that ring. She wanted me in her house. And that knife there. It may be used for cutting herbs or whatever, but it means something."

"I suppose, but you haven't tested the theory," Mick told her. "It's true your magick has changed; you're more like a witch now."

Jax shot Mick a glare.

"What?" The warlock rolled his eyes. "It's true. Pfft. As I was saying, you may be able to trigger whatever spell has been infused into the object."

Katrina's stomach sank at his statement, her patience wearing thin. She didn't have time to theorize. Irritated, she snatched the boline.

"What are you doing?" Jax asked, his words slow and deliberate.

"We can't just sit here and speculate. I'm using this thing

now. I want to know if it'll work again and what it all means. We're here with Mick. There's no time like the present to figure out what's going on." She held the point to her palm.

"Just wait a second. Don't do this, Kat."

Katrina had grown tired of everyone telling her what she could or could not do. *Lost magick. Demons. Mating.* With every breath she took, she lost control of her own life. Rage surfaced fast and hot, and she considered all she'd been through. A survivor, she deserved more than empty questions and 'what ifs'.

"I'm sorry. This is all about instinct. And mine tells me to survive." Slicing the sharp edge across her palm, she cringed, the white hot pain stabbing up her forearm. She swiped her thick blood across its blade. Satisfaction filled her chest as lettering appeared in its wake.

"Read this," she demanded. With a loud clank, Katrina dropped the boline onto Mick's desk. Scarlet drops sprayed across the white stone surface.

Jax accepted tissues from Avery and grabbed Katrina's wrist. His eyes narrowed in on her, angry she'd challenged him.

"I'm fine," she insisted, yanking her hand from Jax. He asked her to trust him, to follow his lead, but he couldn't trust her in return to know her own body and mind. Wrapping her palm, she stemmed the blood flow. She caught the look of disgust that crossed Mick's face, displeased she'd marred his furniture. Ignoring his concern, she gestured to the knife. "Hurry before it disappears."

"You didn't need to make such a mess." Mick allowed

Avery to wipe around the object, absorbing the fluid. "Well, this is interesting. A message from Ilsbeth."

"How do you know?"

"Ilsbeth has a Nordic ancestry. She was always fond of tricking people with her use of other languages. While French is often spoken in the bayou, Swedish is less known."

"What does it say?" Katrina pressed.

"Där de döda lögnen och vattnet stiger vi möter. Dolda men sett, hitta förtrollningen som du söker. Of course this is much more of a rhyme in English. Where the dead lie and the water rises, we meet. Hidden but seen, find the spell you seek."

"Seriously?" Jake rose and rubbed his eyes. "This whole damn area is filled with water."

"Lake Ponchartrain?" Katrina guessed. "It can be dangerous."

"True, but so can the river," Jax countered.

"The river?" Jake asked.

"Yes. The river," Jax repeated. "The last time I was down in New Orleans I was in this bar having a drink."

"You and half the world," Mick commented.

"Are you going to listen? Because I'm in no mood."

"Proceed." Mick gave a broad gesture with his palm outstretched.

"It was around Mardi Gras. I'm sitting there, and the bartender starts telling me about how once a year people are allowed to dump the remains of their loved ones in the river. That people wait all year long."

"Start with the Quarter," Katrina suggested.

"How the hell are we supposed to find something down there? We don't even know what it is or where it could be. I guess we could start with the river banks, but some are covered with hundreds of stones. Are we planning on looking under every one? Not to mention the steps, docks, boats. It could be any damn place," Jake pointed out.

"We do it the same way we did it at Ilsbeth's. Look, I'm not even sure how or why, but she wants me to find this. I think there is something about this ring, maybe this knife...we're supposed to do something with them," Katrina asserted.

"Destroy the demons?" Mick suggested, wearing an impassive expression.

"Maybe. Maybe not. We shouldn't assume Ilsbeth is trying to help us. For all we know we're bringing these assholes some kind of gift. But whatever it is, Kat's right. We need to go find what Ilsbeth wanted us to find. We'll figure it out from there," Jax told them.

"Before you leave, I'd like to have a moment with my little Kitty Kat." Mick bowed to Jax, bending his arm over his stomach. "Please, indulge me, Alpha."

"I'll be all right," Katrina assured Jax.

"Are you sure about this? I think maybe I should..." Jax began, but hesitated as Katrina nodded, her expression tense but certain. Before turning toward the door, he collected the items they'd brought off the desk and shot Mick a glare. "Let me be clear. While I appreciate your input today, I'd better not find out you're lying. You get five minutes. You hurt my mate and you're dead." Jax reached for Katrina, and squeezed her hand. "I'll be right here in the hallway. He does anything and I'll know."

"Thanks. I promise I'll be okay," she responded.

"You're just going to leave her alone with the magick man?" Jake asked.

"I'm not going anywhere. The door stays open. Understand?" Jax growled.

"But of course I will maintain the fine lady's reputation." Mick gave a furtive smile and turned to Avery. "Sorry, darling, but this is private. Please see to all the needs of the Alpha and his friend."

"I'd absolutely love to," she mewled, her palms adjusting her cleavage. She licked her lips and reached for the crook of Jax's arm.

Katrina clutched at the desk, restraining her urge to attack the flirty witch. Her wolf scratched and whined, warning her not to let him go alone. Hearing voices in the hallway, she was assured that Jax had not gone far, but it did little to assuage her beast.

A hand tugged at her palm, uncurling her fingers. She stared up into icy eyes that appeared to swirl into infinity. The limitless depth of the warlock's pupils caught her focus, and she wondered if he wore contact lenses.

"Look at how well you heal, even without shifting." Mick uncapped a bottle of water and poured it onto a clean tissue. "May I?"

"Um, what?" Katrina averted her gaze, afraid he possessed some sort of hypnotic power. "Oh yes, sorry. Yeah. My hand's fine, really."

"Beautiful skin. Such a shame you are to be mated. Had we met in another time, perhaps we would have celebrated life's pleasures," he drawled. "But alas, I fear it is not to be."

"Mr. Germaine…"

"Mick…please. We're almost family." He carefully stroked her skin dry.

"Not exactly, but…" Katrina gasped as her palm came into view. No scar or line remained; the cut had completely disappeared. "How did you…"

"Magick. I'm not the high priest for nothing. You may think me peculiar, but I assure you my intentions are altruistic."

"How do I know that?" Despite Mick's statement to the contrary, she didn't trust his motives for helping them.

"Conjuring demons is a messy business." He ignored her question. "You see, demons aren't content to stay in the netherworld. They seek the life they cannot have. The devil has long possessed humans. This world," he paused and lifted her hand in his, bringing it inches from his lips, "it must have balance. This is one point on which Ilsbeth and I agreed. Imbalance brings chaos. Turmoil. Imagine the implications if demons have the power to become wolves? To create their own pack? The very existence of wolves is at stake."

With an ethereal presence, waves of energy radiated off the mystical warlock. He lifted her hand and kissed the back of it, startling Katrina. Disturbed by his words and actions, she tugged away and crossed her arms, feigning confidence. No matter how much she wanted to run from his office, she forced herself to listen to his oration, gleaning every last bit of information he shared.

"Once your portals close, you may be able to save your own magick, but the witchcraft imposed on you will forever leave its mark. You've been branded by the demon. I'm afraid you cannot remove what has been done. Ilsbeth, she is neither all saint nor all sinner. But I believe she has touched you. Somewhere along the line, she gifted you with a sliver of her power, and now my dear, you must go use it. Find what she wishes you to find."

Awestruck, Katrina stared at Mick, her body relaxing into the trance he'd evoked. She vacillated between believing every single word he spoke and dismissing the entire evening as a hallucination. He smiled at her, his effervescent laughter erupted, and she blinked, woken from her dream.

"I, um, thank you." Katrina flexed her fingers as the suggestive laugh of a female caught her attention. Her Alpha's voice followed, sparking a hot wave of jealousy in her chest. "I have to go."

Without saying goodbye, Katrina took off out of Mick's office into the dark hallway. As promised, Jax had not gone far, but nor had the seductive witch. Her Alpha stood backed against a wall, his hands wrapped around her wrists. The sight of Avery's palms flattened on Jax's shoulders incited her beast into a rage.

"You! Get the hell off of him, now!" Katrina stalked toward them.

"Hmm….why won't you share?" A wicked smile crossed

Avery's face and she waggled her eyebrows at Katrina. "He's delicious. I can feel every last hard ridge." As she attempted to slide her hands lower, Jax lifted her arms away.

"Hey, sorry, Kat, I…this," he stuttered, swiveling his head. "I'm telling you this isn't what it looks like. Where the hell did Jake go?"

"You have three little precious seconds to get away from Jax before I shift and rip out your throat," Katrina growled. She kicked off her shoes and tore off her dress, readying to shift. "One. Two. Three."

Avery threw her hands up and spun in circles away from Jax. With an evil laugh, she reached into her pocket and blew purple and silver sparkles up into the air. "You need happy dust."

Katrina glared at Avery, who continued to smile at them. Her beast threatened to shift, urging her to kill the witch. "You touch him again, and it will be the last thing you ever do with those pretty little nails of yours."

"It's okay, Katrina," Jax coaxed, his voice calm. "Believe me, I get what's going on here. Your wolf, you've been holding her back for a long time and she's not happy. You need to leave the witch alone, though. No matter what your wolf is telling you, you can't just kill her."

Katrina sniffed into the air and grazed her nose into his chest, scenting the witch on his clothing, and growled. Her hand reached between his legs and grabbed his half-hard dick. Although a sliver of her humanity registered the fact that they were inside of a coven, her wolf inside demanded she claim him. Feral, she ignored logic, which told her to wait until they returned home.

Jax gave a small chuckle as Katrina grabbed his wrist and kicked open a door with her foot. She slammed it behind her, paying little attention to the room she'd entered. Set in a seventies theme, plastic beads covered the walls. Prismatic light splintered from a spinning mirrored ball overhead. A kaleidoscope of colors mottled over the shag carpet and furniture.

Katrina stared up into his blue eyes, her gorgeous Alpha looming over her. Stabbing her fingers into Jax's chest, she directed him backward until his calves touched the mattress. She fisted his shirt at the collar, holding it out from his neck. Jax made no move to stop her as she clawed at the fabric with her nails. Tearing it apart at the seams, she discarded it on the floor. With her gaze locked on his, she dragged her tongue over his flat nipple. As he went to embrace her, she bit him hard in warning.

"Don't move," she growled. Wild, her beast ran free. She'd have her way with her Alpha and by the time she was done, no one would ever have him again.

Jax hissed as Katrina raked her fingernails down his chest, marking his skin with fine red trails. Her hands drifted to his belt, and she unbuckled it. With a swift tug, she whipped it out and dangled it from her fingers. As she unzipped his pants and tugged down the denim, Katrina caught the glint of excitement as his eyes went to the leather.

"Off," she ordered, her eyes intense as he complied, kicking off the jeans.

Katrina smiled, soaking in the spectacular sight of her

mate. From the hard lines of his masculine form to his hardened arousal, she sought to own every inch of him. She reached for his dick and stroked it, gliding her thumb over his weeping slit.

"Ah…what are you doing with that belt, Kat?" he groaned, not making an attempt to move.

"This?" She held it up in the air, giving a small smile. Katrina had never indulged as a dominant yet she'd detected his curiosity to explore the unknown. In the split second that she sensed his interest, she fell into her role, determined to push his limits. *Pain. Pleasure.* Her Alpha had sexual tastes that ran the gamut, and she was about to discover how far he'd go. "Is this what you want? You've been a very bad Alpha."

"I'm warning you, you best not go there," he breathed.

"Why's that? Because you might like it?" Katrina released him and reached behind her back, unsnapping her bra. She cupped a firm breast, teasing its tip into a taut peak. "Remember our little deal? Honesty. We're mates, after all."

"You haven't claimed me yet," he baited her.

Katrina gave a small chuckle, cognizant he'd challenged her on purpose. She was well aware that although he indulged her, allowing her to dominate, her submission to her Alpha was imminent. Feral with sexual energy, Katrina proceeded to tease him.

Standing at a distance from her mate, she smiled as he patiently waited, hunger flaring in his eyes. Holding the strap, she hooked a thumb into the side of her panties and tugged them away. As if her lover's hands were on her body, her fingers glided over her breasts and traveled slowly down her stomach. Slipping them through her slippery folds, she cried out in pleasure as she brushed over her clit.

With his eyes locked on hers, Jax stood perfectly still as Katrina approached. She lifted her hand to his mouth and dragged her cream along his lips. He sucked her fingers, and her pussy dampened. She studied her beautiful mate, his teeth nipping at her thumb. A small grin emerged on his face, and her heart pounded against her ribs. This man would break her, and the whole time she'd beg for more.

Jax's eyes went to the leather in her hand, reminding her of her intent. His sexy smile, wrapped around her like an embrace, had distracted her from her task. She moved to his side and widened her stance. Taking his steel-hard cock into her hand, she gripped him. With each stroke, her hips tilted forward. Her wet folds grazed his thigh and she bit her lip. Holding the strap, her eyes went to his and he nodded.

"This is happening now. I'm going to mark you tonight. And do you know why, Alpha? Because you're mine." Wielding the leather, she slapped it across his ass and he grunted in arousal. "My mate."

Jax fisted his hands as his head lolled back. "Again," he begged.

Katrina's breath caught at the sight of her Alpha embracing the stinging punishment. She swatted him again and he began to furiously thrust his stiffened cock into her hand.

"Don't you dare come," she demanded. Jax panted, sweat beading across his brow, but did as Katrina instructed.

"On the bed now. After tonight there will be no doubt who you belong to."

Jax fell back into bed, grinning up at her, and her heart melted. A true dominatrix she was not. But as he let her direct him, she suspected, like everything else he did in his life, he'd done it on purpose. He'd given her the confidence she needed, her wolf needed. Years of being out of control were erased as she descended onto her Alpha. She climbed atop him, straddling his waist and gave him a smile. "Your hands."

She stifled a laugh as he put his wrists out to her, but quickly resumed her work. Binding him with only a buckle, she knew he'd quickly escape. But the act was symbolic of his trust in her. She gently slid her hands up his hardened abs, admiring every little ridge under her fingertips. When she reached his chest, she gently lifted underneath his arms, brushing her palms up along the sensitive inner skin.

Pressing his wrists over his head, she bent forward and deliberately slid her ripened tips across his face. His lips caught her nipple, and she sucked a breath. Although his hands were restrained, he'd taken control, teasing her peak into a sensitive bundle of nerves. Desire jolted through her body and she writhed her hips, not yet touching him. Aching with need, she tugged her breast from his mouth and slithered down his abdomen.

Torturing him had evolved into a painful exercise for her as well. Denying her own orgasm, she seated herself between his legs, letting her warm breath wash over his shaft. Her lips parted, and she gently lapped at his crown, his salty-tasting essence coating her tongue. His thighs tensed around her torso as she swallowed him down her throat. As she sucked, his head teased her palate, his hips lifting to meet her rhythm.

Katrina studied the contours of his beautiful cock as it disappeared, his smooth skin on her lips. Withdrawing his magnificent erection, she stroked it with her hand and set her attention on his balls. Taking his velvety sac into her mouth, she extended her hand underneath his ass. Her fingers traveled down his cleft, teasing his puckered flesh.

His breath grew ragged as she released his testicle with a pop. Taking him deep into her mouth, she pressed a finger into his back hole.

"Ah, Christ," he cried, but made no protest.

Delving deeper, she touched over his sensitive area of nerves. He jolted his hips upward as she discovered his hidden spot.

"Kat. Oh fuck." Jax pounded his hands into the headboard. "I'm going to…"

He was close, she knew, but once again, she'd deny him his orgasm. She withdrew her hand, ceasing her delightful assault. Grazing her teeth ever so slightly down his shaft, she removed it and laved her tongue over its head.

"Please…Jesus, don't stop."

Like a phoenix, she rose up on her forearms, and crawled her way up his body. She brushed her clit over his balls, still stroking his dick. Katrina took in the sight of her virile mate. A fine sheen coated his skin, his heavy eyes lifting to meet hers.

"No more games, Alpha."

"Holy shit, Kat. You're killin' me here. I can't take much more. I need to be inside you. Like fucking now."

"Is this what you need?" she asked, swiping his head through her swollen labia. As his hardness brushed over her clitoris, she moaned. Blood rushed through her veins, arousal thrashing through every pore of her body. His hungry eyes devoured her as she directed his crown into her wet entrance. Unable to wait one second longer, she impaled herself on his ridged flesh.

"Fuck yes," he grunted.

"Jax. Oh my God..." A slight twinge passed quickly as her readied core accommodated her mate, his cock stretching her open.

Katrina rocked forward, her hips against his. The release she'd held at bay crashed over her as she leaned forward, her fingers crushing into his pecs. Her palm went to his cheek and she held his chin in place. Her mouth descended on his, biting and sucking at his lips.

The honeyed taste of her mate drove her wild. *Claim him.* The words resounded in her head. The gorgeous male beneath her body belonged to her and her alone. Commanding and compassionate, the New York Alpha was the only person in the world who could complete her wolf.

He slammed his cock up into her, his dominance rearing. Within seconds, he'd brand her, reminding her of who was really in control. But first her beast would have its due, seeking the unbreakable bond. As she tore her lips from his, she knew marking him would never be enough.

Her fangs distended, and like lightning she struck, her teeth slicing into his shoulder. She heard a faint cry as his powerful blood rushed down her throat. Before she knew what was happening, he'd broken free of his leather bonds and flipped her onto her back.

"Forever," he repeated as he pounded into her. "You're mine. Fovever."

Jax pinned her arms to the bed, demanding her submission. Releasing his flesh, her glistening lips parted. She tilted her head, baring her throat to her Alpha, acquiescing to his command. As his canines punctured her skin, magick ruptured, her essence absorbed by her mate. Her wolf danced in the abyss of her mind, finally sated.

"My Alpha," she breathed as he ground his pelvis against hers. The friction to her clit pushed her over the edge and she screamed his name as the hardest orgasm of her life seized her body.

"Say it again," he ordered, punishing her with his rough thrusts.

"My Alpha. I'm yours…" was all she could manage. Tiny specks of light danced before her eyes, her release filtering through her every nerve.

"That's right, baby. That's right…" His lips crushed over hers, and she surrendered to his will, relinquishing her body, soul and mind to her mate.

Jax grazed his hips over her sensitized flesh, milking every last spasm. With a final thrust, he groaned and erupted deep inside her. As he slowed his pace, he delicately sucked at her lips, making love to her mouth as he'd done to her body.

Connected with her mate, the fiery culmination of their bond enveloped Katrina. All fears vanished within Jax's embrace. For the first time in two hundred years, Katrina's wolf slept calmly, peace filtering throughout her consciousness.

"Jax." As their lips separated, air rushed into her lungs. A whisper of his name escaped. Emotion coiled in her chest and Katrina struggled to articulate her thoughts.

"Kat, ah baby, I'm sorry," he began, giving a ragged sigh.

"Sorry for…are you okay?" Panic set in and she pushed at his chest with her palms.

"Easy, little wolf." Jax shifted onto his back, bringing her with him.

Strong arms surrounded her, his warmth radiating through her skin. Despite the comfort, she grew concerned that their mating had harmed him like she'd been told. *Selfish, selfish, selfish.* The temptation of seeing him with the witch had spurred her frenzy. Guilt for initiating the mating took hold.

"Hey, stop." Jax's lips touched her forehead and he spoke softly against her brow. "I'm fine. I only said I was sorry because, well, look where we are."

Desperate for her Alpha, obscured in passion, she'd forgotten they'd made love inside the coven. She sighed at the realization that probably every witch within a mile had heard their antics.

"I'm the one who should be sorry, Jax. I just lost it out there."

"Don't you dare go there. Ever since I marked you, I've wanted this so bad. It's not the most romantic setting, but I don't regret it for a second."

"This place is crazy." Katrina's eyes went to the peace sign that hung on the wall. It struck her as funny and she began to laugh.

"You do know who you're mated to, right?" Jax asked as he glanced to the brightly colored plaid sofa in the corner.

"You mean *the* Mr. Jax Chandler? Devastatingly handsome. Sophisticated." She drew circles on his muscular chest with the pad of her finger. "Or do you mean the powerful Alpha? I heard he's lethal."

"Is that how you see me?" he asked.

"The Alpha I'm mated to is caring." Katrina pressed upward so she could look into his eyes. Carefully constructing her thoughts, her voice softened. "He's also vulnerable. Knows what it's like to be hurt. He's protective of those he cares about. Willing to put his own life on the line for his wolves, for his mate. He's...amazing. He's mine."

Katrina resisted expressing the feelings that grew exponentially every second she spent in his presence. Love wasn't something that always occurred between mates. Chemistry drew mates together in a juncture of destiny, a formidable force to deny. Only through a serendipitous occurrence would two wolves grow to truly love each other. Despite rationalizing away the feelings that brewed inside her, Katrina had to admit her thoughts bordered on obsession.

"I...you have no idea how much this meant. I can feel you all around me," he responded. "It's like nothing I've ever experienced."

"I feel it too." She paused. "Jax, I want you to know that even though the witch may have pushed my wolf, I've wanted this since the second I met you. I feel like such an idiot for believing their lies. I'm sorry I waited so long. Being with you is everything to me."

As Katrina disclosed her confession, she buried her face in Jax's chest, unable to reveal how deeply their mating had affected her, how much he meant to her. So many years, she'd lived a cold, lonely existence. She'd closed her heart, a deliberate effort to thwart feelings for other men. Everything she'd ever known had been destroyed, replaced by the realization that she cared more for Jax than she'd ever thought possible. The altruistic effort to save him by denying their connection had morphed into a desperate mission to claim their life together.

The gentle brush of his lips on her skin relaxed her mind and she suspected he'd read her emotion. The strength of the bond would keep them in sync, but her magick would continue to weaken, replaced by a perversion of the true spirit of the wolf. Mick's warning played in her mind. More determined than ever, she'd trust her mate to keep her safe as they continued to search for a way to destroy the demons.

❦ *Chapter Nineteen* ❧

"Why the hell is it that we always have to look for this shit at night?" Jake picked up a rock and threw it into the Mississippi. "Nope. Can't be the day. Witchy, spooky-ass message has to be found at night. Of course it does. Nothing is ever easy."

"Who knows. Maybe it's because it glows, or, as you put it, something witchy is about to go down," Jax replied. "It's easier this way anyway. Less people around."

"Don't be a baby. Besides, look at the city all lit up. It's gorgeous." Katrina leaned back onto the metal railing, admiring the lights flickering over the cityscape. A trumpet played in the distance, its rich tones resonating up to the river walk.

"You two...seriously. I love you both, but you're more annoying than ever," Jake huffed. "I'm going to check over there." He pointed to a set of wide boardwalk stairs that led down to the river's edge. Two young homeless men shared a cigarette, their dog lay at their feet.

"We'll be down in a minute," Jax replied, giving it his

best effort to concentrate on their task.

He wrapped his arm around Katrina's waist and tugged her close. Her giggling was music to his ears, happiness evident in her laughter. His nose brushed into her hair, the delicious scent of his mate consuming his thoughts.

It had been over twenty-four hours since they'd mated and with every glance, every touch of their skin, the bond deepened. Making love to her at the coven, letting her dominate and fuck him, had been impulsive. Although he'd suspected Katrina's wolf wouldn't be deterred much longer, he hadn't anticipated the witch's advances. Jax speculated that perhaps she'd deliberately incited Katrina over the edge, but her motives for doing so remained a mystery. Regardless, Jax celebrated the glorious outcome.

After a short respite, they'd dressed and managed to find Jake dancing with a set of twins. Thankfully, the rain had let up and they were able to drive home without incident. Before they returned, the warlock had wished them well, and gave them a final instruction to search at dusk. However, they still had no idea exactly what they were looking for, besides a promise of another clue.

It concerned Jax that Katrina's magick continued to be compromised. Although Mick had advised him to use another Alpha to strengthen her wolf, he struggled with the idea of sharing his mate. He'd never made love to a woman with another Alpha. Both his touch and raging power were to be wielded with caution. He recalled a time when he and Nick indulged, taking a woman together. The experiences had been pleasurable, but his beta had always submitted and neither had claimed the chosen female.

With his wolf sated, Jax considered he'd be less likely to attack another male. On a visceral level, however, the idea of letting another Alpha touch her provoked possessive emotions. *Mine*, he told Katrina and he'd meant it. No other male would command his mate.

As he observed Jake's agile run down the stairs, he knew what needed to be done. An Alpha, the young wolf still hadn't suspected his true nature. But Jax suspected he'd be the one to help him heal Katrina. They'd already successfully experimented. Their sexual interlude in the kitchen had been primal, and Jake had willingly deferred to him, careful not to cross the line. He couldn't be sure if either of them would agree, but the discussion needed to happen sooner rather than later if they were going to help Katrina seal her magick.

"Kat," Jax began, hoping his mate would be open to his proposal. She swiveled her body, facing the river, and snuggled into his side. "How're you feeling?"

"I'm feeling amazing," she breathed.

"I mean your power. Has it changed since we mated?"

"I'm not going to lie to you. After everything," she sighed and tilted her head up toward him, "it feels about the same. I don't feel weak, if that's what you mean. But it still feels like if I'm not around you for any amount of time, I get drained. Like this morning, for example. You were downstairs, and just that hour or whatever when you were away, I could feel it slipping. Then I start to panic. I'm thinking, 'what if I can't shift? What if I turn into something else?' Ugh, I hate this." She shook her head and stared out to the Mississippi, city lights reflecting on its surface. "It's like a bathtub. You know, you fill it up but you can't get the stopper just right. So you lie back and just when you think you are about to relax, half the water is gone and you're freezing cold."

As serious as the situation was, the image of Katrina lying wet and naked in his bath caused his cock to stir. He shoved the picture to the back of his mind, admonishing the thought. *Focus, Jax.*

"Whatever we find tonight, I have a feeling it will be because of your magick." Jax hated that they'd hurt his mate. She curled against his body, reminding him that she was as much a part of him as the arm that held her.

"It's not my magick. I don't know why Ilsbeth chose me," she pondered, her lips tight. "But I guess it doesn't matter. I just want to find this thing...the spell or whatever it is and get it over with. I want to be free."

"You will, Kat. I promise you," he told her. With his lips pressed to her hair, he continued. "The thing is that when we go back to New York, you need to be strong."

"I know."

"What did you think of what Mick said?" Jax hesitated, almost afraid to speak the words. He would never force Katrina into being with another man. If she agreed, it would be her decision. "About needing another Alpha to help us?"

"Jax, I..." Katrina stuttered, and turned to face him, her eyes on his. "I need to tell you something."

"What?"

"It's about an Alpha. My brother. I called Tristan today. I asked him about my mom and dad. But also…I told him we mated."

"You should have told me before you did that, Kat." Jax shook his head, frustrated she hadn't asked him first. Tristan's incendiary reaction would come swiftly, probably assuming he'd forced her to mate.

"You don't understand. He already knows I'm with you. I think he was okay with everything until I mentioned we mated." She cringed and gave a half smile. "Please don't be mad. I needed to talk to him. I had to ask if something happened to me when I was a child…anything that my parents could have done to bring this demon to my feet."

"It's not that I don't understand, but Tristan? It's going to take time for him to accept us, after everything that happened." Jax's mind spun with possible ways of handling the situation. If he called Tristan, he might make it worse, because he'd likely tell him to fuck off if he challenged their mating. "We've got to get home as soon as possible. Your brother is going to be pissed."

"More like, 'is pissed'."

"We'll deal with this together. The bottom line is that he has no choice but to accept the situation. He's not your father and even if he was, it's what you want that matters. He'll get over it." Jax tilted his head and smiled down at Katrina. "He has to. Because there is no way I'm giving you up."

"I'm not giving you up either." She embraced him, laying her head against his chest. "Tristan doesn't know anything anyway. After this mess is over, we'll go see him and make peace."

"Kat, we need to talk about the warlock. What he said about finding another Alpha...I don't think he meant Tristan." Jax let the silence linger between them, waiting for her to draw a conclusion.

"If you're suggesting we find an Alpha just so I can..." She averted her gaze and shook her head. "I don't want to be with anyone else but you. I just found you. Besides, I can't just have sex with anyone. No, I'll just have to face these things with my magick as it is."

"That's not what I'm saying at all. I want you to remember something, little wolf. No matter how bad you think it is, you can always trust me." A stone skipped across the river, and Jax's attention went to the wolf, who gave him a curt wave. "What about Jake?"

"What about him?" She glanced over to Jake and back to Jax.

"Hear me out, okay? We never really talked about what happened in the kitchen. I'll be honest. I wasn't sure how I'd feel about it when he slapped your ass. But your reaction said it all. The whole thing with him there? I enjoyed it and I know you did too. It was hot."

"Yeah it was. And if you don't stop talking about this, you're going to have to fuck me right here on the dock, because you're making me horny. You know that, right?" She laughed.

"You're aroused just talking about it? What do you think it does to me?" Jax brought her hand between his legs to cup his straining erection.

"I love it when you're hard like this…do you know how much I want this right now?" She gave him a flirty smile.

"Not as much as me. Now come on…stay on topic, woman." He laughed.

"How the hell am I supposed to do that?" She stroked him, stealing a glance behind her to make sure no one saw them.

"We're talking about Jake." He coughed. "You keep doing that and I'm going to come."

"Ah…Jax," she sighed. "Do I want to play with him? With the three of us? Yes, someday." Katrina gritted her teeth and shook her head, blowing out a breath. She removed her hand and faced her mate. "Look, what we did the other day was great, but given a choice, like if all this wasn't going on? I just want to be with you."

"Jake's going to be an Alpha. Someday he'll lead his own pack." Jax's expression flattened as he told her what he suspected.

"Jake? But he…he's not even beta."

"It's the reason he and I go at it sometimes. I've been trying, in a most subtle way, to prepare him. When I came back, I was surprised to see him. Logan had sent him to San Diego, and I thought for sure he'd end up staying, taking over that pack."

"Maybe in some ways he did what you thought he'd do, though," she mused.

"How's that? He was with Finn."

"Exactly. Finn wasn't running the pack. Jake was there

for him." She shrugged.

"Just think about it, Kat. I won't ask you or make you do anything you don't want to do. It's just that I'm worried about you. I know you feel stronger, but I also know the reality of the situation."

Jax caught Jake watching them out of the corner of his eye and hoped he hadn't overheard their conversation. Taking Kat into his arms, he gazed down into her eyes and his heart caught. The unfamiliar yearning in his chest was so much more than lust and he struggled to accept the emotions that rooted in his chest.

"I want you to know…this thing between us." His eyes darted to the glistening water and back to Katrina. "I told you that night we met…I've never met anyone like you. I meant that. I mean it even more now. You're determined. Strong. I'm not sure what I'm trying to say, but…" *Goddess, I sound like a fool. Get your shit together.* He gave a small laugh, realizing that for the first time in his life a woman was making him nervous. "I care about you. A lot. I won't do anything to jeopardize our future. As much as I want you completely healed, the ball is in your court. We…us…our relationship is more important. We'll figure out a way to deal with things, okay?"

A broad smile broke across Katrina's face upon his revelation. Her palm cupped his unshaven cheek and she rose to her tiptoes.

"I care about you too. More than you know."

Jax gave in to desire, and kissed his mate. Nothing mattered but Katrina, her happiness and their new journey.

He almost wished he had the control to stop thinking about her, but relenting to the overwhelming need to be with her was impossible to resist.

The rolling waves lapped against the dock, drawing his attention back to their task and he begrudgingly broke contact. Jax opened his eyes, still focused on his mate. In his peripheral vision, he caught sight of Jake holding his palms upward, mouthing the words, 'what the fuck?', and he laughed in response.

"I think that our friend is getting pissed at us."

Katrina glanced at Jake and smiled. "He's patient. I'll give him that."

"Let's go. This could be a long night."

Jax took Katrina's hand and led her down the steps. He turned to the strangers and growled, his eyes flashing red. Amid their screams and the dog barking, Katrina's voice cut into the night.

"What are you doing?" she asked.

"We don't need an audience. Plus, I don't want anyone else getting hurt. I don't know what's down here. Maybe something bad. Maybe nothing." Jax waited until the area cleared before meeting Jake at the bottom. "Okay, you're the local. Where do you think most people throw ashes?"

"Well on Mardi Gras day they usually come on up here with the parade...you know, through Jackson Square to the river. But shit, I mean you know people probably do it other times. That's a human thing. Us wolves...we've got our own rituals. Puff and flush isn't one of them."

"Jake," Katrina admonished him.

"I'm sorry. I'm just sayin' you know we don't do this kind of thing. Back in the old days, who the hell knows what they did?"

Jax and Katrina rolled their eyes at each other, aware that Jake truly had no idea how long they'd lived. She shook her head, smiling, as he continued.

"Take the yellow fever epidemic of 1853, this city was filled with hundreds of dead people. They didn't know what to do with the bodies. Some of them just rotted away in the houses until the stench could be smelled through the burning tar." He sighed. "The cemeteries were full. But hell, I'm sure that through the years, people saw fit to make enemies wear cement boots, if ya know what I mean. And then you have the swimmers. I read just last week that someone died."

"But for the sake of this message," Katrina interrupted. "Ilsbeth did this. I'm pretty sure she's older than even we are. She's old school."

"Traditional," Jax added.

"I'd go with Mardi Gras. The coven house isn't too far from here either. Dumaine Street. So let's say someone—"

"Or something?" Jax interjected.

"Or something came after her. I mean she could get up to the riverfront fairly easily on foot." Jake scanned the area. "She's not going to hide something on a boat."

"No, she needs a safe place. Somewhere not many people go." Katrina bent down and ran her fingers over a smooth gray stone.

"Well, where we're standing right now. It's easy access

to the river, but this place is usually loaded with people during the day."

"Supernaturals?" Jax scrubbed his hand through his hair.

"Mostly humans," Jake replied. "They play music. Sleep. Just kind of hang out here."

"Okay, well, assuming I'm human, I'm not going to go to certain places," Katrina surmised. She swiveled her head around, examining the area. "Dark places."

"Dangerous places." Jax honed in on the docks. Several sets lined the river's edge.

"That one." Jake pointed to a large pier, much wider than the others. "Under there."

"If I were a human there's no way I'd go underneath there. It's dark. Dirty." Katrina nodded in agreement. "Maybe I'd venture in to go to the bathroom or something, but it's not safe under there."

Jax took stock of the iron girders that emerged from the rocks. As on the steps, graffiti splattered their rust-covered surfaces. White drainage pipes caged the entrance but gave a wide berth for access. The gray blocks were littered with trash, clothing and other odd items. A cemetery of sorts, nothing living emerged. In contrast, the cemented river walk above teemed with life.

"We go in and get out. I told Kat that I think whatever we're looking for, it may show itself to just her."

"If Ilsbeth was in a hurry, she may have just stashed it," Jake guessed.

"But she'd planned for me to find the ring. The knife. I was the only one to feel those things. It was my blood. The

282

message told us where to go. Why wouldn't she have planned this too?"

"Maybe." Jax sighed, and reached for her hand. "Or maybe she planned to put it here but ran out of time."

"We could be wrong about all of this, you know," Jake pointed out. "Are you feeling anything," he paused, incredulous he was even asking, "witchy? You know...any tingles?"

"No, smartass. I don't feel anything. I think we have to err on the side of logic."

"Kat?" Jake called to her.

"Yeah?" she asked.

"Sorry about the witchy thing. I know it's not really funny. I'm just frustrated."

"It's okay. And I wouldn't expect you to treat me any different."

"There's only one way to find out what's under here." As much as Jax loathed the idea of exploring the filthy underbelly, they had little choice. "You ready to roll?"

"Yep." Katrina gave him a small smile and squeezed his hand.

"Right behind ya," Jake called over to them.

"Watch your step," Jax warned. "There's broken glass all over the place."

The Alpha ducked as he stepped underneath the pipes. The stench of mold and stale water filled his nostrils, and he heard Katrina cough in response. He thanked the Goddess for his night vision, otherwise they'd be walking blind. Twenty feet into the cavern, he stopped to investigate the grotto. He ran his fingers over the peeling rust, and brushed it off on his jeans. A noise caught his attention. Focusing in, he observed an empty trashcan tossed about in the current that slapped against a wooden piling.

Reluctantly he let go of Katrina's hand as she tugged it away. Scanning the darkened abyss, he reasoned Ilsbeth could have hidden an object practically anywhere. Heavy tires, steel beams and hundreds of mildew-covered rocks blanketed the ground.

"We need a plan," Jax noted. "Jake, why don't you search near the water? Kat and I will look up here."

"Maybe we need to think about Ilsbeth," Katrina suggested.

"How do you mean?" Jake asked.

"Well, let's assume, giving her the benefit of the doubt, that she was trying to help us."

"That's a big assumption, Kat." Jake picked up a stone and threw it into the water. "I know you guys think I'm coming down hard on her but you don't know what it was like for D. She put him through hell. Jax, think about it, you know as an Alpha. What would happen to a wolf who could no longer shift? It's kind of presumed that if you can't shift, your beast is dead or doesn't exist. He would lose his pack. His family."

"True," Jax acknowledged. It was a hard reality. Dimitri would have been an outcast. A friend of the pack perhaps, but he'd no longer be allowed to participate in pack activities. His entire life would have been destroyed.

"I'm not asking you to forgive her, Jake. And I'm

certainly not saying that Ilsbeth is innocent." Katrina's attention went to the far corner of the dock and then back to her wolves. "I'm just saying that in this situation maybe she chose to do the right thing. There have been times that she's helped people."

Jax didn't blame him for harboring resentment. The witch had cursed Dimitri in a most heinous fashion, one that could have resulted in his demise. Yet his mate's words rang true. Jax had already tried on one occasion to get Jake to understand that without the facts surrounding Quintus, there was no way to judge the circumstances of her actions.

"As much as I hate what she did, because it was disgusting, I think we have to also be logical," Jax insisted, his tone serious. "The more I think about this, the more I'm leaning toward her helping us. If Ilsbeth had meant us harm, I'm pretty sure we wouldn't have made it out of that house. No, I have to believe that for whatever reason, she wants us to find something that will help us stop these demons."

"All right. Let's say she was helping. Something attacks her at the coven," Jake theorized.

"Or maybe she knew it was coming?" Jax guessed.

"Ilsbeth wasn't tall. Maybe five three? I'm not aware of her ability to levitate. Demons? Maybe. Not witches. So that doesn't leave her a lot of options if she came down here on her own." Katrina licked her lips and pursed them in thought.

"Even if she climbed up on here," Jake kicked one of the concrete bases that surrounded the beam, "she's not tall enough to reach up in there."

"So either she hid it under one of these rocks or she hid it where she could reach," Katrina concluded.

Jax squatted, picked up a rock and set it aside. "The ground's not safe. Granted, a storm could take it all, but the water could wash it away more easily down here."

"So we're back to the idea that she hid it where she could reach." Katrina raised her hands and began to pace toward the land. By the time her fingers brushed the girders, both Jax and Jake had caught up, flanking her.

"It could be anywhere above us. Spread out," Jax instructed.

"I wish we knew what we were looking for." She sighed.

"It has to be a spell or instructions on how to get rid of these things."

"So, uh, and please don't take this the wrong way," Jake's eyes went to Jax, "but exactly who is supposed to do a spell here? It sure as hell isn't you or me."

Silence lingered, and Jax hesitated to point out the obvious. Although Katrina was still a wolf, her magick had taken on properties of other supernatural beings. He suspected that whatever the demon had seeded had faltered, yet the essence of witchcraft had set hold in her soul. Katrina's voice echoed in the darkness, and his suspicion was confirmed.

"I think it's me." She shrugged, continuing to search. "We already know that whatever they did changed me. I'm not sure why I can feel Ilsbeth, but she knew about me. I'm sure of it. We know that she knew about the demons, and supposedly asked for their help. I don't ever remember seeing Ilsbeth but maybe she *was* there. And Samantha," Katrina paused, "she knows I'm not right. I could see it in her eyes. It scared her. Because she knows it's unnatural."

"Yeah, well, Samantha shouldn't judge. You do know she wasn't born a witch," Jake asserted. "A mage did that to her."

"But Samantha was human. Weak. Katrina's nature is strong; her beast will fight the intrusion," Jax argued.

"What Mick said about Ilsbeth is true." Jake ran his fingers underneath the girder. "Aside from her bedroom antics, she was old school. Traditional. Now I know she helped Léo to get rid of a demon once, but to help one stay? I'm not sayin' she didn't do it, but it just doesn't all add up, why she would bring something here that didn't belong. It's out of sorts with how she was. She was all about getting power for herself, not giving it to someone or something else. Sorry, but that queen bee wasn't giving up the throne to no one, no how."

"Regardless of her involvement, she knew about me and obviously she knows about them. I mean she sent Quint…" Katrina's voice trailed away.

"What is it?" Jax ran to Katrina's side. Jake quickly followed.

"There." She pointed to the left, to where the concrete met the beam. "Do you see how it's cracked? It's almost as if…"

"It's not sealed. The cement's loose." Jax studied the rough surface and swiped his hand over it. Although it had been caked with mud, a crevice outlining a breakage surfaced.

Extending a claw, he skewered it into the dirt and scraped the crusty flecks until the visible rectangular perimeter had been exposed. Inserting his fingers into the fissure, he tugged at the jagged stone and it crumbled away. Reaching inside, he retrieved a rectangular tin box. The partially rusted container sat easily in his palm. Brushing the dust away, he inspected its red lettering.

"Family medicine?" Jake read the label.

"Aids digestion?" Katrina sighed with disappointment. "It's junk."

"It's an antique quack box. It was pretty easy to fool people back then, but when you think about it, not much has changed. Look." Jake pointed to the writing. "Chocolate coated. Guaranteed to work."

"Well it makes sense," Jax said.

"How's that?' Katrina asked.

"You saw that set up she had going in her office. The collections of novelties. All used for spells. She's been around for a long time. This box is simple," he explained.

"Classic," Jake agreed.

"Like Ilsbeth," Katrina whispered. "Open it."

Jax carefully removed the top and set it on the ledge. A single sheet of perfumed paper sat unharmed in the center of the box. A floral motif adorned the heading. As he lifted it out, the familiar scent of lavender drifted into the air. Jax exchanged a quick glance with Jake, and stared at the nearly black surface. A series of dashes and dots read across the page: -....-.. --- --- -.. / .-. .. -. --. .-.-.- / -.. . ... - .-. --- -

.-- / - .... . / ..... .--. .... --- -. .-.-.-.

"What the hell is this?" Jax tilted his head from side to side, stretching the stress out of his muscles.

"That's Morse code, man," Jake laughed. "Now of all the things I expected to see in a witch's fun box, that was not one of them."

"What does it say?" Katrina grazed the pad of her finger over its surface. "You were in the navy, right?"

"Hell, yeah." Jake smiled. "It says...shit, she's as cryptic as ever."

"What does it say?" Jax asked, his voice terse. He grew impatient with not only Jake but the entire situation. The stench underneath the docks intensified. The putrid scent of a dead animal permeated the air, and his instinct told him they should leave.

"It says, 'Blood ring. Destroy the siphon.'...whatever the hell that's supposed to mean."

"We'll figure it out back at the house. Let's get going. Something's not right here. Can you smell that?" Jax glanced behind him, searching for its source.

"Yeah, I thought it was the river," Jake replied.

"It's awful." Katrina coughed.

Jax set the note back into the box. Not wanting Katrina to sense his disappointment, he threaded his fingers through hers and began to lead her back out toward the river walk. Jax startled as Katrina tugged her hand out of his and ran back to where they'd found the box. He called for her to return, but it was too late.

❧ *Chapter Twenty* ❧

Katrina froze as she laid her hand over the forgotten tin cover, which was blanketed in frost. She went still, the apparition appearing before her. As it solidified, she swore her eyes were playing tricks. The beautiful vampire she'd met once long ago laughed, stretching out her arms. Her tight red dress strained against her wiry muscles. Contrasting with her alabaster skin, her red hair had been swept up into a perfectly coiffed French twist. She smiled, revealing her bloodstained fangs.

"Katrina, darling, there you are. You can run but you'll be with us soon enough." Her voice trilled, sickeningly sweet as if she'd been poisoned with saccharin.

"Dominique? What are you doing here?" Katrina blinked. Confused, she turned to Jax. Her vision tunneled and he dwindled into a speck in the distance. "Does Kade know what you're doing?"

"Your magick grows strong. Soon you'll be ripe once again." Dominique's booming voice shook the ground.

Katrina screamed as the gorgeous vampire transformed

into a creature she recalled from her nightmares. Like a scorpion, its tail whipped through the wind. The long piercing weapon slashed at the air, preventing Jax and Jake from reaching her. Its feminine hands and feet sprouted hooves while its face remained a perverted image of a human. Bald, its eyes glazed over, the red hue so piercing it caused her to squint. The unrecognizable mouth distorted into a massive cavern, a black pit of death.

It let out an ear-deafening screech as its tail scored the rafter of beams, setting off sparks. The scent of burnt metal wafted into the air. Smoke thickened underneath the dock until she could barely see through the black fog. She caught a glint of the bladed tail as it whizzed toward her. Darkness claimed Katrina, and the familiar touch of her mate comforted her. She would not die alone.

Katrina snuggled against Jax, dreams afloat in her mind. She stirred and pressed her lips to his skin. The hazy cloud began to lift and she ran her fingers over the familiar grooves of his abdomen. Even with her eyes closed, she recognized the distinctive scent of her mate, his soothing masculine essence cloaked around her.

Memories of the incorporeal being she'd encountered at the dock flooded back, and she struggled to remember how she'd returned safely to their bed. Katrina had met the ginger vampire at a party once. While she'd been a snarky aggressive female, one not to be trifled with, Dominique had never struck her as ill-willed. Devoted to Kade, she'd served him well. The savage monstrosity that had emerged out of the ghostly form shocked Katrina, and she wondered if she'd hallucinated. The illusion had seemed so real, but confusion persisted.

Jax's soft voice drew her out of her contemplation, and Katrina's eyelids fluttered open.

"Hey, baby, you okay?"

"Hmm…that thing," she began.

"I saw the vampire, but she disappeared."

"What? No." Katrina shook her head, disoriented. "The thing. It was a demon. Its tail. You saw it, right?"

Her question was returned by silence and Katrina's eyes filled with tears. *I'm losing my mind.* As if it wasn't bad enough that her magick had changed, that she sensed things at Ilsbeth's house, had been told by the warlock she'd been contaminated, she now questioned her sanity.

"It's okay, Kat. Please," Jax said, holding her tighter still. "I did see Dominique…if that was Dominique. I don't know what the hell it was. So if you saw something else, believe me, both Jake and I saw you. You were frozen, then started screaming and collapsed."

"I'm scared," she admitted. Katrina's strength had been surging ever since their mating, yet it had splintered apart in the presence of her perpetrator.

"What did you see?" Jax asked.

"It was this thing. A monster. This sounds crazy." She sighed.

"I've seen things, Kat. When they captured me," Jax said. "You know I'm a strong wolf. But the beatings, I don't even remember what they looked like…the attackers. At times they looked human. Other times, they looked like something out of hell. So whatever you saw last night, I believe it. Don't go doubting yourself."

"It was so real."

"Black magick can be powerful. That night in the club, when I thought it was you, I touched you and you were as real to me as you are now. If they can fool me into thinking that was you, whatever they are doing is serious."

"I just want to be done with this. I want a normal life. I want to take you to my gallery. I want to show you my paintings and run with you in the pack. I want to be free again. Not just free," she smiled up at him, "but I want to be with you. I was alone for so long."

"Tell me about your mom and dad," Jax asked, attempting to distract her thoughts from what had happened under the docks. He knew that she'd been raised in New Orleans, but there was so much to discover about his mate.

"My mom is strong-willed." Katrina laughed. "And my dad has a hard time keeping up with her. He stepped down as Alpha a while ago, let Marcel run the pack. Tristan had gone to Philadelphia. Hunter left for Wyoming. They wanted to travel, and if you're gone six months out of the year, it's kind of hard to lead a pack."

"How long was he Alpha?" Jax ran his fingers through her hair and brought a strand to his nose.

"He ran it for two hundred years, give or take. Right

now, they're in some remote part of the Amazon. My mom is a scientist, so to speak. Looks for rare species and sometimes gives her findings to research companies. And Dad likes to explore with her, so he goes along for the ride. I wish they were here, though. Because then we could ask them if they know something, *anything* about what happened that would cause them to come after me."

"Still, what Mick said is true. It's rare for one to have so many connections to Alpha blood. Your father. Your brothers. And now your mate."

"My mate." She gave a small laugh. Her thigh draped across his waist, brushing over his dick.

"What's so funny, woman?" He noted that she'd changed the subject, but with his hand finding its way to her breast, he lost focus. Caressing it gently, he circled her areola with the pad of his finger.

"I can't believe it. I know you don't realize how much of a crush I had on you. It's embarrassing," she admitted.

"Embarrassing, huh? Sounds pretty awesome to me."

"I loved fantasizing about you." She smiled and flashed her eyes at him. "But the real thing is so much better."

"Fantasies, huh? Now we're getting to the good part. Let's hear it. Ah," Jax groaned as she cupped his testicles, smoothing her thumb over the crinkled skin. His length thickened as her fingers lightly teased his shaft.

"Let's hear what?" Her lips curled against his skin as she took his nipple between her teeth.

"What did you fantasize about? Like what would happen?"

"Are you serious? I can't tell you that."

"It's making me hard just thinking about it. Tell me, ah shit, yes," Jax cried as she fisted his cock.

"My Alpha," she growled, her tongue laving his chest. "You really want to hear about it? All right. I'd fantasize that I'd be at a museum. Maybe a party. I'd see you across the dance floor."

"Dancing is good. Foreplay."

"Hmm…but soon I'd be the only one there, and you'd…" She giggled.

"Don't stop," Jax breathed, unsure whether he was referring to her story or the fact that she'd tightened her grip.

"You'd undress me right there. No one would be there, but it was the thrill of knowing that anyone could see us."

"What happens next?" He smiled.

"Nothing," she lied.

"Do we need another lesson, my little wolf?" he questioned, sensing she hadn't told him the truth.

"We'd run away together and fall madly in love." Her voice trailed into a whisper as the words lingered in the silence of the night. Still unsure of Jax's feelings, her heart crushed, exposing her raw emotions.

Love. It had once seemed as elusive as catching a ray of a rainbow. Yet as she opened to Jax, becoming more vulnerable than she'd ever let herself be, she discovered the freedom in speaking the secret she'd never told anyone. In the bed of her mate, she no longer dreamed of making love. She dreamed of Jax loving her the way she'd fallen for him.

⤜⚜· *Chapter Twenty-One* ·⚜⤛

Jax delighted in Katrina's playful squeal as he turned the tables on his mate, rolling her onto her back. As he lay between her legs, supporting his weight on his forearms, his steel-hard shaft prodded her core. If only for a few heated seconds, he resisted burying himself deep inside her.

Katrina's sensual confession had turned heartfelt, revealing more than a passing lust. It exposed an exceptional future, one he craved more than the air he breathed. Jax couldn't say he ever thought he'd fall in love. But the raging emotion taking hold of his heart healed his broken world.

"I like your fantasy." Jax gazed into her eyes, a smile crossing his face.

"Jax...I...what about yours?" She blinked.

"You're it, baby. I'm living mine." Jax's lips captured Katrina's as he thrust inside her.

Her mouth parted, gasping for breath, as his cock speared inside her. They gazed into each other's eyes, the sensual urgency palpable. With every ounce of passion he possessed, his lips caressed hers, and she responded in kind.

His simple kiss spoke the intense emotions he couldn't yet articulate. Rocking in and out of Katrina, he grazed her pelvis against his. As she arched upward, taking him deeper, he increased the pressure against her clit.

"That's it, Kat. Just feel me…feel how much you mean to me," he told her, his lips hovering above hers.

"Jax…yes…there…" Her eyes widened as her head tilted back toward the headboard.

Never had he made love with a woman the way he'd done with Katrina. The passion in her eyes as she reached climax tore at his heart, the raw intimacy exposed. Her breath was ragged as she came, her gaze focused on Jax. Fingernails stabbed his shoulders, and he reveled in the pain, her body shuddering underneath his.

As her pussy fisted his cock, the quivering vise ripped his orgasm from his soul. He stiffened against her, whispering her name. Jax's mouth grazed her temple, the salt of her tears on his lips.

Katrina completed his life, and the great Alpha knew that his beast had, in its own way submitted, to nature, to his mate. Falling for the little wolf, a new Alpha was born, and he would give his own life to protect her.

Jax scanned the courtyard, pleased that he'd purchased the Vieux Carré mansion. Gas lamp sconces flickered alongside hundreds of tiny white lights that ran up the side of a massive wall of ivy. In the corner, an iconic three-tiered fountain sat majestically, its gentle stream of water babbled, the calming waterfall echoing through the silence. Potted Palmetto palms lined a brick walkway that ran along the perimeter of the outdoor space. He glanced to Katrina, who enjoyed a swim in the large rectangular pool, and dreamed of a day when their vacation home would be filled with only joy.

Jax's attention was drawn to Jake's voice. They'd been sitting outdoors, discussing the contents of the tin box they'd discovered. *Blood ring. Destroy the siphon.*

"So what do you think it means?" he asked.

"I think we do what it says. I haven't even brought this up with Katrina, but I'm pretty sure she has to do something with that damn ring. My best guess is that she uses the boline to bleed onto it. But honestly, it looks like a piece of junk. I just don't get how this is going to do anything at all."

"Let me see it." Jake picked up the antique piece of jewelry. He ran his finger over its octagonal crown, scraping bits of dirt away from the top, revealing a dark blue sapphire. "Ah, look at Daddy's little pretty."

"Humans are particularly vulnerable to poison. Think about it. Going all the way back in time, nature has always provided means of death long before weapons were designed." Jax studied the object as Jake rolled it in his fingers. "Leaves. Berries. Naturally occurring substances to chemical derivatives. Modern drugs, even."

"This baby makes it easy to commit murder. Suicide,

too. It's easily concealed and often undetectable. But there's a catch, using a ring." He held up the object to the candlelight. "If you're going to kill, you have to get close to your victim."

"True. The murderer would have to dispense it into a drink. But that's not possible with a supernatural. When we confront these things, they aren't going to just drink it."

"Maybe it has to go into them another way. It seems to me that all these things are basically living on borrowed time. They're essentially dead, using the same black magick to shift and get around."

"So what are you thinking? You get one, you get them all?" Jax's lip tugged to the side in thought, and he pinched the bridge of his nose. "But still, what do you do with it?"

"Not sure."

"The whole purpose of a poison ring is to use it. To conceal the murder weapon. Throughout time people have used all kinds of things to poison people. Darts. Knives."

"Really anything can be used if you're injecting it." Jake flicked the side of the ring. "There's something here. Here, feel this."

"I don't want to break it by forcing it open." Jax took it from Jake, and skimmed his thumb along its surface.

"Or worse, spill whatever is in it out."

"Grab me a glass off that tray, would ya?" Jax picked at the rust until it revealed a tiny ridge. As he inspected it, the fine lines of a hinge appeared.

Jake retrieved one and set it in front of Jax.

"Thanks." His eyes went to Jake's as he flicked the small

attached lever. "If it releases the poison, we'll catch it."

Jax held his breath as he worked, giving it a strong shove with his finger. The metal popped as a tiny lancet ejected.

"And the plot thickens," Jake mused.

"Yes it does. So maybe you don't drink anything," Jax surmised. "Maybe you put the poison on this and stab the person. A little bit will do ya, as they say."

"The question is, how is the blood used? Let's assume it's Kat's blood, because let's face it, she's the one who has the craft flowing through her like a river. Does she just open the ring? Mix her blood with the poison?"

"Well, until she actually opens it, I'm going to go with all of the above. I'm curious about what's inside, but I really don't think we should open it here. Instinct tells me that it's best we leave it closed until it's time for the show."

"Yeah, I hear you. It's like opening a tube of toothpaste. Whatever's in there could be much more than just powder. Might not be able to get it back in. Knowin' Ilsbeth, she's got a surprise stuffed in here."

"Let's just keep this under wraps for a while, okay? Tomorrow we'll jet home and talk about it to Kat on the plane. Right now, I just want her to relax." Jax's focus went to his mate, who rested her arms and head on the edge of the pool.

"Is she okay? You guys didn't get up until late."

"She doesn't remember what happened at the dock," Jax disclosed. "And we're not going to tell her."

When Katrina asked him if he'd seen another creature under the dock, he hadn't completely told her the truth.

While he'd seen something that appeared as if it were Dominique, what he hadn't shared was how Katrina had changed. Transforming from solid into a mass of splintered lights, she'd convulsed in a translucent state.

He hadn't thought twice about running to her, and by the time she'd fully materialized, she jolted violently toward the ground. If he hadn't been there to catch her, she'd have cracked her head open on the rocks. She'd remained unconscious until they returned home, scaring the shit out of him. Exhausted, she'd only spoken a few words, before falling into a deep slumber. After sleeping most of the day, she'd finally awoken, but seemed to have no recollection of the entire incident.

"You sure about not telling her what we saw?" Jake tilted his head in question.

"As much as I hate keeping secrets from Kat, I don't see any benefit in telling her tonight. She's already upset that she saw something we didn't. She says she saw some kind of demon thing. Last night, it shook me up seeing her like that."

"Yeah, that was kind of fucked up. Scared me, too."

"We're gonna have to work as a team. I want to get home and get this shit done. We'll bring the pack. I'm going to call Quint in too." Jax reached for his beer. "Tonight we rest. Tomorrow we fight."

"I have to say that Katrina looks no worse for wear. She actually looks happy," Jake observed.

"Yeah, she does. It's not that she doesn't know what's going down, she's just centered." Jax watched as Katrina swam back and forth in the pool, her creamy bottom breaching the surface.

"A late night swim is most definitely a good idea." Jake gave Jax a devious smile.

"She's pretty amazing, huh?" Jax still couldn't believe how hard he was falling for Katrina. The sight of his beautiful mate caused his heart to pause. Katrina completed his life, made him whole. If he died today, this would be enough.

"Look at you," Jake teased.

"What?"

"Hey, I don't blame you. Kat, she's a terrific person." Jake picked up his glass and took a swig of the ale. "You don't know. When she first came down here. She'd been in Philly a good part of the past hundred years. But she fit right in, ya know? Just like she'd never left. Marcel? If anyone messed with his sister, look the fuck out. He didn't fool around when it came to her. When he died, she was devastated. The past couple of years haven't been easy on her."

"She's resilient."

"It's gotta be scary for her to have all this shit going down with her magick, but she doesn't give up. A lot of wolves would have just said, 'fuck it'. But she's tough. She's got that Alpha blood in her, all right."

"Yeah, she does," Jax agreed.

"I just have to ask you something." Jake hesitated and scrubbed his fingers over his hair. "I know it's none of my business, but when it comes to Kat...I can see she's falling for you. So I don't know what your intentions are, but you were kind of a playboy in New York. It's not like some guys just give up that lifestyle. Some wolves, even after they're mated, act like bastards."

"What are you trying to get at?"

"Don't hurt her. It's as simple as that." Jake stared out over the veranda to the cabana on the far side of the pool. "If you do...hey, I know we've kind of become," he half coughed and gave a smirk, "what I think I'd say is friends, but I'll kick your ass all the same."

"I imagine you think you will." Jax laughed. He found it humorous to hear Jake challenge him in such an affectionate manner.

"I'm not kidding."

"I know you're not." Jax took a deep breath and considered his next words. "Jake...I think we need to talk about something."

"Yeah."

"You and I. Remember the first time we met? How you felt about me?"

"Do I need to get a box of tissues for this convo? I'm starting to get the feels." Jake smiled.

"Do you need to be such a jackass? Don't answer that. I already know the answer." Jax shot him a side glance and mindlessly dragged his thumb over the raised lettering on his beer bottle. "I'm trying to be serious here. Do you remember?"

"What about it? We met in New Orleans. You were an asshole. We fought. Saw you again in New York. Still kind of an asshole." He laughed. "Okay, maybe less of an asshole, but still. That kind of makes a nice fairytale, huh?"

"Fuck you."

"I'm still looking for my happy ending." He winked. "What do you say, Alpha?"

"Can you be serious for one fucking second?"

"What?"

"Did you ever stop and consider why you have this incessant need to challenge me?"

"Um, was I not clear about the asshole part?" he joked.

Jax shook his head and glared at him.

"Come on, Jax. What? I don't know. You're just kind of different than most Alphas I've been around."

"You've been around who? Marcel? Tristan? Logan? Am I right?"

"Yeah."

"Tell me what happened in San Diego."

"Why are you asking me this?" Jake's expression turned somber. He rimmed the edge of his glass with his finger.

"Just tell me," Jax pressed.

"After we killed Chaz, you know Logan sent me out there. It was a mess."

"Challenges?"

"Yeah, it's not like they threw me a parade. How would you feel if some strange wolf you didn't know came in and beat the shit out of every male in the pack and declared himself king of the kingdom? They didn't know me. And I didn't know them either. But hey," he exhaled and shrugged, "it didn't matter. I had a job to do. I know what it's like to follow orders, Jax. When you're in the military, you do what you're told. Sure, you may give leeway here and there, but you don't argue. You're an Alpha. You tell your wolves what to do and they'd better damn well do it."

"And you left because?" Jax left the question hanging.

"I left because I needed to help your sorry ass. Granted, things weren't exactly under control when you got home but Finn and I did our best."

"What about San Diego?"

"What about it? I chose a person who seemed decent enough to run the pack and I left." Jake sighed. "Okay, what's with all this cryptic shit? Why does it matter why I left? I'm an Acadian wolf. Always have been, always will be."

"That's true, but you know, sometimes our nature guides us outside our pack. Before you say another word," Jax held up a silencing hand, "just hear me out. I've been Alpha for a long time. Longer than any of the other Alphas you've known. Unlike Marcel, Tristan and Logan, you didn't know me, so our first meeting was a little rough, but," he laughed, "it's to be expected, given the situation. Look, Jake, under different circumstances, I'd keep quiet, let you navigate this by yourself, because I believe you truly will work things out. But given this situation with Kat…"

"What does she have to do with anything?" he interrupted.

"The fact of the matter is that you went to San Diego because you were sent there. That's all well and true. But once you got there you fought. By virtue of that, you became Alpha. Not just an assigned Alpha."

"That's different…"

"No, Jake. It's not. You may have been sent to do a job but you did it in a way that earned you that rank. I suspect that when Logan sent you, he knew what I knew." Jax glanced to his alluring mate and back to Jake. "You've always had the capability to be an Alpha. We're born that way. Programmed to lead. And if we get the opportunity, we snatch the brass ring."

"I belong here," Jake insisted, his jaw tensed.

"Maybe. Maybe not. Hey, I'm not telling you what to do. I'm just explaining the reality of the situation. You can joke all you want but it doesn't negate what happened in San Diego."

"Yeah, well, you're right about one thing. It's not your decision what I do."

"But when it comes to Kat…"

"Wait a second. Does this have something to do with what that damn warlock said?" Jake closed his eyes and blinked them open, registering where the conversation was going. "What we did yesterday in the kitchen, that was fun and all but I'm not going to get in your way. I know you guys are mated. I just want to see her be happy."

"I appreciate that." Jax locked his eyes on Jake's. "Yeah. Yesterday was cool. And it's part of the reason why I think we can take things further, help Kat."

"Take things further? As in you, me…Kat?"

"Here's the deal. Even though you left your pack, the power you have inside you, that raw energy that only an Alpha possesses, it's there. Do I believe every word Mick is telling me? Hell, fucking no. There's something that rubs me the wrong way about him. But I do believe that if we work together," Jax's focus went to Kat and he smiled at her, "I think we might be able to seal up whatever magick gets in and out of her. Tomorrow, we all have to go back and face these things. She needs to be as strong as possible."

"And you really think that if we do this, it'll help her?"

"I know it will. It's not going to change the fact that they messed with her. Hell, she may go the whole rest of her life affected by the witchcraft, for all I know. But I don't give a shit. As long as she can shift, she's going to be okay."

"You sure about this? The three of us? You know I've always loved Kat. Well, not love love, but you know what I mean," Jake explained, his voice strained.

"Calm down, Jake. Yeah, I'm as sure as I'm going to get. In the end, it's up to Kat though."

"I know better than anyone that she's not going to go doing something she doesn't want to do." Jake gazed to Katrina, who had turned her attention to her phone. "Hey, man. Does Logan really know?"

"About you? I'm sure he does. But it's like you pointed out. This is your choice. You've established yourself as an Alpha. I understand your reasons for leaving. Helping me and my pack was a convenient reason to leave San Diego. It made it easy. But I'm challenging you now...challenging you to consider what's going to happen to the wolves you left behind. Maybe after this is all over you might want to take some time off to think about what you want to do. How will it feel as the years go by and your natural tendency to lead pushes Logan's limits? Your own limits?"

Jake drifted into silent contemplation as he brought his drink to his lips. Jax set a hand onto his shoulder, and stood, giving him space. The Alpha respected the young wolf more than he knew. The night of Nick's death, Jax had observed through blurred grief how Jake fought for his own life. Jake had battled valiantly to save his sister. Two wolves had almost died that night.

Jax set his attention on his mate, crossing the patio to the edge of the pool. As his eyes went to Katrina, he knew full well that the connection between him and Jake would intensify, not only by making love to her, but fighting once again, side by side, in battle. He considered that besides Finn, he hadn't opened himself to another friend since the fateful night his beta died.

But as Katrina smiled up at him, his heart tightened and he knew he'd do anything for her. A war would come tomorrow. Losing Katrina or Jake wasn't an outcome he could conceive of nor accept. He'd gladly die first before letting anything happen to either of them.

"You okay?" Katrina asked.

"I was just about to ask you the same thing." Jax knelt down to her. His eyes drifted to her rosy tips. They jutted through the brightly lit water and quickly disappeared underneath.

"Swim with me?" She smiled.

"You know neither of us just answered that question." A small smile formed on his lips. Droplets of water beaded on her chest, tempting him further.

"Maybe it's because we already know the answer. We're both doing pretty well as long as we have each other," she replied. Her gaze darted to Jake and back to her mate. "Is he okay?"

"Yeah, I think he'll be all right." Jax settled onto the concrete, dipping his feet into the water. Her hands glided up his calves, and his arousal spiked. He laughed to himself, thinking that he hadn't been this horny since he was a teenager. All she had to do was smile at him and his dick turned to stone.

"So we go back to New York tomorrow, huh?"

"Once we get back, we'll go meet the pack out in the country. I'm thinking we'll take the ATVs. Trek the rest. Some of us will go wolf." Jax had already strategized the attack in his mind. "How about for the rest of tonight we just relax? Watching you here in the pool…you know you have me worked up."

"Hmm…do I now?" she flirted. "You know, I really could use a lifeguard. Someone to give me mouth to mouth."

"I'm highly trained." He winked.

"Really?"

"Spent my summers at the Jersey shore."

"Should I be jealous?" She smiled, her fingers traveling underneath the hem of his shorts.

"Never, baby."

"So tell me, Mr. Lifeguard," Katrina purred. She withdrew her fingers and reached for his waistband. Unbuttoning and unzipping him, she freed his erection into her waiting hands. "Do you always go commando? Because I kinda like that."

"Yeah, ya never know when you gotta strip down and run." Jax sucked a deep breath and edged toward her.

"Don't you mean swim?"

"Run? Swim? Whatev... Kat," he gasped as Katrina licked the tip of her tongue over his crown.

Jax leaned back onto his palms and took in the sight of his mate. Mesmerized, he froze as she swallowed him into her warm mouth. Her tongue caressed his cock, and his legs tensed as arousal threaded through his body. He closed his eyes, savoring the sensation and groaned when she sucked hard, a twinge of pain running up through his testicles.

Controlling him with only her mouth, she slid her hands around his hips. Jax sucked a breath as she stabbed her nails into his ass, leveraging herself so she could take his entire shaft down her throat. Her teeth teased his sensitive skin as she withdrew and then plunged him back through her lips. She moaned, humming and sucking him, and he arched up inside her.

Holy fuck, I'm going to come. "No, no, no...Kat. I want to be in you." Jax took a deep breath, stemming the explosion that teetered so close to climax. He gave a small laugh as she released him and licked her lips like a kitten with milk. "Enjoying yourself?"

"Hmm…yes." She fisted his shaft and continued to deliver deliberate slow strokes.

"You're trouble." Jax leaned forward. Reaching underneath her arms, he lifted her up out of the pool and shoved to his feet. "The best kind."

She giggled, wrapping her legs around him. Jax kicked off his shorts and crushed his lips onto hers. The cool water soaked through his shirt, her hands tugging at the fabric. Their desperate kiss was interrupted as they heard the sound of a chair grate against the patio.

With his mouth on hers, he gave a sideways glance to Jake, who stopped briefly to give him a small smile. Katrina's line of vision followed his until their lips slowly separated.

"It's up to you," he whispered in her ear.

Sharing Katrina would not come without consequence nor would it come without a price. He'd considered the implications. Over the past week, he'd opened his heart to not only Katrina but Jake as well. His mate gave him a renewed strength, and his budding friendship with the wolf reminded him of the bond he'd had with Nick. Caring for both of them energized his soul, yet it also introduced a new level of vulnerability. If anything happened to either of them, he doubted he'd recover.

His focus went to Katrina, whose expression registered a common understanding. Both excitement and arousal coursed through his veins, and he gave her a small nod in acknowledgement. Bonded with his mate, he knew the power of another Alpha would help protect her in battle.

As Katrina extended her palm to Jake, Jax's cock thickened. Jake never made a move, his eyes locked on hers.

"Come," she called, her voice soft and husky.

"Be good to her," Jax warned.

Aware that Jake would never touch her without his permission, Jax gestured for him to join them. He'd invite Jake to infuse Katrina with the power of an Alpha, but he knew they'd only go so far, that he wouldn't share all of her with him. He planned to carefully control their sensual play, directing their erotic interlude.

Without waiting, he carried Katrina to the cabana and laid her on the bed. She smiled up at him and her happiness resonated deep within his chest. Water droplets glistened across her slick skin. His palms wet from touching her, he stroked his cock. Sensing Jake's presence, he turned to the wolf.

"You sure you guys are okay with this?" Jake asked.

"Isn't my mate beautiful?" the Alpha responded, ignoring his question. Jax wasn't sure if he could honestly answer yes, but his wolf didn't protest. His sole concern was Katrina and Katrina alone.

"She's amazing," Jake replied.

"Come to me, my Alpha," Katrina whispered, reaching for Jax. "So close to the full moon. My wolf, she yearns to run free. I need you."

"We can't exactly run in the city but we can make love in the moonlight," he responded.

Jax climbed atop the mattress, and smiled at her. He settled between her legs, spreading her thighs wide. Her chest rose and fell in anticipation of his touch, and he scented her desire.

In his peripheral vision he caught a glimpse of Jake tugging his shirt over his head. The sight of his bare chest surged his excitement; the anticipation of watching Katrina explore her secret fantasies within the safety of their bond spiked his arousal. He suspected Katrina would enjoy being with two wolves far more than she'd ever expected.

"Come," he told Jake, a devilish flare in his eyes. Positioned between her thighs, Jax pressed his lips to her stomach.

Jake's legs brushed his shoulder as he went to lie next to Katrina. Although the wolf's erection jutted at her hip, Jax sensed his apprehension.

"Touch her," the Alpha directed. Katrina sighed as Jake caressed her with his hand. Taking a ripe tip between his fingers, he rolled the swollen peak. "Yes, just like that. Her breasts...they're so soft. You like that, baby, don't you?"

"Hmm...yes." Katrina arched into Jake's touch, tilting her hips toward Jax. Jake kept his eyes locked on the Alpha, seeking guidance.

"Tell him what you want, Kat," Jax instructed, his lips peppering kisses over her hip.

"Kiss me," she breathed, her eyes set on Jax's. "Ah..."

Jake's gaze went to Kat's, and his mouth captured her nipple. Taking both breasts in his hands, he laved at the pink treasures. Both she and her Alpha watched in fascination as Jake attended to his task, sucking and licking them into hard points.

"That's it. See how much she enjoys your mouth on her? Tonight is all about Katrina," he told him. "We're going to make you feel so good."

Jax slid his thumbs down through her slick seam, and opened her wide. As he dipped his head between her legs, he smiled at Jake. His cock stiffened at the sight of him making love to Katrina. His mouth descended onto her pussy, his tongue darting over her clit. He delighted as she shivered underneath him.

Desire coursed through him, and he sent his power flowing through her. The sweet surrender of sharing was transforming into one of the most intimate experiences of his life. Having bonded with Katrina and now connecting to Jake, he reveled in the moment. With his heart mended, he wondered if it wasn't him who had needed healing.

❧ *Chapter Twenty-Two* ❧

Katrina's heart pounded in her chest with the anticipation of giving herself to both wolves. The sight of her striking Alpha taking control caused her to flood in arousal. Although Jax's commanding nature was possessive, she caught the savage desire in his smile as he watched Jake pleasuring her. Wolves were more sexually open than other species, but she'd never thought he'd accept another male in their bed. Given their new bond, she knew that the only reason he was doing it was for her, to strengthen her magick. Selfless, her loving Alpha had seeded the idea yesterday. Although she'd always been attracted to Jake, and he'd become a good friend, she'd never taken him as a lover…until now.

Her body sizzled as both men put their lips to her skin. Their raw power infiltrated her soul. Katrina gasped as Jake sucked her ripe tips, making love to her breasts. Jax drove a thick finger into her core, and she moaned, rocking her pelvis into his touch. Every last cell ignited on fire as his delicious tongue rasped back and forth over her clitoris, delivering erotic laps to her pussy. Ripples of pulsating waves speared through her, and she wrapped her thighs around his torso, bringing him closer to her. Raking her fingers into Jake's dark brown hair, she lifted his head, catching his heated gaze. His mouth descended gently upon hers, and she pinned her eyes on Jax as he sucked her swollen nub between his lips.

"Jax," she cried, as her mate's teeth grazed over her clit. Her orgasm lingered in the distance and she raised her hips, seeking more.

"You taste so good, baby. Fuck yeah." He speared three fingers inside her, giving no quarter. "I need you, Jake. Come here."

"No, no, no," Katrina protested as Jax withdrew. "I'm so close, I'm so close...ah...."

She fought for breath, clutching at the bed. Jax raised her leg, catching it under her knee.

"Lick her pussy." Tapping her mound with his cock, Jax directed Jake.

"Jax...I..." she panted.

"I want you to taste how delicious she is." Jax gave her a wicked smile as Jake brought his tongue to her clit. "That's it. Lick her just like that. Look at how pink and wet she is."

"Hmm... holy hell," she cried as Jake used his fingers to spread her labia open, gaining better access to her hidden pearl.

"Hold on, little wolf. Things are about to get interesting." He laughed.

"Jax...oh..." Katrina inhaled loudly as her mate

sheathed himself inside her. Inch by inch, his enormous cock filled her tight channel. The sweet twinge she experienced as he stretched her open was offset by Jake flicking over her swollen nub.

Jax secured her thighs, hoisting her legs over his shoulders, rocking in and out of her. Katrina lost a sense of who was touching her. Clutching at Jake's back, she sighed as he sucked her into his mouth, the tip of his tongue ruthlessly laving her clitoris. As Jax pounded in and out of her, she was helpless but to accept the mind-numbing pleasure they lavished upon her.

"I can feel your pussy tighten all around me, baby," Jax grunted. "Oh yeah, she's so close, Jake. Let's do this."

Jax gave a hard thrust, his crown grazing her sensitive band of nerves. Jake increased the pressure on her hooded bead and Katrina screamed, coming hard. She shuddered uncontrollably, her head thrashing from side to side as her orgasm ripped through her.

"Yes...so good. Please, please, please," she panted. Incoherent, she trembled as the last waves of her climax claimed her.

Struggling to catch her breath, she gave a squeak as Jax pulled out and flipped her onto her stomach. Katrina rubbed her face into the bed, still tingling all over her body. Stretching out her palms, she raised her bottom, presenting to her mate. She quivered as he ran his palms up her inner thighs, tracing his fingers lightly through the crease between her legs.

"Hmm...Jake sure does know what he's doing, huh?" he

commented with a wink to his friend. "Do you want to suck his cock? I think I'd like to hear him scream."

She was taken off guard; no one had ever talked so dirty to Katrina. Exposing her inner desires, her Alpha continued to push her, giving her permission to enjoy parts of her sexuality she wasn't ready to admit she enjoyed.

"Get in front of her," Jax ordered.

Leaning onto her elbows, Katrina set her vision on Jake as he settled himself against the back of the bed. He stroked his shaft, running his thumb over the wet opening. Katrina's lips parted, hungry to taste him.

"Don't move," Jax told her. She gasped as he slid his finger inside her core and removed it. "You're so fucking wet. Taste how sweet you are."

Guiding his hand to her mouth, he skimmed his thumb over her lips, parting them. As she nipped at her mate's fingertips, Katrina watched Jake fist his dick. Licking and sucking, she moaned as he pleasured himself.

"You make me so fucking hard. Watching him do that to you? Jesus, you're hot," Jax praised her. "You ready for Jake, now?"

"Hmm." She nodded. Katrina reached for Jake but Jax stopped her.

"No, baby. I'm controlling this show," he told her, his voice low and rough.

Katrina's pulse raced as she caught the interaction between the two males. Jake lay back, submitting to the Alpha. The intense stare between them turned heated as Jax reached for Jake's cock. Jake grunted as Jax gave it a firm stroke before he set its crown to Katrina's lips. She closed her eyes as he swiped her mouth open with the hardened shaft. Katrina lapped at his head, the taste of his salty essence teasing her tongue.

Putting her hand over Jax's, together they guided Jake's cock into her warm mouth. She relaxed, opening her throat, and swallowed him. Jake moaned, and the sound of his pleasure drove her to take him deeper.

Jax retreated and dragged his hard length down the cleft of her bottom, teasing her wet opening. As he entered her from behind, she gasped, but never let go of Jake. He slowly slid inside, and her core tightened with each slow thrust.

As they made love, a surge of their power rippled through her. The added unfamiliar energy of Jake took her by surprise. Her magick intertwined with theirs. Like an orchestra, the individual instruments brought a unique quality to the piece they created together. The weakened portals in her psyche weaved together, fortifying and sealing the breach that had allowed her magick to seep away.

"Yes…" she breathed as fingers teased open her back hole. Releasing Jake, she stroked him as Jax pounded into her from behind.

"I'm going to take you here right now, Kat. Do you understand?" he asked, his tone demanding.

"I…I'm not sure if I can do this." Despite her words, Katrina had already decided to submit to her Alpha's darkest fantasies. She yearned to embrace every erotic lesson he sought to teach her.

She turned her head back to Jax. He withdrew quickly

and reached for his shorts. Retrieving a small tube, he returned, and she knew he'd planned this, regardless of Jake's participation. Her Alpha was calculating, a man who always took what he wanted. Possessing her, he'd claim every inch of her body and she was certain she'd enjoy every second.

Katrina shivered, waiting for him to fill her. As the cool gel dripped down her crevice, she inhaled in anticipation, his head brushing over her back hole.

"You're gorgeous, Kat." Jake gently caressed her hair, gazing into her eyes.

"I'm going to go gently, baby. Just relax into me, and push back," Jax instructed. "Breathe."

"Ah…Jax." Katrina's lips parted, and she did as he said. A slight twinge rippled through her as he entered her tight band of muscle.

"Don't tense. Just let me in. That's a girl. Oh yes…just a little more." His fingers circled her clit, and as he settled in further, pain was replaced by saturating pleasure.

"So full," she cried, patiently waiting for him to move. But he remained still inside her, giving her time to adjust to his dark intrusion.

"Ah fuck. Just give me a second," he pleaded.

"Please…Jax." Katrina sucked a breath, her nerves on fire with desire.

"Easy now." Slowly, Jax pulled out and rocked inside her, all the while caressing her swollen nub.

Jake held her hair as she slid him into her mouth. Overwhelmed with arousal, she laid her head on Jake's thigh as she sucked his cock. Moving in a simultaneous rhythm, Jax penetrated her. He increased his speed and intensity, plunging in and out, until they both shivered on the precipice of orgasm.

"Ah, I'm so close. Please, Kat," Jake begged.

"See what you're doing to him…"

Katrina barely heard her wolves, the rush of her climax teetering on the edge. She tightened her grip on Jake's shaft, fisting him, and still sucking. Jake's hips arched up into her mouth, his body shaking.

"No, no…I'm going to…" Jake tried to pull away, but she held tight.

The power of her Alphas surged through her body. Unable to hold back her release, she removed Jake from her lips.

"My Alpha…" Screaming Jax's name, a wave of ecstasy slammed into her.

"Oh yeah, Kat, fuck yes," Jake grunted, his milky essence spilling onto her breasts.

"That's it. Yes, yes…" Jax gave a final thrust, groaning, his glorious cry slicing through the air. "Ahh!"

Katrina's body went limp as the last remnants of her release rushed through her, the electricity of their explosive energy humming in her body. She'd experienced Jax's extraordinary power, but with Jake's added, her magick spiraled out of control. A warm washcloth on her skin lasted only a minute, before Jax swept her up into his arms. Cradled against his chest, she scented her mate. A peaceful sensation settled around her, the love of her Alpha rooted deep in her soul.

Love. Never in her life had she told someone she loved them. Until now, letting someone inside her heart had never been an option. Waiting over two hundred years for her mate, she'd denied herself precious intimacy. Her perfect match, Jax pushed her limits and gave of himself so she'd be healed, strong enough to fight for both of them.

In her mind's eye, her wolf ran to his, together at last. In the morning they'd face reality, but for tonight, she closed her eyes, content to be within his embrace. *Loving her Alpha.*

Chapter Twenty-Three

Jax's heart contracted as he watched Katrina sleep. Teasing her hair into his fingers, he considered the feeling that proliferated inside his chest. As a boy, he'd thought he'd fallen in love with the human girl. As a man, his juvenile crush paled in comparison to the emotions he held for Katrina. He'd always wondered what it would be like to be mated. While it was true that his wolf's need to bond had been sated, it was his human need for intimacy that surprised him most. More than content, he couldn't stop from smiling.

"I love you," he whispered, the words true to his heart. Saying it out loud exhilarated him. He considered telling her when she woke, but he didn't want to scare her with his confession nor did he want her to think he'd said it because of their dire situation.

His thoughts drifted to their interlude at the pool. Making love with her and Jake had been incredible. Connecting with Jake filled him with a deep sense of satisfaction. Their friendship, because of both the situation and Kat, had deepened to a level he hadn't thought he'd experience again with another male.

Although he'd felt his own power mesh with Jake's, he was unsure how it affected Katrina. He suspected it strengthened her, but it remained to be seen. They might not know for sure until they were confronted with the demons.

Jax glanced to the clock. In another five hours, they'd board the plane for New York. He planned to hold a pack meeting and announce his mating before they returned to the dungeon. He'd need the support of his wolves going into battle. Although Katrina would have to earn her right to remain in the pack, Jax was confident of her ability to lead with him as part of the Alpha pair.

A loud bang to the door jolted him upright. He jumped out of bed and shoved into a pair of jeans. Jax quickly covered Katrina and took off down the stairs to address the source of the menacing noise. The incessant knocking intensified, and as he swung open the door, he was confronted with the angry vampire.

"What the hell did you do?" Luca accused. He barreled toward Jax, shoving his chest with both his hands.

"Out of courtesy to my mate, I'm going to give you one warning. Calm down. Put your hands on me again, and you'll regret it," Jax growled.

"I'm sick of you fucking wolves..." Luca charged, raising a fist.

With preternatural speed, Jax snatched his arm out of the air. Twisting it behind his back, he shoved him up against the wall, and jammed his face between the stair rails. Jax reached for a wooden spindle and snapped off a shard, stabbing it between Luca's shoulder blades.

"You know, I really tried to be nice, but you're lacking manners." Jax's eyes darted to Jake, who walked through the threshold. Holding a white paper bag and cardboard beverage carrier, Jake stopped and assessed the situation.

"Hey, no one told me we were having a barbeque. Are we making shish-kabob?" Jake gave Jax a sly smile. "I brought café-au-lait. Sorry I didn't bring enough for everyone…didn't know you were expecting company."

"Funny thing, neither did I." Jax dragged the point of the stake over Luca's shirt, tearing through the fabric.

"Beignets though? Got plenty of those." Jake set the drinks onto the floor. He slid behind the steps and dangled the pastry bag under Luca's nose. "If you're a good vamp, I might let you have one. But something here tells me you're messin' with my boy."

"Fuck you," Luca spat. "Where is she?"

"See?" Jax commented. "No manners at all."

"Did you ever hear that expression, 'you catch more flies with honey'?" Jake reached into the sack and retrieved a powdery beignet. He took a bite and smiled at Jax. "I think he may have missed that one."

"Here's your choice, Luca. Because clearly we got off on the wrong foot. I can release you and we can discuss this like adults. Or," Jax paused.

"I think you might want to listen to this part, big fella. Bite?" Jake held the pastry to Luca's lips. "No? Okay, suit yourself but they're delish."

"I could take this stake and drive it right through your rude ass. Because honestly, I have a lot of my own shit going on right now, and this? Yeah, I don't need this right now."

"You'd better tell me where she is. I told you that she wasn't allowed around you or Katrina, and now…" Luca unsuccessfully struggled to free himself.

"Um, Jax…" Jax peered up to Katrina, who stood at the top of the steps wearing his t-shirt. Despite the serious situation, the sight of her warmed his heart and he smiled up at his mate.

"What's going on?" She yawned.

"Nothing, baby. Luca here…well, you see, it seems like he didn't get his coffee this morning."

"You know what that does to vamps. It's terrible," Jake added with a laugh. "Just can't do a thing until he gets his joe. Cranky pants."

"Okay, let's try this." Katrina padded down the steps until she was at eye level with Luca. Setting her gaze on him, she brushed back her hair, twisting her ponytail. "What's going on, Luca? And why is my Alpha holding a stake to your back?"

"Samantha," he breathed. Luca shook his head in frustration. "She's been missing since last night."

"Jax, let him go. Please," she pleaded.

"Only if he says he'll behave. Otherwise, I'm good with killing him."

"Jax, come on." She turned to Jake, who rolled his eyes and gave another chuckle.

"Beignet?" He offered her the bag.

"Thank you, no." Katrina stepped around him, making her way to the landing. Standing next to Luca, she put her palm on Jax's arm and leaned to speak to her friend. "Luca, you know we're friends, but you can't just come into an Alpha's home and threaten him. You may be old and strong but Jax is just as old, and please don't take this the wrong way, but Jax will kick your ass. He's Alpha for a reason, sweetie. Now I'm really sorry that Samantha is missing but we had nothing to do with it. You need to calm down so we can talk. Can you do that?"

Luca blew out a ragged breath, and set his sight on Katrina. "Fine."

"See." Katrina's eyes darted to Jax and then back on Luca. She spoke to him softly and slowly as if he were a child. "Now take a few deep breaths and relax. Count to ten. Come on, do it."

Katrina looked to Jax and mouthed the words, 'Put that away', glancing at the stake. The Alpha shook his head no. "Please."

Jax's body surged with anger for the asshole in his hold. The vampire had crossed a line by coming into his home and attacking him. If it had been any other person, they'd be dead already. The only thing saving his sorry ass was the fact he'd been friends with Katrina. Inwardly Jax laughed, considering how his mate was already changing his actions.

"Are you going to behave?" Katrina placed her hand onto Luca's shoulder and he nodded. "Promise. I cannot protect you if you break my trust."

"I promise," he spat.

"Jax, please let him go," she asked.

"I'm telling you right now, asshole. You're extremely lucky that you have such a pretty friend. But if you go after me again, even she can't save you." Jax shoved him one last time before releasing him. He sighed as Katrina rushed into his arms.

"You know, you wake up and you think, 'I'll go get some breakfast.' But you just never expect this kind of shit at seven in the morning. It was exciting, though. I was kind of hoping for shish-kabobs. Guess not," Jake joked.

Luca stumbled back against the wall, and brought his hands to his face. Jax held tight to Katrina, sensing she was about to go to him. It wasn't as if he didn't care that Samantha was missing but the vampire had no right accusing him of wrongdoing, let alone attacking him.

"What happened?" Jax asked.

"Avery called the house last night." Luca closed his eyes slowly then opened them again. Holding his hand to his forehead, he continued. "I didn't want her to go, but you know these witches…everything's been a mess with Ilsbeth gone. She, uh, she was a difficult woman, but she kept her coven out of trouble. This Mick fucker, he's out partying in the middle of nowhere. That might be fine for some of the witches but there's a lot of them who are more traditional. They stay in town. Last night, Avery called. Said she'd decided to move back to the Quarter and wanted Sam's help getting situated."

"Did she go alone?" Katrina inquired.

"No, I dropped her off at the coven house…like I've done a million fucking times before. I told her I'd be back in a few hours…which I was."

"How does she just go missing?" Jax threaded his fingers through Katrina's.

"I went to pick her up and they said she left with Avery to get some supplies. That's not out of the ordinary, so at first, I didn't think much of it. There're a couple of stores in town where they get things for spells and so forth."

"But she never came back," Jax concluded.

"No. I went and tore up the coven house looking for them and there was no sign of either of them. So I drove all the way out to Mick's. He wasn't there but I searched the whole place. I mean," Luca sighed, "I could tell she wasn't there. I didn't even scent her but I had to look."

"So you decided to come here?" Jake asked

"Yes. Look, the other day…at Ilsbeth's." Luca's eyes went to Katrina. "Samantha told me things."

"Like what?" Katrina's tone was terse, and Jax squeezed her hand, reminding her he was there for her.

"Jesus Christ, Katrina. We've known each other forever." Luca paced, avoiding eye contact. "But she said you had magick in you. Not the kind you're supposed to have. She said when she touched you, your aura…this is going to sound crazy."

"Just say it," Katrina pressed.

"She said, ah fuck," he stopped to look at her. "She said you felt like Ilsbeth. Now like I said, you and I, we go way back. If you were Ilsbeth, I think I'd damn well know. But you scared her, okay?"

"I'm not Ilsbeth." Katrina broke free of Jax and crossed to Luca. She reached for his hand. "I'm still me, but Sam is right. They did something to me. There's magick inside me that isn't mine. Something about Ilsbeth's house the other day...it affected me....spoke to me. I don't know why it's happening, but I can tell you that we had nothing to do with Samantha disappearing. I swear it."

"But we will help you find her." Jax approached Luca, setting his palm onto Katrina's lower back. "There's one thing we agree on. This thing with Avery is suspicious and Mick is the only one who might have an answer. We're going back to New York today, but first, I think we should pay Mick a visit before we leave."

"I'll call the chopper," Jake told him.

"But I was already at Mick's place. I told you that she wasn't there. I couldn't even find him."

"Maybe you couldn't find him. Or maybe he was hiding? Or maybe he just was off in the woods? Regardless, I think we should give it a try. Between Katrina's magick and us scenting as wolf...if he's there, we'll find him. My guess is that the warlock knows exactly where Avery went," Jax surmised.

"But Samantha would have never gone with her. She would have called me by now," Luca explained.

"If Avery is a player in this circus, we have to find out."

"Seems like she was his toy," Jake noted. "A mistress, I'd bet."

"More like a prize student," Katrina added.

"Here's the plan. Let's get dressed and we'll copter back to Bayou Goula." Jax reached for his back pocket and checked the time on his cell phone. He pecked at the glass. "Jake, call the pilot and have him shift the departure time to New York. I'm texting Finn to let him know we're going to be late, but he'll have the pack together by the time we get there."

"Are we meeting in the city or how's this working?" Jake asked.

"We'll fly into Newark and take the chopper up to the Finger Lakes. There's a pack house a few hours outside of where they held us. Once we get there, we have to work fast. For whatever reason, these things seem to have better radar on Kat when she's not in New Orleans."

"Could have to do with Ilsbeth," Katrina guessed.

"Maybe. This place is loaded with wards, every which way you turn. At home, you're much more exposed."

"This is our home." Katrina smiled at Jax, who gazed up at her from his cell.

"Yeah, I guess it kind of is now, isn't it?" Jax acknowledged. He glanced to the empty living room and made a mental note to ask her to help him decorate. Although he loved New York City, this was Katrina's birthplace. She had friends and family in the Big Easy, as well as her own gallery. It wasn't lost on him that she hadn't asked to visit it, but he suspected she didn't want to put her employees or neighbors in danger by doing so.

"I have to find her." Luca's voice wavered as he spoke. "Our baby...she's due any day now. She's been through so much. Dominique…"

At the mention of the vampire, Jax's eyes darted to Jake then to Kat, before settling back on Luca. He hadn't planned on mentioning the incident at the docks. But Jax had heard that Dominique had kidnapped Samantha a few months ago, almost killing her. After having experienced shape shifting first hand, thinking he'd seen Katrina in the club when he hadn't, he doubted more than ever that they'd truly seen Dominique. It was much more likely that they'd seen an apparition or a glamour created by witchcraft.

"Luca, I wasn't going to tell you this, but the other night," Jax paused and glanced to Katrina, "we all saw something that looked like Dominique."

"What?" Luca exhaled loudly and closed his eyes, an expression of shock washing across his face.

"Just hold up there, okay? Before you think it was her that kidnapped Samantha again, I've got to tell you, we don't think it was her. This thing looked like her, but that's where it ends."

"What are you saying? It was someone dressed like her? She's been missing for months."

"Just what I said…it looked like her. These things…demons, witches, whatever they are, they're using some kind of magick to make themselves look like other beings. But they haven't been successful with wolves."

"Demons have always been able to possess humans. They're weak," he noted.

"Yeah, well. Apparently they've replicated their little trick with some vampires too," Jake told him.

"I don't know what started them down this path, but Mick seems to think they are looking to take over packs. I personally don't believe one hundred percent of what comes out of his mouth, but that day they took me…that woman on the floor looked like Katrina. In her human form anyway. We don't know if they can transform into animals yet."

"This is too much to process. Does Kade know?"

"No, I haven't told him. Been kind of busy here. You're welcome to text him, but the fact of the matter is that we don't know exactly how or why this is happening. Somehow the witches are involved. I'm pretty sure Ilsbeth had a hand in this somehow. All we know for sure is they've been stealing Katrina's magick over the past three years. What they're really planning long term is anyone's guess."

"I want to help, Kat, but my priority right now is Sam. We've got to find her." Luca paced, his hands on his forehead.

"Let's go get dressed." Jax reached for Katrina's hand and led her toward the staircase. "Jake, you mind keeping watch on the vamp?"

"You got it, boss." Jake gave a small smile and eyed Luca.

As the Alpha ascended the steps, he glanced back to the vampire and shook his head. Before Luca had had a chance to ask for help, Jax had already decided to search for the redheaded witch. With child, she'd never survive the kind of torture the demons had inflicted on him.

He racked his brain, attempting to put together the pieces of the puzzle. Nothing was an isolated incident as far as he was concerned. *His own kidnapping. Dimitri losing his wolf. Ilsbeth disappearing afterwards. Katrina's infusion of witchcraft. The warlock. Avery's role in Samantha's disappearance.* His mind churned the facts, and although he couldn't definitively find the correlation between them, he was becoming more convinced Ilsbeth had instigated a chain reaction of mayhem. Maybe she'd meant to do it, maybe not. At this point, it mattered little. A demagogue, she was powerful enough to spark the trail of destruction.

Jax took Katrina into his arms, kissing her hair. A scant scent of chlorine from her midnight swim still remained and he smiled, thinking about making love with her. Determined to find and destroy the demons, he swore to the Goddess that today would be the day. Their nefarious existence was coming to an end.

Headphones muffled the deafening sound of the whirling blades. Jax concealed his shock as they circled the scene. From the air, he viewed the incinerated remains of the building. Red-hot embers kindled, wispy tendrils of smoke spiraled toward white puffy clouds. The odor of the charred wood seeped into the aircraft cabin.

As they descended, Jax observed a small group of witches on the front porch of the original mansion. He found it interesting that it had gone untouched while the newer structure had completely burned to the ground.

"What the hell happened here?" Jax heard Jake ask as the helicopter touched down.

"I doubt the magick man torched it himself," Jax responded. "But then again, who knows?"

"That guy is an asshole," Luca spat. "Don't get me wrong. Duplicity was Ilsbeth's middle name. But we could count on her to help keep things under control. This guy? He says he's about 'going back to nature' but it's all a bunch of fuzzy bullshit. He's more interested in fucking than developing the coven. He left Samantha and the other witches in the Quarter to fend for themselves. It's been a shit show."

"Couldn't Samantha or someone else have taken over? Kicked him out?" Jake asked.

"Ever since I was turned, Ilsbeth's been in charge. I love Sam, but before I knew her, I wasn't terribly fond of witches."

"Or wolves," Kat added.

"Or humans." Jake smiled.

"Oh please. Vampires are far superior creatures. Humans are…well, they are interesting but I tire of their weak nature." Luca sighed. "My point is that I have come to respect the witches. Samantha…she's strong. An amazing woman. Her power is growing, no doubt, but she's pregnant."

"Back to Jake's question, wasn't there anyone else who challenged him? I find it hard to believe that Ilsbeth hadn't groomed any other witches," Jax pressed, sensing that he withheld information,

"At this time, there is no one who can fight Mick," Luca hedged. "His party slash feel good style approach of running the coven appealed to several of the witches who'd grown tired of living under Ilsbeth's iron fist."

"Luca, you search the house. Kat and I will question Mick. You're too upset right now to do it. I have a feeling you might drain him before we get answers. The last time we were here he seemed to be in a sharing mood. We don't have time to get into a pissing match." Jax turned to Jake. "Go wolf. Run the woods and see if you can scent Samantha. Let's be as fast as we can. If Sam's not here, we've got to look elsewhere."

"You got it," Jake answered, peeling off his clothes.

"Are we on the same page?" Jax asked, pinning his gaze on Luca.

"Yeah," he grumbled.

"Don't fuck it up. Get your shit together for your witch. We're going to find her."

Not waiting for the pilot, Jax wrapped his fingers around the handle and shoved open the door. He stretched out his hand to Katrina and helped her step onto the gravel driveway. Out of the corner of his eye, he caught Jake leaping out of the helicopter, his tail wagging behind him. Jax gave Luca a nod of warning.

The warlock approached, this time wearing only shorts and a fitted yellow t-shirt with a smiley face on it. His face, marred by soot, wore a somber expression.

"Alpha. You'll understand if I don't extend a greeting." He held up his blackened palms. "My wonderland has been ruined."

"I see." Jax hesitated, deciding not to apologize. "Luca needs to search for Samantha. She's missing."

"Yeah, I heard that he came lookin' for her earlier. But Sam hasn't been here. This isn't her scene."

"All the same to you, we need to search. I'd very much appreciate your cooperation." *Or I'll force you, and it won't be pretty.* Jax gave a cool smile, hoping the warlock understood the implications of his choice should he refuse the request.

Mick's eyes darted to the vampire and back to Jax, his lips tense with anger. "But of course. Search away."

"Thank you. I knew you'd understand." Jax gestured to Luca, who set off toward the dilapidated home.

"If you don't mind me asking, what makes you think Sam would be here?" Mick scrubbed a dirtied hand through his hair.

"Avery. She was at the coven house," Katrina explained.

"We'd like to talk to her," Jax told him.

"Avery, Avery, Avery. Fucking turncoat bitch. You think you can trust someone," he sneered.

"Trouble in paradise?" Jax raised a questioning eyebrow.

"She gave me a hard time about being with Elsie."

"Elsie?" Katrina asked.

"Yeah, Elsie. Well, Elsie and Amber...Natalie, too. Look, I'm not tied to one witch. That's the beauty of what I preach here. But Avery, she thought she was my girlfriend." He put his hands on his hips and shook his head, rolling his eyes. "This...this fire. She did this. I know it.

Jealousy is a very ugly emotion. Coveting what others have. No, my love is free. It always has been. She didn't understand."

"You had a fight last night?" Jax asked.

"Yes, it's why I sent her away. She's no longer welcome here. Of course I didn't have the heart to kick her out of New Orleans. This is her home after all. I could be a hard-ass but it's not like I'm channeling Ilsbeth. That's not my style. Fuck, if you pissed off Ilsbeth, you'd find yourself at the end of a nasty spell, like waking without a hard-on for the rest of your supernatural life. Either that or she'd ban you from the entire state of Louisiana. I'm better than her. I'm a compassionate leader," he professed.

"Yeah, I'm sure you're a real Mother Teresa." Jax wasn't buying the warlock's song and dance. Something about the story didn't ring true, yet he couldn't prove it false. "Avery had a hand in Samantha's disappearance. So if you know where your girlfriend likes to hang out, it's time to spill."

"Are you hard of hearing? I just told you she's not my goddamned girlfriend." Mick raised his voice, a tick in his temple visibly pulsated as sweat beaded on his forehead. He took a deep breath, his demeanor switching back to his previously calm state. "Forgive me. Avery is a free spirit. She could be anywhere in the bayou, but I suspect she's held up in a vampire bar in the Quarter. I'm afraid I cannot help you."

"Got a text number?" Jax pressed.

"Yeah, give me your phone."

Jax took out his cell, bringing up the contacts. He

handed it to Mick, who pecked out the digits into the directory. Jax accepted it back and pressed send.

"Direct to voicemail," he commented and proceeded to tap out a text message to Avery.

"Doesn't surprise me she's not answering. Always forgets to turn on her phone," the warlock told them. "Look, I've got nothing else to tell you. But please, feel free to join the vampire. And when I say feel free, I mean, go find him. I've worked hard to keep this a no fang zone, and I'm sure the girls aren't very happy he's sniffing through their things."

Jax didn't bother saying thank you as he took off with Katrina toward the house. After his interaction with Avery, he'd witnessed her mischievous nature. She'd taken great pleasure in making Katrina jealous, deliberately coming on to him. But at no point had he sensed malevolent intentions from the witch.

The warlock, on the other hand, presented as a ditzy mess of a leader. In all his years, Jax had never met a high priest who loosely attended to coven members the way Mick did. The flare of anger the warlock had displayed may have been a natural reaction to the destruction of his club, but was contrary to how he'd acted in the past. Jax doubted that Ilsbeth had ever groomed him, and he wondered who else was strong enough to lead the witches in New Orleans or who might be vying to be a high priestess. Even though Mick had taken over since Ilsbeth's disappearance, it was likely others were staging a coup.

Noting the rotted wooden step, Jax tested it with his foot before ascending. It crackled underneath his shoe but held.

Two women wearing colorful sundresses rocked back and forth in a vintage porch swing, unfazed by the creaking of the rusted chains that secured it to the peeling ceiling above. They gave him a small smile, and Jax thought their placid disposition odd, given the fire.

Instead of making casual conversation, he ignored them and reached for the screen door. He peered inside, scanning the area before allowing Katrina to follow him into the foyer. The stale odor of musty carpets saturated the air, and he noted a faint scent of cat urine. The walls, covered in textured wallpaper, had been partially scraped, revealing teal-colored paint. Large bins filled with debris sat stacked in a corner along with several paint rollers.

"Luca!" Jax kept his sight trained on Katrina, who inspected items that rested on a wooden curio table.

"Looks like they're renovating. Sage," she speculated, picking up a clump of herbs and holding it to her nose.

"Apparently so. Guess it's good they have a place to live."

"You think she did it?" Katrina asked.

"Avery?" Jax shrugged, his eyes inspecting a large antique chandelier that hung precariously from the second floor ceiling. The hundreds of crystals dripped from the light fixture like pearl necklaces.

"She seemed to enjoy causing trouble the other night. But it doesn't quite make sense." She paused and set her focus on Jax. "Why hit on you if she's in love with Mick?"

"Exactly." Jax loved how his mate's mind worked, as he'd been thinking exactly the same thing. "Do you hear him?"

"Upstairs," she responded. "Luca!"

"Let's go up…" Jax stilled, as his cell phone buzzed in his back pocket. Retrieving it, he slid his finger across the glass and froze as the image appeared. Although he was hesitant to show Katrina, he wasn't about to keep this secret from her. "Kat, I need you to come see this. We're going to find her."

"Oh Goddess, no," Katrina exclaimed.

Jax immediately recognized the location, its brownish stone walls stained with the blood of its victims. Sitting, she appeared calm, despite the flecks of fear in her eyes. Her mouth had been duct taped shut, he presumed to keep her from uttering spells. With manila rope bound around her wrists, her hands rested on her swollen belly. *Samantha.*

➸❦ *Chapter Twenty-Four* ❦❖

Jax weaved his way through the crowd, making a concerted effort to personally greet every wolf in the pack. With over a hundred adult members in attendance, he'd been acutely aware of every precious second that passed. Although he knew they sensed his bond, and quite possibly scented her in the building, introducing Katrina as his mate required patience.

Through the A-frame wall-to-ceiling windows of the ballroom, dusk fell over the shimmering lake. While Jax generally retreated to his private luxury cabin, he'd built the mansion for pack meetings and company events. The two hundred and ninety acre property housed a boat house, three swimming pools, a basketball court and a bowling alley. With over thirty rooms, it easily accommodated groups of out of town guests.

What Jax hadn't anticipated was fighting an enigmatic adversary on his own turf. While they'd fought the occasional territorial war over the years, wolf against wolf, he'd known his enemy's weaknesses and strengths. Tonight, however, they were going in on a wing and a prayer. A medieval ring coupled with the promise of a cryptic message. At best, they were theorizing that Katrina would have the power to ameliorate the demons, using the slice of the ring and her blood. At worst, Ilsbeth had set them up for failure, a cruel joke added to the damage she'd already inflicted on Dimitri.

Calming Luca down after he'd seen the image of Samantha had been no small feat. The vampire had been on the edge of losing it completely, and Jax had considered leaving him in New Orleans. A loose cannon, Luca could be more of a detriment than a help if he decided to go rogue. Only after gaining Kade's assurance that the vampire agreed to defer to the Alpha's orders had Jax allowed him to come to New York.

On the flight up to New York, Luca had disclosed Samantha's rapid rise within the coven. Trained under Ilsbeth, she'd hidden her abilities from other witches, concerned that her power would be misinterpreted as threatening. Luca and Samantha had discussed the possibility of her becoming high priestess after Ilsbeth had disappeared, but they'd decided it wasn't in the best interest of the baby to cause any conflict within the coven. With child, she'd retreated, only practicing her craft within the safety of her home. They expected a daughter, and it was foretold she'd be a witch.

Tonight they'd work together to destroy the demons. Freeing Samantha was critical, not only to ensure the safety of her child but for her to help fight the black magick. Jax knew as well as Luca that it was a miracle she was even pregnant. A rare phenomenon; vampires didn't have children. It was only through the magick of his mate that they'd conceived.

As Jax approached the podium, the room went quiet, and he sensed her presence. *Katrina.* Planned to the second, she'd arrived exactly on time. Luca, Finn and Jake protectively surrounded her as she approached. Even though they'd been together just hours before, his heart caught, seeing her. Her long blonde hair had been braided down her back. Jeans and a black leather jacket presented an edgy exterior but he knew in their private moments, his mate softened, fit him comfortably and perfectly.

Intrepid and confident, she smiled at him. Goddess, he loved her. Revealing the secrets in his heart would come soon, he knew. But when he did it, he planned to make it special. No demons or witchcraft, fear of death or war would be involved when the words were spoken. The memory of their love would be an extraordinary, unforgettable moment.

Silence in the crowd morphed into a low roar and Jax tapped the microphone. Katrina, Jake, Finn and Luca joined him on stage. He gave them a small nod before he began.

"Agrestis Wolves. Today is a beginning and an end. An evil has been brought to New York. This enemy, these creatures are responsible for my abduction. They practice and utilize an insidious form of black magick, the likes of which I've never seen. The demons, they seek to shift into wolves." Jax inhaled, pleased his pack had snapped back into obedience, listening attentively. Despite Katrina's presence, they hadn't challenged her…yet. "Their goal is to steal the magick that belongs only to wolves. They don't wish to only replicate our human forms. They seek our beasts. The animals that run free within our souls. They seek to infiltrate our packs."

Jax paused to allow the message to take hold, then he continued.

"They have the ability to cause illusions. They lie. And they're here in our state. Our territory. Our woods. Where we run. Where we raise our pups."

As he expected, muffled whispers rumbled through the crowd. He held up a silencing hand.

"They've taken Luca Macquarie's fiancée, Samantha…a witch who's with child. They're also responsible for impersonating and kidnapping Katrina Livingston." Jax drew a breath and reached for his mate, who placed her hand in his. "You may ask, why should I care about Katrina, a Lyceum wolf?"

Jax brought her to his side and wrapped his arm around her waist.

"As many of you know, Agrestis Wolves have endured a contentious past with Lyceum Wolves. My father…some of you lived under his savage reign. You watched as he incited territorial wars, brutalized wolves and humans alike. You watched as he beat his own son. You watched as I returned to challenge him, to kill him, to lead Agrestis Wolves as your Alpha. However, you were not the only wolves who took notice of my father's sins. Tristan Livingston has been rightfully cautious of me over the years. While I have never been my father, nor will I ever be, his heinous acts continue to leave a blemish upon my reputation. So when these demons lied to Katrina, she asked her brother to keep me away from her. Although the untrue rumors proliferated, Katrina only sought to protect me from what she thought would be my certain death. But the fact of the matter is that you cannot deny what nature demands. If it is meant to be, destiny will bring two individuals back together. That's exactly what happened the day I rescued her. You see, Katrina," he smiled at her and turned his focus back to the pack, "she's my mate. The bond is complete."

Silence blanketed the room at his announcement. After he had killed Arlo earlier in the week, most would think twice about challenging his mating. However, when they shifted to wolf, Katrina would have to establish her own dominance.

"I know this may come as a surprise to some of you, given past events, but I can assure you that her heart is true. Our bond is strong. Unbreakable. I'm giving you fair warning that my mate is tenacious. So should any of you choose to challenge her or our bond, it will not end well."

Jax caught the ire that flared in London's eyes. He'd anticipated that quite a few females wouldn't accept their mating and wished to be clear about the situation.

As expected, Katrina remained quiet, deferring to him. At some point, she too, as part of the mated Alpha pair, would direct the pack. Although Katrina was typically friendly, he predicted she'd kill before letting another female take her place at his side.

"Tonight most of you are running wolf. Some of us are taking the ATVs so we can go human when we get there. Finn's going to break you up into teams. I'll need several of you to stay here to mind the pups and protect the pack house," he directed, his voice serious. "These demons and whatever witchcraft is driving these things will die tonight. It is the only acceptable outcome. Be mindful of the vampire who chooses to fight with us. As I mentioned, Samantha, the redheaded witch, is pregnant. If…" He turned to Luca, and restated, "…When we find her, I expect you to protect her as you would one of your own. She can help us fight these things but only if she is allowed to speak. Okay, let's do this shit. I'm ready to get on with leading this pack and I want these fucking things dead and out of my State."

Diabolical energy whipped through the wind, and Jax struggled to concentrate. As they'd journeyed through the forest's edge, Katrina had warned him of the impending storm, but he hadn't asked how she'd known. She appeared unaffected, her arms wrapped around his waist. Ever since their encounter with Jake, her magick had grown more stable. No longer did it seep away, causing her weakness, or to doubt her ability to shift. But neither did it negate the witchcraft that had broken through her psyche.

Thunder rumbled, and Jax gripped the handlebars. He swerved right, as lightning struck a massive white oak tree and uprooted it. It crashed to the ground, and Jax swiveled his head to check that Luca, who had followed his path, was unharmed. The vampire, undeterred, continued to trail behind him. Ahead, Jake and several other pack members trekked as wolf from the north. Finn headed up a second group, intersecting with them from the south.

Jax geared down the engine and slowed as they approached. He suspected whatever was inside the cave would sense their arrival. Both he and Katrina had discussed their experiences and had no recollection of the entrance. They only remembered the general location of where they'd escaped. Jax suspected the dungeon had more than one entry point. He recalled seeing multiple passageways and theorized that in addition to the torture chamber and adjoining cells, they'd discover a room of worship.

The quad came to a stop, and Jax turned to Katrina. She gave him a small smile, pressed her lips to his and jumped off the ATV. He followed her and scanned the area. Through the tainted air, he sensed his pack. His eyes darted back to Luca, who was already off his bike, his fangs extended.

As they approached the cave, the familiar door he'd shoved through to freedom came into view. Set into a thirty foot vertical cliff, the entrance was partially concealed by hanging vines. Although not visible, the whoosh of roaring rapids reminded him that the river flowed not too far away from where they stood.

"Do you feel that?" Katrina asked, gripping her jacket collar tight around her neck.

"Someone's not too happy to see us," Jax replied. Breaking limbs sounded behind him, and he caught sight of Jake and Finn padding toward him.

"Jake, you come with us. Finn, I need you to stay with the pack. There's got to be more than one entrance and exit from this place. I want you guys to find them. Once you do, set up guard."

Finn howled in response and Jake took his place next to Jax.

"Kat, you ready to go with the ring?" On the flight up to New York, they'd discussed how to utilize the items they'd found at Ilsbeth's house. As much as he loathed the idea of letting Katrina get close to the demon, they all suspected that only her magick would kill it. If it weren't for her, they'd have never discovered the mystical objects.

"As ready as I'm ever going to be." She retrieved the antique band from her front jeans pocket and slid it onto her finger.

"If for some reason taking one down doesn't take them all out, then this is going to be a whole helluva lot harder, but either way, we've got this. If we need back up, I'll call on the pack but I don't want to expose them to these things."

"She's here," Luca grunted, his palms pressed flat to the gritty stone. "Oh Jesus, no!"

"What's wrong?" Katrina ran to his side, settling her hands on his shoulders. He trembled beneath her fingertips.

"Sam's in labor. The baby," he screamed. "I've got to get inside."

Jax swung open the heavy door, easily passing into the tunnel. But as Luca went running toward the entrance, he slammed into an invisible barrier. His nose bloodied, he pounded it with his fists, to no avail.

"Wards," Jax noted.

"For Luca?" Katrina asked.

"I don't know. Could be for him or could be all vampires? Or maybe they're only letting us in because they want us here." Jax glanced down the dark passage, and heard the faint whimper of a female. Although he sympathized with Luca's anguish, time was of the essence. If they could free Samantha, it was possible she could release whatever wards had been set up to prevent his entry. "We've gotta go. We'll find her. She and the baby will make it out of here, Luca. Hang tight and keep trying to break through. If we can get to her, she may be able to help us, or when we kill these things, maybe the walls will come down."

"Swear to me." Luca's voice wavered, his eyes closing tight in frustration. Blood ran down his face and he made no move to wipe it clean.

"I swear to you. We'll get her. Just do what I say. We're running out of time." Jax tore off his shirt, readying to shift to wolf. He reached for Katrina's hand, his energy accelerating through his body in tandem with adrenaline. "Let's kill these things."

❧ *Chapter Twenty-Five* ❧

Katrina breathed in the dank air and fought the fear that threatened her courage. While Jax stripped off his pants and shifted to wolf, she'd peered inside an empty cell and recalled the times she'd been captured, reliving both her fear and rebellion. Never once had she given in, allowed them to break her. Exhausted and racked with pain, she'd endured. Despite the tendrils of trepidation coiling in her chest, she celebrated the chance to mete out justice.

A muffled sob echoed in the distance, and they both took off toward its source. Following Jax, she cautiously navigated the labyrinth. Her steps quickened, seeking the tormented witch who writhed in labor.

As the decades passed, Katrina's dreams of a family had become a painful indulgence, forcing her to accept her childless existence. Admittedly, she'd been envious when she'd first heard Luca and Samantha had conceived. Not only had he fallen in love but he'd been blessed with a family. However, she'd quickly buried the ugly emotion, electing to be happy for her friend. With the child's birth imminent, Katrina was determined to see her safely born into this world. *Samantha can't lose her baby.*

A pinprick of light flared in the distance, and Katrina's lungs burned as she sprinted toward the fluorescent rainbow. Jax and Jake ran ahead, barking in warning. As she stepped into the enormous stone cavern, she squinted, the luminous bursts ceding. Although confused as to what had caused the temporary explosion, Katrina concentrated on her task: finding Samantha.

She stepped carefully into the atrium, taking in her surroundings. Candlelit luminaries flickered, illuminating magnificent hovering stalactites. Like ominous spears of death, the sharp limestone dripped from the ceiling. In the center of the room, she caught sight of a darkened pit. Katrina spied a glass-encased cell, with a crumpled form lying in the corner. At first she thought it was the witch but as she approached she noticed the emaciated figure couldn't possibly be pregnant.

A moan stole her attention, and Katrina's chest tightened as she caught sight of Samantha agonizing on the bedrock floor. Wide tear-filled eyes stared back at her and she dropped to her knees. Reaching for the duct tape, Katrina attempted to remove it gently. Samantha's hands were bloodied from clutching at the dirt. Jax's familiar black wolf padded toward the witch and licked at her brow. Transforming to his human form, he knelt beside her.

"Sam, it's okay," Katrina lied, concerned they were far from safe. As she sat at her feet, the black magick spun in the air and she was certain the demons would soon show themselves.

"The baby," Samantha cried. She clutched at her belly, doubling over as a contraction seized her body.

"We should get you out of here." Jax brushed her hair from her eyes.

"No, no, no…too late…ahh!" Samantha released an ear-piercing scream as the pain tore through her. "I'm going to die."

"Listen to me, Sam. I've lived a long time. I've seen babies born before, and we're going to do this together. You and your baby are going to be fine. You understand?" Katrina locked her eyes on Jax in silent understanding. It had been years since she'd witnessed a birth, but given the circumstance, they had no choice. She glanced to Samantha, waiting for Jax to send her his energy. The power of an Alpha could usually only be felt by wolves, but she hoped for the best as Jax put his hands on her shoulders. "I'm just going to check you here, okay? Just let me have a peek and see how far you are along."

"Where's Luca? I can feel him. Oh Goddess, he needs to be here. I need him. Help me," Samantha cried. "She's coming."

"Yes, she is. She's going to be strong and beautiful, just like her mamma." Katrina lifted Samantha's skirt, taking note that she was almost fully dilated. "This baby is going to be coming any minute."

"Luca? Where is he?"

"There's wards. He's locked out."

"Oh Goddess. It's a trap. It's a trap," Samantha panted.

"He's here."

"It's going to be all right."

"Jax!" Jake's voice boomed across the cave.

"Kind of busy here," Jax replied.

"Dominique. She's in this…uh." Jake rapped on the glass with his fist. "It's some kind of a cage. I can't tell if she's dead or not."

"Sam, are you with me?" Katrina asked. It wasn't as if she didn't care about the female vampire, but a new soul was about to be born, and the child was her first priority. "I'm going to need you to push soon. Jax, just, I don't know….can you keep her head off the ground? Whatever you're doing with your energy, keep doing it. She seems calmer. Okay, let's get ready…" Katrina's voice died away as a flash burst from the center of the room.

Samantha rolled to her side, and Jax shifted back to his wolf. Katrina caught a glimpse of Avery teetering across the rocky surface. While she'd known the witch probably had something to do with Samantha's disappearance, her eye had been blackened and she appeared to be more of a victim than a perpetrator.

"Leave her alone," Avery spat at the cloud of dust that began to take form.

Katrina coughed, fine particulates drifting up into the air. She stretched the edge of her t-shirt over her nose and mouth, using it as a mask. Flecks of light danced, a human shape constructing itself before their eyes.

"So nice of you to join us, Kitty Kat," it cackled.

Mick. Katrina's stomach clenched, nausea setting in as

she realized what was happening. The warlock spun in a circle, holding his palms upward; bolts of electricity fired up toward the ceiling, causing rocks to tumble down onto them. Shirtless and barefoot, he wore only black slacks.

"You should see the look on your face." Mick slowed his pace, spewing maniacal laughter. Abruptly, he went quiet and faced Avery, his eyes blazing in anger. "This is none of your concern."

"You promised. You said you wouldn't hurt her." As if she were drunk, Avery's footing slipped, weaving as she walked toward Samantha.

"What the fuck are you doing?" Katrina screamed at him.

As Mick set his sights on the females, Jax and Jake attacked. The warlock whispered, flinging his hands toward them, causing a mesh of silver netting to fall from above. Both wolves shifted to their human forms, groaning as they attempted to dislodge the web of toxic metal. Katrina's heart dropped as Jax struggled. He shook his head at her, warning her off. In response to his command, she stayed put.

Samantha released a blood-curdling screech, and Katrina focused on the witch. The baby's head was exposed, crowning the birth canal; the child would be born any minute.

"Sam, I need you to push," Katrina told her in a gentle tone of voice, forced to ignore her mate's capture.

"That's right, push, push away, witch," Mick hissed, hovering above them.

"Stay away from us," Katrina ordered, giving him a brief

glare.

"There was a time I was happy partying in the bars, fucking whoever I wanted," he pondered, pacing back and forth. "But Ilsbeth, she helped me see the light."

"Don't touch her," Jax grunted, weakened from the silver.

"You see, the greedy little bitch had to have Dimitri. Yeah, he fucked her good, all right. She couldn't stop talking about him." Mick paused to pick up a sharp rock and hurled it at Jake. "What she saw in him, I'll never know. You wolves are so self-righteous with your pack mentality. The challenges. Submission. The brutality of it all. So uncivilized." He sighed and rolled his eyes, continuing. "Ilsbeth always wanted what she couldn't have. She couldn't handle the fact that he'd find his mate. She was desperate. Pathetic."

"That's it, Sam. Don't hold your breath. Take a breath and blow it out. You've got this." Katrina tried to ignore his oration, but she'd always known this had been tied to Ilsbeth.

"But to steal magick from wolves," Mick kicked Jax in the stomach, pleased as the Alpha spat blood, "it's not very simple. No, no, no. One must find alternatives to spells. In my defense, she asked for my assistance. She needed a very special kind of ingredient to kill Dimitri's wolf. So you see.... demons, they can be very useful at times."

Katrina concentrated on the baby as her shoulders breached.

"It's interesting, that saying, 'be careful what you wish

for'. Ilsbeth got what she wanted. She almost was successful too. But I've always been one to make the most of a party. Of course the demon wanted something from me in return. A vessel. But I'm no fool. I'd never let that happen. I didn't need another master, and demons don't exactly take orders from witches. They can, however, be tricked into teaching us their secrets. Ah….what I learned to do…" He laughed and danced in celebration. "I have learned how to transform myself. Others, too. Sometimes it's an illusion, sometimes it's as real as I'm standing here. The vampire," he pressed a palm to the glass cell and gave a depraved smile, "she was my first. It was so easy to steal her magick. The demon taught me well. Little experiments here and there. I was even able to turn little Avery here into a human, to have her do my bidding. She always enjoyed the fine art of torture. The last time she came for you. Ah, how she loved to hear you scream. Too bad she's been such a disappointment as of late."

"Ilsbeth caught you." Jax clawed at the netting, scraping a section away from his arm.

"Perhaps. But she started it all. I did what she asked. She got what she wanted. Dimitri. The thing is, she didn't care for my methods. When I showed her all that could be done here," Mick gestured to Dominique, "she wasn't as enamored with what I'd created, my transformation. So you can imagine when she saw Katrina. That day, oh, the lecture she gave. I suspect that's when she gave you a slice of her magick. She retreated into the boring purist bullshit she loved so much. A sly little spell, I'll give her that. That ring she gave you..."

"Belongs to me," Katrina retorted.

"Not for long, my dear. How I do wish I could have taken it from you in New Orleans, but her magick is strong. Ilsbeth cursed it."

"Protected it," Jax countered.

"You say tomato, I say fucking bitch...blah, blah, blah," he trilled. "Clever priestess. You would have known if I'd tried to steal it. I could feel Ilsbeth's vibe all over it. So of course, I imparted wisdom that day. Because I'm helpful like that. And the filthy animals you are, you think only of sex...the bonding. It's like training dogs."

"Why let us bond? You knew it would strengthen me," Katrina asked.

"The demon, let's not speak its name, shall we? Its energy...it feels *so* good." Mick ran his fingers down his chest, waggling his shoulders in a delightful shiver. "You know what it's like, don't you, Kitty Kat? Because I put a little of it in you. Took me a few times of capturing you before I realized how to perfect my magick. But I've had one tiny problem. It's like a beer tap. Tap on. Tap off. Well, I suppose it didn't work as well as I planned, because even though you sucked magick from the Alpha, it leaked like piss. But seeing you with your Alphas...ah, all the pieces came together. Your leak has stopped, hasn't it?"

Katrina turned her head, averting her gaze. She wouldn't give him the gratification of telling him that what he'd suggested had worked.

"No need to answer. I can already feel it."

"She's almost here." Katrina blinked, eyeing Mick out of her peripheral vision as he approached from behind.

"But the wolves, shifting into an animal is quite difficult. It takes a great deal of magick. Alpha magick. It's not easy to kidnap and keep an Alpha, as proved the case with Jax. But Katrina? You've been so easy to catch. Like a little fishy, I capture and release, capture and release. The only trouble is…ah, Katrina, these past couple of years…must you have been so difficult?"

Mick yanked her braid, jerking her head backward so he could glare into her eyes. The stinging pain to her scalp came swiftly. Her eyes widened in disgust as his lips crushed on hers. The stench of his rancid breath rushed into her nostrils, the sour taste of him choking her as he forced his tongue into her mouth. She shoved at his chin with the heel of her hand, thrusting him away, but not before his teeth bit at her lip, drawing blood. She thought to use the ring to slash at him but Samantha wailed, diverting her attention.

"Get your fucking hands off of her," Jax growled, his body half freed.

Mick's evil laughter echoed in her ears, and she willed herself not to cry. Unwilling to give him the satisfaction of her tears, Katrina spat iron-tinged saliva onto the dirt, and focused on her task, carefully guiding the baby into the world.

"Don't worry, Kitty Kat. You'll die soon enough. I think, maybe I'll fuck you first. After seeing your little display at the club, I've got some plans for you. That's right, you know I'm good at the torture. I was very satisfied up until recently." He cast an ugly stare at Avery, who clutched at the wall for support. "I can think of at least a half dozen things I'd like to do with that pussy of yours before I kill you." Mick glared at Katrina, his eager eyes watching as the witch labored. "I've always planned on killing you, but then sometimes a plan comes together perfectly. My dear Samantha, you're ripening for me. Birthing a first witch. So I thought 'why just take Katrina and the Alphas when I can kill the child and take her magick too?'"

"Don't listen to him, Sam," Katrina said, her voice strong and calm. She'd die before allowing this asshole to take the child.

Samantha quietly chanted as she pushed.

"Your spells won't work here, witch. The only reason I taped that pretty little mouth shut was so I didn't have to hear you cry." He sniffed. "After tonight, I will have all the magick I ever needed to be able to shift into a wolf. A true wolf, not just their human form. Whenever I want, wherever I want, I will run as beast. Taking over the packs will be a challenge but as I teach other worthy mages, it will happen. Humans. Vampires. Witches. Wolves. There will be no domain that is not under my control."

"You'll never get away with it." Jax struggled for freedom, his legs twitching.

"Let's see." Mick tilted his head and held two fingers to his temple. "I've located a very special wolf. The daughter, sister and mate of an Alpha. I've stolen her magick...learned how to siphon it and store it. Now, I've captured two Alphas and a witch. I'm able to transform into multiple beings at once."

In a flash, seven men appeared. All different ages and races, their eyes empty orbs, black pits. *Demons.* He snapped his fingers and they dissipated. Katrina fought the bile that rushed up her throat. The beings that had tortured her were all part of Mick.

"That's right, Kat. I've become very powerful."

"Neat trick, asshole, but tonight you're going to die," Jax yelled, attempting to redirect his focus away from Katrina.

Samantha gave a final guttural scream, and Katrina eased the baby into her arms, tears streaming down her face. In the midst of evil, the child's newfound magick thrummed, the innocence in her energy rushing through her skin.

"You did it, Sam. Oh Goddess, she's so beautiful." Katrina cleared the infant's mouth with her fingers, and she began to cry for her mother.

As she leaned to put the newborn into Samantha's outstretched arms, Mick stomped toward them. Katrina quickly rested the child onto the witch's chest, and moved to place herself in front of them. Fumbling with the ring, she never took her eyes off of Mick. She flicked at the latch and released the small lancet. *You want me, bastard? Come closer.*

Unexpectedly, Avery ran to Mick and shoved at him with her palms. "No. You promised to leave the baby alone. You swore, just the wolves. Just the wolves!"

Katrina screamed as Mick transformed into the scaly creature she'd witnessed under the docks. Its shiny bladed tail whizzed through the air, slicing straight through Avery's frail neck. Her head whirled across the cavern, blood spraying in a circular motion. The sanguine flecks splattered across Katrina's cheek.

Her eyes widened in amazement as the ancient vampire flashed into view. Katrina jumped to her feet and tore off her jacket, waving it at Mick. Diverting the creature's attention, she lured it toward her, its clawed feet scraping the rocks.

"About fucking time," Jax grumbled.

"Sorry, amico." Quintus reached for the silver netting with his gloved hands and shoved it aside, freeing Jax and then Jake. "Wasn't a picnic getting in here. Lucky for you I'm smooth with the ladies."

"Fuck," the Alpha breathed and promptly shifted, needing to clear the poison from his system.

"Well, yes. Fucking is usually how it's done, but sometimes I can just ask nicely. Some witches can be quite friendly," the vampire quipped.

"Hey, over here, asshole," Katrina yelled at Mick. Slicing the blade down her hand, she concealed the pain. She fingered the gem until it flipped open and smeared the white powdery substance inside over her palms and the knife.

The creature turned its head, realizing the Alpha had been freed. Its tail whipped toward the wolves, and Katrina seized the moment, lunging at its back. Wrapping her legs around the creature, she held tight and brought the ring to its neck. The small but deadly lancet carved through the rough scales like a laser. Katrina slid the ring off her finger, embedding it deep into the beast's throat. It screeched in pain and bucked at the intrusion, flinging her into the air. She landed on the dirt with a thud. Her lungs burned as she shook off the shock, but was given no reprieve as it lunged for her.

Jax leapt onto the demon, his jaws lodging into its neck, tearing at its flesh. It retaliated, scoring the Alpha's back with its talons. Jax howled in pain but refused to let it attack Katrina. Jake struggled to embed his fangs in its legs, and it whipped its tail at the wolf's paw, forcing him to release.

Katrina screamed in horror as its razor sharp tail slashed past Jake, narrowly missing his neck. The savage beast hissed as the poison took hold. Wheezing and spurting blood, it swung its tail at Katrina. Although she'd partially shifted, it caught her torso, slicing its blade clean through her abdomen.

Struck by the searing demon, she stumbled back onto the rocks and fell to the ground. Her magick leaked out with her blood, and she surrendered, helpless to fight as Mick siphoned her essence away. Despite the demon's attempt to heal itself with her energy, it continued to thrash, its form shifting from beast to man and back to beast once again. Lying immobile, Katrina blinked, watching in fascination as the creature squealed in agony. Splintering, it crumbled into hundreds of pieces, falling into the pit. She smiled as Jax's familiar blue eyes came into view.

"Kat, baby. No, don't leave me…I need you. I love you. Please Goddess, no," she heard him tell her.

Don't cry, my Alpha, she thought, his tears warming her

face. With no discernible spirit inside her wolf, Katrina submitted to the inevitable. Death beckoned, its peaceful blanket embracing her in its arms.

"I love you," she whispered.

Final words, she would never regret giving her life for her Alpha, for the child. As the light called for her, she prayed Jax would find love again.

⤳❦· *Chapter Twenty-Six* ·❦⤶

Jax gingerly placed Katrina's body onto the grass and cradled her head to his chest. The turbulent spring weather had calmed, the sky clearing, stars shining bright. His wolf howled uncontrollably as the grief crushed his chest. Being Alpha was all Jax had known up until the moment he'd met Katrina Livingston. He'd never anticipated the soulful connection he'd forge with his mate. A life-altering experience, the incredible female now consumed his thoughts.

"I love you so much." Numb, he rocked Katrina, whispering in her ear as if she were still alive. Her wolf completely gone, there was no detectable magick left within her beautiful spirit. Ignoring Jake's plea to release her, he'd lost track of time, refusing to let her body go.

A baby's cry broke his trance, and he lifted his gaze to the redheaded witch his mate had died saving. Samantha carefully knelt beside him, Luca supporting her arms as she joined him. Wrapped in Katrina's leather jacket, the infant quieted in his presence.

"She needs her," Samantha stated.

"Kat's gone." Jax turned his focus back to his mate, brushing his lips to her cool forehead.

"Kate. We named her after Katrina," she told him.

Jax sucked back a sob. While he appreciated the gesture, he couldn't bring himself to say a word. His thoughts spiraled. After he buried his mate, he'd step down as Alpha and become a lone wolf. There was nothing left for him to give anyone. Not his friends, not his pack.

"Katrina needs her. Please Jax," Samantha pressed.

"I...I can't right now," Jax managed. His bloodshot eyes met hers, tears fresh on his face.

"Her magick..."

"It's gone. She's gone," he cried. "Sam, look, I need to be alone with her and say goodbye. Please..."

"Katrina needs Kate," Samantha repeated.

With no fight left, confusion twisted through him as she reached for Katrina's hand. Her limp arm rolled onto the grass and he choked as her lifeless fingers touched the ground.

"No...what are you doing? You need to leave her alone," Jax pleaded.

"Just please, let me do this," Samantha told him, her voice calm.

Jax licked the salty moisture from his lips, perplexed by her actions. She unwrapped the child and kissed her forehead. Samantha smiled up at Luca and gently placed the baby onto Katrina's chest. As the infant cooed against his mate, he immediately sensed the surge of magick tingling through Katrina's fingertips.

"What is she doing?" He wore a stunned expression, his eyes widening at the sensation.

"Our little Kate is very powerful, much more powerful than most witches suspect. But Mick, he must have done his research. He knew what kind of magick our special miracle would bring to this world." Samantha set her palm to the Alpha's cheek. "It's true that Katrina's magick was siphoned. But our little Kate, she didn't let him have it. She took it. It's inside her. And now," she smiled to Katrina, whose chest rose in a shallow breath, "her magick has been restored."

Jax, too tired to argue with Samantha, closed his eyes. Emotionally and physically exhausted, he threaded his fingers through Katrina's, a scant quiver of life flittering over his skin. Jax jolted upright, observing his mate's eyelids flutter.

"Jax," Katrina breathed, a loud gasp escaping her lips.

"Kat," Jax cried. His palm grazed over the baby's back in amazement. "How did she do that?"

"She's a very special child. A first witch. An old soul." Samantha scooped the infant into her arms, giving him a broad knowing smile. "Luca and I are going to have our hands full with little Kate."

"Sam...tell me this is real," Jax blinked, terrified to believe his own ears and eyes.

"It's okay, Jax. She needs to shift. You're her Alpha. Call to her." Samantha focused on her infant, playing with her tiny fingers.

"Baby, can you hear me?" Jax gave a small laugh as Katrina squeezed his hand. A small smile formed on her lips. "That's it. Oh Goddess…"

"My Alpha…" She wheezed, a hand moving to her bloodied abdomen. "I feel awful."

"You need to shift," he told her.

"Help me," she managed.

Jax carefully removed her clothing. Shocked Katrina was alive, he lifted her into his embrace. Skin to skin, their energies merged. He smiled as she opened her eyes, his chest tightening in emotion.

"Let's go for a run, little wolf." With a gentle kiss, he breathed in relief as Katrina shifted. The small white wolf gave a bark and he laughed.

"You're beautiful," he told her and transformed, freeing his beast.

Elated, he sprinted, quickly catching up to Katrina. Full of life, she pranced under the moon, her shiny coat reflecting its light. Within seconds the pack surrounded them, and concern they'd challenge her so soon after her recovery surfaced. Establishing her rightful rank within the group, Katrina stared down each and every member. Her ears and tail erect, she stood firm, refusing to back away. Asserting her dominance, she ran a circle around her mate. Jax gave a bark and was pleased as his wolves lowered their bodies in submission to their Alpha pair.

Satisfied, he howled in celebration, but his exhilaration was short-lived as an unfamiliar wolf answered. Katrina took off toward the rustling leaves, in search of the intruder. He cursed, promising to continue her lessons in submission. Within seconds, he surpassed her stride, and was not surprised at his first scent of the wolf. *Tristan.*

Jax hesitated, seeing the great brown wolf tear through the forest. Although Tristan was formidable, the Alpha knew he'd crush him. Jax glanced back to Katrina. The joy in her eyes was soon replaced with fear as her brother ran directly toward her mate, and she realized he planned on attacking.

The black Alpha growled in warning but it didn't deter Tristan. The Lyceum wolf lunged at Jax, and they both barreled down an embankment. As they settled at the creek's edge, Jax's nature demanded he take action. Tristan attempted to lodge his teeth into the Alpha's neck, but Jax easily maneuvered out of reach. Refusing to back down, Jax had little choice but to force him into submission. Leveraging a strong paw into Tristan's flank, he shoved his opponent into the mud, his fangs settling into the soft fur of his throat. Katrina would never forgive him if he killed her brother. He exercised restraint and snarled rather than tearing open his skin.

"Let him go!" Jax heard the panicked voice of his mate call to him.

His eyes darted up to Katrina, who had taken on her human form. Wolves from both packs stood on alert, but didn't dare to intervene.

"Tristan, stop this. He's my mate." Katrina cautiously walked toward them and held her hand to her brother's snout. Tristan sniffed and licked at her fingers, and she fell to her knees, placing her palms on each wolf. "Our mating is meant to be…Goddess, please stop."

Sensing the shift in Tristan as the Lyceum wolf calmed, Jax released him. Waiting for him to shift first, he followed as Tristan shoved to his feet.

"I'm not going to let him do this to you, Kat," Tristan began.

"Tris…I already explained this to you when I called. I know you haven't gotten along with Jax. Please. The past is the past. He doesn't run his pack like his father. He's not like that." Katrina glanced to her Alpha and back to her brother. "I love you, but I'm not letting Jax go. You need to accept this. This male is mine. He belongs to me."

It was a serious moment, but it struck Jax as funny how bluntly she spoke to Tristan. Unable to restrain his emotion, he laughed and shook his head at her words. *This woman is going to kill me, and I'm going to love every goddamned minute,* he thought. Her dominance would not be mistaken by a single wolf in either pack. An Alpha's mate through and through, she spoke her mind with truth and conviction and no one would mess with her.

"What's so fucking funny?" Tristan asked, smearing the mud from his eye.

"Apple. Tree." Jax shrugged and winked at Katrina. "Or in this case. Apple." He pointed to Tristan and then his mate. "Apple. She's pretty awesome, isn't she?"

"What kind of mate did you think you'd end up with, my Alpha?" she purred with a sexy smile.

"Ah fuck." Tristan sighed and threw his head backward,

his hands on his hips.

"What?" Katrina pressed.

"You really are mated for real, aren't you?"

"Yes, of course I am." She laughed. "I keep trying to tell you that."

"I've only ever wanted to see you happy," Tristan insisted.

"I love you, Tris. I'm sorry for everything that happened. You need to know that Jax isn't his father. I love him."

Tristan stared at Jax for a long minute and extended his hand. "Don't hurt her."

"I will protect her with my life. I promise you." Jax clasped his palm, giving it a firm shake, but his attention was quickly drawn to his mate.

A broad smile crossed his face, his heart pounding so hard he thought it'd explode. *I love her so much.* Strong and compassionate, she professed her feelings for him, her statement spoken loud enough for every wolf to hear.

Without a care as to what anyone thought, Jax released Tristan and reached for Katrina, pulling her into his embrace. Passion for his mate flooded his chest as his lips captured hers. The sound of wolves serenading echoed through the trees, and Jax lost himself in the moment, so in love with the little wolf who owned his heart.

⋖⋗ Chapter Twenty-Seven ⋖⋗

Katrina took a deep breath, willing the butterflies in her stomach into submission. She glanced in the long mirror, and adjusted the edge of the plunging neckline. Sleeveless, the black ribbing fit her like a glove, the silver pleated skirt flowed easily, its hem brushing her calves. She reached for her lipstick, and smiled, pleased that her auburn locks had returned. Upon Mick's death, fully healed, she no longer experienced the foreign magick.

Twisting the gloss upward, she gently applied it to her lips, grateful that she'd not only met her mate but that they'd both made it out of that hellhole alive. It wasn't until after she'd quelled her brother's fears that they'd returned to the cave. Jake, not belonging to either pack, had stayed to watch over Dominique. The extent of her friend's compassion never ceased to amaze Katrina. Despite his misgivings, he'd fed the vampire, assuring her survival. While his blood had instantly regenerated her body, Dominique remained despondent.

Because she was sired of Kade Issacson, he'd been

contacted right away. But it was Quintus who'd offered to return her to New Orleans. Under any other circumstances, she and Jax might not have agreed to the transportation arrangement. Given her condition, however, Jax permitted the ancient vampire to assist them.

As planned, Jake had set off the C-4 explosives, collapsing the entrances to the cavern. Without inspection, it was difficult to ascertain the condition of the interior, but the former Navy SEAL assured them no one would ever be able to enter. Katrina prayed to the Goddess that whatever demon Mick had summoned had been entombed forever.

The reality was that if he'd allowed it to breach the earthly realm once to grant favors, there was no guarantee it hadn't escaped. A deal with the devil was not one where the debtor set the terms. It was likely he'd overestimated his ability, bringing a great atrocity into the world. At Jax's request, they'd conducted an ecumenical service to bless the land and restore it. The ministers, from both human and supernatural religions, had assured them the area had been cleaned. Cautiously optimistic, Jax had allowed wolves to run on the property.

Thoughts of Ilsbeth haunted Katrina. Although her magick no longer sang in her body, she couldn't help but wonder what had happened to the witch. Mick had never disclosed what he'd done to her but whatever it was, Katrina suspected she'd met a torturous existence. Not convinced Ilsbeth was dead, she'd hired a private detective to search for the witch.

Neither Jax nor Jake had been pleased, but they'd

accepted that Katrina sought closure. Despite the high priestess's heinous attack on Dimitri, she'd gone to great lengths to help Katrina, which had led to Mick's demise. Convinced the witch regretted her actions, she wished she could thank her.

Katrina's mind drifted to Jake, who'd asked to stay in Jax's remote cabin. While she'd thought it odd he didn't immediately return to New Orleans, she suspected Jax had influenced his decision. An Alpha, Jake would have to decide his own fate. Now that Jax had called him out on leaving his San Diego pack, he'd been given confirmation of what he'd probably known all along. Katrina understood the conflict, having grown up in New Orleans. It had been difficult moving to Philadelphia. Taking her rightful place with her Alpha in New York City, she drew comfort from knowing they'd visit and stay in their French Quarter home on occasion.

Katrina dabbed her lips with a tissue, and wondered what Jax had planned. They'd been home for a week, and he'd worked nonstop, catching up on business. When she'd come home from her new gallery, she'd found a note on the bed instructing her to meet him on the roof at seven. It was the one place in the penthouse he hadn't allowed her to see yet, and she suspected he'd been planning something special ever since they'd returned to the city.

Remarkably adventurous, her Alpha had a delightful habit of taking her off guard. She'd learned not to expect anything but the unexpected. Falling for the charismatic wolf had been easy, but since the night of her death, they hadn't professed their love to each other. Although disappointed they hadn't exchanged the sentiment, she'd never doubted his commitment. Aware of how Nick's death had affected Jax, she'd patiently wait for him to open his heart fully. There was no place else on the entire Earth she'd rather be than in his arms.

Wearing the dress he'd laid out for her, Katrina stepped into the elevator and pushed the button. As she arrived and the door slid open, she smiled, hearing Mozart play into the night air. The sight of her Alpha took her breath away. Katrina's eyes were drawn to his clean-shaven face. Sophisticated and debonair, he'd dressed in a suit and tie, his hair once again styled short.

"My queen." Jax extended his hand with a broad smile.

As Katrina placed her palm in his, she gave a nervous laugh. The sexual tension sizzled between them as her skin touched his. Her face heated, and she brushed her fingertips over her cheek. As he led her out onto the veranda, she smiled, taking in the gorgeous scene.

White cushioned outdoor furniture sat adjacent to a stone column corner fireplace. The spectacular space had been designed with a modern flair yet the potted trees and plants gave a warm impression. Her heels tapped along the marble floor, and she noted a section of grass on the far side of the patio. In the center, a rectangular pool sparkled, a series of fountains dancing upward.

Her eyes went to a set table, and she smiled, realizing he'd planned dinner. As she turned to Jax, she accepted a glass of champagne.

"A toast?" His eyes darted to the string quartet. "The classics always were my favorite. Eine Kleine Nachtmusik."

"A Little Night Music. It's beautiful," she replied.

"We think alike, my sweet mate." He held his glass to the air. "To a thousand more nights together."

"I'm looking forward to it." She gave a sexy smile, the effervescent drink bubbling over her tongue.

"Come." Jax winked as he took her glass, setting it aside.

Katrina breathed deeply. Aroused simply from being in his presence, she couldn't conceal her attraction.

As he swept her into his arms, she sighed. Within his embrace, she rested her head onto his chest, breathing in the masculine scent of her mate. His freshly showered skin registered first, a faint touch of cologne detectible, its mint and lemon scent adding to his allure. She resisted the urge to rub against him as his hand caressed her lower back, teasing her bottom. Dancing slowly, offbeat to the music, her body ignited in desire.

"Jax." She lifted her head to make eye contact with her sexy wolf. "This is beautiful."

"I wanted it special for you...for us." He glanced to the fountains. "The pool has always been here, but the rest? I worked on it this week."

"What?" Her eyes widened at his confession.

"This place...uh, Nick and I...we used to come up here. We'd have a drink. A cigar. Guy stuff." Jax looked to the furnishings and back to Katrina. "It was time for a change. You deserve a home, Kat."

"We'll make a home together." Katrina's breath caught

as he turned serious.

"Everything I have. Everything I ever will be…it's yours. Always."

"Jax…I…"

"Katrina," Jax paused and gestured to the musicians. They ceased playing, but within minutes of them leaving, the music continued, filtering through speakers. Her Alpha took her hand and placed her palm to his chest, his eyes locked on hers. "You are everything to me. How I feel…" He laughed and continued. "I feel amazing. I never knew what it would be like to find you. When we first met…that rush? I can still remember feeling obsessed. And when you didn't want me, I was so angry. I couldn't understand how it could be possible to have this chemistry with someone…it was so strong. It didn't make sense that you couldn't be my mate."

"I'm sorry…"

"Making love with you. Finding out you are my mate. Getting to know you…falling for you…I told you when you were sleeping." He smiled. "When you died."

"Told me what?"

"I love you, Kat. I've never met anyone like you and I never will. I love you more than I ever thought was possible."

"Jax…" She smiled, her heart melting.

"I should have told you I loved you when we got back but I just wanted it to be special. I wanted you to remember this moment forever. No death. No evil. Just you and me." He glanced to the cityscape and back to Katrina. "I want to share my life with you."

"I love you, too." Katrina's eyes fell to his lips then returned to his eyes. "You are the only one I've ever loved...will ever love."

"I love you." Jax leaned in toward her, closing the distance between them.

"Jax..." her words were silenced as his lips took hers.

Katrina wrapped her arms around his neck, drowning in his passionate kiss. His soft mouth made love to hers, his tongue seeking and tasting. Breathless, she gasped as he broke contact, his heated gaze undressing her.

Without speaking he led her over to the edge of the lawn, and circled around her to her back. His strong hands weighed down onto her shoulders, his fingertips stroking the hollow of her neck.

"You look stunning tonight."

Katrina went still, recognizing the dominant tone in his voice, his erection brushing her bottom. His warm breath teased her ear.

"I love this dress on you, but there's a problem with it, I'm afraid."

"What...I..." The sound of her zipper being undone silenced her. She smiled, aware of what her devious wolf had planned.

"Your skin...it's," Jax trailed his tongue behind her ear, eliciting a barely audible moan, "delicious."

Gooseflesh broke over her skin as he peppered kisses onto her neck and hooked his thumbs over the thin straps, drawing the fabric away. The cocktail dress pooled at her feet. Bared, her nipples hardened into points, the cool evening air caressing them like a lover.

"No bra?" he growled, nipping her shoulder. "And what is this fine surprise?"

A broad smile broke across Katrina's face. She'd bought the panties especially for her Alpha. A thong designed of delicate crystals hung low on her hips by black satin ribbons, adorning her as if she were wearing a necklace.

Like a panther he stalked around Katrina, and drank in the sight of his mate. The feral look in his eyes sent a jolt to her pussy and her thighs tensed.

"For me?" He smiled and raised a questioning eyebrow at her.

"Only for you," she responded, her voice breathy.

She sighed as he cupped her cheeks, his thumb tracing over her bottom lip. Darting her tongue over his fingers, she sucked it.

"You are a naughty, little wolf, aren't you?"

"On the contrary, Alpha. I'm very, very good."

"I'm not sure about that. After all, you have caused our dinner to be delayed."

"Hungry?"

She gasped, as his hands moved to her waist. With lightning-fast speed, he pressed his lips between her breasts.

"Jax, ah…"

"I'm ravenous." Taking her swollen peak between his teeth, he tugged it.

Katrina cried out. The sweet pain morphed to pleasure, his tongue laving and sucking. He focused his attention on her other breast and she stabbed her fingers through his hair.

"And this…"

She sucked a breath as he tugged on the strings, and the gems pattered against the stone floor. He dropped to his knees, and she blinked, never once caring that she stood bare in the night.

"No clothing will ever be as beautiful as this," he told her.

Katrina's head lolled back as Jax dragged his tongue through her wet slit.

"That feels…yes," she managed. Wearing only her heels, she widened her stance, seeking his touch.

"So fucking sexy," he hummed. "And this…"

"Ahh…" Katrina tightened her grip on his hair. Her clit tingled as he sucked it into his mouth, and her body quivered in response.

"I love every single part of you, baby. You taste," he drove two thick fingers up inside her, "so good."

Unrelenting, his wicked tongue lashed over her swollen nub. As his fingers curled inside her, grazing the thin strip of nerves, Katrina screamed in ecstasy. Her release came fast and strong. She teetered in her pumps, struggling to remain balanced. Jax's hand clutched her hip, steadying her.

She heaved for breath, her heart pounding in her chest like she'd run a marathon. As he raised his eyes to meet hers, she shivered, watching in fascination as he smiled. With slow deliberation, he dragged his tongue up through her seam, pressing his lips to her mound.

"Jax…make love to me," she breathed.

He pushed to his feet, taking her in his arms. His mouth descended on hers, and their lips collided in a desperate attempt to become one. Their tongues intertwined, and Katrina swore she could feel his love through every cell of her body. His savage kiss drove her wild, and she tore at his jacket, tossing it to the floor. Within seconds, she'd removed his tie. Desperate to have him inside her, she tore at his shirt, buttons scattering across the tiles.

They fell to their knees onto the soft grass, and he kicked off his pants. She reached for her prize, gripping his hard cock in her hand.

"Katrina," he called into her lips as she stroked him.

Taking control, Jax flipped her onto her back. A small cry escaped her as he settled between her thighs, his broad head prodding her core. She wrapped her legs around his, urging him to take her. As he slammed inside, she moaned, her fingers clawing down his back.

"Ah, Kat," Jax laughed into her mouth. "You're a dangerous woman."

"You feel so good."

Jax rocked out and thrust back inside her slick channel. "I fucking love you."

"I love you too…don't stop…just like that…keep going. Ah…"

"Hmm…bossy little mate."

"Fuck me." Katrina smiled in his lips as he plunged inside her, increasing his pace. "Yes, yes…"

Jax tore his mouth from hers to gaze into her eyes. He wrapped his fist into her loose locks that had come undone.

The twinge of pain focused her attention and she tilted her hips up to his. Thrust for thrust, his pelvis grazed over her clit, her orgasm building. Feral, she dug her nails into his ass and he cried out. The sound of flesh smacking flesh echoed in her ears as he fucked her even harder.

With each forceful stroke, Jax pounded into her, hurling her over the edge. Helpless to fight the wave of ecstasy, she surrendered. Trembling, her thighs tightened around him, bringing him deeper inside her.

With a guttural cry, her Alpha stiffened against her. He slowly made love to her lips, refusing to separate from his mate. Katrina reveled in his branding kiss, a reminder that she belonged to him. Infinitely connected, their energy merged, forever as one.

"I love you," she whispered, her voice cracking with emotion. She smiled against his bare chest, her heart bursting with happiness.

Jax Chandler. Her dominant, loving Alpha commanded her heart and soul. She'd waited centuries to find him and had almost lost it all...her life, her mate. Within his arms, Katrina smiled up at the stars, her love for Jax certain and true. *My Alpha.*

Jax smiled as Katrina cuddled into his embrace, his heart crushing with emotion. He breathed in the ambrosial scent of his mate and pressed his lips to her hair. Intoxicated with love, he accepted the loss of control that came with loving someone so completely.

A lifetime of thinking he'd happily go through life unmated had been proven utterly ridiculous. He inwardly laughed, realizing that as Alpha he'd insisted on her submission, all the while knowing that she'd done the same to him. Fiery and tenacious, Katrina completed him. Exuberant that he'd found his mate, the beast celebrated its glorious bond.

She stirred in his arms and he peered into her eyes, still laden with passion.

"I could sleep here all night," she told him, her small hand caressing his chest.

"Hmm…me too. You can't see the stars as well as in the country, though," he noted. "We never did eat dinner."

"Why did you put in all this grass? It's super soft."

"You mean it wasn't obvious?"

"Somehow I don't think you planned for us to make love on it."

"I had every intention of making it though dinner." Jax laughed. A romantic evening was as far as he'd thought. Telling her he loved her had been special but he should have anticipated that he wouldn't have been able to control his libido around his mate. She'd looked spectacular in the dress he'd bought for her, but hell, she'd looked even more amazing wearing only heels. "Did I tell you how beautiful you are?"

"Hmm…I love you in that suit. So handsome," she purred. "Seeing how hot you look, I might have to make you go to the office in gym shorts. Those girls go crazy over you, I'm sure."

"Is my mate jealous?"

"Never," she denied with a small chuckle.

"There's only one woman for me and she's in my arms. And as for this grass..." Jax hesitated, unsure if he should divulge the real reason he'd had it installed. But he'd decided long ago that they'd never again have secrets. "Truth?"

"Truth." Katrina pressed up onto his chest, catching his gaze.

"I love you. You and I," he sighed, "we've been alone a long time. You're my family now. And I'm not talking about the pack. Yeah, that counts, but you're my blood. I know we haven't talked about kids but..."

"You want to have a child?" Katrina asked.

Jax nodded, detecting her heartbeat race at his revelation. Concerned he'd scared her, he decided to back off and let her know that regardless of her desire to have children, she alone fulfilled his dreams.

"Kat, we don't have to..."

"Yes," she interrupted, a small smile forming on her lips.

"Yes?" he asked, excitement in his eyes.

"Yes." She laughed and hugged him. "My big silly Alpha...you put in the grass for our kids?"

"Yes...it's crazy, right?"

"Not at all. It's brilliant. Our pups need a place to run."

"Pups?" His voice went up an octave in surprise.

"Pup. Pups. Whatever." She laughed.

"I love you, baby. So much."

"I love you, too," she whispered, her voice sleepy.

Jax smiled as slumber claimed his mate. With her in his arms, he relaxed into a blissful state of contentment. Loving Katrina had nearly broken him. Losing her, even if only for minutes, had been devastating. His little wolf, the one who'd denied and protected him, had stolen his heart.

~⚜· *Epilogue* ⚜~

Jake raced through the woods, his wolf agitated. Ever since his talk with Jax, a gnawing guilt had eaten at his gut. *Alpha.* Becoming a true Alpha didn't sit well with him. He didn't even know anyone well enough in California to call them a friend, let alone consider them family. When he'd left, his conscience had been clear. It hadn't mattered that he'd fought and won every single challenge in San Diego. Loyalty meant everything to him, and he owed everything to his pack, the Acadian Wolves.

Fucking Jax Chandler. *Asshole. Mentor. Friend.* Jake couldn't stop thinking about what the Alpha had told him, his words playing in his mind, confirming that he'd earned his right as Alpha. It wasn't as if he hadn't always known about the aggression that lurked inside him. He'd concealed it well from everyone. In the navy, he'd let it loose, rewarded for his remarkable fighting and shooting skills. After several years, he'd returned home, only to retrain his mind.

Jake never imagined living anywhere else but New Orleans. He'd deliberately subdued the will of his wolf, burying his desire to dominate. Challenging Logan would bring certain death, and there was no way in hell he'd ever hurt his friend.

Conflicted, he'd grown used to going off for long periods of time in the bayou. Resting his mind had become his only coping mechanism to sate the wolf that sought submission. In his solitude, his beast calmed, accepted his fate.

But in the presence of others, it took all his energy to pretend to be something he wasn't: a follower. He'd succeeded in his masquerade until he'd met Jax. The more experienced Alpha pushed his buttons, seemingly challenging him on purpose. At the same time, his wolf submitted to Jax, sensing the overwhelming power the older wolf possessed.

Forging a deep friendship with the Alpha had been both unexpected and surprisingly comforting. No longer did he have to hide his true nature. Jax hadn't pressured him into making a decision. Rather, he offered words of acknowledgement, imparting his vast wisdom about what it meant to be Alpha.

Making love with Jax and Katrina had been an extraordinary experience, but he needed time to think about his future. Alone once again, his wolf ran free, content to be without others. Jax had given him full access to his cabin and Jake planned on staying for as long as it took to clear his head. Although spring, the morning air remained crisp, winter lingering on its heels. The foliage, waking from its frozen slumber, sprouted buds, birds serenading above.

His ears pricked in awareness, detecting a human

presence, and Jake crouched down in the bushes. Through the thicket, he spied a reflection in the water. He patiently listened. The sound of rushing water swooshed over the rocks. In the absence of voices, Jake's curiosity piqued.

He caught a glimpse of movement behind the waterfall, and instinct drove him to investigate. His stealthy strides through the muddied creek went unnoticed as he approached. The small figure made no move to escape, and he went still, peering behind the trailing water.

Jake shifted as she came into sight. *What the fuck?* Shocked, he rubbed the moisture from his eyes. The emaciated female shook uncontrollably, shivering on the rocks. Her arms clutched protectively around herself, shielding her bareness. He called to her but she didn't respond. Burning hate was soon replaced with an uneasy compassion as she stared through him as if she'd lost all memory of who he was.

Conflicted, Jake despised her, but knew he had no other choice as he took action. A small whimper was the only sound she made as he scooped her into his arms. Taking her back to New Orleans wouldn't be easy. When it came to her, nothing ever was. The female had nearly ruined his friend, yet she'd saved another. With her skin against his, no magick emanated from the pathetic creature. She'd been evil. She'd been kind. She'd been powerful. She was *the* witch. *The* high priestess. *Ilsbeth.*

Romance by Kym Grosso

The Immortals of New Orleans

Kade's Dark Embrace
(Immortals of New Orleans, Book 1)

Luca's Magic Embrace
(Immortals of New Orleans, Book 2)

Tristan's Lyceum Wolves
(Immortals of New Orleans, Book 3)

Logan's Acadian Wolves
(Immortals of New Orleans, Book 4)

Léopold's Wicked Embrace
(Immortals of New Orleans, Book 5)

Dimitri
(Immortals of New Orleans, Book 6)

Lost Embrace
(Immortals of New Orleans, Book 6.5)

Jax's Story
(Immortals of New Orleans, Book 7)

Club Altura Romance

Solstice Burn
(A Club Altura Romance Novella, Prequel)

Carnal Risk
(A Club Altura Romance Novel, Book 1)

Lars' Story
(A Club Altura Romance Novel, Book 2) Coming 2016

About the Author

Kym Grosso is the New York Times and USA Today bestselling and award-winning author of the erotic romance series, *The Immortals of New Orleans* and *Club Altura*. In addition to romance, Kym has written and published several articles about autism, and is a contributing essay author in *Chicken Soup for the Soul: Raising Kids on the Spectrum*.

Kym lives with her family in Pennsylvania, and her hobbies include reading, tennis, zumba, and spending time with her husband and children. She loves traveling just about anywhere that has a beach or snow-covered mountains. New Orleans, with its rich culture, history and unique cuisine, is one of her favorite places to visit.

• • • •

Social Media/Links:

Website: http://www.KymGrosso.com
Facebook: http://www.facebook.com/KymGrossoBooks
Twitter: https://twitter.com/KymGrosso
Pinterest: http://www.pinterest.com/kymgrosso/

Sign up for Kym's Newsletter to get Updates and Information about New Releases:
http://www.kymgrosso.com/members-only

Made in the USA
Middletown, DE
31 March 2016